Richard Lunn ... with Helen and ... Australia, Asia and Europe trying to find, among other things, his first novel. He found it in Italy and called it *Feast of All Souls*, an earlier version of which won the Alan Marshall Award. His stories have won the State of Victoria Short Story Award and the *Age* short fiction competition. He currently teaches Creative Writing at the University of Western Sydney, Macarthur.

Also by Richard Lunn:

Pompeii Deep Fry (poetry)
The Divine Right of Dogs (short stories)
The Taxidermist's Dance (short stories)

FEAST of all Souls

RICHARD LUNN

vintage

A Vintage Book
published by
Random House Australia Pty Ltd
20 Alfred Street, Milsons Point, NSW 2061
http://www.randomhouse.com.au
Sydney New York Toronto
London Auckland Johannesburg
and agencies throughout the world

First published by Random House Australia in 1997
Copyright © Richard Lunn 1997

The detail from the right panel of the triptych *The Last Judgement* by
Hans Memling used on the cover is reproduced with the kind permission
of the Muzeum Narodowe Gdañsk.

All rights reserved. No part of this publication may be reproduced, stored in a
retrieval system, or transmitted in any form or by any means, electronic,
mechanical, photocopying, recording or otherwise, without the prior written
permission of the Publisher.

National Library of Australia
Cataloguing-in-Publication Data

Lunn, Richard.
Feast of All Souls.
ISBN 0 09 183453 8.
I. Title.
A823.3

Design by Yolande Gray
Typeset by Asset Typesetting Pty Ltd, Sydney
Printed by Griffin Press, Adelaide

10 9 8 7 6 5 4 3 2 1

To my mother, Joan Lunn, who has also told a story or two in her time.

ACKNOWLEDGEMENTS

I would like to acknowledge the help of the following people at the birth of this baby: Helen, my wife, because she's so smart and calm; Gary Langford, the most truthful of liars; Helen Daniel, who gave the book such great support and wouldn't lose faith; Lyn Tranter, who knows what's what and never says die; Ron Pretty, the kindest of supervisors, who helped make it part of a doctorate; and Linda Funnell, who has very sharp eyes and still sharper judgement.

CONTENTS

Flotsam

In which Tuccio di Piero Landucci encounters a monster 3
Jacopo Passero seeks his fortune 14
Tuccio goes hawking 24
The Tartars come to Kaffa 35
In which Brother Corvo finds new work 47
An invincible enemy 65
Tuccio visits his carders 77
Jacopo sails to the Bosporus 87
Tuccio gives alms 107
In which Jacopo tells a tale and then grows silent 116
Cardinal Rollo da Parma hires help 129
Jacopo jumps ship and meets a holy man 139
Tuccio becomes a politician 165

Jacopo and Fra Lippo discuss religion,
then meet some unbelievers 179
Cardinal Rollo da Parma has
unpleasant dreams 188
Jacopo and the friar encounter
Wolf Schwanhals 191
The fall of Frederico dalla Montagna 202
In which Fra Lippo makes an
unpalatable suggestion 209
Tuccio parleys with Wolf Schwanhals 217
The cardinal hears bad news and Corvo
confronts the cook 223
In which Jacopo comes to Topomagro 229

A Sport of Kings

Guido Cupa takes the fleece in the
carders' secret chapel 237
In which Brother Corvo finds disciples 250
Jacopo Passero meets Lucia 262
The carders discover an unexpected ally 275

In which Brother Corvo builds a kingdom
and Jacopo steals a gift 283
The King of Cats and plans
for a charivari 292
Guido leads a charivari 299
A trial and counter-trial 307
Lucia meets Brother Corvo and
Tuccio meets the Priors 315
In which the carders choose their
Carnival king 322
The worthies put on a show 334
Mardi Gras riots 340
In which Brother Corvo reaps a harvest 353

The Lord of Light

Brother Corvo prepares for battle 359
Lucia takes Jacopo to Corvo's kingdom 362
Tuccio eats orange sherbet 372
In which Corvo considers the Pestilential
King and Jacopo attends an execution 383

The pestilence comes to Topomagro 390
Jacopo discovers the means of
his vengeance 404
The sickness spreads and Tuccio
mourns a daughter 414
In which Jacopo pursues Marina and
Brother Corvo pursues a vocation 424
Marina braves the plague 432
In which Jacopo is faced with a difficult
decision and Brother Corvo
takes control 443
In pursuit of Marina and Jacopo 453
The beatification of Brother Corvo and
flight into the north 459

Epilogue 471

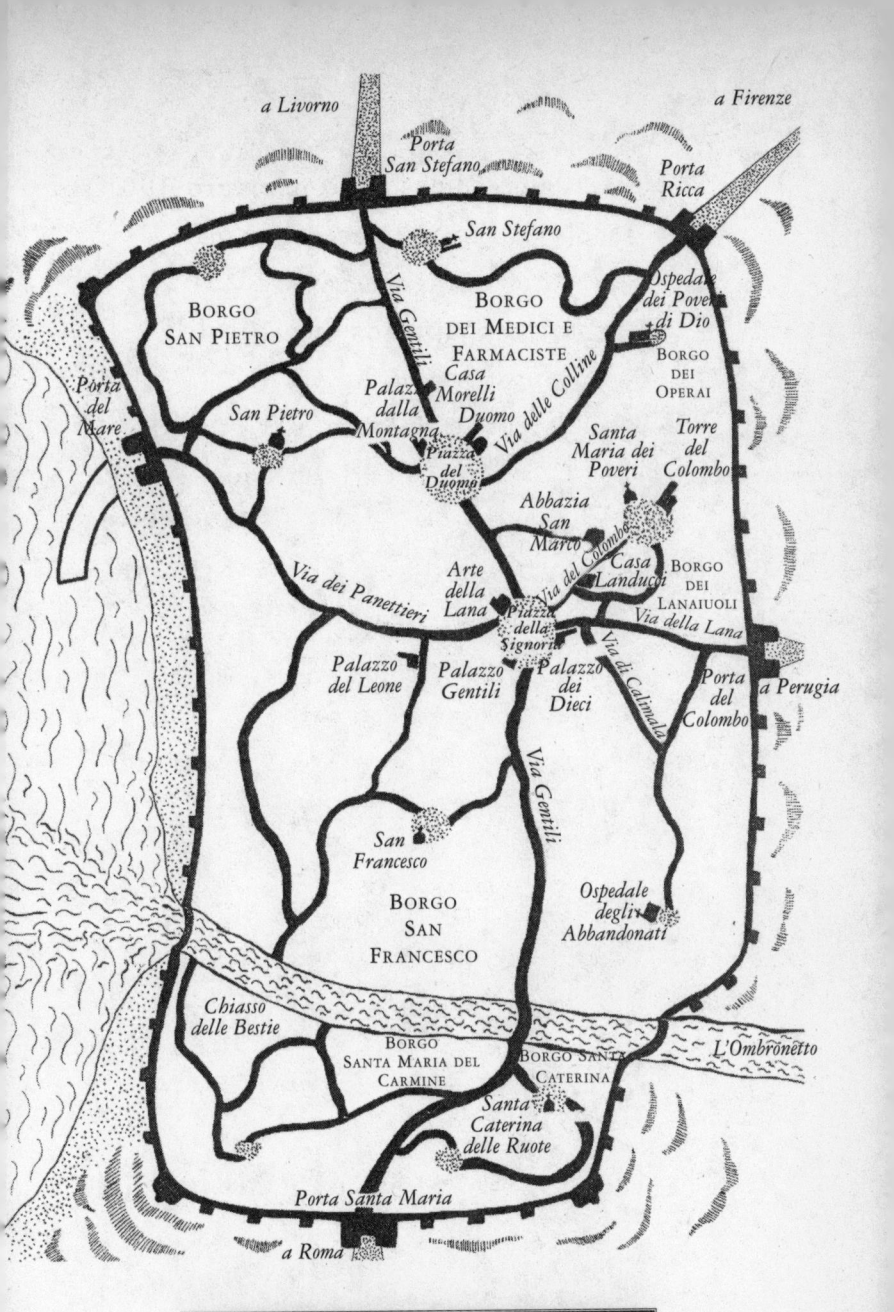

LA CITTÁ DI TOPOMAGRO

FLOTSAM

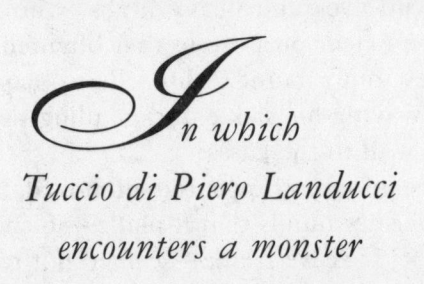

In which Tuccio di Piero Landucci *encounters a monster*

THE MONSTER LAY BREATHING BENEATH THE WALLS OF the town. It was huge and black, with a tail that might swat a knight clean off his horse with one casual flick. Topomagro's idlers were jostling on the walls for a better view, though none had yet ventured from the parapet, through the Porta del Mare and onto the beach. The monster was far too monstrous, almost thirty *braccia* in length, and looked capable, had the mood taken it, of downing the town's largest boat at a gulp. And yet, against the vast pewter plain of the evening sea, it had the shrunken look of any fish out of water, while its great rolling eye, the girth of its barnacled belly and, above all, the sardonic twist of its curious clownsmile, made it look almost comical.

From the walls they could hear the faint, bubbling hiss that came from the slits in its back. They saw the small crabs go scuttling like sinners in the nave of its shadow, while they watched and waited, shuffled and sighed, and felt boredom grow in the depths of their wonder. Then some spoke of marvels abroad in the land, strange happenings, bad harvests, omens and auguries. One, with bright, wild eyes and heavy limbs, who carried a sickle to no clear purpose in that blighted countryside, threw out a taunt to his fellows, cajoling and chiding, waving his sickle and goading them down from the wall to the gates.

Yet the monster appeared unmoved, unaware. The twittering sounds that it made—so small in the midst of its massive frame—seemed not to respond to the changes about it, as if governed only by vague inner urgings. There were occasional, sudden mouse-squeaks, which the priest of San Stefano later compared to the shrieks of infernal apes, as if the beast had been spewed from some sidegate of Hell in the watery deep to the west of the town. But the seamless sheets of its teeth still held their ambiguous smile, and its shoreward eye betrayed no feeling, only movement. Even this—apart from its eyelid's momentary avalanche—was the movement, not of a living eye, but a mirror, a giant form of those convex reflectors used in shops to cast light on account book and abacus. Reflected here was the town itself, its walls transformed to the cliffs of alien harbours, its towers the tips of a sunken city, and there, on the walls, a weird horde too strange to imagine. And now this army swelled forth, its sickles and rakes, its blades and axes, aglint in that living mirror like hosts of aqueous stars.

Tuccio di Piero Landucci sat in the room at the top of his house. He liked to think of it as his library, though he wasn't reading now. Far from it. He was sitting, pen in hand, the ink of his greeting already dry, trying to think out the right form of words with which to chastise Sandro dei Fiumi. He'd had such hopes for the boy, such good reports from his *fattore* in Pisa. He'd rarely heard old Bartolomeo wax so lyrical, except perhaps about a good wine— 'A natural *fattore*, young Sandro; not only can he do the books without supervision, but he's got a nose for good product, and what a way with people!'—as if they'd been trying to offload the boy. But no, they wouldn't have dared, not once they'd known that Tuccio himself was taking him under his wing to train for Ibiza. Indeed, Sandro was his own mistake, though an understandable one. The boy had talent and knowledge beyond his years, but once away from the steadying sway of his homeland, alone among slaves and sly traders, his youth had prevailed. It was Ibiza that was to blame.

It grieves me, Sandro, to find how ill you are faring in the job I entrusted to you, he wrote, growing angrier as he went. *I can barely believe that you could place our cargo with Cristo Bedoya. The man is notorious. He borrows money as I breathe air and, like all such captains, borrows on the surety of his cargo, preferring to let his ship sink than pay his debts. You can pray to Messer Domeneddio that our bales and sheepskins arrive in port, though I fear that even God will not see fit to mitigate such folly.*

He stopped, suddenly hot at the thought of that Catalonian wool, all those bright florins—like the golden fleece itself—lying useless on the bottom of the sea. A story he'd recently heard invaded his thoughts—of how three young Florentine *fattori*, playing *zara* in Venice with letters of credit drawn on their companies, had squandered thousands of florins and nearly destroyed their masters. He scribbled more furiously still, as if shouting with his quill, reminding Sandro of other cargoes he'd failed to insure, of yet another arriving in Pisa without any sign of a bill of lading having been written. *If you are hell-bent on ruining the company,* he concluded, *let me assure you that my notaries will draw up a contract that will leave you liable, so that you may ruin only yourself. I mean what I say, and well you know it.*

Yet he could not totally harden his heart to the boy. He himself had been the San Matteo agent for the Pecora company in his early years, and knew how lonely and lost a youth of twenty could feel in such outposts. It had been hard to keep up his spirits till God and Giulio Pecora had seen fit to make him *fattore* in Barcelona, something which would never have happened had he been careless like Sandro. Still, his aim was not to demoralise the boy.

I know it is not easy work, he added, *but that is why I have chosen you, Sandro. Nor am I unaware of how alone one can feel in such places. Yet remember that God in His mercy and wisdom is everywhere, and that we who turn the fleece of sheep into cloth are also His flock.* He paused, hesitant, then scrawled, *And let me remind you that I do not disapprove of my* fattori *seeking comfort from a pretty slave or two, though I would frown upon bastards being kept on company property.*

Tuccio signed the letter and sealed it, suddenly tired of the business with Sandro. In fact, he felt tired of business in general. It had been a long day, and he'd go down shortly and have some wine. The letter had made him think of his youth, of San Matteo and, better still, of Barcelona. He got up, stretched, tried without success to stamp the stiffness from his legs, and wandered across to the tall Venetian windows pushed wide to the night.

Topomagro lay shadowed in the dusk, falling away to the sea where flocks of gulls went wheeling, while larger birds, buzzards perhaps, came circling out of blood-red cloudbanks. Tuccio leaned against the wooden frame and let his gaze skim smoothly over terracotta tiles, following the inclination of the hillside to the east, where the Torre del Colombo rose before the walls. And then he let his eyes glide back toward the north, settling on the belltower of the Duomo, where flights of swallows went tumbling through the turquoise air. He sighed and, for a moment, even as he watched those little birds below him on the slope, seemed also to see them from the cool arcade upon the courtyard of the trading post in Barcelona. For a moment he smelt the moist leaves of mint and rosemary, the sharp Castilian wine, the heavy scent of herbs in Netta's hair and, in that same instant, felt her smooth black arms about him, her laughter warm against his ear.

Again he sighed, swept with a sudden envy of Sandro's youth, of his own youth, of Netta, his Moorish slave, and that other girl—the Berber— whose name he had forgotten, and the world's uncertainty, its strangeness and the sense of possibility ... But how ridiculous, he thought, to be jealous of yourself. You might as well start railing at your teeth for being sharper than your brain. What he had said to Sandro was true. It had been a lost, confusing time. Yet there'd been a certain freedom, the sense that nothing mattered so long as he maintained his profits. His reputation had been a product of the mails. But here, now, at the outset of the year 1346, established as he was in Topomagro, the town's greatest cloth-maker and merchant, an international trader of some repute, well known in Florentine and Venetian business circles, even, at times, a Prior ... well, he could hardly afford to court scandal. Nor could he afford to indulge in misplaced nostalgia. Barcelona was no paradise, and he wouldn't be the feckless youth he'd been for all the French Pope's luxuries.

He craned his neck a little further out the window and peered downward, his thoughts disturbed by a sudden hubbub in the street below. There were voices and the sound of bagpipes and a shrill piccolo. He saw a crowd come marching up the Via del Colombo from the direction of the sea. They were shouting to each other as they went, and some were even dancing. At their head was a boy with hair the colour of greasy straw, a grin glued from ear to ear. He was moving at a great pace on a pair of battered crutches, his withered-looking legs barely touching the ground, while his wooden ones, thrust beneath his armpits, strode forward like the limbs of some lopsided wading bird. Beside him was a tall and raw-boned man in a great loose tunic that might have once been scarlet but was now the colour of dried blood. He flung out his arm as he went, as if driving the boy on, though he may just have been pointing to the Ospedale dei Poveri di Dio, to which Tuccio assumed they were headed. If these two moved with a manic intensity, the throng behind them seemed exhausted, struggling to keep up, many walking with the stiff-legged gait of the starving, eyes dark in parchment faces, their limbs in rags like so much mummy-cloth. Above them, the notes of the pipes unwound like the cries of a cat's carnival, the balloon-faced piper puffing up his bloated cornemuse while the piccolo player—a stout girl of no more than ten—stabbed at the air with stiletto squeaks. And there were dancers, skeletal in the evening light, whirling with wooden-doll steps, smiles stitched to the bones of their faces.

Tuccio drew back from the window. His office seemed suddenly dark. He'd get Lucia to light the lamps. But as yet he hadn't moved, staring at the glaucous sky above the rooftops. He didn't like these crowds, these glowering, shadowy mobs. Throughout the last decade conditions had worsened, the freezing winters, the bad harvests, the slow, continuous famine driving them over the roads to the city's stored grain and the fish scraps that littered the markets. Though even the fish had seemed to grow fewer, as if God were truly chastising them. And now, just yesterday, when the hake and mullet, even the sardines and anchovies, were leaving the shores of the town, the ocean had sent them a monster, as the ill-informed were calling it.

Tuccio leant on his desk and smiled. During his years in Spain he'd learnt of the great Biscayan whales, but that one should reach a beach in Tuscany … such a thing he'd never heard of. These truly were strange times. Wasn't it just last year, in the heaviest snows of his generation, that a fever in the earth had caused the town to shake, the bells of the Duomo and all the churches ringing as if on the Day of Judgement? Perhaps that day was nearer than they thought, and perhaps the poor would wreak God's vengeance. During winter he'd noted more than one corpse hugging the warmth of a dungheap, and doubtless the harvest would fail this summer. Even those seeds that the weather had spared had been eaten by the peasants. There would be more processions of the poor, more corpses, more desperate anger. Do what they might with confraternities and hospices, foundations and charities, the piles of the dead would grow, and they could not allow the flood of migrants to continue.

Tuccio groaned, his hand caressing the Psalter that lay on his desk. Lord, had he worked so hard and built so much to let it come to nothing? Clicking his tongue at his cowardice, he shook his head. He was tired, unsteady. He needed a sip of good Carmignano. To fear those famished souls was the height of pitilessness. There was more to fear from Montagna and His Eminence, Rollo da Parma. And these, too, could be overcome.

He opened the Psalter, then snapped it shut and strode to the stairs. What he had worked for and what he had built was the strength to determine the fortunes of Topomagro.

•

It was long after prime the next day when they started to climb the stairs to the parapet. Tuccio wished to see the creature before he did anything else, instructing Gino, his steward, to ready their mounts for an early excursion. He'd reckoned without his accountant, Luigi Pucci, who'd arrived in his usual panic, this time about some dishonoured bill of exchange. Tuccio had silenced him at once, inviting him to come and see the whale for himself, on the proviso that he made no mention of bills of exchange. Indeed, he'd rather have gone alone, but three burly servants were the minimum safeguard in days such as these, so there was little point in forbidding Luigi.

The captain of the Porta del Mare was keeping people away from the parapet—there'd been too great a crowd in the last two days—but of course he made an exception of Signor Tuccio, and allowed Luigi to follow him up. As he climbed the stairs, Tuccio was somewhat surprised by the sense of excitement he felt at the thought of the whale. Certainly he knew of the creatures, had seen drawings in bestiaries and the marginalia of manuscripts, but to see the leviathan in the flesh—it was a bit like seeing a centaur or unicorn, or some other beast from the tales of the ancients.

'They suggest that … well … it's quite hideous,' Luigi blurted. 'Are you sure it's—'

'Yes, yes, Luigi, of course it's all right. The thing's hardly going to leap on the wall and gobble you up.'

'Well …' he began, as if anything might be

possible with such a beast, but one look from Tuccio made him keep his own counsel.

The merchant did not feel like talking. There was something about the thought of the creature that unsettled him in a way not altogether unpleasant, as if the sea's disgorging of so strange a thing were a sign that all the dull business, all the flat, intractable surfaces of life, might suddenly open to reveal something marvellous. He mounted the stairs two at a time, Luigi grumbling worriedly in his wake. And then they were there, on top of the wall, with the sea stretched out in quilted blue ripples, and down below them, the leviathan.

It was a mountain of bleeding meat, a pile of red bone and flensed blubber. Great strips of flesh now hung from the ribs, which rose from the sand like the arches of some rough cathedral. Festoons of sinew and huge sheets of muscle steamed in the early air; gulls made screeching circuits around the untouched head, where the mouth continued to give its crimped grin, as if somehow amused at the violence rendered upon it. Tuccio grimaced, wrenching his gaze from the butchered monster and watching the crowds now thronging about it. They were gathered round two rusty cauldrons that looked like cloth-dyers' vats, from which clouds of greasy smoke unfurled through the sky. Some, astride their fellows' shoulders, pushed at the contents with long wooden poles. An army of onlookers crowded about, some with their hands raised for bits of boiled meat, others already with smoky trophies; further along the beach, smaller groups huddled round bonfires, cooking gobbets of whale fat over the flames on sharp, blackened sticks.

Not all were eating, however. At one of the fires the paupers were laughing and clapping, the look of sated burghers on their haggard faces, though the food was clearly too rich for some—even as he looked, he saw one man turn retching into the sand. There were also three dancers—a woman and child, and a thickset cripple who heaved about on a flat wooden tray. Tuccio watched a group of small children play chasings amid the great ribcage while, perched overhead on the tip of a tail-fluke, a crow raised its head and moaned like a sad-hearted conqueror. He looked at the whale's dull eye, noting the thick yellow muck that oozed from the canthus, as if the creature wept tears of candle wax. He glanced behind him at Gino, his steward, and the two burly servants, at their well-groomed mounts and his own plump mule—the sort bishops rode, for which he'd paid over two hundred florins, shipping it all the way from Cadiz. He thought of his house, of his farm in the hills, then looked at the whale with its fat hacked away, and shivered with cold in the sharp morning air.

Jacopo Passero seeks his fortune

HAD YOU BOARDED A GENOESE GALLEY FROM THE mole just north of the Porta del Mare, sailing south to Civitavecchia, then on to Gaeta and Naples, through the Straits of Messina, south-east across the Ionian Sea, past Kithira, Crete, Khios and Lesvos, north through the Sea of Marmora, threading the needle of the Bosporus, past the smoky domes of Byzantium and over the Black Sea, it would not be too many months before you reached Kaffa, the Genoese trading post at the foot of the Crimean mountains. Here, with its century-old walls and its fortress, its tiny Armenian church and, at its heart, the proud marble of its Catholic baptistery, it funnelled the wealth of the East toward Christendom, keeping at bay the hordes of Tartary. Tuccio had an agent—Francesco Corsani—in the Genoese enclave, who often sent him consignments of spices, alum and brazil on board the galleys and cogs that plied southward. Yet the figure we see in the alley below the Fanfani mansion is neither a friend, nor even an acquaintance, of Tuccio di Piero Landucci. He is Jacopo Passero, one-time shepherd, salt-scraper, jongleur, now turned burglar, and he's watching the lights go out.

He seems edgy, his eyes glinting quickly beneath the new moon. At the rear of the house, on the second of the building's four storeys, the last yellow light is extinguished. It's most likely the room he wants, the master bedroom, and he makes to step from the shadows just as boot heels ring on the stones at the end of the alley. There's the glow of an oil lamp swung with the stride of its owner, the mutter of voices and a grunt of laughter. Jacopo hugs the darkness more closely, and the clink of steel fills the gaps in their speech as the night-watch sway by in the drunken lamplight. No good to be caught out just now, not after the trouble in Tana, and with the curfew so strictly enforced. He waits till the light, the words, the blows of boots are lost to the streets. Then he slips through the thin stream of moonlight to the foot of the mansion's wall.

He pauses a moment, no more than a lanky shadow with eyes like slivers of mercury, eyes that slant slightly up to mimic the corners of his mouth, even his nose's thin tip, as if he never stopped laughing at some sly joke. He touches the rope at his throat, the small bag of tools on his belt and, hung at his hip, the larger pouch for his secret weapon. Throat, right hip, left—a thief's benediction. He uncoils his rope and hurls it upward. Two flukes of its hook catch high on the coping with the faintest whisper of metal. He pulls down hard, smiles as it holds, then hauls himself up. It wasn't for nothing that he'd earned his keep in Savoy as a jongleur and acrobat. The perfect training for a burglar, and what better way to taunt grim Death than to hang from a tightrope, juggling with oranges, the hungry crowd uncaring if you fell, just so long as you dropped the fruit. He glances up as he goes. It's not like he's lacking a plan. There's a reason he's failing to try these shutters he's climbing past: just before the light failed completely, he saw a small window with one open shutter at the top of the house. So, humming, he climbs by the silent rooms until, sure enough, he finds the shutter still hooked to the wall, where it's been for some time if one is to judge by the webs and dead moths that hang from the rusty fastenings.

The window is closed, but it's only a light, oiled linen stretched tight on its frame. Jacopo tries to peer through, but all is in darkness. He presses his ear to the cloth—there's no sound to be heard. Then, aware that he might be seen from the street, he makes a slit with the tip of his knife, slips his hand through the stiff, scratchy fabric and unfastens the inner catch. Now is a dangerous moment, yet more dangerous still if he waits, so he eases the window open, bracing himself for the intake of breath, the sudden cry—'Thief!'—and the clatter of weapons. But there's nothing, just the scrape of the frame as he brushes past and the hiss of the waves on the distant beach. He lifts the window as far as it goes, squeezes awkwardly through, then slithers on his belly to the rough plank floor. He glances about him, allowing his eyes to adjust to the deeper night of the room. Then the vague forms of grain sacks, of earthenware jugs and bales of cloth, the trestles and planks of makeshift tables, emerge from the dark. His grin glimmers white in the faint-hearted light. He sits up, brushing the grit from his hands. It's a storeroom, and the dust on the floor suggests how rarely it's entered. He stands, treads, squints at the creak of the plank at his feet, and steps across to the door. Scimmia. Now is the time for his secret weapon. He touches the pouch upon his left hip, gives it a squeeze, but it doesn't respond. He sighs a bit then joggles it harder, unhooking the flap and peering inside. A pale, splayed paw with tiny, sharp claws stretches out, a green eye glitters, there's a yawn with needlepoint teeth. She arches and shivers herself awake, then nuzzles his hand with her whiskered muzzle. Scimmi, his secret weapon.

Suddenly she leaps to the floor, tense and alert, lifting her nose to the grain sacks.

'Well, my fine cat,' he whispers, 'what's the matter with you?' She looks up sharply, mews at him quizzically. 'Scimmi, you demanding little brute.' And he pulls some pork jerky out of his pocket, breaking off just the tiniest bit, then holding it down to her. One claw flashes out, drawing it back with a suave ferocity. It's gone in an instant and she's up on her hind legs after some more. Jacopo puts out his hand and, seeing it empty, she sits neatly back on her haunches, blithely accepting his stroking. She's small, thin and silver, as if carved out of moonlight, and lithe as a monkey with an acrobat's balance and wicked green eyes—a true jongleur's cat. A soothsayer said she was born of an imp and a scion of Saladin's infamous tom, but Jacopo never trusts soothsayers, not after being one himself for six months in Marseilles. He pats her head once more and she purrs her squeaky purr. 'Come on, Scimmi, we've got work to do.' He loves her smug look when he pats her. She'll drop a gutted rat at his feet, then look up into his eyes like a child at its first communion.

'Time to go, cat.' He picks her up, opens the door just a crack and pops her through to the room beyond. In a moment she's back, squeaking worriedly. Clearly there's a problem. Jacopo puts his eye to the crack, knife in hand. He can see a narrow, shadowy corridor, but little else besides. He opens the door wider; it squeaks but he perseveres. Gripping the hilt of his blade, he eases his head through the doorway. Empty shadows to the left, and to the right? Sickly moonlight that seeps through the slats at the end of the passage, bright enough to reveal a Tartar asleep on a palliasse. He falters and Scimmi weaves knots of squeaky purrs round his legs.

'A fine time for that,' he mutters, glancing left and right. There's no-one to the left, but any stairs in that direction will lead him past bedrooms and kitchens, where he's bound to find more sleeping servants. Whereas if he goes to the right and risks the Tartar, his way will more likely lead through the large, empty rooms at the front of the house. He decides to take the immediate risk, creeping on tiptoe toward the right.

Scimmi shoots on ahead, vanishing down the corridor. At times Jacopo would like to turn himself into a cat. So little noise, so few needs. Still, he moves more softly than most mere men, sliding along the shadowed wall, past the slave with the moon on his face, which—even as he stares—twists in a sudden frown, as if in the grip of a dream. Jacopo feels the blade on his thigh, then peers hard at the quivering face. But the Tartar remains in his dream and Jacopo rolls his eyes with relief, slipping along to the spot where his cat disappeared. It's a narrow stairway and he's halfway down when he hears her soft mew. Barely audible though it is, its meaning is clear, and when he reaches the room below he sees that it's empty.

In fact, there's almost no furniture, just a huge open space with a handful of chairs, a sideboard and narrow table, all enclosed by tapestried walls. A reception room, only used by the family for public events. Though, from his knowledge of the Fanfanis, there'd be no shortage of those. Indeed, it was in another fine house, at one such event—to which he'd cozened an invitation—that he'd first seen the Fanfani diamond. He'd almost spilled his wine on his foot. A beautiful stone, as cold and bright as the evening star, and clasped in a choker of wine-dark rubies. There it was on the neck of Monna Fanfani. And what a poor, pouchy neck, the diamond virtually smothered by chins and fat dewlap, the rubies glinting amongst those folds as if some old hen had just had its throat cut. Sacrilege, pure and simple, and only needing one such as he to set it to rights, so this jewel might adorn the throat of some Florentine beauty. One thousand ducats at least in the shops round Saint Mark's. Yes, and he knows the captain who'd buy it.

Scimmi squeaks at his feet. He follows her down a far wider staircase, one of fine stone, till he sees from the table and heavy brocades that he's reached the mansion's main dining room. He knows where the merchant's treasures will be. A man like Fanfani would never sleep unless his wealth slept with him. Two separate doors lead out of this room. Scimmi slips through the one on the right. He would have guessed the other, since the last light extinguished was on the south side. And who, in the house of a grasping merchant, would burn the last light? Who else but the master? He darts through the left-hand door, past two small chambers, then comes to the dark master bedroom.

He peers in, stands listening. Oh, for the eyes of his cat! There's a chest by the wall—a painted *cassone*—and a picture to the left. Close by the door he can make out the edge of a dresser and a smaller chest on the other side. A crucifix hangs on the right-hand wall, while the dresser holds a number of boxes and caskets. But the single thing that commands the whole room is the huge curtained bed almost eight *braccia* wide. Its curtains are drawn of course, but he doesn't need to fling them apart to know that within are the master and mistress. His basso profundo croaks through the night, while her dainty snores go fluttering up like soft, plump pigeons. Yet there's something else beyond this duet, on the room's far side, a barely audible twitter of breath that must be a maid on a truckle bed. There, he's got it mapped out, and no Scimmi to help him.

The diamond should be in one of the dresser's

caskets. It's just a matter of care, like a cat with a bird. His eyes dart about. No pause to the snores. He tries a small casket of carved, painted bone. Some bits of lace braiding, half-a-dozen gilt buttons. Trust him to find the sewing box. He opens a larger one—a handful of silver *grossi* and a lady's gold belt. He pops the coins in his pocket, tries the belt in his pouch. It's far too awkward, so he buckles it round his greasy old smock and goes on trying the lids of the caskets. There are ducats, some florins, a guilder or two, a very small sapphire on a thin silver ring, and something like a cornelian, though it's hard to tell in the gloom. No matter where he looks, from the exquisite ivory box to the chests full of cloth, there's no diamond to be found. At last, desperate, he goes to the massive crucifix hanging on the wall, his fingers groping across it to seek out encrusted jewels. There are none, but just as a knuckle brushes the nail through one of Christ's palms, he feels the tiniest movement, hears the faintest of clicks and sees the Lord's chest spring open. The ribcage has miniature hinges and, as he parts the sternum further, he sees—aglow with the faintest yet purest of lights—the Fanfani diamond.

Jacopo crosses himself, mutters a quick thanksgiving and grasps for the jewel with a trembling hand. Just as his fingers graze the bright facets, a hideous cry erupts through the night. There's a deep, rumbling snarl and a stutter of feet from the rear of the house, then a second yowl, a sound like that of a riven baby or a demon confronting the Cross. Hand frozen before it can close on the jewel, he swings to the door as Scimmi tears through with a squeak of relief. Not pausing to aim, she leaps for the pouch and lands in a shiver of jewellery and coins. Jacopo has no time to think, there's already something there at the door, something snarling, rabid and black—a massive dog, perhaps a fanged horse. Now the maid pops up by the bed, then the curtains fly wide and, with a cry of, 'Shut up, you stupid animal!' Fanfani gapes out, quite naked except for his nightcap, while the fat, capped form of his wife is already drawing the covers back up, whimpering as she stares at Jacopo. But Fanfani's too busy mastering the dog, which rumbles low in its throat, every muscle aquiver since it's seen the intruder. Then Scimmi, peeping over the edge of the pouch, starts to splutter and hiss like a choleric kettle. The dog leaps, roaring—Fanfani bristling, transfixed—as Jacopo springs for the window, flings out the shutters, squats on the sill, then jumps for the rope's thin shadow asway on the wall. He grips in a welter of slobber and shouts, slithering down with smoking hands, winded an instant there on the stones, then scrambling away up the alley.

He turns back once and sees at the sill not the man, but the hound like some monstrous householder, belling and biting the mild, dewy air. He unbuckles the belt, hurriedly stuffing it into his shirt, then sprints north-east as fast as he can, keeping to shadows under the walls, making no effort to steady the pouch that bounces on his hip. Serve her right to get a bumpy ride, nearly bringing him undone, and he grins to himself as she squirms amid trinkets and ducats. He pauses at last by the wall of a shuttered bakery. She pokes her head out of the bag, mewing reproaches.

'You should talk,' he mutters, 'after giving us away like that. How do you think you'd like it in prison?'

She watches him with her bright green eyes and utters a sharp miaow.

'Plenty of rats? Well, that's a comforting thought.'

He shakes his head then gives her a pat, and her face takes on its virtuous look.

Then they're hurrying on, past San Giovanni, the silk merchants' rooms, the consul's palazzo, coming at last to streets where there's movement, a trickle of pilgrims heading for inns and the cloisters round Santa Croce—wherever they might find relief from the present troubles. Here, he knows, the presence of so many others will help keep him safe. Nevertheless, he stays in the shadows, hurrying on till he sees the gate. He stops to observe the refugees, carts buckling under the weight of their goods as they're processed by guards. The reports of the killings in Tana are bad. There's even talk that the Tartars are raising an army. They've long resented the Genoese. And the Greeks won't help their fellow Christians, not after the slaughter at Romanais. For a moment his chest seems to tighten, then he looks at the column of refugees, their belongings half off their carts for the taking. He pats his cat, smiling.

'Rich pickings, eh, Scimmi?'

Tuccio goes hawking

They rode their great horses in the green morning and each young man had a hawk at his wrist. Tuccio, however, rode his black mule and had no hawk. He couldn't stand the sport, with its feudal trappings and its birds that bit at your glove and looked like fierce little knights in their leather hoods. 'At least ride one of the horses,' his wife had sighed. 'You'll be like a cripple at a dance on that mule of yours. They'll be galloping all over the countryside, and you stumbling along trying to keep up.' Needless to say, *she* hadn't come. Beatrice disliked the sport as much as he, but she was jealous of his dignity. Nevertheless, he'd informed her, as if it were his favourite pastime, that falconry was not like hunting a fox or a boar. One didn't go hurtling up hill and down dale. It was a noble sport—the hawks did all the work while you simply trotted along behind and gathered up the quarry. Besides, his Spanish mule was his pride and joy, worth more than one of Baldassare's chargers any day. So here he was, once again bringing up the rear on his gentle mule while the others sat waiting.

'You'll have to bleed him, Tuccio,' Baldassare

chuckled, 'your grooms have fed him too much.'

'He's a wise beast,' Tuccio replied, scratching the mule between its ears. 'He sees little reason to go chasing after prey fit only for knights and falcons.'

It was an old chafing post: Baldassare's love of his bird and Tuccio's pride in his mule.

'Wise?' Baldassare smiled, reining in his impatient mount. 'He's lazy from all those honeyed figs.' And the others chuckled knowingly, since these were Tuccio's favourite snack.

'Wise indeed,' he insisted, 'and the palate of a gourmet.'

Baldassare laughed, the falcon calm on his hand as he cantered off through the grass, the others close at his heels. Tuccio watched them go and ambled along behind. They were a handsome group, no doubt about it, all merchants or the sons of merchants, better off than they'd ever been and playing at the game of country lords. Baldassare himself was noble, both in blood and bearing, and Tuccio held an almost fatherly affection for him. He watched him on his black horse, his blond hair, cut longer than the fashion, flying out behind him. Like the others, he simply wore a doublet with his tight linen hose, and Tuccio shook his head ruefully. Even when he was young, he would have felt uneasy to be so scantily clad; but now the young were different, more readily given to immodesty, though he couldn't agree with Friar Tommaso that this was a sign of the coming Apocalypse. Surely God would require more than tight hose to trigger the end of time.

No, on such a beautiful day it was hard to

imagine this ending would ever happen. He leaned back in his saddle, enjoying the sun, the darting of finches and wrens in the air, the clink and bright brass of the harness. It was perfect June weather, with everything held in a blue-green depth—the long grass on the hillside, the woods toward which they were riding—and down in the valley the shouts of the mowers wielding their scythes, or a woman singing as she raked in the stalks, or the banter of those who were pitching the load on a high-piled wagon. To the east were the wheat fields, still not quite ready for reaping; to the west, the sea glittered blue, Topomagro hidden behind the low hills. On such a day it was also hard to believe that food was so scarce, but one look at the size of the unripe crop was enough to tell him how much of the seed had been eaten that winter. The beauty of the scene belied its danger. At present the thought of the threshed, heaped grain made the farmers hopeful. Yet what remained in the city's bins was now closely guarded. He glanced at the village on a ridge to the north and guessed that some of its number were boiling up grass for their dinner. The harvest would not feed them all.

Tuccio felt hot and, compared with the others, a little stuffy in his long grey cloak and *gonnella*. If not for the heat of the sun and the gait of his mule, he might have been up on a hobbyhorse back in his study, his face flowing forth from a painter's brush. He smiled derisively at the thought and fixed the *berretta* square on his head. Beatrice was always at him to have another portrait done, to commission a Nativity—with *them* cast as shepherds—for the chapel in Santa Maria dei Poveri. In fact, he didn't like portraits. With his sharp chin, scant hair and pinched, narrow nose he looked like some satirist's vision of Parsimony. He glanced at his daughters ahead of him—hanging back so their father wouldn't be left behind—and thought how lovely they were. God knew, they didn't get their looks from him. Then again, nor did they get them from their mother, who was a wonderful woman in her way, blessed with an unusual degree of wit, but as plain as a Lent larder.

Gaia, the elder of the pair, looked splendid upon her white horse with its harness of scarlet and brass. She was a tall, pale, dark-haired beauty with anthracite eyes and a degree of pride that was doubtless a sin, but which was, perhaps, what Tuccio most loved about her. It seemed so unassailable, an inner redoubt from which she repelled each indignity, mockery or shock. Though, as she was Tuccio's daughter, such confrontations were rare; and at eighteen her pride had already stood in the way of more than one marriage offer. This, he knew, was his weakness. He could rule the wool trade with an iron fist, command shipping from Cathay to Catalonia, keep his factors in stammering trepidation, but control his daughters? In this he displayed less skill than many a peasant on the brink of ruin. Other fathers organised everything—brokers, betrothal, wedding—and the girls simply had to accept it. But here, as in no other part of his life, Tuccio allowed his will to desert him. For this he received muttered disapprobation, though very softly muttered indeed. He loved Gaia for her pride, had let her have her way in all things, and simply couldn't bear to break her. It would have felt like breaking himself.

And Marina, fourteen-year-old Marina? Well, just look at her there in tunic and hose astride her bay pony. She wanted to ride like a man, not side-saddle like Gaia, and so she must dress like a boy. It embarrassed him, but again he couldn't say no, despite his wife's protestations. He was just too weak. He couldn't resist the girl—she had more life than all his apprentices added together, as brown as a nut, with squirrel-bright eyes, and as skinny and quick as a whippet. How could he stop Marina? Yes, these daughters of his—Gaia, surmounting her horse like a plinth, while Marina rode hers like a jockey—they were his pride and his source of humility.

Tuccio breathed a sigh of relief as they entered the shade of the woods. Tall holm oaks tented the narrow track, their dark, prickly leaves rustling stiffly above. Baldassare's farm was woods more than meadows, one hundred *staiora* of land—surely no more—at four florins a *staioro*; with a rough shack under the shade of a chestnut tree, a few vines, some olive trees and a dovecote. Gaia was why they were here, not the urge to launch hawks at small birds. Baldassare was clearly attracted to her. Tuccio had known it for quite some time, and was even a little anxious on his behalf, as she'd seemed unusually cold to him, even by *her* cool standards. And much as he liked Baldassare, he wasn't convinced he provided the best match for Gaia. Certainly he was a delightful fellow, adventurous, clever, good-hearted and honourable. But his father had been the least prudent of men— a noble, in fact, thrown out of the town and too proud, or obtuse, to succeed as a merchant. He'd simply frittered away what remained of his wealth in his exile in Venice. Baldassare had cut his old ties and tried hard to make good—he'd even been Tuccio's Balkan agent, dealing in iron, furs and wax from Roumania. Yet, though his trading ventures often made money, he seemed to lose far too much. His talents, at best, seemed erratic. And what a curse to their families such men could be. No, even had Tuccio felt able, he would not have promoted the match, no matter how much he liked Baldassare. As a man he was charming; as a business proposition he was a bad risk.

In the deep green light of a tiny glade he caught up with the company. The dogs and beaters had waited there for them, along with a flask of wine and some olives. No-one dismounted but Marina, who ran over to pat a big tawny hound that was flailing its tail in the brush. Tuccio finished his cup of red wine and sighed. He glanced at the trim young falconers, the birds on their wrists like little blind bishops in their bright leather mitres, and felt a surge of distaste for this fruitless parading about.

As if reading his thoughts, Baldassare gave a sign to the beaters, who went striding off down the path, belabouring the scrub.

They rode in a long, loose column, Tuccio forced to increase his pace, finding himself between two men who were clearly keen to see the first flush. He watched Baldassare and his friend from Livorno,

Aldo del Palagio, who rode together at the head of the group. He knew they harboured a friendly rivalry over their birds, but noticed that neither Fiera, Baldassare's purebred peregrine, nor Aldo's big gyrfalcon had yet been unhooded. Instead, a brown goshawk was glaring about, eagerly bating with short, stout wings on its handler's gloved fist. Though the others held their birds by conventional jesses, Baldassare kept no such check on his peregrine. But for her hood, Fiera was free to move as she would, yet maintained her motionless stance on her master's wrist. Before Tuccio could give it any more thought, there were wings all about him as the dogs flushed a brace of woodpigeons, which went beating away in every direction like so many feathery Roman candles. The goshawk's owner gave a shrill whistle, and it lunged from his wrist, pushing him back in his saddle, already weaving between the trees in pursuit of its prey. In a matter of moments one of the pigeons, which had seemed to move so fast through the air, was just in front of the hawk's sickle beak. And then it was caught in the talons' curved hooks, the creature embracing it—the cruellest of lovers—and gripping its flesh to the very heart.

The dogs now belled through the tangles of holly, and the beaters came after, the hunters all smiling high on their horses. The goshawk's owner whistled, loud and insistent, and his bird soon settled back on his wrist, its beak still bloody beneath the plumed hood. When they got to the pigeon they found it half plucked, head holed like an egg by the goshawk's beak.

'She's a bit eager,' smiled Aldo, though his friend just shrugged, saying nothing.

Tuccio looked at the corpse appraisingly. Perhaps it had been an untidy kill, but it was a lovely plump bird, and he found himself already thinking of dinner.

It wasn't long before they emerged into sheets of bright sunlight where a steep meadow, quite silvery in the sudden glare, rustled its grass round their horses' gaskins. At the top of the hill, surrounded by chestnuts, was Baldassare's farmhouse; some way below, the fields fell away to a thin, bright ribbon, a tributary of the Ombronetto. Tuccio lazed dreamily in the saddle, gazing ahead to Marina and Gaia now riding with Baldassare. At present he spoke with Marina, but even from where he was, Tuccio saw how his glance strayed to Gaia. Perhaps, after all, he would make a good son-in-law, even an excellent one. He was smooth, a good talker, quite shrewd at times. With Tuccio's help he might make a fine merchant, though this may not be enough for Gaia, who rode with that typical air of assurance that charmed and frustrated her father, her eyes fixed ahead, a faint smile on her face, as if accepting the sun's due obeisance. Even had she liked Baldassare, his path would not have been easy.

Indeed, were Tuccio to allow himself any anxiety over the man, it would not be on Gaia's account. Baldassare had genuine enemies, much the same as Tuccio had, yet for Baldassare their enmity seemed more bitter, even though twenty years had passed since the exile of all those old nobles, including the young man's father. That he too had been one of the victims only made their resentment greater. Frederico dalla Montagna, Odofredo Moltogalante, the Gentili, and all the other clans of their faction, saw Baldassare as a traitor to his family traditions, to his caste and, although he'd only been ten at the time of his exile, to his Ghibelline past. They simply couldn't stomach the fact that a noble would turn his back on his faction and go with the Guelphs, insulting his father, banished for fighting that very party. It enraged them to see a man of his blood working as a wool merchant's agent, aspiring to be a bourgeois, and not a very good one at that. Yes, Baldassare had to watch his back in the streets, especially now that bad harvests and growing disorder had made Montagna more cocky. He was even said to be plotting with factions in Florence.

Tuccio watched Baldassare and wondered whether he liked him because they shared so much in common. They were both despised by the nobles, had both spent their youth in foreign trading posts, and both their fathers were exiles; though Tuccio's father had, in fact, been a voluntary exile from his native Pisa, becoming a partner in a rundown tavern in the Borgo Santa Maria. Still, this meant that neither man—unlike the rest of the merchants— had a network of relatives in the town, so that each must count on the friends he could find. Yes, they had much in common. So why not Gaia? But his thoughts were interrupted by a sudden shout from the falconers.

A great flock of pigeons was wheeling in circles over the hills, approaching the party like a piecemeal cloud, turning in slow, solid arcs, their wings to the sun, then seeming to vanish as they changed direction. Aldo drew the hood from the head of his bird, which bated and stirred on his wrist. Fiera, Baldassare's peregrine, stayed quite still when her hood was removed, only blinking a bit in the dazzle of light. Slate-blue on her master's scarlet doublet, she looked like a small, fierce statue, and though the gyrfalcon seemed far bigger, Tuccio noted the length of her wings, the notched beak, the sharp, alert eyes with the black bars beneath them. As the wings of the flock came and went in the sun, her face was a mask of watchful ferocity.

Its ties released, the gyrfalcon flew, springing from Aldo's arm, its talons ripping free of the glove. It climbed till it soared like a shadow above the flock, which was drifting over the green valley floor. Then Fiera too soared, but so swiftly, so soundlessly, that Tuccio felt he'd hardly drawn breath before she was high at the sky's blue summit. He watched the still birds and briefly pondered on what they saw so far from the ground. He and his fellows would be mere ants, and away to the east— the far hills and Perugia—would they see Venice, perhaps? And further still, to the lands of the heathens, or those described by Marco Polo? To the west, Topomagro, then Spain, the far islands, and beyond? Over the sea? Would such birds see the edge of the world, then the great singing spheres? Or did they think just of the kill? He smiled, bemused, but was interrupted by the horsemen's shouts. In a burst of bright song, a pair of skylarks soared over the valley, their flight above the slow-flying pigeons. He put all his musings aside and thought of those skylarks, their sweet, juicy flesh, packed with white truffles. Oh, a food for the gods and rich gluttons.

Both falconers whistled shrilly. But their birds were already stooping, dropping so fast they slipped out of sight, and likely beyond their masters' signals. Fiera, though she'd stooped second, was ahead when her flight seemed to falter, to warp in the air like a damaged arrow, veering short of her target. And sure enough, the gyrfalcon hit, taking a pigeon mid-flight in its talons. The broken bird was fluttering down to the ground already. A second cry made him turn to Fiera since, at that very moment, at the end of a fast, arcing fall that might almost have torn her wings from their roots, she'd caught one skylark a blow with her claws, pursuing it down as it plummeted.

The dogs and the beaters descended the hill as the gyrfalcon flew like an angry white ghost, swooping back up toward Aldo's fist. But Baldassare didn't move. Instead, he gave a curious, trilling whistle. Then Tuccio heard an intake of breath. 'I don't believe it,' someone was saying. 'What peregrine ever does that?' For there was Fiera, sweeping toward them, the skylark clasped in her claws. But her master just smiled—rather smugly, in fact—and took some raw meat from the pouch at his belt, holding it out to the fluttering falcon.

The Tartars come to Kaffa

JACOPO PASSERO LIVED NEAR THE EAST WALL OF KAFFA, in one of the rooms of a large but ramshackle house on the edge of the Armenian quarter. It might be more true to say that he *slept* in that room, since he spent most of his time in the kitchen, talking with his landlady, Monna Simona, nibbling at the tasty bits she was chopping, or sitting on the big rear balcony, hoping for a soft southern breeze while he gossiped with Lapo Tromba, his landlord. You didn't actually talk with Lapo, you listened to his endless soliloquies on the slyness of the Venetians, the stupidity of the Turks, the clannishness of the Armenians, the lechery of the Genoese, indeed, on any subject guaranteed to raise him to a slow and satisfying rancour while his voice grew slurred with his homemade grappa. 'The Tartars,' he might snarl, since this was a subject that preoccupied the town at that period. 'Don't talk to me about Tartars. A race of degenerates, drunk all the time when they're not raping virgins. Bloody Tartars.' And he'd mumble his way to apoplexy, while Jacopo nodded, watching his fleshy, vermicular nose grow bright with conviction as he drained his full cup.

It's not here, however, that we find Jacopo Passero on this fine spring morning, but at the door of the long Tromba larder in the foundations of the house. It's cool here, half underground, though this is not why Jacopo's picking the lock. He likes food, and so does his cat, small though she is. But Lapo insists on keeping the best of the larder strictly within his family. It's a small failing, the sin of gluttony, and Jacopo could do worse than relieve his landlord of the need to confess it. He slips the door open carefully, peers into the dimness, while Scimmi darts through like a little grey phantom. 'No,' he hisses, as she crouches to spring beneath the hung ducks, which have charged the cool air with a sharp, gamy smell. 'Have some of this, you greedy thing. No-one'll notice.' He carves a thin slice from a long leg of ham, then throws it down so she pounces hungrily, shaking her head as if killing a mouse. There's no point in stealing a feast if you wind up in prison, or even if it means you can steal nothing more. The larder is always left looking just as it did, so Jacopo can visit for judicious snacks whenever he pleases.

'No, Scimmi,' he whispers as she props once more beneath the ducks, and cuts her a second thin slice of ham. He looks about him, carefully wiping his blade, takes off the bag slung over his shoulder, and carves out a piece of *marzolini* cheese, a few hunks from a hacked mortadella—two of which he tosses to Scimmi—then fills a small flask from one of the barrels of homemade red wine, takes a handful of olives from a pottery jar, some imported figs, some goose-liver pâté, a bit of pork jelly, a pair of oranges, and—though he hesitates here—a small capon that somehow has slipped from its hook and lies on the stones. Then he stuffs it all in his bag, gathers up Scimmi and hurries outside, locking the door while she stretches her neck for the buried capon.

Passing through the kitchen on his way to the street, he finds Lapo bent at the table, wiping his bulbous nose with his hand, eyes aflame as he munches at chillies and garlic.

'He's unwell,' says his wife, and Jacopo finds himself wondering once more how small, fair Monna Simona wound up with an ogre like Lapo. 'There's a surfeit of sluggish humours. Maestro Tomassi says he needs dry, hot food.'

'Worms,' moans her husband, coughing wetly. 'My body's a city of worms.'

'Worms?' Jacopo repeats, feeling the bag at his back to see that it's properly closed.

'Yes, may they roast in Hell with the Tartars.' And, cradling his stomach, he groans once again, then quickly adds, 'Not that I mean it, Jacopo. They're all right—the worms, I mean, not the Tartars—so long as they're kept contented, well fed, not jostled about or attacked with poisonous medicines, just resting there happily in the guts with nothing to disturb them. Between the mouth and the arsehole it's their own little fortress, and God help you if you try to lay siege to it.'

'Then what are you doing with all those chillies? They're a weapon against worms, aren't they?' And, indeed, Monna Simona is coming with reinforcements—a cup of fiery grappa.

'No, no,' replies Lapo, snuffling up the fumes. 'Oh, they like that,' he chuckles, and tosses back a mouthful. 'It's them, my guests, who need all this heat. It's their humours, not mine, that are out of balance. We have to cure our vermin to cure ourselves. Woe betide the man whose worms grow sick or start to die, spewing their poisons into his blood. My own have grown melancholic with phlegm, and so the blood becomes thick and the heart grows sluggish.'

Scimmi has jumped on the table, where she sniffs at the chillies and springs back, blinking. Jacopo removes her before his landlord can give her a clout with the back of his hand.

'I could get you something to expel them,' he says, 'down at the apothecary's on Via Malocello. I've heard of a woman at Tana who produced over three hundred worms, which she kept in a bottle like grey vermicelli.'

'The devil you will! Just the mention of it makes the beasts writhe within me. The surest sign of a dying man is his worms begin leaving. No, nothing like that. But if you're going out, could you get me a few of those hot ginger sweets? I think they'd like those.'

Jacopo readily agrees, taking his leave and strolling to the door. On the street he heads north along the east wall, toward the north-eastern gate. But it's clear that something is wrong. The town militia is manning the parapet, soldiers are running toward the gate, and every face holds a look of muddled or knowing urgency. Jacopo grasps a knowing one's sleeve and asks him what's happening.

'You're a bit behind,' the man grunts. 'It's the Tartar army, one of their forced marches. They've advanced more quickly than anyone thought possible.' Then he pulls away, rushing off to wherever he's going.

Jacopo opens Scimmi's pouch, and she peers up at him, yawning. 'Well, my girl, it looks like we're in for it.' She stares blankly up, then yawns once again. 'No,' he grins, 'you never were a political animal,' then closes the flap and hurries on to the north-eastern gate.

Now the church bells are ringing all over the town—Santa Croce, San Pietro, Santa Maria—as if proclaiming the Lord's Second Coming and not the descent of the Golden Horde. The gates, of course, are locked tighter than Heaven to armies of sinners, and soldiers are guarding the stairs to the wall like armoured Saint Peters. Some paradise, Jacopo sniggers, with burglars included. 'Would I ... ah,' he begins, '... be able to go up and have a quick look?' But the corporal glares and waves him off with his spear. So, what's he to do? He wants to see for himself, and not out of morbid curiosity, but because he feels blind behind these walls. If only he could see—no matter how big the army—he wouldn't be feeling so helpless. And then the great pealing announcing the siege makes him think of Santa Croce. The belltower. He goes rushing off, retracing his path till he gets to the church with its tall campanile. No priest, no people, only the sacristan ringing the bells. Jacopo ducks through the doorway and runs up the stairs, one flight, two then three, more panting and weak-kneed the higher he climbs, engulfed in the thick waves of sound that roll through the air. And when he gets to the top—his fingers stuck in his ears, the very stones ringing around him and Scimmi abruptly awake, peering out of the pouch with fright in her eyes—he first sees the Tartars.

They're coming down through the hills on the road from the north, a seemingly endless column of horsemen, more horses than men, each rider clad in a leather cuirass or in mail with a breastplate of oxhide and iron—all bristling with javelins, bone bows, fletched arrows—hefting maces, hooked lances, an axe or a scimitar curved like their drooping moustaches; and above the blank discs of their shields, as if their emblem were Nothing itself, are their faces' flat masks. The column winds back to the top of the foothills where a signal fire burns, answered by one in the valley beyond and beyond that another, till they're lost in the haze whence the army emerges: warriors, horses, carts bearing mangonels, trebuchets, rocking beneath the weight of tall siege towers. There are camels loaded with bamboo ladders, the poles of low tents, fat-bellied drums to beat out the rhythms of battle. Oxen drag fodder, provisions, equipment; and along with it all comes the history of slaughter—Bukhara with its thirty thousand corpses; Zhongdu, its palace turned to a mountain of bones; Nishapur's three mystic pyramids, one for men, one for women, one for children, all of skulls. The record of conquest trails through the mountains to Kaffa, where even now the chiefs of that army are just beyond arrowshot, their squat horses solid beneath their thin banners—

no longer yak-tailed, but made out of fine corsac brushes—and behind them four riders, each with a long wooden lance, one spiked with the head of a Franciscan friar, one with a merchant, one with his wife, and one with the head, still trailing torn veins, of the Genoese consul in Tana.

Jacopo doesn't want to see any more. Nor does he feel like the food he has stolen. Yes, he knows that they use the tactic of terror, and now he's convinced it works very well. He walks numbly down and heads home, feeding Scimmi the slices of ham as he goes. 'The trouble with you, my girl,' he mutters, watching her bolting the mouthfuls, 'is that you're insensitive.' But she pays him no mind, and he can't be bothered continuing. This apathy lasts to the Tromba kitchen.

'The Tartars are here,' he says flatly, as if they were some expected guests. 'I saw them from Santa Croce's tower.'

All three of the family stare at him. Lapo, already in his cups, tries to get him in focus. Monna Simona looks alarmed, and her little daughter, Caterina, at first looks blank, then starts to respond to her mother's anxiety.

'What ... what did they—' begins the mother, but Lapo bursts out, 'Oh Christ, here come the heathens, sew up your daughters' slits.' His voice is heavy with grappa, not fear. 'Sic all the old sex-crazed nuns from Santa Dolorosa onto them. Exhaust the poor bastards, whittle their savages' cocks, give 'em the—'

'Would you stop!' cries Simona. 'You're frightening your daughter.'

And, indeed, Caterina is looking upset, though more from her mother's urgency, Jacopo suspects, than from Lapo's obscenity.

'Trina ... here,' he says, holding out one of the oranges. 'I got you a present.'

'Oh,' says the girl, gripping the fruit in both hands. In fact, as a man more taken with thieving than eating, it's not the first time that he's raided their larder only to make them a gift of the food.

'Oh, Jacopo, you shouldn't have,' says her mother, pleased to be able to change the subject.

'And ... well, here are a few other things I got for the pantry.' So saying, he takes out the olives, the figs, the other orange and the capon, leaving the pâté and jelly since they might well recognise them.

'Any, um, wine there, Jacopo?' mutters the landlord and, for an instant, Jacopo almost takes out the flask, then thinks better of it.

'This is too much,' says Simona, smiling. 'You're really too kind.' Then she turns to her husband. 'We've never had a lodger like Jacopo, have we, dear?'

Her husband dutifully shakes his head, while Jacopo smiles benignly. 'But it simply shows how hard the times have become,' she continues. 'I mean, no matter how many of these little presents you give us, the larder just never seems to grow full.'

It was not long before the Tartar army had established its camp near the city, extending across the plain to the east and to the foot of the northern hills. They swarmed beneath the walls, locust-like in their lacquered armour, erecting tents, catapults, siege towers, while the heads of the consul, the friar, the merchant husband and wife, stared at the town from the tips of their pikes with melancholy eyes. They had some banker from Tana, one Giuseppe Tantabella, deliver a speech beneath the eastern wall, saying that the Genoese should open their gates to the conquerors, that they would be treated well if they did, that should they resist, history showed the fate that awaited them. But the townspeople answered his words with silence. Late in the night some thought they heard cries, and at dawn an object was lobbed through the air, landing in the Piazza San Piero. It was the moist, bloody skin of Giuseppe Tantabella, and when the guards looked into the trench below the walls they saw the banker's body huddled in the dirt like some pink and violet pupa torn from its chrysalis.

This heralded a rain of missiles, the mangonels firing massive darts across the walls, the trebuchets lobbing rocks onto rooftops, streets and squares, while volleys of arrows pierced timber and flesh alike as they fell in random showers. Jacopo scurried beneath an arcade on the Piazza San Piero, stepping gingerly out when the arrows ceased clattering onto the tiles, and quick to duck back when a set of large stones came crashing about him. One rolled close to his feet as he huddled behind a pillar. He looked at it, and it looked back. He looked still harder, but it didn't blink. This stone had eyes, a nose, a mouth and trimmed beard. Despite the chance of further arrows—and, God knew, further heads—Jacopo went scuttling for home.

In the following days came a rain of human limbs, the putrid bodies of oxen, and Simona recounted a tale of a dozen limbless babies falling over the Borgo San Antonio. The Armenian quarter suffered a torrent of skulls that landed on the pavement like huge, fragile hailstones, exploding as they fell. It was as if the sky were one great charnel-house pouring its contents down on the earth. But such excesses dwindled as the town showed its resolve and, presumably, as the army exhausted its most ghoulish missiles.

Thus, the first wave of terror over, the Tartars now used conventional tactics, launching massed attacks against the walls with their ladders and towers, pounding at the gates with iron-shod tree trunks; their bows streamed with arrows and the mangonels flung fiery darts. But the town militia was alert and well armed, chopping off the hands of their agile attackers, raining arrow storms down on their heads, pouring hot pitch, boiling oil, molten lead through the walls' machicolations till the Tartars, in the tight iron scales of their armour, were fried like shoals of metal fish. So it wasn't long before their generals were admitting that the siege would be slower than they'd all first hoped and that, though the town would soon fall in one great offensive, they might have to let hunger smooth their path.

Hunger, however, was something the Genoese could stave off for some time to come. They had long known the Tartars' intentions and were well prepared with granaries full to the brim and richly stocked warehouses. A fast galley was sent to the west, though the Turks were unwilling to help, while the Greeks would doubtless feel well rid of them. Yes, help would be slow in arriving, if it arrived at all. Yet they had food for the interim, and so they held out, glancing back over the southern wall toward the Black Sea with their swords held north and east. As the Tartars dug in for a longer siege, life resumed the bulk of its normal rhythms. People returned, as much as they could, to their daily routines, never free of the sense that they played out a part, doing their best to ensure that the mask of order and calm was kept in place, knowing all the time it might break to bits with the fall of a stone, or the flames of an arrow kindling the roof, or the breach of the wall by ten thousand soldiers.

One morning, for instance, Jacopo is walking down the street, doing just what he always does—keeping an eye out for a likely purse to snip from its belt. He's looking quite jaunty, since the times have been kindly to burglars, what with the siege distracting all and so many merchants given commissions. The only hitch is their fear for their houses. With those bamboo-tube rockets fired like arrows, and those big flaming darts, everyone thinks their houses will burn. They no longer leave their valuables at home, at least not those that are portable. And where do they put them? Why, on their belts, of course. So this is the reason he's sauntering along, seeking the right purse to cut. And here it is now, fat with the clink of gold florins and dangling from the belt of a dapper bourgeois, oblivious to the siege, it would seem from his air of complacency. Well, if the Tartars can't ruffle his smugness, let Jacopo see if *he* can. Sidle up through the crowd in the square, slip out the knife, take care lest the bustlers nudge you against him. Now step alongside, feel the weight of that purse, heavy with florins and big as a bull's testicle. Then reach with the blade, draw down the cord, and *thonk*! the fellow's been hit by some massive black rock that's come through the air, crushing his skull like an empty eggshell, while everyone turns and your hand's on his purse.

It's now that Jacopo clings to the man, beginning to cry, 'Oh, my friend, my poor friend,' cradling his head while slipping the blade up his own loose sleeve. 'Quick!' he cries to one of the starers. 'Those bastards have done it! Can't you see that he's hurt?'

The man obeys Jacopo's gestures, putting his arm round the victim's shoulders. But hurt? His head's like a plate of spaghetti. Yet no-one objects when Jacopo says that *he'll* find a doctor, perhaps because he runs off so smartly, wiping his brow and releasing his breath, barely recalling that, in the chaos, he didn't think to take the purse.

In which Brother Corvo finds new work

Rosso Gitti, a little light-headed with wine, walked down the track that led to the woods from the Under the Star. Normally he would have thought nothing of this walk, but tonight, with the crescent moon turning the cypresses lining the path to funereal stone, and the beech woods looming ahead like a tunnel of darkness, he felt oppressed by some vague threat. He tried to focus his mind on the conversation that had taken place round the table that evening, but the words kept drifting aside to reveal, through the inn's open window, a figure seated in the dusk, face shadowed in the folds of his cowl.

'The cardinal's trying to increase the labour that's due to him!' These words swirled up in eddies, obscuring the dark figure, as Giuliano, the farrier, mounted his hobbyhorse for the second time that evening.

'Cardinal Rollo da Parma,' he'd spat on the inn's dirt floor, receiving a scowl from the taverner. 'He's the greediest vulture in that flock of vultures, and I don't mind telling him to his face.' The farrier had jutted his chin, cheeks flushed with wine and belligerence, as if Rosso himself were responsible for his master's actions.

'That's right,' said Girardo, another chin-jutter. 'Last year the tithes, this year the work-dues.'

Rosso was sick of the way they badgered him about the cardinal's greed, as if washing Rollo da Parma's dishes made him privy to his every decision. Yet he couldn't help himself: whenever they started criticising, he always ended up defending his master's actions as if they were his own.

He shook his head at himself, bowing beneath the palpable shadows of the great beech trees and glancing back across his shoulder at the pathway, pallid with moonlight between the cypress columns. There was nothing there, and he breathed a slow, giddy sigh, once again shaking his head at his own reactions. Like a child, he thought, and returned to the farrier's words. 'Everybody knows he had trouble at Avignon. And now he's come back to make trouble here.' This was something that was often said, though Rosso saw no proof of it.

'Oh, people talk, Giuliano,' he'd said, draining his cup, 'but I don't know. He comes up to his palace from Boccaperta because it's cool in the hills. Tithes get increased because life gets more expensive for everyone, even the cardinal.'

It was at this point that Girardo had slapped him on the back and laughed. 'You're an innocent, Rosso,' he'd grinned unpleasantly. 'You could clean out the devil's shithouse and think him an angel. Rollo da Parma's going to screw us, and then he's going to go across to the coast and screw Topomagro. But it's no good arguing with the innocent.'

Rosso felt his face go hot, even in the cool of the thick night woods. 'I'm not innocent,' he had said, gulping down yet another cup of oily red wine.

'Then you're guilty!' roared the farrier, pounding the bench. 'And what are you guilty of, young Rosso?'

But Rosso had felt confused, and it was then that he'd seen the stranger in the dusky light, sitting outside alone, face framed by the small, square window, and staring directly at him, or so it had seemed, though it was hard to tell with his features shadowed as they were by the rough grey wool of his hood. 'I—I'm not guilty of anything,' he muttered, turning back toward the room.

'Oh, well, that's a shame,' Girardo had snickered, facetious as ever, till Rosso—again defending his master with no real intention of doing so—had blurted, 'And I don't see what Topomagro's got to do with it.'

He turned. A shadow had moved in the depths of the trees behind him. He was sure of it and stood, unmoving, watching the bend of the path where moonlight trembled in thin little slivers. All was still, there was nothing there, he was drunk. Slowly, turning his head uneasily back to the section of track before him, he hurried on through the wood. Such fears were childish, and he tried once again to focus his thoughts on the talk at the inn. But it was all too confused. There was something about the Priors in Topomagro taking over church land and renting it out at a profit, but he'd grown bewildered by the wine and mockery, and couldn't properly understand what they were saying. Instead, while their words swarmed round his ears and the alcohol fumed in his skull, his eyes had turned to that person no-one else had appeared to notice, the figure now dark in the deepening dusk, framed by the window like Death himself and shrouded in grey *romagnolo*.

It was the way this person—a Minorite friar to judge by his robes—had been staring so silently into the room, at Rosso himself ... it had jangled his nerves. Again he wanted to look back behind him. But he wouldn't. To do so was feeding his fears, making them worse by letting them win, and he held his gaze firmly before him. Yet slowly the shadows closed in, building like waves at his back, till he had to look once, and there, behind him, secreted amongst the branches, was nothing. He breathed and went on, recalling the final words that they'd flung as he'd stumbled out the door. 'What are you walking for?' the farrier had cried. 'Why don't you get da Parma to give you a barge for one of those canals he's building all over the country?' Intent on the friar alone in the night and on keeping his eyes averted, he had hardly heard him. Yet he couldn't resist one swift, secret glance as he walked down the road, peering back at the silent man now watching after him, exhaling two quicksilver columns of steam—though he couldn't be sure— and grinning an intimate grin.

The track went funnelling down under trees, their foliage rustling like sniggering imps. Rosso considered the inn no more, but kept his eyes on his feet, on the roots and hollows that threatened to pitch him onto his face, on the branches scraping his skin, on his hurry. Fear stretched time with its tenterhooks and, as he stared through the dark, he heard the footfall. Despite the rustling of leaves, the sounds of his progress, it came with the force of a sword drawn in anger. Once more, he knew he was letting his fears win, and held himself rigid, refusing to look though the phantoms might gather behind him, until he could hold out no longer and, turning, knowing the path must once more be empty, saw the hooded figure pursuing him down through the trees.

He panicked, almost cried out, and walked briskly on with small gulping noises. As he hurried round a corner in the track, he took one more glance and was frightened to see that the thing was still rushing behind him, the Minorite robe whipped back by the speed of its progress. Though nothing was clear amidst the shadows, he felt sure that he'd seen no feet touch the earth, nor face in the hood. He began to bolt, when a sudden voice cried, 'Lad!' He slowed, and then it came again—'Hey, lad!'—a rich, smooth, fatherly voice, the very voice to protect you from dangers and dreams. He peered behind, seeing naught but that friar's habit which, even as he looked, was raising one arm to push back the hood, revealing a face that seemed to be laughing ruefully. 'Hey, lad,' the friar puffed, 'slow down a minute. I've been trying to catch you up.' And the boy felt suddenly foolish, no more than half grown, as if the others were right to laugh at him.

He stood and waited for the man to reach him. 'Sorry if I gave you a fright,' the friar said, adjusting his habit. 'I'm trying to get to the cardinal's palace. I thought you might know the way.'

Rosso heard the smooth voice and nodded, still shaken. 'Yes, I'm going there myself.'

'Oh, good,' the man chuckled, resuming his progress along the path, so that Rosso fell in with his footsteps as if it were he who followed the friar and not the other way round. They walked for a way in silence, then the man turned toward him and said, 'You work at the palace, I take it.'

'Yes,' the boy mumbled, 'I'm one of the scullions.'

The friar nodded, and again there was silence, only broken when he added, 'Good food there, I suppose?'

'Keeps body and soul together.' The boy glanced up with a diffident smile.

'Ah, but thus they never were,' sighed the cleric suavely. 'And the black comet already mounts the earth's rim.'

'What?' asked the boy, slowing his stride.

'I am that comet,' said the patient voice.

'You're ... what?'

Rosso stared at the shadowy road, eyes wide, mouth making a breathless rattle, the knife already buried up to the hilt in his chest.

'Your humble servant—Brother Corvo,' said the friar, bowing, as he let the boy bow too, all the way to the ground, then tore out the blade.

The palace of Cardinal Rollo da Parma lay in the midst of the wooded plains to the north of

Boccaperta. Though this port town, the largest in his see, contained what was technically his most magnificent residence, he loathed the way its windows let in the scent of brine and fresh-gutted fish, and so spent whatever time he could within the honey-coloured walls of his country palace. It lay like a topaz set in the cleft of two low hills, surrounded by a park of elms and oak trees, no more than eight leagues south-east of Topomagro. It formed the hub of an incomplete wheel, whose spokes were a series of half-built canals by which His Eminence purposed to travel throughout his see, unimpeded by brigands, towns or bad roads. As if to follow the countryside's fashion, it had the look of a castle about it, with the crenellated parapet ringing its roof, its tall twin towers, its heavy bronze gate, and its moulded grille to ape a portcullis. Yet it lacked real fortifications, designed to give only a sense of severity while hiding its luxury behind high walls.

Isolated though it seemed, it was really a little city unto itself, housing an army of guards and servants, chaplains and chamberlains, lawyers and notaries, deacons, physicians, carpenters, masons, goldsmiths, jewellers, cooks, grooms and washerwomen. Gardeners tended the shrubs and the lawns, keeping the moss off the statues, scrubbing the sculpted saints as if they were Heaven's bath attendants. And at the centre of this splendour sat Rollo da Parma, late of the Curia at Avignon, late of the Papal Consistory, late of Pope Clement the Sixth's inner circle, and lately returned to the tidal mudflats of Boccaperta. Squawking gulls and stinking fish—on the wharves of his own home town he might almost have been in the council chambers of Avignon.

On the night of the visit of Pope Clement's envoy, with flickering torchlight tormenting the faces of saints in the garden, the cardinal wore the mask of a statesman along with his best samite robes. His figure was like a squat red ball in the glistening fabric, and beneath the crimson biretta his teeth shone whitely at the envoy. He'd had the servants light a small fire in the corner of the room and, though it was rather a crisp autumn night, the fact that he'd worn his finest robe, lined as it was with ermine, was making him sweat and dab at his face with a linen napkin. By contrast, his guest—Dom Pietro Carrara—looked sharp and cool in his long black habit. He peered smoothly about the big chamber, noting especially the tall, gaunt figure that stood stock-still in the shifting light, as if it hung from the wall in its motley, a Carnival puppet. He turned to his smiling host and then nodded.

'You were wise, Your Eminence, to return here. It's a place where works more lasting than the intrigues of Avignon can be achieved.' He raised the golden goblet to his lips, then paused, seeing that it was almost empty.

'Like ordering another jug of wine?' smiled the cardinal, raising his finger into the air, where a ruby flared in the firelight. The gawky clown came slowly to life and crept off toward the kitchens. 'Or deciding whether to have the partridge or the hare?'

'No, Your Eminence,' said Dom Pietro softly. 'I think what the Holy Father had in mind were those works on canon law that the duties of the Curia had prevented you from writing.'

Rollo wiped his brow and stared at his guest. It was no mere exercise in modesty to concede that the Benedictine knew canon law with a depth and subtlety that he, even were he to live forever, could never achieve.

'Yet even here, Dom Pietro,' he said, dismissing the charade, 'in the peace and silence of the countryside, where one would expect to be able to devote oneself less ... distractedly ... to Christ ... even here one meets intrigue and faction.'

The Benedictine toyed with the empty goblet, watching his reflection twist and flicker on its golden surface. 'You are speaking of Schwanhals or Topomagro.' There was an air of getting suddenly down to business in his voice.

'Well ...' the cardinal began, keen to continue, yet allowing his words to trail off as the lanky jester re-entered the room. The fellow looked like some ungainly stick-insect, his crown of bells ding-a-linging in the air, the tray perched high on a spidery hand and, in the other, his fool's sceptre, a curlicue of wood with the moth-eaten head of a grinning monkey. He bent to the table, setting down his load, and it was only now that the Benedictine realised just how tall he was. Briefly surprised at the figure's height, he proffered his goblet for filling. But the jester turned with his wry, bony face, gently waving a finger, soliciting his patience. Instead of filling the goblets, he poured some wine in the small silver cup beside them on the table. As if proposing a toast, he lifted the tasting goblet, incised as it was with serpents' tongues, and tossed back its purplish contents, swilling them round in his mouth. He might have been gauging their vintage, not testing them for poison, since he smacked his lips and sighed, apparently uncertain, lifting the jug to pour out a second draught.

'Tozzo, enough!' said the cardinal sharply, yet with a small, indulgent smile, so the clown could sneak a few more drops before ambling off on his skinny legs to his corner by the fire.

'As you were about to say, Your Eminence,' suggested Dom Pietro, his voice betraying impatience, 'the Priors of Topomagro are setting a dangerous precedent. The Holy Father would be pleased if you could teach them a lesson, and by then your problems at Avignon might well have abated.'

'Oh yes, I could teach them a lesson all right.' And Dom Pietro saw a helpful glint of pride in the cardinal's eyes. 'In so many places, men's faith in the Church has been compromised, even among the clergy. But most, it benefits the jumped-up town magistrates and the more rapacious of the merchants.'

'How true, Your Eminence. They think that by casting off the guiding hand of the Holy Father, they can gain control of their local bishops and use the Church to their own advantage.'

'And once again we see the Devil working through the avarice in men's hearts.' The cardinal, warming to his subject, wiped at his glistening face and sucked at the bones of the anchovies lodged in his teeth. 'So many of these parochial townsmen have sought to discredit His Holiness simply because he is now at Avignon. They claim that he has deserted them, and these little men of Topomagro are like all the worst of their breed. They nod piously at whatever rantings they hear against the wealth of the Church from some wandering Fraticelli, and then steal whatever they can from her. As you know, the Priors of the town have taken over Church land merely because it had lain unused for a few years. But now, Dom Pietro, they've let it out to a gang of peasants on a sharecropping basis, spending nothing on it and making a small fortune in the process.'

'Have these peasants got the land back into full production?'

'Oh yes, you can be assured of that,' Rollo sneered. 'They're paying none of their dues to me but they still get to hoard a share of the profits.'

'You mentioned Bernardo Moltogalante in your letter.'

'Yes, he remains exiled in Florence, where I'm helping him to negotiate some loans. He's eager to aid his brother, Odofredo, in rescuing Topomagro from that overweening clutch of—' He stopped to draw breath, then picked up an olive. 'They'd gladly hand Our Lady herself into the claws of the Devil if it meant a few florins for them.'

'Yes, I believe you're right,' nodded Dom Pietro, watching him closely. Then his voice grew softer, more probing, as he added, 'And you're in contact with Wolf Schwanhals?'

'He's the best means of bringing the town to its knees.' And now it was the cardinal's turn to probe. 'But his services don't come cheaply.'

'Pope Clement is aware of that,' the monk said in a voice as silky as Rollo's robes. 'And he'd be willing to contribute to your costs, partly as a token of his sorrow at what's happened.' He leant back slowly in his chair, adding in a thoughtful, almost dreamy, voice, 'These mercenaries—these *condottieri*, as they style themselves—are possibly a sign of things to come, and a dangerous sign at that. There's no richer gem for them to pluck than Avignon. Schwanhals is just reckless enough to try it, and perhaps even able enough to succeed. Clement would rather that you kept him here in Tuscany.'

For a moment there was silence, while both men reflected on Dom Pietro's words. 'Is Clement's enthusiasm for my plans great enough to induce— to some extent, at least—his funding of my construction projects?'

The Benedictine stared into the depths of his wine, then smiled as if to himself. 'Yes, I think I could properly say that he has shown some interest in these canals of yours.' He looked up slowly at Rollo, eyes replete with sincerity. 'He has always held the utmost respect for your abilities and affection for your person ...' But any further words were cut short by the noise at the doorway, as the jester, Tozzo, wrestled a salver of roasted quail from the servant newly arrived from the kitchens.

In the massive kitchens of the palace, it seemed that all creatures of land, sea and air, each herb of the forest and plant of the field, every tuber, fruit and leaf were grist to the mill of the cardinal's belly. Here, in the glare of the great fire, where the spitted silhouettes of pheasants and partridges were roasting, the high-vaulted dome was painted with ducks, geese, hares, rabbits, boars, deer and all the other totems of the table; copper pots and saucepans, hanging on the wall, glimmered in the smoky air like the armour of a troop of trenchermen. It was here that Strappo the cook held court, bouncing his ladle off the heads of lazy kitchen-boys, marching through the lurid blaze of hearth and oven, squat and ruddy as a terracotta general. And it was here, on the night of the papal envoy's arrival, that he was poking at the parboiled cubes of carrot, dipping his finger into the blood-red sauce of *savore sanguino*, upbraiding the sauce-cook for the abundance of sumach, and generally throwing about his not inconsiderable weight beneath hams, mortadella, trussed fowls and spiced meats that hung from the ceiling like warped chandeliers.

Brother Corvo, minus his habit and dressed in a scullion's tunic, peered about as he plucked a small capon. He watched the figures bent to the massive pie at the long central table, the shadows that toiled at the spits with their burden of birds, the strutting Strappo who gestured and snarled in the hell-glow. He walked across to the hot metal plates, past the pots that were boiling in furies of steam, to some gently simmering white *camellina*, the cardinal's favourite sauce. For a moment he thought of the scullion buried out in the woods, then glanced at the scurrying kitchen-maids, at the glassy eyes of a hanging rabbit, at the long-necked goose that craned from its cage; and then, with an almost invisible flicker of fingers, spread some fine herbs on the bubbling sauce, grinning with quick delight at the ease of it all.

Strappo watched as Brother Corvo spoke with two of the wenches. He didn't like this new addition to his kitchens. Certainly the man had been there at just the right time, almost at the instant they'd realised the boy—Rocco, Rosso, whatever his name was—had run off. But this new one ... there was something unsettling about him. With his long billhook of a nose and his lank greasy hair—the way it fell to his shoulders from his bare white pate—he sometimes looked as hard and tough as an eagle. Yet at other times, like now, peering about with a quick, wily look, he seemed more like some ancient buzzard perched on a carcass. Though he couldn't say what it was, and though the fellow seemed a good worker, Strappo felt sure he was up to no good. There was nothing for it but to keep an eye on him, and kick him out at the first sign of mischief.

'You watch out for him,' hissed one of the malkins, glancing toward the cook. 'He doesn't like you, Naso,' which was their nickname for him, on account of his great beak.

'You're right, Speranza,' said the other, taking him gently by the arm. 'He can be horrible when he wants to.'

'Even when he doesn't want to,' smiled Brother Corvo, pressing closer against them while they crushed the roots of *galinga* to make the cardinal's comfits.

'Yes,' nodded Speranza, then chuckled softly. 'Though that isn't often.'

'He's beaten some of the boys pretty badly. Even sliced the finger off one with a kitchen knife.'

'Well, he'd be wise not to try it with me,' Brother Corvo said, and his words were neither threat nor boast, but a simply stated fact.

'You might be right,' murmured Speranza, looking searchingly into his eyes. 'But just remember, his soul's as black as that pot, isn't it, Fiducia? And just as filthy.'

Her companion nodded, giving Corvo's arm another solicitous squeeze, but he peered boldly at the staring Strappo and seemed to take their warnings lightly.

'His soul? As black as that pot, Speranza?' he smiled, licking the fragments of herb that remained on his fingers. 'Then if his soul's his only strength, I've little to fear.'

The women remained silent, looking blankly at him, until Fiducia shooed some pullets that came pecking round her feet.

'The Church speaks of the soul and devours God's body.' Corvo gazed down at them, smiling, his tone more solemn than when they'd been speaking of his safety. 'And the Cathars say that true good is the good of the spirit. But believe me, ladies, the path of the spirit lies through the body's prostration.'

They gazed at him, bewildered, as if pondering some mistake they may have made, when suddenly he laughed and ran his hands round their waists, squeezing Speranza's chubby flanks. 'I, for one, have a yen for prostration,' and Fiducia giggled at his words, though unsure of what they meant, just as Strappo shoved her away, grasping a fistful of Corvo's neck.

Though the cook was not a tall man, he was as solid and hot as the oven behind him, and with only one hand seemed easily to hurl the thin Corvo toward the sputtering hearth. Speranza made to grip his arm, but he brushed her aside, springing quickly after his victim, shouting, 'That's enough of your heretical filth,' and flung him once more at the flames. A group of pullets went scattering under the tables, while the cat on the mantle opened one eye and a bevy of scullions patiently plucked some plump quail on a bench.

Brother Corvo brushed the hot bricks with his hand, drawing it back as the cook strode in, bawling, 'You're paid to work here, not gabble your smut.'

Mid-stride, Strappo found himself twirled in a dance with the lanky scullion, who whispered into his ear. 'If that was smut,' he was hissing, waving his arm at the rabbits, sausages, pheasants and hams, 'then your kitchen's a temple to smut,' a knife he'd plucked out of nowhere now pricking the cook's thick throat as they stumbled back to the blaze. 'And if you ever try that again, I'll slice your fat heart like a turnip.'

When the table was finally cleared of plates piled high with brown bones, of the pie dish where remnants of crust still smoked like a crater, of jams and jellies scooped into careless curlicues, of half-eaten comfits and empty wine jugs, the cardinal lurched from his chair, a little shaky on his legs. With a quick, nimble skip, Dom Pietro Carrara came to his side and took hold of his elbow.

'It's all right, Dom Pietro,' Rollo muttered a trifle peevishly, 'this blasted cope gets caught round my feet.'

'Ah, the theatre of the Church, Your Eminence,' smiled the monk. 'It can turn so quickly from spectacle to farce.'

Rollo glanced at him sharply, fussed at his robes and straightened his biretta, then stiffly marched to the door. The Benedictine strode after him, and the jester, lounging by the fire, pulled down a torch and led them along a high, vaulted hallway hung like an old Roman highway with crosses.

'Tozzo,' cried the cardinal, 'for the love of Heaven, slow down.' And the jester did, checking the pace of his stilted legs, now lunging forward in slow-motion tumbles and cartwheels with such easy grace that at first Dom Pietro had thought the smoky torchlight was playing tricks on his eyes.

'My trouble here in the country, Dom Pietro ...' puffed the cardinal. 'I don't know why ... perhaps it's too quiet after Avignon ... I get bad dreams ... terrible things that wake me up in a sweat in the night.'

'Dreams, Your Eminence?'

Rollo felt a sudden urge to push him down the stairs, for there it was again, that supercilious formality to which the man retreated whenever he grew uncertain.

'Yes, Dom Pietro, dreams. Dreams that hold

such terrible force that the waking world seems pallid and shadowy.'

Dom Pietro glanced at the shimmering form that waddled ahead of him up the staircase; beyond, beneath the torch itself, the jester turned a spidery cartwheel.

'They may be the echoes of Avignon's upheavals. The intrigues of the French prelates, Rollo, those accusations about the murder of the Grenoble cardinal, Guy de St Marcel d'Avançon ... I'm convinced that Clement was right to give you this respite. Bad dreams, like the pain of a bad wound, are sometimes a part of the soul's healing.'

They had reached the top of the stairs and the cardinal was nodding, partly in agreement and partly, it seemed, from sleep. He lunged out abruptly and gave the monk a rough embrace. 'You may be right, Dom Pietro, you may be right. But at present I'm too tired to think with clarity. We'll speak further on it in the morning.' And he plucked a torch from its sconce as he headed off into the darkness, his last words flung over his shoulder, 'Tozzo will show you to your chamber.'

The jester was already vanishing down the dim corridor. When Dom Pietro arrived at his room the clown was there at the doorway, proffering a torch, his hollow, bony face stretched tight in such a grotesque grin that the Benedictine wondered if he, too, would dream a Carnival of nightmares.

An invincible enemy

For some weeks the people of Kaffa stayed caged in their town like a colony of mice surrounded by an army of cats. The Tartars' deluge of stones and darts did not diminish, their assaults on the walls grew daily more violent and the volleys of their rocket-arrows hissed through the town like erratic, smoky comets. For all this, it was perhaps the growing sense of the impossibility of rescue, of the inevitability of defeat, of the relentless decline of food and will and energy that was the Tartars' deadliest weapon. It was a weapon secreted in the hearts of the people themselves and, as such, was all the harder to combat. With each fresh offensive on the outer walls, this sense of doom gnawed deeper at the walls within. As they watched the wagons descend from the mountains to bring the invaders fresh troops and supplies, the townsfolk increasingly felt themselves part of some failing mechanism, some piece of clockwork wound tight at the Tartars' arrival, now slowing, dulling, losing momentum—despite their best efforts—in a ceaseless winding down.

It was only after the bombards' arrival, after

evenings spent hearing the truncated thunder as the balls hit the ramparts in grey clouds of stone, that they first discovered the Tartars too had their own inner enemy. For a time its nature remained unclear; since it firstly made itself known through the catapults' spasmodic firing, until whole days went by with barely a missile launched at the town. Then there were cries in the night and great fires burning over the plain. Some way to the east the Tartars set up a second camp, a tiny island of tents cut off from their army, quite baffling in its placement since it was neither on the supply route nor close enough to help in the siege; yet it grew till its size soon rivalled that of the principal camp. Once, during this time, the Tartars launched an assault on the walls, charging forth with their ladders and towers behind a torrent of fiery arrows. It was their most concerted effort since the earliest days of the whole campaign, but their least successful. The militia told stories of Tartar troops so exhausted by scaling the walls that they'd simply stood panting, almost thankful, as they watched the pikes lunge down at their throats. Many said that they'd seen their enemies cling to their ladders, eyes glassy and feverish, swords dangling from their fingers; others told of Tartar leaders running their dazed troops through. Needless to say the army had skulked away to its tents, humiliated.

It was during the following days, when columns of ox-drawn carts filled to the brim with corpses went rattling out to the Tartars' makeshift graveyard, that the rumour of plague took hold in Kaffa. There seemed more dead than the failed assault could account for, and most signs of life, save those that dealt with the transport of corpses, were gone from the camp. What the Genoese assumed to be massive pyres now draped the air with smoke palls as heavy as velvet, as if town and camp were the coffins of giants laid out together beside the sea. The thick summer heat hung damply about them, and soon long spirals of flies began to mimic the coiling smoke that rose from the plain, while the heavy stench of corrupted air wafted over the walls with each hint of a northern breeze. Refugees from the mountains and Tana told tales of a pestilence out of the east—something of which most had heard—a sickness afflicting Cathay with a cruelty unknown to even the hordes of Genghis Khan. They pointed at the thinning, desolate smoke of the pyres, the wagons of dead, the silent camp, the great-winged vultures now flown from their mountain fastnesses, and nodded their heads with the grim satisfaction of those who know truths far worse than others imagine.

The roles of besieged and besiegers reversed with the plague's sudden advent, until it seemed to the people of Kaffa that now it was they who awaited with patience the end of their enemies, watching the signs of their slow decline. It was an irresistible inversion, too like a mighty and vengeful God's justice to be passed off as mere good fortune. So the city's preachers gave thanks to the Lord for His wrath at the heathen, and merchants donated more of their profits to charity, still keeping a wary eye on the missiles that rained spasmodically down. In fact, Jacopo was walking along the Borgo Sismondi when the fateful assault occurred. It plummeted from the sky, crashing through tiles and cloth awnings, and then—as if transformed in the air into some softer substance—striking the ground with a dull, muffled thud. When the barrage appeared to be over, he ran with the others to the scene of destruction, finding not only broken stones, but broken bodies fallen from the heavens, as if the charnel-house rains from the first days of siege had started all over again.

Jacopo fled the spot almost immediately, though not before he had time to observe that these were infected bodies. Certainly, they were beginning to rot. There was a livid quality to the flesh, and bits had broken off where they'd crashed to the ground. Nor was this all. He had seen dead bodies before and had smelt them, but never any like these, which gave off a stench that was more than the start of decay, something cloying and heavy that made the onlookers gag. Something like the smell that had come from the Tartar camp, but a thousand times worse. Even the briefest inspection revealed that some had lumps on their bodies—behind their ears or on their necks—many of which had burst, staining the skin about them with putrid black oozings, now dry, yet which seemed to be the principal source of that nauseous stench. Some of these lumps were no bigger than chestnuts, others the size of eggs, and a few were almost as big as an apple. Jacopo didn't stay to learn more of this sickness. He neither knew what it was nor what had caused it, just that it vanquished whole armies, and if indeed it were God's wrath, then he saw no reason why he should be spared. Like an earthquake or flood or any other token of God's displeasure, it was wisest fled and questioned later. Thus the city's doctors took some time to pronounce it a Heaven-sent pestilence, best kept outside the walls, where God intended, so that troops of soldiers were ordered to cart the bodies through town and to dump them into the sea from the southernmost point of the parapet. It was also said that the worst of the lumps had been found in the armpits and groin where, according to Lapo, they sprouted up 'like an extra ball as big as a melon'.

In the days that followed, more bodies plummeted down onto Kaffa, falling from the clouds like infected angels, splattering in pieces on the squares and courtyards. No sooner had they fallen than platoons of labourers scraped them up, piling their bits into ancient carts then hurling them into the harbour. Here was what seemed an endless supply of missiles, an army immune to death, yet whose very numbers measured the Tartars' destruction. Talk of God's wrath and prayers of thanksgiving dwindled, perhaps in the sheer frenzy of dumping the noisome corpses, and once the first symptoms began to appear in the town, all talk of heavenly justice ceased.

The early cases of plague seemed more like rumour than reality, a myth so frightening for what it implied that they chose to pretend its very intensity made it seem real, even though it remained just a nightmare. As the corpses began to mount up, its truth became undeniable, although for most it stayed just a series of facts reported from a distance. It made its initial appearance in the crowded Turkish community, then spread among the Armenians and then to the artisans' quarter. There were tales of entire families dying, delirious with fever, of streets where every window echoed with groans and cries, of whole neighbourhoods in which the terrible stench of the sick made every attempt at entry fatal. Priests were known to have perished in the act of absolution, physicians to have died while ministering to the ill. The authorities tried to isolate the worst-affected quarters, but it wasn't long before the telltale symptoms—the boils or buboes, the lethargy, pain and delirium—were seen in the wealthiest streets. The town's two graveyards could no longer cope with the dead, and pits began to be dug, though some maintained that the bodies would have to be thrown in the sea like those of the Tartars, and others even suggested lobbing them over the walls in answer to their enemy.

The plague's pattern was devilish. It seemed to make no sense at all. For a time it would devastate a neighbourhood, then vanish abruptly, occurring instead in some far part of town, where perhaps one family might be affected before it was gone from there, popping up like a puppet-show demon in some other quarter. In the midst of such curious danger there was little attempt at explanation, though most agreed that corrupted air was to blame. Magister Cosimo Simonetti swirled his red cloak before the town council, announcing the cause to be an effluvium spread by decay of Tartar corpses; whereas his colleague, Magister Salimbene di Michele, picking nervously at his vair-lined hood, suggested that this would fail to explain how the army itself was infected, and that the pestilence sprang from the earth as a noxious vapour resulting from recent earthquakes in the Caucasus. Some thought it might pass from person to person, but the Turks maintained that this couldn't be so since the plague was God's punishment and one man's deserts could hardly apply to another. Fra Giacomo Lanfredi was apt to agree, asserting that any infection occurred in the individual only through God's direct intercession. Such explanations failed to console the townsfolk, who discovered their own ways of coping, according to what their physician might say and what their wealth could afford.

Jacopo Passero has neither wealth nor physician. Yet he knows the sickness more closely than most. One morning Lapo Tromba comes howling down the hallway toward him.

'She's hatching an egg,' he cries, grasping Jacopo's shoulders. 'Caterina, our little Caterina, hatching an egg.'

For a moment, taken completely off guard, Jacopo is silent. 'An egg,' he says at last, confused by Lapo's weeping. 'Caterina's infected?'

'Yes,' the man sighs, then grips his arm tightly, steering him through to the rear of the house. 'Come, we must hurry!'

Jacopo isn't sure just why they must hurry, but lets Lapo take him to a low, narrow chamber where the little girl lies on a bed by the window. He can't think of what he should say. She's writhing about in a knot of sheets, whining to herself, her small blunt features twisted in pain. Her skin, quite shiny with sweat, already hints at the cloying stink of the pestilence.

'Are you sure?' he says, turning at last to his landlord and only now seeing Monna Simona huddled on a chair in a corner of the room. 'It could be a chill or some other infection.'

'A chill?' Lapo snarls, and looks as if he might strike him. He seems about to say something else, but instead he lunges toward the bed and hurls back the sheets, revealing his child's naked body. Then he takes both her legs, pulling them roughly apart, till she screams a single, thin shriek of anguish. She draws legs, arms, all quickly together, shrivelling up like a crushed white insect, yet already Jacopo's seen the red tumour, the size of a duck egg, tight in her groin. 'You call that a chill?'

Jacopo looks at Simona, then turns back to Lapo. 'No,' he says softly, shaking his head.

Soon the house of Lapo Tromba is thick with the stink of the sickness. It fills the bedrooms and kitchen, it drifts through the hallways and out through the windows, infecting the street and the alley. Simona becomes invisible, tending her daughter, bringing her fluids, mopping her face and sharing her cries. The child is now quite delirious, mumbling to herself and moaning, screaming at shadows in the corners of the room, then breaking out into devilish laughter.

If his wife rarely moves from the sick room, Lapo seems glued to the kitchen, drinking himself to a stuporous melancholy, urging Jacopo to join him. Once the landlord asks him to take up some food for his wife, saying, 'I can't go up there, not today. The child seems so tiny to bear so much pain,' and with trembling hands holds out the tray to his lodger.

Upstairs the air is so heavy that Jacopo can barely go in. It's as if the room were filled to the ceiling with dense, foetid water, a choking fluid deadly to breathe, yet he struggles through, placing the tray by Simona asleep near the bed. Caterina also is sleeping, though she's thrown off her covers, fretting amid some dream. A second egg has hatched—this in her armpit—and seeps a black fluid. As he watches, she moans in her sleep, twists, writhes, then cries aloud as a thick brown slime pours out beneath her, filling the room with such a stink that Jacopo begins to gag. But Simona has already sprung to her feet, upsetting the tray, eyes half closed as she wipes at the child with a filthy cloth. He lunges after the gushing wine, the tumbling loaf, rescuing one piece of cheese and holding it dumbly to him. 'She's too young,' the woman says, more to herself than to him, 'too much a child—' but pauses, not sure how to put it, 'to be punished like this.'

It gets so Jacopo can barely stand to be in the place. Now old Carlo, another of Lapo's lodgers, falls ill with the plague, a goose egg under his arm and that of a pigeon behind his left ear. Their physician, the self-styled 'Maestro' Bernardo, tries to have Lapo agree to his treatment with gold and crushed sapphires, but since it's too dear he simply bleeds them all, as both cure and preventative.

Jacopo's had enough, taking off with Scimmi to rob vacant mansions. Yet, after a handful of days, this gets on his nerves as well, and he wanders aimlessly round the streets while carts come carrying Tartar or Genoese corpses down to the sea. He winds up back at Lapo Tromba's, where the man comes lumbering down his front steps, his daughter's body held in his arms.

'She's dead,' Jacopo murmurs, his voice containing no hint of a question. But Lapo says nothing, not a groan, not a sigh, just the steady dribbling of his bulbous nose onto his daughter's hand. Her eyes are black glass, and her skin is mottled with livid splotches like queasy marble. 'We'll get the priest round, Lapo, and the sextons.' But the man just keeps walking, nudging him out of the way with the girl's pale body. 'Come on, Lapo, you want to do it right.'

'Wake up to yourself, Jacopo,' Lapo mutters, not even turning to look. 'There's no-one to bury her, except in a pit under hundreds of others. I'll do it myself. And don't you worry, *I'll* do it right.' And he reels away round the corner, under the weight of more than the child and the grappa he's drunk.

Jacopo stays staring, then hurries inside. 'Monna Simona,' he cries, 'Monna Simona,' moving quickly through the house, opening doors and peering into rooms, finding only old Carlo and Luigi Garzoni—both sick—in the kitchen. He goes to the door of his landlord's bedroom, knocks, hears a groan then a cough and, casting aside what manners he has, walks in. He finds what it was he expected: Simona, writhing about on the bed as if on a griddle, her face thickly smeared with sweat that already has the smell of the gravepit about it. And it's right there and then that he knows, no matter what dangers, no matter what penalties hold for deserting the town, that somehow, even if he has to swim all the way to the Bosporus, he's going to get out of Kaffa.

This is not a unique resolution. The town's richest traders, bankers and prelates have made it before him, their departure delayed by Venetian and Genoese companies unwilling to risk their goods in the siege. Thus there are only two galleys in port. Jacopo's problem is more basic still: he has neither money nor contacts to secure his passage. Then comes his first real piece of good luck since coming to Kaffa. His search for the fare now leads to a small but elegant house in the centre of town, a place quite open to the world. Here, as in so many other such houses, he finds a corpse in the fluids long burst from its buboes. He does not pause to admire the smell, but ransacks each room as fast as he can.

In a cluttered desk he finds a letter that tells him the name of the corpse: Giorgio dei Sapori, who was clearly a man of no small means, a trader from Bologna only recently arrived. It soon becomes plain that the fellow was prudent, the kind who deposits his cash in a bank, since there's barely any around the house. Jacopo goes back through drawers, chests, caskets, desks, cupboards, purses, bags, and ... the satchel, the expensive leather satchel with the small brass clasps, where he finds his good luck. At first he passes over it, missing its significance; but then notes the size of the sum—

over a thousand florins—recorded on the scrap of parchment. He looks more closely at it and, for the hundredth time that year, gives thanks to the great Orlando, who'd taken such trouble to teach him to read. For now he sees that the scrap's a receipt made out by 'Giuseppe Pozzi (Master) on behalf of E. Argenti & Co.' for the carriage of pepper and saffron, as well as smaller amounts of oil, salted meat, loaves, fowls, oranges, vinegar, wine, cassia, comfits, rosewater, garlic, onions, ginger, pots, bowls, candles and—here he gives a shout of joy, 'for the passage of Ser Giorgio dei Sapori aboard the *Santa Margherita*.' Yes, this is his passage, his way out of Kaffa, and Jacopo gives another loud whoop, so that Scimmi comes hurrying in, nuzzling his legs and purring, divining a feed in the warmth of his voice.

He picks her up and spins her round in the cool, bright moonlight that streams through the room. Yes, it's Giorgio's fare to Genoa, the pepper and saffron his cargo, while all the rest was what he would need for the trip. Good old Giorgio, the burglar's friend. Jacopo can't believe his luck; before the trader can rise from his bed in vengeance or Fortune change her mind, he wrestles Scimmi into her pouch, pockets the receipt and flees the house without looking back.

It is only three nights later, with a bag of stolen finery and Giorgio's receipt, that Jacopo Passero and his dapper cat embark on the *Santa Margherita*, slipping forever out of Kaffa and south across the sea.

Tuccio visits his carders

SEXT WAS ALREADY RINGING WHEN TUCCIO RODE HIS fine Spanish mule past San Francesco, where the friars inside were doubtless beginning their midday office. Via Gentili was crowded with carts and wagons, and even the bullying tones of Gino, his steward, and his two hefty servants failed to clear the road before him. So by the time they approached the Ponte alla Porta Santa Maria, the old, inadequate bridge was jammed with lunchtime traffic and Tuccio was cursing himself for dallying that morning over a shipment of gall-nuts. He dismally watched how the Ombronetto swirled round the bridge's plinths in its final descent to the sea. The foaming water looked much like those veils that he'd recently bought from Perugia, all somehow torn in transit. He glanced at his mule's twitching ears. Nothing seemed pleasing today, and now his grumbling carders would have finished their midday meal and he'd have to interrupt their work to talk to them. It still annoyed him to think that his *fattore*, Niccolo di Lapo, had needed him to deal with it. Things had reached a pretty point when a man of his standing, a *lanaiuolo*, who'd been a consul of the wool guild and already served a term as Prior, must haggle with his own wool-washers.

He glanced down the hill to the Chiasso delle Bestie, where the tanneries hunched by the river. Even here, up on the bridge, the stench of their lyes infected the air. He cast a more sanguine eye on the Borgo Santa Maria del Carmine, where the dye shops jostled for space on the bank with labourers' crumbling cottages. A picture came briefly to mind of the great vats brimming with all the world's colours—violet orchil, crushed from the lichens of Majorca, Catalonian saffron, Indian lak, yellow arsenic and the Red Sea's orange realgar. He saw vats of madder and black burnet, brazil from the trees of the Indies, a cauldron of woad like a huge blue eye, and bright scarlet grana, leached like blood from the myriad bodies of insects. He thought of the mordants for fixing the dyes, the red and white tartar and Black Sea alum, knowing the pleasure of one who possessed not only the town's biggest dye shop, but the only real network of transport and agents to import dyes in large quantities. He had spent his term as a guild consul putting an end to the wool guild's plans to build its own dye shop. He'd thought long and worked hard to get his business where it was, and was in no mood to hear the complaints of a handful of carders.

He watched the river flow past the dyers', tinged with spilt madder. He peered upstream at the scourers' and carders' rickety hovels. They leaned at strange angles over the water, which glistened with oils, fuller's earth and old soap from the washers and fulling mills. Beyond were the sheds with their tenterhooks, and those shops where the cloth was teazled and shorn, and further yet the looms of the piecework weavers, and out past the walls, the spinsters who'd spin their own weight in yarn for a bushel of grain. All this set in motion by Tuccio's hands, and here he rode to talk pennies with carders. Of course he knew life was hard for them, especially with the shortages. However, it was he, and those like him, whose efforts provided the work that they needed. It was people like him who'd freed such men from their bonds to the soil, who'd helped them escape the likes of Montagna. To think that they might be consorting with those mutterers. Yes, this was the rumour: that some had found common ground with the nobles in their envy of the merchants, and that even a few subcontractors—people who'd made good money from their fulling mills and mending shops—were joining the agitation. Not, of course, that there *was* any real agitation, just that the merest hint made the guild consuls nervous. Something was afoot with Montagna and the others, and the poorest carders were doubtless feeling the pinch of famine. If the nobles and clog-wearers somehow joined forces ... well, then blood would flow.

Indeed, it already had, at least in minor ways. For instance, there was the death of Guccio di Leonardo, one of Tuccio's best wool sorters, whose body was found at the back of a tavern in the Borgo Santa Caterina, throat cut and head battered almost past recognition. Niccolo di Lapo had suspected some of the workers and had mentioned a carder named Geri Pinza as an unsettling influence. It might well be that such events formed no part of a planned campaign, that they merely served as the passing emunctories of the time's infection. Briefly he thought of the idlers who gathered at the fountains in the town's piazzas, of Frederico dalla Montagna awaiting his chance, of the vengeful cardinal plotting in his palace. The world seemed to lurch toward chaos. And yet it was this very feeling, this fear of impending doom, that contributed most to the madness. He shook his head—more at himself than anything else—as they rode through the lane to the river, approaching the walls of the carding shed. Above all else he must seem patient with these carders.

Geri Pinza stood at the carding bench, pulling the fine metal teeth of the card across the dense wool, drawing out the long fibres, untangling the knots, removing the burrs and small seeds that lay trapped in its depths. He was one of those men whose very bulk seems to make them look short, with squat, solid legs and a barrel chest, like a dwarf who had somehow, by some freak of nature, managed to reach average height. He was frowning now, as if at the task of straightening the fibres with twin metal cards, his beard and thick dark curls resembling the wool that he worked, giving him the look of a sombre black ram, head bowed to the bench as if ready to charge. In fact, he was seeking an answer to give his companion, who worked at the bench next to his.

'Well, I was right, eh, Geri?' the man urged once more. 'He's not going to come.'

Geri glanced up, saying nothing. Alfredo Crostadura, as long and sinewy as Geri was solid, as nervy and choleric as he was phlegmatic, could annoy him almost beyond all patience. He passed his hand through his hair, which was wet with sweat. As always, the long room was hot because of the fire that blazed at one end, where the fleeces were hung to soften their oils for the sorting. The door was wide open, revealing the scourers rinsing the wool, foamy with soap in the chilly river; but in here it was hot as a new-baked loaf.

'Well, he might still come,' said Ciuto di Dino, a rather gentle old man whose bench faced the others. 'A man like Signor Tuccio is bound to have things cropping up, you know.'

'Like a lunch that takes the whole afternoon, when the rest of us can barely afford the price of a loaf?' snapped Alfredo, not taking his eyes off Geri.

'You might be right,' Geri conceded, 'but let's not get ourselves all steamed up before we're certain. It's hot enough in here.'

Alfredo leaned from his bench. 'Maybe somebody *should* get steamed up, Geri.' After all, how long could they live on a wage that wouldn't buy enough food? 'I'm sick of not getting steamed up.'

'Yes, I've noticed,' he smiled, and turned his gaze from Alfredo's face, avoiding his urgency. For a moment he watched Leonardo and Rocco over by the door preparing the wool to make worsted yarns, drawing out the short, furry fibres and straightening the long with their sharp metal combs. On the room's far side, nearer the heat, a pair of sorters worked on the fleeces, hurling them onto the high wooden bench, plucking good wool from bad and dumping the pickings in big graded bins.

'Geri, you're as impatient as I am. You just hide it better.'

Geri gave Alfredo a level look. Impatient? Because the shortages drove up the price of bread? Because their wages stayed the same? He shrugged. 'Of course I'm impatient. But getting hot-headed won't do any good.'

'We've held back too long.' Alfredo thought of them all, the clog-wearing mobs that couldn't pay rent or buy enough food and who, because they worked hard, remained unregistered at the city's poor tables. 'The paupers live better than we do.'

'So you'd rather beg, Alfredo?'

'I'd rather work and get paid a decent wage. I'd rather not have to pay a deposit on these cards just for the pleasure of making Tuccio a profit. I'd rather be a member of the wool guild, Geri, instead of simply having it tell us what to do. Or better still, I'd like us to have a guild of our own where we'd have a chance to hold office, or at least have some sort of say.'

Geri slowly nodded his head, but old Ciuto di Dino, looking alarmed, said, 'That's dangerous talk, Alfredo. Carders were killed in Florence for trying to form their own guild.'

'No-one's formed anything yet,' said Geri. They'd simply asked for a meeting to discuss their conditions. He glanced at Alfredo. 'And there'll be no talk about forming a guild or holding office. We simply want wages in keeping with food prices.'

'Yes, I know, all very humble and reasonable. But you ask me if I'd prefer to beg. Well, what are we doing now but begging, holding out our caps and pleading for Tuccio's charity? It'll be like this again and again—always begging for crumbs since we've got no power. And do you think we'll ever get more than crumbs from the Signoria?'

'All right, Alfredo!' Geri snapped, losing patience at last. 'We all know that power lies in the hands of the *lanaiuoli*. It goes without saying. But we're talking about real possibilities, in the real world, about getting food in our bellies and a roof over our heads, not about getting thrown into gaol or hanged for sedition.'

'But if anyone's hurting the commune it's some of these bastards that get themselves voted as Prior.' Yes, there were Priors—everyone knew it—who ran the town into debt and then lent it money at huge personal profit.

'Keep your voices down,' put in Ciuto, bending harder to his work. 'Niccolo's just come back in.'

'I'm not criticising you, Geri,' continued Alfredo. 'But the only others excluded from office like us ... I know you mightn't like the comparison ... but it's the nobles. And that was because they tried to keep power by violence. But what have we—'

'All right! But we can only get what's possible. Now keep your voice down.'

'What's possible is up to us,' hissed Alfredo. 'Maybe Montagna's message is worth—'

'Come on, let's get some work done,' boomed the voice of Niccolo di Lapo. 'We don't want Signor Tuccio coming in and finding you chatting like a bunch of old washerwomen.'

Geri glanced at Alfredo, who was watching him sideways, a pointed smile on his pointed face, then bent to his work.

The meeting with Tuccio was all too brief. He came sweeping into the shop in his long grey cloak and hood, flanked by his burly attendants, glaring around at the fleeces and rovings. Niccolo fussed about him, thanking the merchant for coming to see them, then presented a number of carders by name.

'Ah, Geri Pinza!' barked Tuccio. 'You're the chosen spokesman, I hear.'

Geri raised his eyebrows and nodded, not humbly, but discreetly. 'Yes, Signor Tuccio, I suppose I am.'

'You *suppose* you are?'

Geri frowned and said softly, 'I am.'

'Hmmm.' Tuccio gazed quizzically at him. 'Well, Signor Spokesman ... speak.'

Geri glanced about him, looking a bit embarrassed. 'I suppose you will have heard the gist of our ... requests.' He waited for some response, but received a noncommittal stare. 'Well, uh, they concern the fact that life is getting harder every day ... that grain is now four times the price it was two years ago ... that rents have gone up with the poor coming in from the country ...'

'Yes, you're right, Geri,' said Tuccio sadly, 'life is harder for everyone these days.'

'Harder for some than others,' Alfredo muttered, getting a frown from Niccolo. He received no response from the merchant.

'The problem is, Signor Tuccio,' blurted Geri, as if to cancel further comment from his neighbour, 'that our wages can no longer purchase the means to live. We receive six *soldi* a day, minus the deposit on our tools, while grain is now more than sixty *soldi* a bushel. Two years ago it was often less than fifteen.'

'You want me to increase your wages,' said Tuccio flatly.

'Yes, Signor Tuccio.' Geri looked to his fellows hopefully, some of whom nodded agreement. 'Ten, perhaps even nine *soldi* would help to alleviate the problems we find ourselves in.'

Tuccio looked grave. He closed his eyes as if making calculations, then heaved a sigh and nodded. 'Yes, it's true,' he said, 'life is now far from easy, even for those who have work. You'll have your increase.' Tuccio's eyes stayed fixed on Geri alone. 'Seven and a half *soldi* should just be possible in the present climate.' And his features thawed to a generous smile.

Geri looked anxiously round the room, noting Alfredo's silent glare, then shook his head slowly. 'Even nine *soldi* would still leave our families hungry, Signor Tuccio. Seven and a half would change nothing.'

'It would change everything by one and a half *soldi* a day.' And here, raising his voice in a tone near anger, Tuccio turned to address the whole workshop. 'These last two winters have profited no-one. People are not buying cloth the way they did. They buy less of everything. It's as if the bare fields leach their purses of money. Our markets in the north are being drained of wealth by war. If we made cannons instead of cloth I could, perhaps, afford nine *soldi*. But at present we'll be lucky if the business survives. Even seven and a half is reckless.'

'Then we'll be lucky if *we* survive,' said Alfredo bitterly.

'You'll survive.' Tuccio's voice was loud and stern. 'If worse comes to worst, the Priors will feed you from the commune's granaries.'

'If I was a Prior,' said Alfredo, voice shaking with anger or fear, 'I'd feed the people now.'

'Then you'd starve the whole city when the famine got worse. But you're not a Prior,' said Tuccio, pausing as if he would add something more, then simply said, 'and I'm no magician. I can't change the world with the wave of a wand. Seven and a half is the best I can do.'

This time his announcement was met with silence. Some stared numbly, others with sullen eyes. Unexpectedly, he added, 'But as a sign of good faith, I'll undertake to provide you with a brace of pheasants and a suckling pig for your feast next Carnival. And I hope it may allay your hunger.' Then he nodded, twirling on his heel, his servants scurrying to catch him up, while Niccolo di Lapo thanked him for his kindness and the carders simply stood looking glumly at each other.

Jacopo sails to the Bosporus

THE GALLEY SAILS IN THE SUNLIGHT UNDER SKYWIDE flocks of cirrus cloud. A mild north-eastern breeze puffs at its canvas and the oarsmen lounge at their drawn oars, chatting like lords on a pleasure cruise. Jacopo sits at the bow, taking in the sun, his legs stretched before him; Scimmi perches between his feet, leaning into the wind of their passage like a small ruffled figurehead. Once again he swivels around on his elbow and glances over his shoulder, as if he might see, beyond the fat sails and low poop, and the shimmer of cirrus streaming out of the north, the great black shadow of the plague pursuing them from Kaffa. But all is sunlight there and, warm as he is on the mild blue sea, he finds it hard to imagine that, past the horizon, the townsfolk are huddling away from the Tartars while Death piles corpses inside their high walls. He slipped away in the night, he and the others, the shallow hold crammed with provisions and a limited cargo of spices and silks—for all, with just one exception, are prosperous merchants—leaving only the promise of further galleys to cheer their fellow townsmen. After all, there's been word of a dozen vessels, perhaps, from the many rich ports to the west; and, indeed, fourteen passengers are more than the limit, and that—owing to the captain's greed—now makes them dangerously overcrowded, what with the archers and twenty-two oarsmen required.

The larger of the two galleys, *Lo Storione*, which left a day before them, carries no more than the *Santa Margherita*, since its captain was more cautious and his passengers included the cream of the town—the consul, the bishop, the magistrates, guild consuls, the wealthiest merchants. Those aboard the *Santa Margherita* have seen no sign of it, and probably won't, at least till their first port of call, as it's clearly the faster ship. Jacopo regrets that Giorgio dei Sapori lacked the prestige for *Lo Storione*, for the passenger list includes the Fanfanis and he might have had one more crack at that diamond. 'And no dog this time, eh, Scimmi?' He scratches the fur behind her ears, and she rolls back her head, making the burred, squeaky sound that's her version of purring.

Jacopo glances around at the poop, where a number of passengers stand with the captain, their long *gonnelloni* blowing about them, like sails luffing loose in the wind, while one or two others sit at the rail, legs dangling over the water. One old merchant, Guglielmo Carogna, who could buy and sell the rest put together—and probably would, given half the chance—has taken exclusive control of the captain. Even now he has him in a huddle, as if discussing some secret deal, though Jacopo's observed that he treats the most everyday chatter much like a transaction of spies. He might take you by the sleeve, glance slyly about him, then squint at your face like a co-conspirator, hissing, 'Hey, Giorgio, pass the salt,' or something like that. Anyway, ludicrous or not, the old man and his wife have nabbed the one cabin other than the captain's. And this captain, Giuseppe Pozzi, is a man who looks like he knows what he's doing, dark, stout, his beard sprinkled with grey and his skin with the look of well worn leather. His mate, Aldo, however, has a bit too much of the pirate about him for Jacopo's liking, flinty and lean, with a hungry gleam to his eyes, though perhaps it's just that he's surly at having to give up his cabin to Carogna, most likely for the captain's sole profit.

Jacopo prefers the plump cogs that ply the peninsula's waters. The *Santa Margherita* might be quicker, but it's built for war and the speedy transport of cargo, not for conveying more than a dozen passengers between one sea and another. And such passengers—all of them, save himself, used to the comforts of wealth; and all of whom will doubtless be full of complaints about sleeping on deck, especially if the weather turns cold, once the relief of getting out of Kaffa fails to hold their tongues. If things get bad enough, with gales or sudden snowstorms from the north, how will sleeping in the narrow, sopping dark below-decks appeal to such a bunch of pampered cats? 'Sorry, Scimmi,' he says, stroking her throat. 'I'm not including ratters like you. You'd love it in the bilge.' She stares primly up at him and he smiles to himself. So who's complaining now? Barely a day out of port and already forgetting to number his blessings. He shakes his head, lounging back on the boards, once again giving thanks to God, to Fortune, to whatever it was that had led him to Giorgio dei Sapori. After all, it's not wise to take such things for granted. A little thanks, at least, seems prudent.

Yet, in the midst of this feeling, there is also regret, or perhaps something more like self doubt, since he sees that the circle of leaving has started once more and that, just as before, he feels almost nothing for the place left behind. Kaffa, Lapo, Monna Simona, Caterina ... perhaps there's a twinge of sadness, though it's really an emptiness, a blank that he feels whenever he knows that the weeks or the months that he's stayed in some place might never have been for the little they've touched him. He stares at the sea, suddenly tired, lost in the dazzle of sun, the flickering light that sparks in the swell just as the salt had seemed to catch fire on the plains at Hyères—those thirsty salt marshes— in the years after his father had died. His thoughts drift back through that time, after the loss of their land to the Lombards, after the years of vagabondage, his father's death, when he'd scraped raw salt for a living, piling it up into friable pillars like hosts of Lot's wives on the ice-white plain. The boat rocks beneath him, and he thinks of the salt tax, the hated *gabelle*, grinding his teeth till Scimmi looks up at the noise. He sees the salt workers forced from the land, wandering foodless over the roads in their salt-stiffened rags, like knights' errant bones, mail brittle with rust the colour of snow.

He looks at his hands, still callused from days scraping salt. Perhaps leaving breeds its own kind of calluses. Perhaps each departure's reduced by the sum of those other departures, which flood back to mind at each new leaving, just as he now recalls his flight from Provence, then the hills of Savoy where he'd worked as a shepherd, and the freedom he'd felt when he'd first led his flocks to the high spring pastures. At first it had seemed to provide a fine life, no longer hammered with heat on the salt flats, but tending the sheep—just like the Good Pastor— beneath the mild stars. Yet in winter, when he freelanced down in the meadows around the low towns, not only did some nights half freeze him, but he felt the distrust of the people, and grew sick of the other shepherds, infected as they were by the stupidity of their flocks. At last he'd found the itinerant lifestyle, the suspicion of strangers and the dearth of his wages conducive to odd bits of thieving—usually from some rich peasant intent on defrauding him—and so had begun his latest vocation, though not before his time as an actor ... and now he is smiling, not quite ironically, nor with nostalgia, but with a wry sort of pride.

He thinks of his ramblings back through Liguria, the land of his father, then down toward Tuscany and north into Lombardy, where he met Orlando the Great, who'd annoyed Archbishop Visconti with some bit of *mistero buffo*—his famous Clown Cardinal—and was fleeing Milan with his troupe. It was more than their lives were worth to remain in Lombardy, and he remembers Orlando believing his tale about being a tumbler escaping the archbishop's tyranny. Politically astute, perhaps, but acrobatically unsound, he pratfell through Tuscany, then dropped on his head all the way across Umbria, juggling eggs that burst in his face, till his views of the Po and the ruins of Rome were seen through a haze of egg yolks. Yet he beamed like a dozen beatitudes, silly as a saint in an ecstasy, so people thought him a clown and happily echoed his idiot's grin. Even Orlando seemed taken in, which was hardly surprising, since half the time his drunken tumblers performed like a troupe with the falling sickness. And sure enough, as time went by, he'd not only learnt the rudiments of reading, but could twist in the air, juggle hot turnips and walk a rope with the best of them, even when they were sober. But their slanderous satires, their warped mock-parables, their *misteri buffi*, made them move fast through Calabria, Basilicata and Puglia until, pursued by a choleric lord of Aspromonte, they crossed the Straits into Sicily. It was here that Jacopo performed the feat of walking on air.

He smiles to himself, leaning back in the sun while he strokes Scimmi's flanks. He thinks of her as she was then, at the time he performed his most difficult feat, no more than a bundle of fur in his pocket. It was at Colpatorta, soon after the patriarch, Catania's archbishop, had brought a group of latter-day Arnoldists before the Inquisition. The court was set up by the local priest, as well as a zealous Dominican friar who'd gone to the town; they tried the priest's foes with a vengeance, burning a handful, gaoling some others, while most had to wear the heretic's yellow cross. Just as

Orlando's actors arrived, the place erupted around them: the townsfolk and peasants joined forces—not in the cause of heresy, but against the Church's work-dues—accusing the priest of simony, then driving away the friar. They held their own court, trying the Church's servants and condemning the priest to death. The pyre was built in the central piazza, though it wasn't a solemn affair, more like some riotous Carnival, with masks and dancing and feasting in the streets. Orlando and his troupe were pressed to perform, their payment made from the priest's corrupt profits. It was here, after much drunken juggling and tumbling—as the priest went up in smoke—that Jacopo walked on the air.

He shakes his head, recalling the smell of the burning priest, still seeing the rope stretched over the flames from the tall campanile to the towered Palazzo. Even now the aroma of blackening meat can bring back the terror he'd felt. Yet the townsfolk prevailed, their extortion and gold too much to withstand, and Jacopo found himself up in the air, knowing nought but the rope that was under his feet and Scimmi's warm piss in his pocket. He remembers little of his exploit, though Orlando later recounted that, just as the fire started to roar, the people looked up and saw him, not on a rope, but walking through empty air. All round the blaze was ashimmer, the tower asway like the drunken crowd, and he seemed to appear from nowhere, drifting in vapour over the stake, until many—forgetting the terms of their entertainment—were terrified, as if *he* were the cleric's spirit, or a vengeful visiting angel.

He pictures that cowering crowd, himself on the rope, unneedful of vapour to make him tremble. It was the best-earning trick he had ever performed and, fleeing the troops of Catania's archbishop, Orlando kept muttering, 'Miracles, yes, miracles,' as if racking his brain for a way to exploit the miraculous. Then, perhaps for the lack of burning priests, he'd forgotten all about it, and they were back in Rome with their usual routines.

'He's a nice cat,' says a tiny voice, making Jacopo turn in surprise. A tiny girl stands before him, staring into his eyes. She seems nonplussed by the startled look on his face, and mutters uncertainly, 'Is he a boy?'

'A girl,' he says softly, inclined to ask if she herself is a girl or a doll, her face is so perfect, her hair, the colour of sunflowers, so neatly arranged in its tight little bun.

'Oh …' she nods, then seems not to know what to say. Jacopo waits, seeing the boy, a little older—perhaps five or six—who's standing behind her, as dark as she's bright.

'How old is she?' he asks in a manner so solemnly adult that he seems almost sulky.

'Oooh … I'm not sure,' Jacopo sighs, counting off years on his fingers. 'Not as old as you, I'll bet.'

The boy's face lights up for an instant, then resumes its stolid demeanour. Meanwhile, the girl hasn't taken her eyes off the cat.

'Can I pat her?' she says at last, as if she can wait no longer, and totters up at a nod from Jacopo, while Scimmi regally lifts her head to the child's plump fingers. 'Oh, she's nice and soft. What's her name?'

'Scimmia,' he smiles. 'Scimmi for short. Why not try scratching under her chin? She likes that too.' Then he sits up straighter, folding his arms round his knees. 'Aren't you going to tell her your name?'

'I forgot,' she apologises, looking more closely at Scimmi. 'I'm Tessa.'

'And what about you?' he coaxes the boy. 'Cat got your tongue?' But the child looks more serious still beneath his dark curls.

'Bruno,' he mutters quickly. As if to cover the sudden sound of his name, he adds, 'Is she playful?'

'Well, sometimes. It depends on her mood. Right now, while Tessa's patting her, I don't think she'd feel very playful.'

'They seem to have made a friend,' says a deep female voice.

'Yes,' he laughs, turning to find the one that he'd thought might be there, the tall, dark woman with the elegant hands and the face of a sombre Madonna. He stands and slaps at his rumpled clothes. 'Though she's a fickle little creature.'

She looks at him, and seems to smile to herself. He thinks that perhaps it's his accent. Though he'd worked hard on his voice in his time with Orlando, he's never felt sure that it hides his true origins.

'For a moment, I was sure you were going to say "*like all women*",' she laughs, watching her children play with the cat. 'I'm glad you didn't.'

'Then so am I,' he smiles, and leaves it at that.

After watching some more she turns to him slowly. 'I'm Laura della Bosca.' He raises his eyebrows. Her manner is very direct—what some would call *modern*—though he wonders if this might have something to do with what they've all been through, since not just their health, but formality too, seemed consumed by the pestilence.

'Giorgio dei Sapori,' he says with a bow.

'Funny,' she smiles, 'I met a Giorgio dei Sapori at one of Raffaello Moretti's parties.' She glances blandly over the sea swell. 'He was a trader from Bologna. He looks nothing like you.'

'And it's not a common name,' he says softly, clucking his tongue. 'Oh, Monna Laura, it's a small world we move in.'

The galley sails into the south, loaded with its cargo of spices and fugitives. It seems that they've left the plague safely behind, and a more relaxed mood prevails as they skim lightly over the calm blue waters, their banners rippling like the wake of their passage. From time to time a flock of gulls comes squalling round the mast as they pass some invisible island, or the sea beneath them winks with the shimmering flanks of mackerel, or turns to flexible glass with a jellyfish flotilla. Jacopo spends much of his time with Laura. Indeed, on the very day he'd embarked he had noticed her thick dark hair and her face of a pale haughty saint, made paler still by her black widow's weeds, and he welcomes the way they've grown close as the days go slowly by.

Still, the fact of her mourning sets limits on just how close they may grow, while the definite, yet friendly, distance between them gives him no chance to slip off the mask of Giorgio dei Sapori, not even a little. Though she makes no further mention of having met the man, it remains a hinted suspicion and keeps him on his guard. Nor, he suspects, is the nature of her mourning any real impediment to their intimacy since, not that she ever says it directly, there seem to be resentments toward her dead husband. This man was a merchant of great wealth, and of still greater years, and it was only in the final hours of his life, when he lay in the grip of the pestilence, that she learned how much of this wealth he'd devoted to saving his soul. He'd bequeathed almost all his property, his shares in his companies and over fifty thousand florins to the Church and its charities, leaving to her and the children no more than a house in Genoa and bequests of a few hundred florins a year. Almost twenty thousand florins were to go to families against whom he feared he'd made usurious loans, so that all she carries with her, apart from her copy of his will, is a cargo of cinnamon, nutmeg and cassia. 'So, with the grace of God and the Pope's good will, he may enter Paradise,' she says softly, gazing out to the eastern horizon, not the least trace of irony marring her words.

Most of their conversations, however, are happier than this. For indolent hours they sit at the stern, feet dangling above the lacy trails of their passing, while he speaks of the strange events he has witnessed, now cast in the form of a rich trader's tales; and she in turn conjures the luxuries of Avignon and the watery mazeways of Venice, until he thinks that, perhaps, they're displaying their lives through coloured, eccentric lenses. He sometimes surprises himself and the lady when, turning from watching the children, he catches her gaze on his face, a gaze which, if anything, grows fonder still when he speaks of his wealth in Perugia.

Whatever these hopes and doubts, schemings and impossibilities, all is changed by a single cry from one of the oarsmen, a sound not of shock or of pain, but of simple despair as he slumps from his bench to the boards. At the bow the archers stop their dice game, the passengers fall silent, every heart gone cold as the mate leans over the fallen oarsman. Even he, dour though he is, can't stifle the groan that comes to his lips as he turns the man over and finds the hard tumour under his arm.

Now the voyage grows dire and frightful. No more do they feel they've fled Kaffa's closed trap for the freedom of the sea. Instead it seems that they're caught in narrower confines still, with no way at all of escape. The sun, which had seemed so friendly and warm, beats on the deck like a hammer. The heat that they feel, the sweat that they drip, might well be the fever's first fatal signs. The water, some insist, has a strange, metallic taste. Even the fleas, which all had ignored, begin to feel like an infestation. The oarsman is kept at the front of the ship, and yet, as if to prove that it plays no favourites, the sickness lights on old Guglielmo and his arthritic wife. Since they have their own cabin they're easily isolated, and those who'd been wooing the elderly pair now leave them alone, their only company the crewman appointed to serve them. The door is shut, except when this fellow brings them the food they won't eat; yet their groans haunt the ship as they hatch the great eggs in their groins, as do those of the oarsman who shouts at the prow. The stench of the fever blankets the deck from bowsprit to stern, a drifting miasma beneath the blue sky.

The others' one-time indolence becomes an anxious, watchful torpor, as if they too tossed in the throes of the sickness. When they speak they do so more softly, yet with greater purpose, responding to jokes with uneasy laughter, observing their fellows more keenly since they know that they number more than fourteen, that the ship carries one not listed, a stowaway stalking their dreams, breathing into their faces, sharing his meals with the rats and the vermin, hiding by day in the ship's dark places. For Death nestles somewhere amongst them, and there's nothing to do but wait and be watchful. Then the wind from the north, the first wintry wind, turns sharp and cold, cutting over the sea like a scythe. Its blade bears away, with the foam and the spindrift, the souls of the merchant, his wife and the oarsman, sweeping them up in the starless dark so that all that remains is their hunched, cradled husks. These are quickly consigned to the sea and sink with a sound less harsh than the wind round the witnesses' ears as Captain Pozzi sprinkles a handful of prayers on the waves.

Now come days spent waiting beneath the slate skies. They rug themselves up in their coats against the loud wind, yet will not huddle, scattered on deck like so many islands, eyes peering out between hats and tight scarves, watching their neighbours for signs, for hints of their sickness, quaking at every twinge behind their walls of wool. The rain comes sweeping in slow, icy drifts, urging them down below, to gather deep in the creaking gloom. Most refuse, remaining on deck to breathe the wet air, the sheets of rain lashing over the waves, soaking them all to the bone as they silently sit in the tents of themselves. The curious thing is that when the weather turns bad, the plague disappears. Watch though they might, it does not return. None of them—passengers, sailors, oarsmen or archers—fall sick with anything worse than a cold. Once, during the rain's easing, Jacopo watches Scimmi play with a rat that she's caught in the hold. It's a tiny black creature, little more than a baby, and she pauses after she's mauled it, waiting for movement, patient despite the urge to strike that trembles within her. She gives it time to grow bold, to make a bolt for freedom, then pounces, hurling it through the air on the tips of her dainty needles. Jacopo wonders whether the sickness too is like this, waiting, allowing them to recover, to lose their fear, poised like a claw above them.

Whether or not it's just playing, the plague remains absent for long enough to allow the return of fine weather, to enable the travellers to loll on the deck and regain their habits of conversation. The sun is cooler and the north-eastern wind, though gentler than it was, is far from a summer breeze. It's as they turn hopefully southward to seek out Byzantium that the sickness returns, felling a second oarsmen, then his neighbour, and still unslaked, taking two further merchants and the first of the archers.

Captain Giuseppe Pozzi acts decisively, commanding the ill to be taken down to the hold.

This decision, however, is not good enough for the ship's first mate, whom Jacopo and Laura have overheard in dispute with the captain. At first they had spoken so low that the burglar and lady, engaged as they were in their own conversation, heard only the tone of their voices. It was a change in this that caught their attention, the mate's voice growing especially heated.

'We can't afford to let it get worse!'

The mate was vehement, and he leaned from the rail to glare at the captain, who replied with restraint, 'I know that, Aldo.'

'But what action are you willing to take? Trying to isolate them in the hold may do no good at all. You saw how things went in Kaffa.'

'I did,' said the captain, and Jacopo sensed that his calm was actually anger, barely contained. 'And I saw too that no-one could find a satisfactory reason for what happened.'

'Maybe not, but the fact remains that the more who are sick, the more'll become so.'

'Just what are you suggesting, Aldo?'

'That it won't be long before everyone on board falls sick, and even if the *Santa Margherita* lands at Constantinople, it'll bring nothing but a cargo of corpses.'

'But you keep implying the need for some action other than what I have already done. Have I misunderstood you, or do you have something better you wish to suggest?'

Jacopo and Laura leaned closer together, aware that their silence betrayed their interest, yet eager to hear more.

'No, you haven't misunderstood me,' said the mate, too immersed in his argument to notice anything else. 'What I'm saying should be perfectly clear. That if we have any further signs of infection—and preferably *before*, in my opinion—we should rid ourselves of those who endanger the rest.'

'Put the sick overboard, you mean?'

'Yes.'

The captain drew himself up, his response so ready that he might have rehearsed it. 'I'm afraid I could never resign myself to so ruthless an action, and I'm deeply disappointed to find an officer in my charge recommending such a course.'

'Well, then let it be—' but here the mate stopped, unyielding in his gaze if not his words. Jacopo waited for someone to break the silence and was shocked to find it was Laura who did so.

'I entirely agree, captain,' she said stoutly. 'It would be a mortal sin to cast the helpless into the sea to avoid the risk of sickness ourselves.'

'If God infects them with plague, then it's His will that they die.' The mate spat over the rail. 'Whether His will is done by drowning or pestilence seems of little issue, especially if it means saving the rest of the ship.'

'I can't believe that anyone who suggests killing the sick, when it's our charitable duty to care for them, could possibly be the best person to interpret God's will.'

The captain had smiled, the mate had glared, and Jacopo, staring out to the southern horizon, had started to whistle.

Most of the times he descends to the hold, Jacopo averts his eyes from the dying. Once, however, when he goes to retrieve a bottle of malmsey, he sees something move at the edge of his vision. He peers into the gloom, through the dusty gold shafts that fall through the boards, and sees a sick oarsman up on his pallet, his arms extended as if in prayer. The man's face seems rapt and his lips move too quickly for words to emerge, yet his eyes are so fixed on the depths of the hold that Jacopo follows his gaze, expecting to see he doesn't know what—some demon out of the man's delirium, an angel arrayed for battle, or the great, grim shadow of Death himself towering in the silence. But then, as his eyes adjust, there's only the body of one of the sick and, beyond, their fur slick with bilgewater, a group of glistening rats that are eyeing him cautiously out of the shadows. When the man falls panting back on his rags, Jacopo grabs at the malmsey, snatching it up and scurrying off for the hatch.

Though Death may not have appeared that morning, his presence is palpable down in the hold as one by one he takes his victims. Indeed, from among the sick, only the archer remains alive when Captain Pozzi himself falls ill. He can barely stand with the pain of the egg between his legs, yet addresses them all from the steps to the poop, claiming they're close to the Bosporus and insisting that he too be placed in the hold. He almost falls down the steps, and the mate, showing none of the satisfaction Jacopo's sure he must feel, has him carefully carried below. Now, its corpses still bobbing behind it, its captain adrift in the tides of delirium, the *Santa Margherita* has the stench of a death ship. It sails in the warm autumn sun, across the blue sea, like a tiny island black with corruption. Yet Aldo, the mate, ensconced in the captain's cabin, seems swollen with confidence, wearing his smartest outfit and strutting the poop like an admiral. Late the following afternoon comes the cry of land to the south.

It's dusk by the time they are sailing beneath the walls of Constantinople. Jacopo gazes across the Bosporus at the fat-bellied domes and smoky towers, feeling truly secure for the first time in weeks. The Emperor's palace and Santa Sofia rise in the evening sky, which glows like a gilt and crimson mosaic, till he dreams up vistas of shutterless windows and opening caskets. But the promise of such easy invitations is quickly belied at the harbour's gates. The watch, arrayed in brass armour—more like trumpets than soldiers—stand armed on the seawall. Their captain comes forth to challenge the galley in blustering Greek. As it happens, no-one aboard speaks more than its most basic phrases, so Aldo's reduced to gestures and grimaces, while the Greek commander points with contempt at their Genoese banner and waves them off with his sword.

'We are friends of the Emperor!' Aldo cries hopelessly. 'We trade with the patriarchs!' All he receives are peremptory gestures and volleys of babble, in which can be heard only 'Kaffa' and, possibly, 'Tartar'. Then an outburst of Greek erupts behind Aldo's back as Captain Giuseppe Pozzi, up from the hold and trembling with fever, delivers a speech to the wide-eyed watch. More intent on his looks than his words, they barely seem to listen, edging away with a nervous clanking of spears. The speech of Captain Pozzi quickly peters out, and he pants at the rail while Aldo, sidling toward the helm, gives him more than adequate breathing space.

'It's no good,' he says in a barely audible voice, sounding as if he might weep. 'You didn't understand ... but what they were saying before ... they're allowing no vessels from Kaffa to land because of the plague ...'

'But that's not right!' cries Aldo. 'We could keep the sick aboard and quarantine them in the harbour.'

'They don't see the point,' he sighs, almost slumping to the deck. 'What their commander was saying ... I think I got it right ... was that *Lo Storione* tried to land two days ago ... it was riddled with plague ... they'd sent it on under threat of setting it alight ... So the only—' But he pauses, peering shoreward with everyone else.

The docks are lost in the gloom, and the first stars are out, studding the indigo depths above thousands of shimmering lamps. A flurry of torches and clattering armour is rushing toward them.

'Cast off!' shouts Aldo, almost shrieking with frustration. 'Hurry up! Lay to those oars!'

Already the archers are out on the seawall with fiery bolts in their bows. Captain Pozzi collapses amid all the shouting, and arrows like ill-omened comets arc through the air, hissing into the water, burning between the boards or catching at sails and shrouds, where men and women douse them with brine. Jacopo leaps to a bench where an oarsman is missing, drawing the oar with all of his strength as the *Santa Margherita*, festooned with bright fires, crawls through the night for the Sea of Marmora.

Tuccio gives alms

FURTHER BACK ALONG THE BEACH, AT THE BASE OF THE high wall, the river spewed from the water-gate's wide, grated mouth. Ahead, there was something down on the sand, where gulls and waves and a single barking dog competed for its possession. Tuccio glanced round at the troop of riders following at his back, men like Baldassare d'Aquila and Bernardo Cuorevero, all mounted on spirited horses except, of course, for Luigi Pucci, his accountant, Gino his steward, and the rest of his servants, whose nags, though healthy enough, were hardly the stuff of romances. Yet here they were, trailing meekly along the beach behind his sedate black mule. The only person riding at his side was Francesco Morelli, also mounted on a Spanish mule, a purchase which Tuccio could not help considering a slavish copy of his own.

'They're like an army of buzzards and stray cats,' Francesco was saying. 'At present, the whole countryside's full of them.' He pointed at the makeshift lean-tos that huddled by the wall. 'And there's not one of them who's not a leper or convulsive, who doesn't suffer some malignant fever or catarrh, some rash of boils or ulcers. To treat such mobs would be like trying to catch ...' and here he paused, extending an arm to include the waves beside them '... to catch the ocean in a thimble.'

Tuccio nodded at him slowly, knowing that nothing could tempt Francesco Morelli, physician and commune Gonfaloniere, to treat that indigent mass of suffering. Not that Tuccio would recommend such charity. The quicker these vagrants knew there was little for them in Topomagro, the better.

'They run from famine in the north to famine in the south,' Tuccio said, pausing for a moment to peer at the shallows where the dog did battle with the gulls for a bundle of wave-tossed rags. 'And the winter looks like being a cold one. There'll be even more deaths than last year.'

'The thing is, Tuccio, we can't afford to keep them in the town. There've been troubles elsewhere already—disorder in San Gimignano, insurrection in Florence, food riots in Pistoia. These vagabond armies are prey to every false rumour of plentiful communes and lands of Cockaigne. Yet when they arrive, only to find the granaries guarded by the town militia, then things can turn nasty. We're going to have to get rid of them.'

'Perhaps ...' said Tuccio doubtfully. He glanced at the scene about them, at the gloomy clouds of the late afternoon, at the ragged shacks below the wall and the great white ribs that rose from the beach before him. 'Yet the Church enjoins us to charity.'

Francesco smiled and reined his mule past the

first of the whale's pale bones. 'But it doesn't require that we care for all the poor of Lombardy and Piedmont when their own cities neglect to help them.'

Tuccio nodded absently, his attention drawn by the massive ribcage. Unconsciously he slowed his mule to observe the remains, the entire party behind him coming almost to a standstill. He realised that he'd virtually expunged the creature from his memory, something that underlined for him just how long it had been since he'd ridden on the beach. It was this very absence, this withdrawal from public attention, that had provoked their impromptu procession. It was time to assert their presence and wealth once more. And it surprised him to find how much better he felt; here, riding through town with his friends and his followers, he sensed his own strength with a pleasure he rarely let himself feel. Still, just at this moment of rejuvenation, as he looked at the ruined whale, he returned to those feelings he'd had when he first set eyes on it. For the briefest of instants, as the wind-picked ribs rose overhead like the spars of one of his ships, he felt a curious bond with the creature, as if he himself were lying there, a dilapidated giant picked clean by a rabble of gulls.

'Come on, Tuccio,' called the physician, who was already some way ahead.

The merchant didn't move, thinking of that pile of rags beside the water, the bands of hungry vagrants, and suddenly seeing an image of Marina, his young daughter, galloping down a sunny highway. She was smiling and excited, full of boyish, brash self-confidence. He thought of her eagerness to face the world, and of what that world was like. Was it just a road of bones? He feared for her youth and hopefulness among it all.

'Tuccio!' Francesco called once more. 'It'll be night before we get back, and then we'll never—'

'Look!' shouted someone in the group behind them, interrupting Francesco. Tuccio turned from the bones to the men at his back. He saw Baldassare point to the Porta del Mare, and followed his arm till he saw the horsemen riding onto the beach. It was Frederico dalla Montagna with his friends and retainers. They rode at a canter across the sand, coming quickly toward them, so that Baldassare, Bernardo and a number of others started reaching for their swords.

'Leave your weapons where they are,' called Tuccio, annoyed by the unwonted squeak in his voice. The approaching riders had already slowed to a walk, their horses tossing their manes and snorting out steam in the cool evening air. He urged his mule a little harder, attempting to match their pace, watching the face of Montagna, its features obscure in the dimming light. There was no doubt about it, the man was impressive on his heavy black horse as it sidled and propped and sprayed up the sand. He held its head upright by sheer strength, despite its wild mettle, baring his teeth in a smile at the merchant, a grin as glib as a gypsy's except for his arrogant eyes. His sons rode behind him on horses almost as wild, and Tuccio felt that he himself cut a small, timid figure astride his plump mule, no matter what it was worth; then wondered if all that shying and prancing wasn't merely for show. But the horsemen were almost upon them.

'A nice evening, Tuccio ... Francesco,' said the noble, smiling once more, though the merchant could see that some of his men had their hands on their hilts. 'Just take care that your mule doesn't bolt.' And he came straight on, not pausing at all as his stallion slid by breathing steam.

'Yes, he looks pretty wild,' crowed one of his sons, the other shouting with laughter, close on their father's heels, while Francesco and Tuccio nodded tight greetings, reining in their uneasy mounts. And now the groups were mingling, the horsemen merging their ranks like stormbanks clashing in mute confusion. As Tuccio turned in his saddle and Montagna's retainers scraped past, there was something about that hushed, tense watchfulness, those stiff, sidelong glances, that made him think of a pair of street dogs passing each other, hackles raised and snarls buried deep in their throats. There were mutters and bumpings, the jingle of harness, till even the merchant gripped at the dagger under his cape, expecting the hiss of the first drawn sword. But the final rider was by him, and Montagna—he could see him high on his mettlesome horse—was already past old Luigi Pucci dawdling at the rear. Just as the danger seemed over, he heard a loud cry and a thud as Gino, his steward, fell to the sand amid skittering hooves. Baldassare and Bernardo Cuorevero had their swords out already, and his servants glared darkly about them. The nobles, in turn, drew their weapons in one hissing sigh.

'Stoldo!' bellowed the patriarch, voice cleaving the air like a blade.

The elder son lowered his head, then his sword, and swung his horse around with the jerk of an arm. 'Your pardon,' he murmured, leaning down to help up the steward. 'My arm caught on your coat as we passed.'

There were grumbles from Tuccio's men, who made no effort to sheathe their weapons, and Baldassare came forward. But Stoldo had already turned, he and his brother cantering off in a flurry of riders, leaving the merchants to mutter indignantly on the sand.

'Forget it, Baldassare, all of you,' said Tuccio softly, reclaiming his authority. 'He said it was an accident, so we'll treat it as one.'

There were murmurs of protest, but they put up their swords and knew he was right. This was one more stain on their pride, which some other day must wipe clean. That such a day would come seemed no longer in doubt. It would just have to wait until Tuccio, Francesco Morelli and the other town worthies deemed it necessary. For now they'd be prudent, keep their swords sheathed, and follow Tuccio's mule to the Porta del Mare. For here they were, so distracted by their anger that they'd hardly heard how their horses' hooves now clattered on stones.

Tuccio gazed at the tall gate above them, urging the mule beneath the dark arch. He nodded stiffly at the guards and cast one final glance at the beach, where Montagna's party seemed to have turned back already. Then he entered the Borgo San Pietro, quickly immersed in the quandary of streets that twisted beneath the city walls, his nose assailed by the stench of dead fish. The party wound through the quarter past groups of young men, some of whom nodded. Others seemed churlish, turning away or mumbling together with quick bursts of laughter. They came to the Piazza San Pietro, hemmed in by low walls and the heavy, squat form of San Pietro itself. Thin streets and laneways gave onto the square that had, at its heart, a dry stone fountain in which there sat a decapitated goddess.

Approaching this fountain, Tuccio paused for a moment, finding it surrounded by a group of vagrants who lounged on its steps like the pauperised apostles of its ruined deity. The church's porch seemed filled with a still larger crowd, though the growing gloom made it hard to distinguish shadows from their owners. Tuccio went forward. His mule had not gone far when a pair of figures rose from the fountain and slowly approached, and others sat up with expectant glances. Before he was able to make them out, they were almost upon him, a man and a boy, the child no more than six or seven, leading the other by a rope. The man seemed ageless, and anxiously stretched out his hands despite the boy's ministrations. Indeed, with his wide, gaping mouth and eyeless sockets, the whole of his form seemed to grope at the air before him.

'Coins,' cried the child in a practised wail, 'a few coins for God's poor, signore!'

'Yes, signore, a few humble pennies for the blind!' the blindman blurted, then stumbled forward, hands clutching like suckers, and caught at the reins. The mule shied, wheezing, but the man held firm, staggering round on his great flat feet while the boy kept up his plaintive wailing. Francesco Morelli admonished the pair and the others gathered about, demanding the fellow loosen his grip. But Tuccio put up his hand.

'Here,' he said gently, placing a silver *grosso* in the palm of the boy, who handed it to the blindman. 'May that make the winter a little warmer for you.' He made to ride on, yet the man kept hold, as if afraid to let go now that he held something solid. The others rose from the steps, coming quickly toward them. Already a figure was hopping across like a featherless crow on a big wooden crutch. One leg was gone and his head was completely devoid of hair, his features collapsed as if eaten away from within. 'A penny for the poor!' roared the leper, while an ancient woman—flesh thin as spiderweb over her bones—trembled and whined at the feet of Francesco.

'I don't like this,' hissed Baldassare in Tuccio's ear.

'Nor I,' said Bernardo beside him, while the crowd closed tighter still.

'Go on, get away,' cried the voice of Luigi from somewhere behind them, followed by the sound of a scuffle as a pair of Tuccio's servants shoved at a group who were jostling the old accountant.

Tuccio caught the glint of a blade, unsure of whose it was. Others swarmed from the steps of the church and the blindman wrenched at his arm. He tried to pull free, watching the swelling crowd, some hobbling on rickety legs, some on crutches, others wheeled headlong on small wooden trolleys, all seeming so ragged and shrunken and thin that they swarmed through the square like a mummified army. 'My purse!' cried a voice behind him, and just as the merchant turned he noticed one of the beggars sliding his steward's sword from its scabbard. Francesco was rowelling his mule for all he was worth, and Niccolo followed suit, lurching forward across the square. Baldassare was yelling, 'Come on, let's get moving!' and all of them battered the ribs of their horses. Tuccio jerked away from the blindman, kicking his mule till it lunged through the crowd with a harsh, wheezing cry. More people, beggars perhaps, clung tight to the walls as the riders sped north up a laneway. Wheeling round once in the saddle, he saw the child stretched out on the ground while the blindman, tied to his wrist, gaped after them dumbly.

Across the piazza, at the start of the street leading back to the beach, Montagna watched with his men ranged behind him.

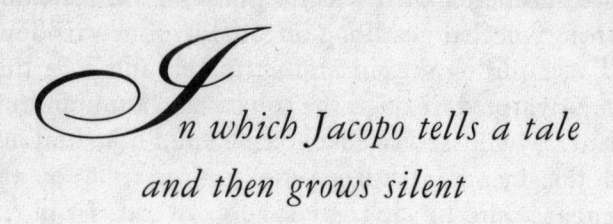

In which Jacopo tells a tale and then grows silent

CROSSING THE SEA OF MARMORA THE LAST OF THE sick, including the captain, died. The death of Giuseppe Pozzi unsettled Jacopo more than he had expected, and he wondered if, perhaps, there'd remained in the back of his mind the notion of some authority that he could appeal to, someone whose sense of good service might somehow banish the plague if a passenger protested loudly enough. Clearly the captain was not that authority. Nor was Aldo, strutting above the oarsmen and barely attempting to hide his panic when a pair of Greek war galleys appeared to the north, sailing from Byzantium. These trailed them for almost ten leagues in the Hellespont. 'Some Christians, these Greeks,' snarled Aldo at last. 'They don't want us landing anywhere in the Emperor's domains. But don't worry, they'll keep their distance.' And he was right. Even before the *Santa Margherita* had left the narrow straits, the galleys had vanished.

Soon they were sailing out on the sparkling Aegean, under fleets of big clouds drifting north through the air. The sun, glaring down in great pallid sheets, seemed to echo the swell of their three-cornered sails, which rippled and luffed in the strong southern wind. Here they sailed for some days, awaiting the first sign of fever.

None occurred. Under the cold, searing light of the early winter sun, with that wind from the south blowing hard in their faces, they stood on the unsteady deck as if the sickness were being blown from them.

Long weeks of crisp, fair weather passed. They put in at Lesvos and Khios, Tinos, Milos and Kithira, replenishing their food and water and, above all, their sense of membership amongst the living, of oneness with the squabbling mass of fishermen and other clients of the dusty, dark tavernas. Not once did they mention the sickness, but instead smiled like merchants on a well-stocked pilgrimage, till it almost seemed they'd forgotten their danger and the fatal stowaway down in their hold. The villages ringing the high blue harbours, each cross on the white basilicas, the men who mended fishing nets, and the ancient women with their seamed brown faces and widow's weeds—all seemed to say they were slowly drawing nearer to home.

It did not take long for such a sea change to work its influence. The torpid fear which had gripped the ship now relaxed its hold. The children, boisterous at any time, now peppered him anew with questions about Scimmi. At first, his chief pesterer was Tessa, asking whatever she thought of concerning his cat—'Does she eat mice, Giorgio?', 'Does she have a mummy?'—but later he was quizzed by Bruno, who gained in confidence, and grew impatient of his sister as he did so. He liked to ask what he felt were grown-up questions, while Tessa looked on wide-eyed, hoping for a story. For instance, there was the matter of Scimmi's worth.

'How much did you pay for her, Giorgio?' asks Bruno, hands behind his back and looking very solemn, much as Jacopo imagines his father might have, bargaining over a shipment of spices.

Now it's Jacopo's turn to look solemn, wrinkling his brow and rolling his eyes, as if doing difficult sums. 'Well, I didn't pay anything for her,' he says at last, 'at least not when I got her. But after that I paid over six thousand gold *scudi* for the little beast.' And he gives her a scratch behind the ear, till she cranes up primly, waiting for more.

Laura looks dubious, Bruno confused, and Tessa, glancing at the others, starts to pout.

'Six *thousand*?' asks Laura.

'What do you mean, Giorgio?' adds Bruno.

'What's a *scudi*?' lisps Tessa.

'A gold *scudo* is a lot of money,' says her mother, raising her eyebrows as if to accuse him of boasting or lying, or possibly both.

'*Sicilian scudi*,' Jacopo explains, then pauses to gather his thoughts. 'It was on the Canary Isle,' he finally says, 'with Orlando the Great.' He gazes at Tessa. 'I've told you about Orlando the Great, haven't I?'

'Yes,' she nods quickly, shoving her thumb in her mouth, her listening-to-stories pose.

'Well, this time,' he says, rolling his eyes up once more to refer to some codex kept in his head, 'Orlando was taking his troupe on a ship, all the way to the Canary Isle.'

'Mice?' says Laura cryptically.

Jacopo smiles at her slyly, but Bruno turns as if she's gone mad. 'Canaries,' he insists, shaking his head at Tessa, who's waiting for more, thumb in her mouth.

'That's right, Bruno,' Jacopo chuckles, patting the boy's dark hair, 'the Canary Isle it was.' And he too turns to shake his head at their mother.

'Well,' she says, 'what happened on this Canary Isle of yours?'

'Oh, it wasn't mine. It was the king's. King Agapanthus. He invited us all to dinner the night we arrived.'

'Were you going to juggle there?' asks Bruno. 'In his palace?'

'Clever boy,' he says, then glances at Tessa, giving her cheek a soft pinch. 'And you're clever, too.' He rolls up his eyes to read his mental manuscript. 'Yes, all of us, all of Orlando's troupe, were going to perform at the palace. So King Agapanthus, who was a very nice king, gave us a banquet the night we arrived. The ship's captain and his mate were there as well, and one or two of the other passengers. So, there we were, seated at the king's big banquet table, with napkins in front of us and ... well, what else would you expect?'

'A cake!' splutters Tessa, dragging her thumb from her mouth.

'A knife and spoon?' laughs Bruno, 'A bowl? A cup and a big piece of bread?'

'Well, you would. And I'd have loved a cake there, Tessa. But you know what there was?' And the children shake their heads. Jacopo waits, then looks at them, chuckling. 'The only thing before me on the table was a club, a thick wooden club as big as my arm.'

'A club?' says Bruno. 'How can you eat with a club?'

'Well, that's exactly what I was wondering. I thought they might bring out a chicken, a live one, and put it on my plate for me to bonk on the head.'

Bruno and Tessa erupt into giggles. 'Bonk!' says Tessa, pulling out her moist thumb, then reaching up to hit Bruno on the head, while he lurches away and Laura shushes them to silence.

'Yes,' laughs Jacopo, avoiding Laura's eye. 'Well, I was a bit worried, I can tell you. But my fears were needless. The food, when it arrived, was not only dead, but delicious—great steaming bowls of veal with spicy sauces and vegetable dumplings, roasted woodcocks stuffed with figs, then plates of pork jellies and bowls of coloured jams. Oh, it makes me hungry just to think about it.'

'But how could you eat it with a club?' Bruno insists.

'Well, no-one did. Everyone, including the king, used nothing but their fingers, which is probably the most sensible way to eat anything. After all, animals get on perfectly well without spoons, don't they, Scimmi?'

'Then why did they give you the club?'

'Oh, I thought you'd never ask.' Now Jacopo leans forward, as if to impart a secret. 'You see, almost as soon as the food was brought out, and certainly before it reached anyone's mouth, the floor began to move as if it were alive. There was a squiggling and scuttering and squeaking everywhere—along the wainscot, under the chairs, even on the table. And this was because, the instant they smelt the food, a horde of mice, hundreds of them, an entire city of mice that lived in the walls, came rushing out to join the banquet, scurrying amongst the dishes, stealing bits of food, practically nipping the mouthfuls out of your teeth. It was then, when I noticed the king and all of his courtiers reaching for their clubs, that I saw what they were for. Suddenly the whole room was in an uproar, with people lashing out—even as they chewed their dinner—at the tiny, rushing creatures, sometimes scoring a hit, but more often than not, either missing or hitting their neighbour by mistake. It was a battle, and I'd no doubt the mice were the winners.'

'But,' says Bruno, 'but ... didn't they have any cats?'

'Like Scimmi?' cries Tessa.

'Yes, that's a very good question.' Jacopo shakes his head sadly. 'You see, I'd left Scimmi back on the boat, out of courtesy to the king—and as the poor man apologised, lamenting how they'd found no better way than the clubs to deal with the troublesome creatures, I realised I could do these catless islanders a favour.'

'What did you do, Giorgio?' says Tessa.

'Well, the next night, when the king invited us back again, I made sure that I had her tucked in my sleeve. Then, when dinner was served and the mice came swarming out of their holes, running under the chairs and up the legs of the tables, just as the king and his court were reaching for their clubs, I opened my sleeve and Scimmi came bounding out. King Agapanthus sat there open-mouthed, his crown atilt. His court seemed stunned. And the mice, who'd never seen a cat before, seemed even more so. For a moment they didn't move. Scimmi, on the other hand, who'd not only seen but tasted many a mouse, hurtled amongst them like a knight amongst peasants, killing more than forty before she drew breath.'

The children stare silently at her as she snoozes in Jacopo's lap.

'So, right then and there, the king made an offer of three thousand *scudi*.' He rubs the back of her neck, though she doesn't even stir. 'For this skinny little alley cat. Well, fool that you may say I am, I didn't want to sell her.' The children shake and nod their heads, unsure of how to agree with what he did, but certain they do. 'She's my cat and I simply didn't want to sell her, not even for that ridiculous sum. So the king offers four thousand *scudi*, then five, but still I shake my head, until he begins to look unhappy. Finally, he tells me to think it over and to bring her the following night. He invites everyone back, looking at the heap of mice and declaring that another night or two like this might see him rid of them forever.'

'Did you sell her, Giorgio?' asks Tessa.

'Of course he didn't,' says her brother, then turns to Jacopo. 'But did you take her back again?'

'Yes, Bruno, I did. But not because I was thinking of selling her. I just didn't want to leave her alone on the ship, not now that she was worth so much. Someone might have stolen her.' He looks down at Scimmi and shakes his head ruefully. 'Yes, five thousand *scudi* ...' Once again his eyes roll up as he pauses. 'Now, where was I?' he says absently. 'Oh, yes, that's right, at the following evening's banquet in the palace. This time I didn't even bother hiding her, but simply waited with her there in my arms till the meal was brought out. Of course nobody made a move toward the food, nobody except the mice, which once again came rushing out across the room and up onto the table. Nor did anyone reach for a club. The only other thing that seemed to move was Scimmi, who leapt, snarling, at the nearest mouse. She was already pouncing on her second victim when there was a scrabbling and a hissing from somewhere in the room, and the fat ship's cat came charging right out of the captain's coat, sliding then falling from the greasy table and killing half-a-dozen mice beneath her as she landed. The overfed thing caught nothing else by the time that Scimmi had gobbled a score. Still, inexperienced as he was, King Agapanthus showed no discernment on the subject of mousers, and he offered the captain six thousand *scudi* on the spot. *Six thousand scudi*. Ah, Scimmi, I could almost say you've ruined me.'

'But did he take it? Did the captain sell his cat?'

'Did he take it?' cries Jacopo, wide-eyed. 'Bruno, do cats eat mice? My boy, he thrust that cat so hard into Agapanthus's hands that he nearly caused a diplomatic incident. And not only that. He did a deal with the king to sell him a *shipment* of cats, to keep the kingdom free of mice forevermore. Oh, I tell you, children, this cat has kept me in the poorhouse.'

Tessa giggles behind her thumb at his grimacing face.

'Well may you laugh, my pretty one!' he cries, tickling her ribs till she splutters and wriggles. 'But when I said that Scimmi cost me six thousand *scudi*, well, I wasn't even thinking of the fortune I could have made on all those other cats. She's probably cost me half of Florence.'

'You poor man, Giorgio,' laughs Laura, squeezing his elbow with mock sympathy, 'and to think I never knew what a hard life you've led. What you need is a cup of good malmsey to sweeten things up.' Before long, the children are gorging on comfits and cordials, slipping a share to the priciest cat in all the known world, while Jacopo and Laura consume the best part of a bottle of Levantine malmsey.

They were not long out of Kithira when a violent gale blew up, screaming over the swells and taking the galley with it. For some days they ran at great pace before the wind, covering league upon league, passing far beyond the Peloponnesos, across the Ionian Sea. At last the gale abated, giving way to a time of unseasonable heat which reddened their flesh and reduced the oarsmen to thirsty silence. The passengers lolled about in the sun, watching the waves roll sluggishly by, losing themselves in pleasant dreams of Venice and Genoa, of country villas in the hills, until, one evening, from the stern of the galley, they heard a cry of purest terror.

A crewman, who'd been pissing beside the tiller, was gripping his pizzle with one trembling hand while he prodded his crotch with the other. For there, amongst the tangled hair, was the tender redness of a budding tumour. 'An egg!' cried the mate. 'He's hatching an egg!' No-one on that ship gave thanks that it was someone else; all felt as if they themselves had hatched that bubo, as if it grew between their own two legs, announcing their own deaths. And, indeed, it was the start of a further cycle of sickness. Within a day, two more had brought forth tumours; like the crewman, lapsing quickly into fever. Captain Aldo, whose skill and prestige seemed to grow with the plague's disappearance, was once more discussing their need to be rid of the sick. However, for now, he followed Giuseppe Pozzi's example, filling the hold with victims.

The galley might almost have sunk, so great was its weight of despair. Having felt that they'd escaped, having rejoiced in their freedom and harboured thoughts of home, it was almost too much to accept that Death now held them once more in its grip. For two more days the sick lay down in the hold, delirious with fever, before another victim—the wife of a wealthy notary—fell ill. And this was the start of what split the ship for the rest of the voyage. They carried the woman below, and found that the first of the victims, the crewman, was lying as if he were dead. The captain quickly pronounced him so and proceeded with his removal. Some protested—the notary most of all— that the sickness never ended so soon, that a sturdy man should last more days before dying, and that the crewman was merely unconscious. But Aldo claimed that he heard no heartbeat, that the man was dead and that besides, it was now his ship to command. So they bore the body up to the deck, where Aldo pronounced a perfunctory prayer amidst a clamour of protests, the archers alert on the stairs, their weapons at the ready.

Jacopo, watching it all, said nothing. He tried to distract the children with small bits of magic since Laura had joined the protesters, who were shouting at the captain, decrying his prayers as hypocrisy. At one point, noting the archers up on the stairs, he tried to warn her to silence, but she wouldn't acknowledge his glance. In fact, her face was white and sweating, her eyes quite glassy with the ardour of her anger, and when she brushed him aside, her hand was burning as if with passion. The crewman's body was hoisted aloft in a riot of cries, where it hung suspended a moment, then toppled into the sea. There was an instant hush. The crowd stared down at the flat blue water, as if trying to fathom the depths of the crime. Then the body bobbed back up, appearing to move one arm, and just as quickly vanished. The hush erupted with shouts. 'You killed him!' cried some, and 'Murder!' yelled others. Some defended Aldo: 'It was the tide that did it,' they cried, 'a wave, just a fish!' But Laura wasn't shouting at all. Jacopo saw she was crying, clutching her side and weeping in loud, hoarse sobs, tearing the sleeve of her dress, turning toward him and lifting her arm to show him the red, fierce tumour.

Laura lies drifting in the ship's dark infirmary, its air like a single flame folding her tight in a pocket of heat then flaring out till it licks at the walls' damp planking. Sometimes it seems to run through her veins in red, wriggling streams. It seeps through the cracks of her skin, melting her thoughts till she floats through the hold, choking and light as burning sulphur. Sometimes her flesh is a wineskin of vinegar, a bloated thing that rolls with the ocean in restless anguish, as if her one hope were to be slit open. She feels transparent to pain, like a stained-glass saint where the sun comes streaming, searing her innards with red-hot fingers and filling the air with crimson light. This place is not vacant: its edges shift with familiar strange things. Troops of black rats wait in the corners, slimy with brine, their eyes pale pearls in the swimming light. High on their backs are the fat black fleas, their dark armour glinting and whetted heads turning. Sometimes they wait while she blossoms with fires, then suddenly swarm: Berich in purple armour, Gemer sheathed in his ebon helm, Azazel with banners and fanions flaring; some leaping, some hopping on squat, jointed legs as they mount the red giantess, silent as spirits, crueller than armies, spitting her flesh and sucking her blood with their bladed heads.

A change now comes to the hold. At her side there is whimpering, sobbing, then screaming, till the air seems to ache of itself. Tessa and Bruno have been lain beside her. She sees them lifted in fingers of flame, their bodies ash-pale, pocked black on the arms and mottled with tumours. Tessa begs her to come, while Bruno writhes on his sheets as if bound. Laura strains to sit up, and the rats come staggering out of the bilge to group in the shadows. Their riders—among them spined Moloch, Asmodeus shrouded in jagged black plumes—scuttle across her children's pale limbs, bursting the skin, nuzzling and suckling like venomous babies. She cries, feebly twists, while a hand dabs her brow with soft, moistened silk, a knife of smooth ice that slices her nerves.

Cardinal Rollo da Parma hires help

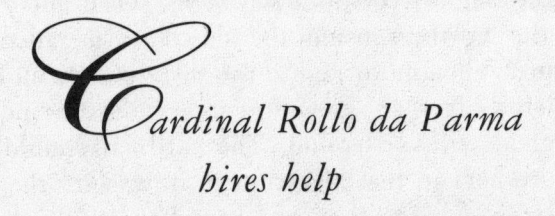

BENEATH THE NEW MOON'S WAXING CRESCENT THE palace of Cardinal Rollo da Parma, deep in its cleft between oaken hillsides, was little more than a hint of pale masonry in forests of guttering torches. The cardinal's expected visitor was now so late that it seemed unlikely he would come, and all the servants—with the exception of a handful of grooms and serving-maids—had been sent to bed, leaving the windows in darkness. Carvings—dark friezes mottled with moss and weathered by time—were striped with the moonlight that played on the walls. Angels cast demons from dense granite clouds, the bodies of saints sprouted patches of mould like the guilt of old sins, and high on the walls, between tall upper windows, the damned burned in flames that were yellow with lichen. The carven limbs of these figures, which appeared to twitch with each shift of moonlight through the dark leaves, were framed by the arch of a pair of thin legs that belonged, so it seemed, to some guardian demon carved on a far grander scale, yet which, even now, ran a hand through its hair to catch small, crawling things between finger and thumb.

Brother Corvo shone with cold sweat and gazed to the north, sensing the dawn of a rancorous Saturn. Then he turned to the eastern horizon from which a black comet would soon be ascending. He laughed with no sound. The cardinal should feel secure here in the hills, though now, with the help of strange herbs that had found their way to his kitchens, he sensed the furled chaos almost as clearly as Corvo himself. But he would not see it for what it was. For him it was no change in the cosmos' fabric but a fraying at its edges, a shift in circumstance, not substance; something to be fought with swords and gold when, in fact, it demanded no less than total obeisance. Rollo's solution was as yet all wrong, and Corvo awaited its arrival.

This solution, though late, was unmistakably imminent. At first it was a rumbling in the darkened woods, then a thunder and, at last, a trembling in the ground that clanked like metal as it raced toward the palace through moon-coloured dust. Corvo pressed closer against the cold stone, watching the riders approach in full armour, their horses hideous in metal masks, as if they were here not to bargain but to ransack. Red light from the torches passed over their forms till they seemed to well up from the darkness of sleep, the first a massive armoured swan with his neck of tight mail and long-beaked visor, and behind him others with bear's-head helms or snouted bevors tusked like boars. They came to a halt at the walls, banners aswirl with the rush of their motion, and stood like a herd of heraldic beasts. Their pennants' emblem—a swan that breathed fire—nested in flames like a newborn phoenix; their captain himself wore a bright steel aventail, and climbed from his horse, shouting commands in a harsh German tongue, stamping and clanking beneath the high walls. The others dismounted and dragged off their helms, as Brother Corvo noted the squeal of the big metal gates and the voice of a palace guard. Then the leader, Wolf Schwanhals, vanished from sight, and the rest of his company with him.

The north-west wind picked up, blowing so cold that it might have been breathed by the moon itself. But Corvo would wait till his blood turned to frost, since he wished to confirm how the dreams he had stirred into Rollo's food affected the Cardinal's actions. Yet more than this, the demise of His Eminence, Prince of the Church, was a prelude to something far greater. The thrill of conviction fired his heart, spreading at last to his numb, livid skin as the window beside him glowed suddenly yellow with torchlight.

He peeped through the gap where the sheets of waxed linen failed to meet squarely, and saw the cardinal enter the room ahead of the soldier. Rollo was wearing a taffeta gown, which shone so bright in the smoky light that he looked like the ruby that gleamed on his finger bloated to monstrous proportions. Wolf Schwanhals, minus his helm, had remained in his armour, clanking along in the wake of his host, the flickering torchlight glinting and sparking about the steel edges, giving him also a bright, gemlike look, though his was the hardness of diamond. A servant entered behind them, setting a tray with a brimming ewer and two golden goblets upon a low table. Rollo's fingers waved him away and the two men waited, mouths set, like jealous fops at an opulent masque.

'Help yourself to some wine, Baron.' The cardinal's words were barely muffled at all by the panes of waxed cloth.

'With pleasure ... Your Eminence,' his guest replied, hesitating at the honorific, perhaps through uncertainty, perhaps through pride. His chiselled, beardless face gave nothing away. He moved toward the low table, pausing over the goblets, bending his long and sinewy neck. He filled both goblets with wine, and offered one to Rollo, who led the way to a pair of chairs on either side of the table, bunching his robes as he sat.

'Please, Baron, feel free,' he said, pointing at the goblet which Schwanhals held to his lips. 'It has already been tasted.'

The man paused, sniffing at the wine before sipping. 'A fine wine, Your Eminence, by the aroma.' His Tuscan was larded with thick German vowels. 'More subtle, perhaps, than that of Swabia.' He smiled at the wine but still did not drink. 'Not as sweet, yet not, I think, as potent.'

The cardinal grinned at him knowingly, raised the cup to his bared white teeth and tipped it up in a lingering draught, keeping his eyes on his guest all the while. 'Your health,' he said, lifting his cup in a tardy toast.

Schwanhals mirrored the gesture, his features stony, and took a quick sip at his wine. 'Well, Your Eminence, to business, eh? It's been a long ride and I'm eager to know your terms.'

'You know the larger part of them already.' The cardinal frowned, as if at a thick-witted scribe. 'We've spoken of Topomagro, of its overweening burghers and their need to be humbled.'

'Oh, yes, we've spoken of that. I'm perfectly happy to teach the town some respect for the Church.' Rollo winced at his tone, which seemed to imply that the Church could garner respect in no other way. 'But it's time we said more about payment.'

'We've spoken of a sum, I believe,' said Rollo severely.

Wolf Schwanhals finished the wine at a gulp and put down the goblet. 'Yes, we spoke of a sum.' He laughed abruptly. 'But that was a joke, I think.' The cardinal didn't respond. 'Ten thousand florins, Your Eminence, is nothing for such a campaign.'

'Oh come, Baron. You'll gain almost as much again from the countryside.'

At this Wolf Schwanhals laughed out loud. 'My dear Cardinal, with all due respect, you are no soldier, unlike some others of your rank.' He now stood up and went clanking about the room. 'We are talking of storming a fortified town. For this I will need far more than my German knights, warriors though they are. At present I can count on a core of little more than eight hundred horsemen of the finest calibre. To take such a town, which will be well apprised of our intentions—let's have no illusions there—I will need at least another thousand men-at-arms and no fewer than six or seven hundred foot soldiers. I will also require siege machines and bombards for breaching the walls. Such things cost money.'

Rollo stared blankly at the man, who was standing arms akimbo on the rucked, frayed rug, his head lolling sideways upon his long neck.

'It will amount to little more than twenty thousand florins,' he announced, and gazed down sardonically.

'I don't have that kind of money.' The cardinal looked quite flustered.

'Well, that's how it is. There are rich pickings elsewhere and other, richer lords. You say the Priors themselves are wealthy.' The soldier shrugged, then smiled. 'And of course there's the Emperor.'

He bowed, turning as if to leave, but Rollo blurted, 'Wait!' just shrilly enough to make Schwanhals pause, brows raised in a question. 'Naturally I myself don't have that much to spare. But I know for a fact how concerned Pope Clement is to protect the prestige of the Church. In times such as these—surely you've noted it, Baron—men turn from the Lord to gold and material pleasure, from the wisdom of the monasteries to the vulgar tongue and the superficial learning of the universities. The Pope requires great knights to mount a new crusade, not in the infidel lands, but in the traitorous hearts of our fellow Christians.'

'I know what you mean, Your Eminence, and I'm ready to help. But, of course, even crusades need more than the Pontiff's *blessing*. I'm no alchemist. I can't simply turn the blood of the vanquished to gold.'

'So you first take the gold and then wring the blood from it?'

Brother Corvo was grinning as Rollo jerked forward, bumping his cup with a thrust of his hand and spilling the dregs on the table.

'No,' sneered Schwanhals, turning away, 'there's no point in trying to sound as if you're above the process. You can't snatch the victory and leave me the blood. Face it, Your Eminence, it's God's *strength* we worship, and it's the strong that God rewards. The Emperor knows it, and the Pope. The great kings always have. God's on the side of the sharpest sword. He despises the poor and the weak. Why else would He have them live as they do? The peacemakers will only be blessed if they submit. The meek might inherit the earth, but Paradise goes to the strong.'

Rollo was showing the whites of his eyes. 'That sounds dangerously close to heresy, Baron Schwanhals.' His voice betrayed the lameness of the statement. The mercenary's words were heretical. Heresy must be punished by the inquisitor. Thus, the syllogism insisted, the inquisitor must punish the mercenary. But what inquisitor could try Wolf Schwanhals?

'Well, perhaps ... perhaps not.' The man shrugged impatiently. 'Can you pay, or can't you?'

The cardinal opened his mouth, either to speak or in bewilderment, but was saved from making any response by the opening of the door. A bowl of *zuccate*—pale gold pumpkins boiled in sugar and hardened with honey—had entered the room, perched on the jester's splayed fingers. A hush now fell as the long, gaunt figure crept through the shadows. Besides his bells' truncated tinkling, the only sound was Rollo's breathing. He wheezed and panted like a winded organ, his eyes fixed white on the silent clown as if on a vision of doom come true against all odds. Brother Corvo glimpsed the jester as Rollo now saw him, the eyepits hollow above his bleak smile, the ape's head twisted on the summit of his sceptre, and his hands so quick and pallid that they scuttled through the air as if on webs. The figure seemed transformed from the awkward, gawky mime of the previous few moments and was now a thing that might have stepped—with its loose, skeletal limbs and leering grin—from some entablature of Death itself got up in cap and bells. Brother Corvo rubbed his hands with glee. It seemed his cookery was good, his recipes for Rollo's dreams correct and well prepared.

The jester, Tozzo, produced his tasting goblet. He was reaching for the ewer when Rollo shouted, his words both hoarse and shrill: 'Tozzo, get out! Go on, get out!', plunging a hand beneath his robes as if to find some weapon. 'Get out, or I'll have you beaten.' But Tozzo was slipping from the room already, heading through the door in a horizontal lunge which should have ended in broken bones. Yet he might have continued, levitant, through the halls of the palace for all that was heard of his fall to the stones, and this silence served to stress the cardinal's wheezing.

'I'm sorry,' Rollo blurted at last, 'but sometimes he goes too far.' Wolf Schwanhals did not try to ease the tension, simply sitting, staring at the red-faced cardinal, fingers tapping at his sword-hilt till Rollo hurried on: 'And I've not been sleeping well. To tell you the truth, Baron, I'm plagued by dreams, such dreams as I couldn't explain to you ... But they're all the fault of those apostates in Topomagro, of that I'm certain.'

Schwanhals gave him time to settle down, to ease his flustered breathing which made him rattle like a fat red bellows. Finally the soldier said: 'An army of apostates? There's no problem, Your Eminence. We'll crush them like so many bugs. Oh yes, and whatever ... bad dreams they may bring.' As the cardinal started to speak, he held up his hand for silence, and Rollo closed his mouth. 'But I'll need that twenty thousand.'

'Oh, there'll be no problem there. I'm certain of it now.' Rollo raised his arms, palms open and empty. 'I wasn't really quibbling. You see, I have some influence with Clement. He'll be willing to help with funds, just as he's guaranteed to finance my canals. Besides, I've apprised him of your usefulness. No, with you to sweep the country clean of treacherous hearts, and canals to secure safe passage, all our fears will be over.'

'Well,' said Wolf Schwanhals, reaching for a glistening *zuccata*, 'if you hire my company you'll be safe enough without canals. You might save yourself some money.' Further debate was curtailed by a scuffling outside the window. The cardinal turned, peering at the shut wax panes. Schwanhals reached them in a single stride, sword sighing from his scabbard. He unfastened the cinched frame and flung it wide, thrusting first his blade and then his head into the dark, where he found nothing but the weathered frieze beneath his hand and the cold, pale crescent of the waxing moon.

Jacopo jumps ship and meets a holy man

THEY SIGHTED HILLS TO THE NORTH-WEST TEN DAYS after Laura's death. At the lookout's cry, Jacopo barely raised his eyes to see. She had died in a mess of stench and fever, soon followed by her children, first Bruno and later little Tessa, screaming at a deathbed host of nightmares. Jacopo had gone to see them, mopping Laura's brow, helping the children drink while they were able; still, he'd hesitated, more often than not remaining on deck, afraid of that hold so harrowed with plague it was like going down to death's antechamber. Now his memory saw her corpse, and those of both her children, thrown time and time again into the sea. There was an oarsman who'd sickened the same day as Laura. He was taken to the hold and given up for dead with all the rest. Yet, though she and her children were now beneath the waves, this man was back on deck, having risen from the hold as from the grave, and showed no further signs of sickness. He was the only one to have recovered, and Jacopo could barely look at him for wishing that he was dead and Laura living in the sun and salt spray. Once, quite near the end, she'd opened her eyes wide and spoken with great clarity, saying that what was hers upon the ship she left to him. He'd nodded, knowing he would take it, knowing also that he'd long since failed some kind of test.

Messina and the Straits now lay before them. People laughed and shouted, spilling wine into each other's cups, unknowing that *Lo Storione* had put into the port some days ahead of them, full of the plague's infection, and had there been burnt to ash. Before the *Santa Margherita* could approach the shore, a pair of swift corsairs sailed out, flush before the wind. Only once did they draw close enough to loose a flight of arrows. The galley's archers tried to answer, receiving in return a second enfilade which wounded several crewmen. They harried her toward the north, driving her along the mainland's western coast, while Aldo raved that they must leave the sick behind, causing wild debate among the passengers.

Meanwhile, their pursuers urged them onward, falling back upon the evening of the second day when, near to dusk—as if to multiply their woes—they saw a storm approaching from the south. Great bleak thunderheads rolled over the horizon, blades of lightning flashing from their bellies, and a wind came coldly across the dark waves. Jacopo watched the small corsairs beneath its shadow, the sudden way they pitched and bucked, their sails appearing to ignite in bursts of luminosity. While they jerked about as if on strings, the clouds engulfed them in their darkness, coming quickly on across the whitecaps. The *Santa Margherita* made no attempt to land since the coastline was too rocky to be safe, swept as it was with breakers; and the storm stalked forward on its bright blue legs, bursting over them with foam and thunder. They rode upon that sea of lead, swirling and groaning, crushed then torn apart, until the sky became the white-flecked sea beneath them, and the sea the boiling sky, all things inverting, so that fish went flying through the clouds above and gulls screamed in the depths. The well became sick, their insides out, and the sick grew still until it seemed that they were well. Days went by, or weeks, or hours, so crammed with motion that whole lifetimes might have passed without their owners knowing. And, indeed, the lives of all the sick—and of numerous others too—*did* pass. It was only when the storm died down, diminished to a gale that whipped them northward, that they tallied up the dead. All those stricken with the plague now lay as stone-cold corpses in the hold. Three crewmen and four passengers had drowned, and one of the archers lay below, dying of a head wound. As winds went tearing at the shredded sails, the bodies were dropped overboard and each survivor stared behind into the waves. Even their pursuers might briefly have seemed welcome had they not already vanished in the emptiness.

One night, however, the wind abated, the furrowed sea grew smooth and reflections of the stars shone softly in the deep, whose unwonted calm shocked sleepers from their dreams until they thought the calm another, stranger dream and sank back into sleep. In the half-light before dawn, staring at the peaceful bay to which the helmsman brought them, they saw that it was real. The forms of ships were all about them, bobbing on the swell or creaking in their tethers at the jetty. A town of tiered houses climbed the cliffs about them, rooftops hinting at a maze of twisting laneways. Barely a lamp shone anywhere, but this was no impediment to Aldo, who turned toward his mate, declaring, 'It's Amalfi,' then shouted out to any who would hear, 'We've reached Amalfi.'

Jacopo no longer heard him; he'd slipped down from the side some time before, tired of his travels on that sorry ship, and was already reaching out to take a hold upon the jetty's steps, a bag of sodden florins at his waist and Scimmi like a rigid, wild-eyed collar round his neck.

At Amalfi, Jacopo bought ship's passage as far as his florins would take him. This was Civitavecchia and, though the last thing he felt like was setting out on yet another voyage, he wished to put as great a span between the galley and himself as he was able. So he and Scimmi embarked that evening, using their own names to avoid complications, and keeping to themselves throughout the voyage. The vessel was a trading scow, taking goods and travellers up the coast at a tranquil, steady pace. They called at Naples, Gaeta and numerous other, smaller towns along the way, passing by the ancient Roman port of Ostia as the weather grew bitterly cold and sleet fell silently upon the waves. Only a few days before Christmas they reached Civitavecchia, where Jacopo left the ship with no more than his cat, a handful of silver *grossi* and a bundle containing a shirt, some bread and a bit of old cheese. If he'd set out on the sea at Kaffa as a prosperous merchant, provided with wealth and reputation, he landed as a vagabond in Latium, trembling with the cold, eyes open to embrace whatever Fortune offered.

He certainly did not regret this change of status, and tramped among the slushy streets with a hopefulness he'd virtually forgotten on the galley. The very act of walking wherever he might choose, his freedom from the plague's grim spectre and the gunnels of the ship, the sound of Scimmi purring in the pouch against his side, all made him want to keep on going, to leave this last reminder of the sea behind. He rested in a tavern, baked beside the fire and drank a cup of wine, but his urge to hurry on would not be quelled so easily. The road kept opening out before him, leading on toward the north, to Tuscany, and further yet, so that he left the inn and stepped into the drizzle of the streets, hurrying beyond the great palazzi, the shops and houses of the master craftsmen, the cottages of artisans, until he'd left the town behind, walking on a muddy road past smoky farms and fields devoid of crops.

It was not too long before his legs began to ache, unused to such unbroken bouts of exercise, and he slowed his pace, already feeling the first blisters where his feet now rubbed inside his merchant's boots which had seemed to fit so well within the confines of the galley. The discomfort did not prevent his thoughts from flowing freely, as they always did when he went walking. Not that these thoughts were pleasant. One question had kept returning since the death of Laura and her children. He simply couldn't understand why he—a cutpurse and a burglar—should remain untouched by pestilence, while she and her two innocents were ravaged by it. He rolled up his sleeves as he walked, almost expecting some belated sign of plague, as if justice, though slow, were still relentless. Yet there it was, his skin, unblemished and white as if he'd spent his life in cloistered purity. Of course he'd long decided that if there's any Godly justice in the world, then it's a thing past human understanding; and yet the agony of Laura, Bruno, little Tessa, seems far too brutal to permit such easy words. Nor, try as he might after witnessing their plague-corrupted bodies, can he picture them beatified and cleansed in Paradise, no matter how far off the place might be. So once again he seeks the comfort of his perilous friend, Dame Fortune, and labours on her wheel.

Despite relief at being back upon dry land, he soon discovers just how scant the pickings are along the roads he travels. Numerous of the towns have near-empty granaries, the fields seem strangely bare of livestock, and even the doorways of the houses lack the usual cluck and strut of chickens. Some places appear to have lost the bulk of their inhabitants, and those remaining look hollow-eyed and hungry. In such villages Jacopo doesn't even try to look for loaves or cooling pies to steal, but hurries through, head lowered to the falling rain or sleet. Needless to say, a thief can hardly flourish where there's nothing left to steal, and the pleasures of the road are mired fast in slush. More often than not he has to hunt his meals in scrub or hedgerow, something at which his cat is far more capable than he. So it is that, in the poorest places, he's obliged to her for almost every mouthful, and sometimes he must chase her while she darts from spot to spot with quail or dove or tiny mole between her teeth and a growl deep in her throat. Yet finally they share the meal, whether it's a pigeon that she's pinioned in a tree, or a hedgehog curled into a ball of spines that she's hit and worried at until he's come to kill it.

Some villages seem better off, and in these he exploits what talents he can to fill the gaps in both their bellies. It's at a crossroads, just after they've devoured a juicy pigeon pie plucked from a roof in one such hamlet, that they hear the beat of hooves. Shouts of urgency approach along the road. Jacopo darts behind a rock, fearing that the owner of the pie is after them. But the voice cries out again, and this time there's no doubt about the fear it contains. Jacopo pokes his head out slowly; his cat peeps from her pouch. Both gape in some amazement at the figure there before them, almost tumbling from its donkey, it reins it in so hard. The beast is wheezing, walleyed, as the rider clambers from its back. This person is devoid of proper clothing; like some gigantic bird, it wears a pelt of ruffled feathers stuck on—so it seems—with treacle or molasses, since nothing else could cause the thick, sweet smell or swarms of flies and bees that hang about it. Jacopo simply stares, unsure of what to say, or even of what language he should use. But this comes clear at once when the figure hits out at the insects on its face—failing to dislodge the feathers that are stuck there—and blurts out, 'Help me!' in a hoarse male voice.

'What?' says Jacopo.

'Please, I need your help,' the man continues, brushing at the plumage round his lips. 'I'm being chased by madmen, a gang of cut-throats. They'll kill me if they can.'

'Well, I—'

'Quick!' he urges and grasps Jacopo's arm with silky, sticky hands. 'They're right behind me.'

Jacopo sees the frightened eyes that blink out through their feathers. Already there's a ruckus back along the road.

'All right …' he says doubtfully. 'Take your donkey into the bushes and I'll see what I can do.'

'Oh, thank you, thank you!' gasps the stranger, rushing for the bushes with a bandy, stiff-kneed run, leading his beast behind him and stepping through the foliage, though Jacopo still hears buzzing and a sudden bee-stung yelp.

No sooner have they hidden than a gang of flustered men comes storming up the road, most of them on foot and bearing flails, scythes, pitchforks and other makeshift weapons. Their leader, a huge man with a rusty sword, is riding a small ass. At the middle of the crossroads they come to a sharp halt, glaring round them with surprised, ferocious looks upon their faces. The fellow leading them leans down from his exhausted ass and, eschewing introductions, nails Jacopo with a narrow stare, demanding, 'Where is he?' as if their quarry might be hidden on the burglar's person.

'Who?' Jacopo says, eyes wide with consternation.

'That scum! That turd!' the man erupts, waving the sword's brown blade above his head. 'That simoniacal Minorite who fled before we finished with him!'

'I ... don't know. There's no-one here but us.' He hoists his cat out of her pouch, rubbing her soft fur against his whiskery cheek.

The man rolls up his eyes and asks more loudly, as if shouting at a halfwit, 'But did you see anyone before we got here?'

'Oh! Oh!' Jacopo nods vehemently. 'I see what you mean. Yes, yes.' He shakes his head with equal vehemence. 'No, I didn't. I didn't see anyone.'

'Christ, man,' snarls his interrogator. 'Then which way did you come?'

Jacopo puts his finger to his mouth and ponders, scratching at himself, then seems to discover a louse, which he takes so long in cracking that the group looks fit to burst. 'Uh ... from Friuli,' he says at last, as if he'd just recalled the question.

The man leans down and grasps him by his coat. 'On the northern road? Here?' he urges, pointing up the road. Jacopo slowly nods and the leader jerks his arm. 'Come on,' he cries, kicking at the sagging ass, 'he must have headed this way.' Without further ado, he leads them grumbling down the eastern road.

Once they're out of sight—and a good while after that—the feathered man emerges from the trees. He stiffly turns his head and gazes to the east, waddling to the centre of the road to stand beside Jacopo.

'Thank you,' he mumbles, flailing at an eager bee. 'You've probably saved my life.'

Jacopo stares at him, then bursts out laughing. 'You'll need to get cleaned up before someone tries to pluck you and stick you in a pot.'

'Yes, I think there's a creek a little way ahead. Otherwise I'm going to set like toffee.'

'Tell me, what were they chasing you for?'

'Oh, I don't know—cacciatore, a casserole, a stew.' The chicken gives a brief hysterical cackle.

'No, I mean it,' insists Jacopo. 'I was running a risk then. I'd like to know why.'

'Oh.' The man seems suddenly sobered, arms sagging at his sides like tired wings. 'I'm not sure that I can properly explain it myself.' He reaches for the bag that's hanging from his saddle, drawing out of it a rumpled robe of stained and faded brown, a Minorite's long, coarse wool cowl. 'Incredible as my present state might make it seem, I follow the Rule of Saint Francis. It was my zeal, I'm afraid, which caused me to run foul of those cut-throats ... no pun intended.' He quickly folds up the habit and crams it back into the sack. 'But who is it I must thank for saving me from their indignities?'

'Jacopo,' says his saviour, 'Jacopo Passero.'

The friar smiles painfully beneath his feathers. 'Fra Filippo Peppo at your service. Fra Lippo for short.'

Jacopo returns the smile, while Scimmi wriggles from her pouch and leaps down to the ground.

'Why did they object so strongly to your zeal?'

'Oh … well, who can fathom the motives of such vicious souls?' He pauses, as if to plumb the depths of their depravity. 'I think it was a kind of moral envy, mixed with shame.'

'What do you mean?'

'Well, it had to do with my preaching … in a village just south of here. I'm a very … ardent preacher … and I was dealing with the Acts of the Apostles, trying to clarify for the villagers the nature of their sins when, without any obvious reason I could see, a group of loiterers started calling out comments of various kinds. I mean, really, it isn't normally like this.' He bows his head and spreads his arms to indicate his wretched state. 'Anyway, to cut a long story short, their interjections grew more rowdy until I felt obliged to reprimand them, at which a series of worsening exchanges ensued, followed by my being set upon by members of the gang you saw. The other villagers were too afraid to help me, and I found myself subjected to various indignities, culminating in that thug, their leader, claiming that, since I was so angelic, I'd need some feathers. And so you see me in the state I'm in.'

He stands there, arms akimbo, legs apart, his feathers shining whitely in the wintry sun.

'But they were still after you, and you said they wanted to do more.'

'Yes, yes, that's true,' Fra Lippo mutters thoughtfully. 'I'm not sure what would have happened had they caught me. They kept making jokes about tests for angels … about whether I could fly. I suspect—though I can't be certain now—that they were thinking of some nearby cliff.'

'Yes, I see,' says Jacopo slowly, glancing down the eastern road. 'Well, perhaps we'd better hurry to that creek.'

'You're going south, though, aren't you, from Friuli?'

Jacopo simply grins, shakes his head and takes the feathered friar by the arm. After walking on in silence for some minutes—the donkey trudging gloomily behind while Scimmi, dog-like, weaves between its feet—Fra Lippo turns to his companion with a smile. 'You know, you're a smart lad, Jacopo—the way you fooled them, I mean. In truth, you had me wondering too if you were simple-minded.' He glances sideways through his plumage. 'I could use someone like you—indeed, the Lord could use someone like you—to bring His word to these rough villagers.'

'No, thanks all the same, Friar, but I've no wish to sprout feathers.'

'Look, my boy, believe me, this is one of those rare trials the Lord inflicts upon His children. It's not normally like this at all. Most times it's like a pilgrimage, spreading the Gospel and the teachings of Saint Francis, wandering through the countryside, meeting a host of good souls and sleeping in warm inns.' He notes Jacopo's doubtful gaze. 'Really, Jacopo, do I look poorly fed?' He pats his belly with his hand. 'I should say not. Usually people respond far better to my preaching and shower me with alms, sometimes more than I can carry. I eat well and live well, and generally with a minimum of risk. Whereas you, my boy, look in need of a good meal. I can guarantee it—with me you'll get one ... in fact, a good deal more than one. Right now I could do with a helper who can use his wits.'

Jacopo observes Fra Lippo, his expression still sceptical. Yet when he considers the friar's portly form, and when he recalls those moles and hedgehogs, and scrambling through the bushes after Scimmi, the thought of being showered with alms by faithful peasants takes on a more appealing lustre.

'You wouldn't expect me to do any preaching, would you?'

'Oh, good heavens, no,' the friar chuckles. 'No, it's just a matter of assisting with the props I use to make the message more accessible to simple minds.'

Jacopo ponders, weighing up his words, then bends as if to whisper in the ear of his cat. 'What do you think, Scimmi? Should we do it?' And after further muttered counsel, he turns round with a grin and says, 'Why not?'

At that moment they come upon the creek, the merest little rill that trickles at the bottom of a ditch across the road. Fra Lippo pulls at one embedded feather, peers at his image in the water, and then sighs. 'Oh, dear.'

Fra Lippo Peppo stands ringing a bell in the centre of the village. It seems more prosperous than some Jacopo has passed through, with flocks of chickens scrabbling in the mud about the little timber houses, and the smell of baking bread that wafts across the afternoon's cool air. The few cows that he sees appear to have some fat between their ribs, and there's actually a rubbish heap where a plump pair of pigs are rooting through some rinds and rotting vegetables. Fra Lippo stands ringing his bell, like a one-man chapel, to bring the people to him. Slowly they gather, the idle and the curious, the suspicious and the querulous, all coming from their evening tasks with tentative, slow steps as the friar draws his breath and yells, 'Hear all you sinners the word of the Lord. Hear all you sinners the word of the Lord,' till every person in that place is gathered round in watchful silence.

Jacopo stands with Scimmi by the donkey, ready to plunge into the tethered sacks at Lippo's asking. At present he requires nothing but this silent, goggling crowd, its old men and matrons, its strong-backed peasants and its children jostling for a vantage point. The place seems suitable enough, with few signs of hunger or disease, and none at all of a resident priest. Fra Lippo plants his sandalled feet, flings out his arms and starts to bellow.

'Hear all you sinners the word of the Lord upon this eve of judgement. Hear you men puffed up with pride and women full of vanity. Hear you angry, choleric souls, and you made vicious as a snake with envy. Hear you slothful and you bloated gluttons, you misers who embrace your wealth as if it were the Lamb of God, you lechers writhing in your secret dreams. Hear and know your judgement is at hand.' Jacopo's impressed to hear the soft-voiced friar come bursting forth like a thunderclap, eyes drilling into every listener's gaze in turn, as if he saw the very sins that nestled in their hearts. 'And do you tell yourselves that you are meek and poor and thus exempt from the Almighty's wrath? Then know at once that none remain exempt. Both kings and paupers are a prey to their own sinfulness. Do we not see the corruption of the Neapolitan queen, Joanna? The self-styled tribune, di Rienzo, squatting like a spider on the Roman throne while the Pope delays in Avignon? In Naples, Rome and Venice the churches crack with earthquakes; rain and floods and icy winters cause the crops to shrivel till grain is nowhere to be found but in the rich man's granary. I've heard people in the countryside beg Christ to turn them into asses that they might eat the grass ...' At this a group within the crowd begins to giggle, and Lippo swings upon them, saying, 'And there are those who turn to asses without the aid of prayer,' which brings smiles among the others and the quick return of silence as he turns his gaze on *them*.

'Oh, Lord,' he cries, as if in pain, 'did You die in agony that they might laugh at You? Was iron driven through Your hands and feet that they might think it funny?' He glares with narrowed eyes and notes their looks of horror, then falls upon the ground before them with a supplicating gesture. 'What purpose is there in the harvesting of corn when it's the harvesting of hearts that matters? Why save money when you might save your soul? Do you think that you can buy God's grace with gold?' He rises to his feet and stares at them with fixed intensity. 'Now, on the very eve of judgement, as the world collapses around us, there are two undoubted ways, revealed to us by God, to save ourselves from the destruction. But do you wish to save your souls?' His eyes alight on individuals in the crowd. 'Do you?' he pursues. 'Do you?'

Some look frightened and confused, some nod dumbly, still others answer, 'Yes,' or 'Yes, I do,' or 'That I would, good Father,' until they all seem desperate to save that which, till then, they'd never realised they were close to losing.

'But what is the best way to salvation, Father?' one cries out.

'A vital question,' he replies, 'and one which I can answer with no hesitation since this answer is recorded in all the great authorities and in the holy words of God Himself.'

Here he pauses, giving people time to wonder and to ask more of him. Yet nothing comes to fill the silence, no word, no question, just a hushed, confused expectancy, until Jacopo shouts, 'What is that answer, Father?'

'I'm glad you asked,' says Lippo with a smile. 'The best way to salvation is through good works and charity, through the witnessing of things most holy, and the granting of donations to the order that enables you to witness them.' But Jacopo is no longer listening, too busy opening up the sacks and sorting through them as Fra Lippo has shown him. 'For the Holy Order of the Minorites has granted me the dispensation to bring—at least for those who truly wish it—salvation to this region and, in so doing, has placed at my disposal certain relics of a sanctity beyond all words.'

Taking this as his cue, Jacopo draws a stoppered vial of fluid from a sack. One or two among the crowd move forward, and when the rest surge after them, Fra Lippo rings the bell for all he's worth, shouting, 'Get back! Stand away!' and peers timidly toward the heavens. 'Do you want to draw God's fiery vengeance down and turn this place into another Sodom?' He glances doubtfully about the muddy clutch of hovels, waving back the people with his bell. Jacopo hands him the small phial, which Lippo lets them glimpse before he palms it.

'What is it?' asks one, nudging forward past his neighbour.

'It looks a bit like oil,' suggests another.

At this, Fra Lippo springs at her and says, 'Beware lest it be oil in which the devils roast you.' She cowers back, and he smiles quite beatifically. 'And yet, perhaps its power may be such that, despite your ignorance, you sense its nature without knowing it.'

'Tell us what it is, Father,' cries one.

'Yes, what is it, Father?' implores the woman he has frightened.

'Ah, but do not think to penetrate this mystery without sacrifice. The saving power of these relics depends upon what each will give to see them.' At this, Jacopo makes as if to tie the sacks back up. 'The Lord is not profligate. Grace does not come free. There is no salvation without sacrifice.'

'But what must we give, Father?' asks an ancient man who looks more prosperous than the others. 'We're just poor farmers.'

'The Lord asks only what you're certain you can

give,' replies Fra Lippo, clutching the relic to his breast.

At this, several of the peasants break off from the crowd and hurry to their hovels, emerging with trussed chickens, muddy carrots, famished-looking purses and deflated wine-sacks, whatever they can find to offer. Others follow suit, till the friar is surrounded with so much shouting, clucking and squawking that it's like a fair or feast day. He points to where Jacopo holds an empty sack, and when most of their donations have been safely placed within, displays once more the little phial of oil.

'Indeed, this woman knew far more than she suspected, for here,' and he holds the fluid up to catch the light of the low sun, 'is a portion of that oil in which the Emperor Domitian sought to boil Saint John the Evangelist.' The crowd steps cautiously forward, peering hard into the fluid's depths, as if they might observe some bit of John within.

'And just as the saint was saved from those cruel fires, so those who sacrifice some earthly thing to see this relic have made more certain their salvation from the flames of Hell.' A murmur passes through the crowd, and Lippo smiles to hear the satisfaction in it.

'But ... but how can you be certain it's that oil?' ventures one. 'It was so long ago.'

'Do you think the Father does not hear your doubts?' roars Lippo, peering fearfully toward the sky. More gently, he adds, 'Poor fellow, don't you realise how exact the Church's records are to account for all its holy objects? This oil, blessed by God Himself in the salvation of His saint and thus more full of virtue than the holiest of chrisms, has descended from the early Church of Rome, through the Holy Fathers, to Constantine's Byzantium, to Antioch, where it fell into the hands of infidels, only to be rescued by the Knights Templars who, to save it from their enemy, King Philip, gave it to our Order. Does that satisfy your curiosity, or do you want yet further detail?'

'Uh, no,' says the man dully, shaking his head, while the crowd casts disapproving looks his way.

'But, please,' Lippo implores them, 'can't we take the word of God on faith?'

The crowd nods emphatically, aiming vicious glances at the doubter. With the eyes of an eager monkey, a tiny woman watches Lippo, saying, 'Do you have any more such holy items with you, Father?'

The friar smiles benignly down on her. 'Yes, my child, I do. But surely you have given all you can. Besides, it might seem unfair that the people of this village should get so great a start on Heaven's stairway when other villages may have no chance to see these relics.'

They protest so pitifully, and rush so quickly to their shanties to find yet more donations, that Fra Lippo simply can't refuse them.

'Don't forget that coins are preferable,' he calls after them. 'Bulky objects, such as hens and wine-sacks, are awkward for lone pilgrims like ourselves to carry.'

Jacopo's sack is bulging fit to burst and he must

stuff the heavier items—loaves and cheeses, pullets and turnips—in amongst the sacred objects. The friar has now found his stride, snatching relics from anywhere he can as quickly as the villagers can find donations. They, too, seem to have reached some sort of rhythm, darting here and there, laughing out loud, oohing and aahing, competing with their neighbours, while Fra Lippo displays, with no apparent schema, the handle of the windlass round which Saint Elmo's viscera were wound; a feather plucked by Jacob from the angel's wing; three hairs cut from the beard of the maiden Wilgefortis; and, torn out of the Cross itself, a nail which suddenly appears in his hand as if he, Fra Lippo, had been stigmatised. Perhaps the most amazing thing of all, remarkable for both its preservation and its power which, as Lippo says, 'Contains the surest remedy for sin because so near to the source of sin itself,' is the core of the very fruit that Adam ate. After the crowd has stood about, staring at this final revelation, some shaking their heads in wonderment, others gazing at the friar with beatific smiles upon their faces, he thrusts the Holy Core with all its Blessed Pips into the sack, and Jacopo gathers up the other relics.

At last, as darkness falls, Fra Lippo holds his hands out in a benediction. 'May each and every one of you, when your time comes, be lifted up to Heaven by the faith you've shown today.' Then he blesses them amidst much cheering, the children dancing as if Carnival has come, while one old lady grabs his hand to kiss it. Most are murmuring in hushed, excited tones of the marvels they have seen, as if these things had passed already into village lore. One man emerges from his cottage with a drum, another with a flute, and yet another with some pipes, so that the friar, his assistant and their overloaded donkey are paraded from the village with a makeshift band, as the people wave farewell beneath the now fortuitous stars.

Later, sitting by their fire in the woods, they tally the donations—those that they don't eat. They have provisions to last them for a well-fed week, and the bags of silver *grossi* and *denari* come to about three florins. Jacopo sits with Scimmi in his lap, thoughtfully stroking her silky fur, watching as Fra Lippo beams above the booty.

'A village of the faithful,' he intones at last. 'Salt of the earth and pillars of Heaven.'

Jacopo gazes at his moving hand. 'How can you lie to them like that?' he says. 'And you a holy man.'

'Lie to them?' the friar rumbles threateningly, trying one of his glances at the heavens. 'Are you saying that there's something doubtful about these holy relics?'

Jacopo laughs out loud. 'Doubtful?' he chuckles, recovering his breath. 'If that stuff's holy we'd better give up going to church and start praying at the rubbish heap. Besides, I know for a fact that the feather of Jacob's angel was one of those chicken feathers you had stuck on you.'

For the first time that day, Fra Lippo's speechless.

'Well,' he says finally, patting his companion's

shoulder, 'you're a clever lad, Jacopo. I knew that from the moment I saw you. That's why I chose you to be my assistant.'

'Then don't take me for a fool like you did those peasants.'

The friar glances up more sharply, his gaze descending solemnly on his assistant. 'I don't take them for fools, my boy; at least, not for greater fools than anybody else. They had a day that'll last for years in their memories.' He turns away and peers at the fire. 'Don't let your cleverness rob you of understanding. It doesn't matter whether the relics are true or not. What counts is whether these people believe. We're giving them the chance to prove their faith, and thus, just as I assured them, to save their souls.'

Jacopo stares at him, taking his turn to be speechless, while the friar watches Scimmi.

'And on the notion of saving souls,' says Lippo slyly, 'I have a proposition to make to you concerning this fine creature of yours …'

Jacopo and Fra Lippo are rummaging through their bags in the centre of Santa Rocca. It is a moonless, starry night, and a bonfire is raging at the top of the bare hill on which the village stands. People gather as close as they dare to the blaze, which throws their shadows on the houses' muddy walls. The friar and the thief wait motionless, as if surrounded by a host of spectral dancers. Scimmi is nowhere to be seen, and the donkey stands off to the side, free of his sacks full of miracles, while Lippo starts preparing his performance. A small, elaborate platform stands upon the friar's left, and to his right is a yet smaller table on which there sits a statue of the Virgin. All the previous day he's been absorbed by these two items, fussing with the platform in particular, making sure that the collapsible joints are firm enough to hold, testing the trap, increasing the size of the concealed compartment in its base. He has apprised Jacopo of the relics' natures, so that now, standing below the rise where the friar waits to speak, he feels decidedly more confident.

'Good people of Santa Rocca,' Fra Lippo commences mildly, 'this is indeed a perilous time, a time of the Great Adversary and his legions, and of the Antichrist already rising in the west.' He lets a silence fall upon the crowd, during which no sound is heard but the hellish crackling of the fire. 'It is a time when all those great in power fall, when shepherds desert their flocks and the farmer leaves his crops to rot upon the earth. Has not the Pope abandoned the throne of Saint Peter and gone to live in luxury at Avignon? Does not Philip of France expose his people to the depredations of invaders? And does not Edward of England reduce his subjects to penury to pay for his vainglorious war?' Here he stops to let his eye fall gently on the crowd. 'And do they not, these great ones in their folly, like men who teeter on the brink of an abyss, send all those nearer to the edge careering down before them? For it is you who must lose all when they increase their rents to ward off bankruptcy, and it is you who suffer the depredations of their armies when they are not paid, and you who starve when they hoard the grain within their granaries to push the prices up.' He glares around the ragged crowd, the crumbling houses of their village. 'So is it not the wealthy and the great who must account to God for that vast rioting of sins throughout the world?' More deeply still he stares into the crowd, as if to read the answer in their eyes.

'Oh, madmen and sinners all!' he bellows with such fury that many of his audience lurch back. 'Oh, yes, I can read it in your faces—others are to blame, others are the sinners, it is others who must meet the Lord's eternal punishment upon the Day of Wrath.' He leans forward, face contorted in a mask of anger. 'But do not think your follies can delude the Lord. He sees all, and can see the sins that lodge like worms within your heart, sins to which you're blinded by resentment, sins which even now, as I am speaking, grow fat upon your rancour. For is not that humility which takes solace in itself another form of pride? Is not that hunger which thinks of naught but food another form of gluttony? Is not …? Is not …?'

And so he continues to batter them with questions to which they have no answers, forcing them to face the sins they'd half suspected in themselves, yet never found the words to formulate, until at last their eyes are begging him to offer some solution, some means by which they might absolve themselves and face their judgement unafraid. Just when it seems that he's abandoned them as lost, has proved the irredeemable nature of their wickedness, he finds a possibility, a tiny pathway through their swamp of sins by which they might achieve salvation. Jacopo rifles through the pile of relics, discovering the oil, the hairs, the feather by which they might reach Paradise.

Now Lippo hints that here, this very night, for offerings of coin alone, they might see not just the sacred, but something drawn up from the depths of Hell. Muttered wonderings arise out of the crowd as they ponder what the friar means. Indeed, they had not realised that remission of their sins could be such fun, and some discover tiny piles of worn *denari*, while one or two come bearing single, tarnished *grossi* in their hands. Only then does he reveal to them the guilty stone that was among those used to lapidate the deacon, Stephen, and which, even in the shifting shadows of the bonfire, seems to weep red blood-drops for the crime. So impressed with their donations is the statue of the Virgin that, despite Fra Lippo's grip upon the table where it stands, it consents to break in pieces when he murmurs, 'Cross.'

Yet only when he steps behind the platform, carven with elaborate painted angels, does his audience go silent with expectant relish. The friar starts to rave. 'Oh people of ... this village,' he intones, and grips the peeling paint as if behind a pulpit, 'do not let yourselves imagine that the Devil has abandoned you. For there is no-one who is safe. Not the Pope or the Emperor or the least significant of serfs. I have performed the rite of exorcism upon a proud *podesta*. I have drawn an imp of gluttony, like a coiling, scarlet worm, from the body of a bloated nun. And there was once a newborn infant I delivered of a demon passed to it at birth by its adulterous mother.'

The crowd stares, mesmerised by Lippo's rhetoric. Looks of horror alternate with grins and indrawn breaths, while his sudden, watchful silence spreads among them all like slow hysteria. 'And now,' he pounces, 'I will reveal to you, the people of Santa Rocca, the demon I have captured from a miller's wicked soul.' In a puff of saffron smoke, bright as a blast from the mouth of a bombard, a creature arrives on the platform before him, a bearded demon red as fire, hissing and spitting in the burst of light. Its fangs flash like silver, its eyes glitter crimson in the bonfire's glare, and at every sweep of its lashing tail the crowd backs off with a gasp.

Jacopo stands, suffused with doubt, watching the demon chained to its ring—fangs fastened to its teeth, horns on its head, a chicken's wattle tethered like a beard to its chin—and wonders if he's made a horrible mistake by letting Lippo talk him into this. After all, they'd never used flashes and smoke in rehearsals—the friar was all too sparing with his props—and Scimmi looks so frightened. Scarlet powder colours her fur, thickens in the air; she starts to sneeze, then vanishes from sight in a saffron flash while the friar delivers an arm-waving speech, an impassioned plea beseeching the crowd to give him the means, the rude coin, to travel the land saving souls from such horrors. Somehow, as Jacopo loads up the sacks and the donkey, the villagers find still further donations—tarnished *denari* from long-ago harvests—and stumble to Lippo, their treasures in hand.

Tuccio becomes a politician

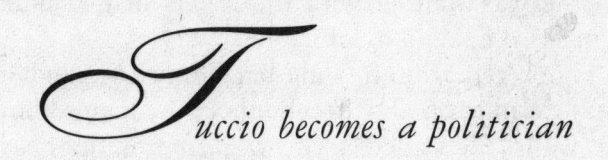

FROM THE TOP OF THE DUOMO'S CAMPANILE OR THE Torre del Colombo, Topomagro looked like a web of winding streets and laneways surrounded by a wheel of walls. At the hub of this webbed wheel lay the Piazza della Signoria, with its benches of old men and its air full of pigeons. Here were the Gentili and the Chiaudano palazzi, the church of San Giovanni del Agnello and the Arte della Lana, headquarters of the wool merchants' guild. Shadowing them all were the high stone walls and massive tower of the Palazzo dei Dieci, home of the commune's government. It was here, in the centre of this building at the city's heart, that Tuccio now sat—and, indeed, would sit many times during the next two months—making executive decisions with the other Priors. It was only ten days previously that the commission of scrutators had once again declared him an eligible candidate for the Signoria, two days after which his name, along with those of his nine fellows, had been drawn from the bag of fifty names. So now he was a Prior for the second time in his career, his belly still churning from the feast he'd enjoyed with the outgoing office-holders, and he was waiting with the others in the fading light for old Agnolo del Leone.

He peered around while Bartolomeo Chiaudano went droning on and attendants lit the lamps about the walls. He stifled a yawn, gazing at the heavy blocks of stone, the great Guelph lion roaring on its banner and, of course, the walnut table with its sixteen chairs. Tonight the ten Priors and the six Gonfalonieri were meeting in joint session to deal with the approaching crisis. Yet Tuccio was thinking more of Baldassare and Gaia than about the plots of Frederico dalla Montagna, Odofredo Moltogalante, the Gentili and their rebellious friends. For Baldassare, dispensing with the formalities of marriage-brokers and go-betweens, had approached him personally to ask for Gaia's hand; indeed, had approached with so much sudden circumspection that, for a moment, Tuccio had thought he might be asking for a loan. He'd felt immediate relief, amazement and, yes, delight upon hearing that hesitant request, since he'd always treated Baldassare as the son he'd never have and now, it seemed, he might soon have that son. He had watched the man's solicitous blue gaze and briefly pictured, standing beside him on the steps of the Duomo, Gaia in a gown reflecting sunlight like a second moon as she smiled above the wedding crowd. He had wanted to confirm the vision that instant, yet demurred to his friend's request that he first ask Gaia's consent. To his surprise, after all her haughty aloofness, she had seemed struck dumb, then set her lips in a straight, tight line and breathed out, 'Yes.'

'No, Bartolomeo,' Marco Martello was protesting, 'the cost of so much veal would be exorbitant at this time of year. And it'll be poor, tough meat from the Maremma or worse.'

'Marco, you've just been voted Prior,' Bartolomeo patiently explained. 'Stop thinking like a shopkeeper. The Priors' high table is no peasant's trencher to be stocked with bargains. We should have the best veal available, and who'd be fool enough to charge excessive prices to those who set the taxes?'

'Oh, I see. How naive of me. You mean use our position as a threat?'

'No,' sighed Bartolomeo, 'of course not. But we must maintain the dignity of that position.'

And so the debate went on, though Tuccio was not in the mood for listening. He kept thinking about Gaia, and peered round the assembly, wondering what they'd make of his willingness to let her choose her own destiny. Now that she'd accepted Baldassare, he himself was beginning to doubt his own wisdom, fretting over his friend's predilection for hunting-birds, high-priced horses, poetry, and all the other things that made him so amusing as a friend and dubious as a son-in-law. In seven days' time would be the *impalmatura*, when he and Baldassare, standing on the Duomo's steps, would clasp their hands above the contract before both town and notary. Perhaps it was for the best that a third of the dowry of two thousand florins would pay for the trousseau, and that all must be returned if Gaia, God forbid, should die within the first twelve months. After all, extravagant dowries could expose well-meaning fathers to even higher taxes.

Nor could he free his mind of the anxiety caused him by events no more than two days old. To think that a woman of his wife's good sense could be so foolish, and in times such as these. Certainly the Via dei Speziali was no great distance from their house, but it was a dark and crowded laneway at the best of times, and the afternoon had been so late and overcast. To go there with Marina, protected by no-one more formidable that his accountant, Luigi Pucci ... well, he would be kind to label it merely imprudent. He could see them now in that dim lane outside the apothecary's, Beatrice in her monkish cloak of rough brown *monachino*, helped down from her gelding by Luigi, who is wearing, under his long coat, his absurdly gilded Turkish dagger, as if to advertise his physical ineptitude; and Marina, who has done her mother's bidding and worn a stiff wool gown, leaping from her bay before the man can reach her.

He could see the shop's interior as they entered, the lamps that burn in two dark corners of the room, the dull grey daylight seeping through the doorway to glisten in the oils and pots of glazed majolica. Further in, beneath a mirror to reflect what light there is, Gianno Benini's accountant scribbles in his ledger, a young apprentice handing him his counters from a clutch of little bowls. He imagined old Gianno as he'd often seen him, insubstantial as a shadow in that gloom, mixing powders on a trestle table, a huge, squat mortar on the floor beside him, and high above his head, like some instrument of execution, a massive pestle dangling from the roofbeams.

He watched him peer up and smile his oily smile, heard him murmur, 'Monna Beatrice,' nodding at the others, 'a pleasure to see you on such a gloomy day.'

'Good afternoon, Gianno,' she would say, quite crisp yet not unfriendly. 'We've just called in for one or two small things.'

One or two small things! Enough to get you killed, he fumed in silence, thinking of the way the excursion had turned out. Saffron—a bit of coloured saffron—and a few tasty tidbits to ease the boredom of a dreary afternoon, with no more than Luigi for protection.

'Do you have any *pinocchiati*?' he heard Marina blurt, since he knew how much she loved to tease her mother, who found Marina's taste for such cheap sweets too vulgar.

'Oh, not *pinocchiati* again,' his wife would likely say, interrupting the apothecary's nods. 'Gianno has such lovely jelly. Yes, quince jelly, nice and pink, and firm enough to slice with a knife.'

'Indeed, Monna Beatrice, indeed.' The man now turns his nods on her. 'A freshly made batch with the finest quinces.'

'Quinces!' Marina wheels upon her heel to face Luigi, standing silently behind them. 'Do you like quinces, Luigi?'

Here, he would look confused, glance rapidly at Beatrice, then reluctantly admit, 'Well, yes, I'm afraid I do. But then, why not get something for everyone?'

'That's the kind of thing my father says.' Marina flips her hair across her shoulder, and mutters to her mother, 'Tuccio the diplomat.'

'That's enough, Marina,' Beatrice would say then.

He smiled, imagining the looks upon the faces of Luigi and Gianno, seeing the flasks of embalming fluid, the thick ropes of liquorice, the shelves of paints and dyes, the pepper from Cyprus, the sugar for heartache, the cassia for clysters, the nutmeg for nightmares, the parchment, rat poison and church wafers, all ranged upon the walls about them as they walk into the street, Luigi carrying the saffron, jelly *and pinocchiati*.

Tuccio glanced round him and felt his face go hot. Half aware of the dispute that still went on between the Priors, he saw his wife come slowly from the shop toward their horses, moving through the crowd that throngs the lane. Marina walks behind her, stonking on the flagstones, awkward in her heavy woollen gown, while Luigi balances the parcels in the rear. Beatrice gasps, then screams, her arm tugged sharply sideways. There's the quick flash of a knife, her purse strings cut and dangling as the thief darts off among the crowd. 'Oh, oh, look …' His wife stares after her assailant, gaping like a fish, while Luigi stands there, wild-eyed, anchored to the shopping. But Marina's scrabbling at his coat, saying, 'Quick, come on,' snatching at the dagger in its gilded sheath, then rushing through the people, yelling, 'Thief!' Men stare, bemused, at the skinny, shouting girl who pushes past them, long gown tangled, brandishing a knife.

At length, she returns, shoulders slumped, lips pursed, defeated, pulling at the wool that clings about her legs. 'This stupid dress!' she spits. 'This stupid, stupid dress!'

Tuccio leaned back against his chair, face reddened by his thoughts. What would have happened had she caught the cutpurse? The notion of Marina, his sweet monkey, coming to real harm, and all because of Beatrice's rashness ... he couldn't bear to think of it. The girl was an eccentric, there was little doubt about it. She would need to learn discretion. Just as he was starting once more to doubt the wisdom of the way he'd brought her up, Agnolo del Leone came into the room.

The bickering between the Priors ceased so sharply that Tuccio glanced up from his thoughts and saw Agnolo standing in the silence, handing his hat and long fur coat to the boy behind him. Four times elected Prior, and this his seventh term as Gonfaloniere, he was watching them with all the ruddy, stout authority that such experience commanded.

'I'm sorry to be late, gentlemen,' he said, not sounding sorry in the least, and remaining on his feet as if the meeting were now his. 'But I wanted to apprise myself fully of the matters you're expecting me to speak of.'

'So what's the story, Agnolo?' said Francesco Morelli, his fellow Gonfaloniere.

'Not a very reassuring one, I'm afraid.' There was a small dramatic pause as he took off his kid gloves. 'At least, if the information of one of our spies in Florence is correct. And there's no reason to think it isn't.' Tuccio watched him silently, as they all did, allowing him to take his time. His four-month commission—twice as long as Tuccio's—included the detecting and exposing of conspiracies against the commune. Right now it was a full-time job. 'Our informant has learnt from Orfeo Beccanuggi, son of the Ghibelline exile Buonaccorso Beccanuggi, that our enemies within the town are plotting against us with—well, we might have guessed it—Cardinal Rollo da Parma, who just happens to have hired the services of the Swabian *condottiere*, Wolf Schwanhals.'

There was a momentary silence, not stunned so much as crackling with such a mass of questions that, for an instant, none was asked. Then the deluge came:

'Schwanhals?'

'They're dealing with da Parma?'

'Which of our enemies exactly?'

'Isn't Schwanhals still in Latium?'

'Spy?'

'What spy?'

'How reliable is this informant?'

Agnolo raised his chubby fingers as if to say, 'Enough,' and the cries diminished into muttered conversations.

'We're all aware of da Parma's spite,' said Francesco Morelli. 'And no-one believed that he'd do nothing. But that he's hired Wolf Schwanhals and his company ... and that some within the town are dealing with him ... well, surely none of us suspected this. They'd be sealing their own fate with someone such as Schwanhals.'

'Perhaps,' Agnolo murmured doubtfully. 'But then again, they might feel that they can come to some accommodation with him. The livestock of half the commune's peasants, the gold of the richest and most troublesome merchants—such a price may not be too great to control the town once more and, with it, the drafting of its laws, the imposition of its taxes and forced loans, the disposition of its militia, the—' But here he stopped, raising his hands and eyebrows to indicate the obvious.

'This informant you refer to, Agnolo,' said Poggio Cerini, one of the new Priors, 'did he confirm the names of any of these traitors? Did he speak of Frederico dalla Montagna, Ludovico dei Gentili or Odofredo Moltogalante?'

The grizzled red face of the Gonfaloniere stared blankly at him. 'These are the names he mentioned,' was all he said.

A momentary hush descended, till Tuccio broke it. 'Did you get any idea of how advanced the *condottiere* is in his preparations?' he said softly. 'Or whether things have even gone so far as his making preparations?'

'Oh, yes.' The old man's tone was grim. 'He's made preparations all right. As far as I know, he's gathered a force of several thousand horsemen and foot soldiers which, at this very moment, is settling like a horde of locusts on the marchlands of Tuscany and Latium. If they wished, they could be here in twelve to fifteen days.'

Tuccio leaned forward in his seat, nodding his head like a thin, sharp axe-blade. 'Then there really isn't any time to lose. I don't think we can afford the luxury of quibbling about guilt or innocence. If any of these traitors are allowed the freedom to continue with their plans ...' He knew how heavily the commune limited such men, refusing them access to political office, doubling their punishments for crimes of violence, requiring them to post a bond for good behaviour. He swung around, addressing the whole company. 'Just think what you would do in their position ... You'd rise in armed rebellion as Schwanhals neared the city. Then, if you succeeded, you could honour all the guarantees of booty you had made. And if it looked like you were losing? Well, you could open as many gates as possible to the mercenaries.' He peered slowly from one to another, daring those who would to refute his logic. When it appeared that Marco Martello was about to try, he quickly added, 'No, there must be no delay in placing these three men, at least, in chains.'

Around the table there was muttered affirmation, yet Marco cut across it. 'But nothing here is certain,' he protested, speaking like the only sane man in a madhouse. 'We have no real notion of the *condottiere*'s plans, no clear confirmation of how far this treachery goes, no word at all on how well armed the nobles are. To act too hastily could precipitate events that otherwise might never happen.'

Tuccio could feel the blood rush to his face. It was always Marco who found objections, pushing himself forward, trying to find something to say, irrespective of its worth, just like the jumped-up silk merchant and importer of cheap veils that he was.

'I agree with Marco,' put in Poggio Cerini, another would-be trader with the heart of a shopkeeper. 'We need to proceed more prudently. Unless we can be sure of every detail, we may engineer our own downfall.'

'These fears may even play into Montagna's hands,' added the silk merchant.

'Prudence is a cardinal virtue,' nodded Pandolfo Salutati, the apothecary, 'there's no denying that.'

Tuccio had thought the old goat was asleep but, true to form, he'd opened his eyes just long enough to deliver up a platitude. 'Perhaps it is,' he began, 'but—'

'But virtues depend upon their context,' interrupted Francesco Morelli. 'Prudence and temperance may be vital in the daily running of a business, yet on the battlefield such qualities can be misplaced. They—'

'Must we be so eager to find ourselves upon the battlefield?' cried Marco Martello.

'Must you be so eager to avoid it?' demanded Tuccio, losing all patience.

'Exactly,' nodded Ser Gianozzo Lamberteschi, the notary and scholar. 'It appears that we'll have no choice. And besides, Maestro Francesco is correct—the hierarchy of virtues changes according to the situation. When Edward of England defaulted on his debts and the banks of the Bardi, Peruzzi and the Acciaiuoli fell, do you think it was the prudent, waiting to hear if the rumours were correct, who survived the collapse? No, in situations of such extremity, one must simply react as quickly as one can according to one's instincts.

As the Yorkish Alcuin said in the days of Charlemagne—'

'Just so,' said Agnolo del Leone. 'We must act quickly.'

'With as little unnecessary quibbling as possible,' added Francesco Morelli.

'And this needn't preclude attempts to gain further information.' Tuccio's smile was both conspiratorial and conciliatory. 'Such inquiries can proceed while we're preparing the militia and passing the necessary legislation.'

'Yes,' said Agnolo, 'and then, with the conspirators in prison, we can have them confirm whatever information we may gather.'

Around the table there was muttered laughter, cut short as Tuccio cleared his throat and rose to speak. 'But we mustn't lose sight of the situation's danger.' His smile was gone, his voice now tight and anxious. 'In the south we have Wolf Schwanhals and his company. In the town we have sedition that's been festering too long to be discounted as mere bluster. Either would be parlous on its own. Together? Well, they spell disaster. So, we must inform the captain of the people and the *castellani* of the city gates as soon as possible, and kill the rebellion in the womb.'

'What, you mean attack the nobles' houses?' demanded Marco.

'No,' replied Agnolo, 'not *attack*. Well, not unless we lose the advantage of surprise, or their resistance is too great. It should be a matter of sending three strong forces to the three key households—those of Frederico dalla Montagna,

Ludovico dei Gentili and Odofredo Moltogalante. There, before they can mount any sort of defence at all, we'll arrest these men and those amongst their dependents who might pose a threat. Thus, by the time Schwanhals arrives, any help he might have counted on will be imprisoned or demoralised.'

'Then we'll need to move very fast indeed,' said Francesco Morelli, 'since surprise is of the essence.'

'Mmmm.'

'Yes.'

'He's right.'

'No doubt about it …'

The murmurs of assent passed round the table while the noddings fanned the air.

'I see,' Agnolo smiled at last. 'Well, we'll put it to a vote. Though I doubt that we can move as quickly as we'd like on everything, since we'll need to pass the legislation for some levies and forced loans to meet the approaching army.'

'I can't see that we'll have time to raise an army of our own,' said Francesco Morelli, incredulous.

'Of course not,' agreed Agnolo.

'No, we'll have to rely on buying Schwanhals off.' Tuccio's frown relaxed a little. 'Not that he'll be pained by moral scruples. It'll simply be expensive.'

'But you know the record on rejecting forced loans,' said Poggio. 'With such bad food shortages, the Council of the People will need to be convinced.'

'I think they'll be convinced by this,' Bartolomeo Chiaudano smiled grimly.

Marco Martello gave a cynical snort. 'Well, if we

keep talking about it there'll be no call to convince them. The army will already be here.'

'Exactly,' nodded Tuccio, surprised by Marco's acuteness. 'We must decide on the timing of the arrests, and find some form of words for the legislation on the loan.'

'Then come on,' said Agnolo gruffly, 'you're the Priors. How about getting the voting started?'

Jacopo and Fra Lippo discuss religion, then meet some unbelievers

The inn appears round a bend in the road like an answer to a prayer. Though what god would provide such an answer remains obscure. A light snow has begun to fall, hazing the ground about their feet, and the sight of that inn, sprawling over the frosty fields and billowing smoke like a hoary old dragon, makes both of them grin through the steam of their breath. They tie the donkey to a pole in the stables, where it noses a manger of mushy hay while they head for the door. They open up and stumble in, noting the blaze at the heart of the room and the heat that catches them up like a hug. Jacopo closes the door behind him, beginning to notice the numerous groups that huddle together beneath the low roof. Passing the hearth, he turns aside—the heat of the fire hurting his eyes—and bustles toward a low table.

The innkeeper strolls across and takes their order of wine, bread and cheese. He's a surly fellow and grumbles away when Jacopo shows him the sleeping Scimmi, saying, 'And some milk as well, for the cat.' Nor is he quick to return, trudging along, still muttering, and shamelessly overcharging them. But Fra Lippo, feeling generous after their profits in Santa Rocca, seems happy enough to pay for the lot, doling out coins and dismissing their host with a nod.

Once they've drunk some bitter red wine and fed the now wide-awake Scimmi, they relax in the hubbub and heat of the smoky room.

'Tell me, Friar,' Jacopo yawns at last, leaning across the table, 'how is it that a man like you, learned and clever with his words—or so it seems to me—can end up flogging fake relics to poor villagers?'

Fra Lippo looks up sharply, casts his companion a judicious glance, and seems to wonder whether he's one who grows obnoxious with wine. 'That's a rather unflattering way to put it, Jacopo,' he says at last.

'But true,' the thief insists, 'isn't it? I mean, I'm not trying to insult you or anything. It's simply how it is. And I'm curious to know.'

'Well, I've explained that the relics' true nature leaves their virtue intact as a test of faith. Indeed, to insist on their authenticity is, perhaps, to fall into the trap that such literal-minded peasants are apt to stumble into, and that some unscrupulous souls can—'

'Lippo!' The cry brings a halt to the torrent of words. 'I'm not an inquisitor. I'm sorry if I put it bluntly. I simply want to know how one who speaks like a scholar can be living like a vagabond.'

Once again the friar observes him coolly, though this time his gaze is more sardonic. He edges forward and fills up their cups, draining the pottery jug. He waves his hand at the innkeeper, but the man looks away as though he hasn't seen.

'He seems to resent making money,' he says, sipping his wine, but Jacopo won't let him change the subject, and raises his eyebrows expectantly. 'Oh, well,' the friar sighs, 'it's not a very salutary story, nor even particularly interesting. Just the tale of a man whose learning made him reject the path he'd taken and who, some years later, rejected that for which he'd rejected it, merely to find that the only place left was the road.'

'These are riddles, Friar. What do you mean?'

'What do I mean?' Fra Lippo peers into his cup as if to discover his meaning there. 'I mean that I spent a decade of my youth in a monastery of Conventuals, who believed that men could own in common, where the things we owned of greatest value were books and where, through books, I came to believe that the Spirituals were right, that nothing may be owned, and even, eventually, that the Spirituals themselves were wrong to countenance the wealth of the Holy Father.' He swills the wine around his cup, then stops before it spills. 'So I joined a group of Fraticelli who were wandering through the country.'

'But they were called heretics and sorcerers,' says Jacopo, 'and burned as such.'

'You're not wrong there,' the friar nods, gazing into his wine once more. A man leaves the dice game over by the door and saunters past their table. He glances quickly at Lippo, and just for a moment Jacopo feels sure that he's seen him before. He thinks of the towns that he's passed through,

Civitavecchia, the boat, Amalfi, but cannot seem to place him and, besides, he's already gone.

'The Fraticelli,' he murmurs, 'were said to have looted churches, to have made peasants burn castles and kill their landlords.'

'Oh yes, they were said to have done that, and more besides. Preaching Christ's poverty and the greed of the Church ... well, let's say they made some enemies. I spent a number of ... interesting years ... you know, wandering the woods like a vagrant, preaching in towns where I lived by begging, condemning the sins of the Pope and the cruelty of the lords, until we were declared anathema and hounded from town to town by the agents of the Inquisition.' He pauses, searching Jacopo's gaze with eyes that now, instead of warmth or feigned anger, hold the kind of pain the thief remembers in Laura's eyes as her children were dying. 'I saw three of my brethren burned in Rome, and my closest friend was drowned by thugs in a lake near Perugia.' He waves once more at their host. 'Ah, he's coming,' he smiles without joy. 'After that I fled all contact with the Fraticelli.'

'You want something?' the man inquires. Jacopo notes the fat purse that peeps from his smock.

'Some more wine,' says the friar and hands him the empty jug, which the man takes, grunting, and carries off to the barrels on the far side of the room.

Jacopo observes his retreating back, running his fingers over the blade of his knife. 'You know, now that I think of it, I could almost have guessed from what you were saying at Santa Rocca. Your past, I mean. All that stuff about the sins of the great—I was wondering where that was heading.'

'Yes, well, not where I would have taken it when I was a Fraticello. Not that there's much danger in it now. Clement the Sixth has other fish to fry.' He glances up as an argument erupts at the dicers' table, then turns back, smiling. 'No, it's just a means to an end with me now. I know how some of those people feel, especially in times like these when the wealth of the towns is waning and taking the peasants with it. To them, such sentiments make *all* I say seem true. But I can't really preach them with much conviction. I used to believe in the God of the Fraticelli—the simple Christ who lived in the hearts of ordinary people and wandered the roads like a pauper. I'm not sure that I do any more.' He ceases talking, as if from a habit of secrecy, while the taverner thumps the jug down before them.

'Why?' says Jacopo after he's taken his turn to pay for the wine and the man's left the table. 'What do you believe?'

'That each day follows the next—at least, if you're lucky. Stay sharp and you might stay alive.' He smiles ruefully, leaning closer over the table. 'Sometimes I could almost give credence to the Catharist heresy, or something like it anyway. I mean ... when you look around you, doesn't it seem like the Devil's more than a fallen lieutenant, a flunkey no longer in Heaven's favour?'

Jacopo had known a Cathar contortionist in Orlando's circus who'd maintained that Satan was God's twin, His evil opposite. And indeed, when he thinks of Laura and both of her children shrivelled with sickness, he seems to understand. Yet he simply says: 'You'd know more about that than I would, Friar. Like you, I get by day to day.'

'Oh, don't get me wrong,' puts in Lippo, glancing narrowly at his companion. 'My own beliefs have grown far closer to the Pope's than they once were. As I said, I can no longer believe in a pauper Christ.' He gazes absently at Scimmi, who purrs beneath his fingers. 'If He were a pauper, could He really be so heartless to His fellows? No, like the greatest of popes or emperors, God lives far away in heavenly splendour and will only descend to assert His might when He has to. So now, in my own humble fashion, I seek to emulate His spendour by selling—as you say—fake relics to peasants.'

The conversation goes on, trailing off into tactics for use in the towns, until they finish their wine. They get up to leave, the taverner scuttling across, collecting their cups in surly silence.

'Excellent meal,' says Fra Lippo, retrieving his paunch from under the table.

The man merely grunts and doesn't turn round as a sudden flurry of movement attracts the friar's attention. But Jacopo's just there at the taverner's back, tucking Scimmi into her pouch.

They head for the door, passing the hearth and the dicers, and Jacopo stares through the smoky air, seeking the face that he thought he'd known, wondering if possibly one final look might solve the small puzzle. As he does so, he sees not only this man, but his runtish companion, whose features too seem strangely familiar. They nudge and mutter as the friar goes by, yet Jacopo still can't place them.

Outside, the cold air hits with a thrill, then starts to settle into his bones. A light snow is falling, but they keep on going. 'After all, we've got money enough to satisfy the greed of any peasant farmer,' says Jacopo, comfortably patting the innkeeper's purse under Scimmi's curled purring. Just as he's grinning with self-satisfaction, he knows where he's seen those faces before: in the gang that was after Lippo.

The next village they reach seems very poor, a mere huddle of shacks under scrub oaks and pine trees. One of the hovels lies broken in two where a big old cypress has plunged through its roof, and not a single fire appears to be lit. The place looks so unprepossessing that Fra Lippo almost keeps going, just giving the bell a tinkle or two if only to warm up his arm. In fact, he feels a bit unsettled after this morning's struggle with Scimmi, and then the dispute with Jacopo, when all that he'd done was powder her fur and do her up as the demon. No sooner had he tied the chicken wattle to her chin than she started to squirm, wriggling out of his grip when he'd only stuck on one horn, while Jacopo hissed, 'There's just no point. She won't do it.' Then the imp—demon indeed!—had scratched at his hands and vanished into the brush, refusing to come no matter how they cajoled her. So now she has gone and he jangles the bell, half hoping for no response, when abruptly, hey presto! the people are there, expecting a show. So he gives them whatever they want, Heaven and Hell, sin and salvation, two sacks full of relics, even resolving to drop his demand for hard cash, since it seems fairly clear that, here at least, such demands will gain nothing but anger.

Nevertheless, there's a curious fact. At first there's no more than a dozen, but as Lippo proceeds, the numbers grow, until there are twenty—perhaps even thirty—people gathered about him. Nor do they seem to come from the houses, but drift through the trees, each hooded so carefully against the cold that he can't really make out their faces, though all of the later arrivals are men. Indeed, the place appears to contain at least five times more men than women. Jacopo's feeling uneasy, especially with Scimmi refusing to come, sulking alone in the bush; and he sees, from the way Fra Lippo keeps glancing toward the donkey, that he feels the same. Still, the friar goes through his medley of relics—Elmo's windlass, Saint John's cooking oil, the hairs of Wilgefortis, the collapsible Madonna, Adam's apple core, Saint Barbara's gallstones, the feather of Jacob's angel—until he gets to the bit about demons and exorcism. He leans at them over his flaking pulpit, caught up in his rhetoric, unaware of the pair who have slipped through the trees. But Jacopo sees them and knows who they are, despite their deep hoods. One, thin as a weasel and holding a rope, is the first man he'd recognised back at the inn. The other, big, with stumpy legs and a barrel chest, was the leader—he's certain it's him—of the men who'd been chasing Fra Lippo, the one on the ass.

The friar tears right on, caught up in the stream of his eloquence. 'And now my good people,' he cries, 'I would, if I could, have shown you the demon I snared in the soul of a miller. But let such imps lay hidden and sly in their shame. It's the devils that clutch at your own sinful souls that I seek to show you, the devils of avarice, envy and lust, of anger and—'

'He's the one!' a loud voice breaks in, and Jacopo sees the big man step forth from the crowd, his finger pointed at Lippo. 'He's the one who came to Sottile, the one who seduced my poor niece.' His grinning companion's unwinding the rope. 'He said he'd show her the Virgin's girdle.' Lippo looks pale, as if bled. 'But he showed her his stinking prick!'

Just as the crowd closes in, Jacopo darts to the friar. There's a saffron flash from the pulpit, another beside it. He snatches at Lippo's arm and drags him toward the donkey. He tries to heave him up, but Lippo can't do it. He's too heavy, too scared, and Jacopo pulls him away, flinging him backward between the hovels, pushing him on through the trees. Meanwhile, the gang from Sottile gets tangled up with the villagers, who are racing to ransack the preacher's baggage, tripping over each other's feet until no-one's quite sure which way the pair went. Fra Lippo pauses for one final moment, glancing back at his things, while Jacopo tries to see Scimmi but can't, not in that melee, and wrenches the friar up through the pines.

Cardinal Rollo da Parma has unpleasant dreams

THE CARDINAL'S PALACE, DESPITE ITS SIZE, WAS NOW invisible. It might almost have been there to mimic those spirit worlds hidden from sight were it not for the sudden eruptions of light that blazed from its casements at curious intervals. Hours of darkness lay between these, which abruptly ignited and flew at great pace from window to window, as if some strange Mardi Gras, rushed and spasmodic, had started. Yet, since none beyond the domains of the palace were near to see, its mystery remained unwitnessed, if hardly unexplained. The only ones who saw it were those who knew its meaning or, at least, had some small part to play in it. Perhaps its one true witness, hiding in an upper chamber presently unused, leering through the doorway's narrow crack and raddled with foul unguents, was Brother Corvo. Though he played no part in its performance, he understood it with a greater clarity than anyone who did.

At that very moment he crouched beside the doorjamb, watching, trying so hard to suppress his own laughter he fell to the floor. A short way down the corridor, two guards with halberds flanked their master's room. They wore breastplates and morions, and their weapons were hung with Rollo's colours. Dream warriors, Corvo sniggered, to frighten the cardinal's dreams. The unguent glistened in his pores and sang inside his blood. Oh yes, he understood His Eminence's dreams all right. In fact, he crafted them the way that artists craft paintings, as if the herbs he crushed and mixed in Rollo's food were pigments that made nightmares. Like all true terrors of the night, they left their traces upon waking, so that Rollo knew no respite from the figments of his fear, sensing plots in every half-heard conversation and assassins at each door. There might be killers sent by Topomagro's Priors or hired by his enemies at Avignon. And killers, as any child would tell you, strike in darkness.

Abruptly, Rollo's door burst outward in a blaze of torchlight, and the cardinal came rushing through surrounded by his servants. Almost at once the doors that flanked it, and those directly opposite, swung open to admit yet further squadrons to the hall, each waving torches in the air like banners of bright flame. One of Rollo's deacons, swathed in a rumpled almuce, hastened to his side; a chaplain, whipping off his nightcap, stumbled through the servants forming into ranks. Barely had the armed guard taken their positions than their captain bellowed 'Balthazar!' and all marched down the passage glazed with light. Brother Corvo couldn't say which room was Balthazar, since the guard changed code words every night, but he waited till the glow had faded round a corner and then went creeping after them. The oil felt warm upon his skin, and shadows swam like fish about the walls. He giggled, stumbling in the dark. Poor Rollo, he mouthed, poor Cardinal da Parma, reduced to wandering his nighthalls in a panic. His Eminence must change beds, since demons and succubi hide among his sheets and murderers haunt his cupboards. Poor Rollo, running a gamut of bedrooms to baffle his phantoms. Brother Corvo slid around a corner, hiding in an alcove.

The torches were wreathed in circular rainbows. Soldiers and servants, groggy with sleep, collided. The deacon scolded, untangling their halberds, and Rollo watched, disdainful. At last the captain unlocked the door, the guards were at the ready, and the others adjourned to adjoining chambers. The cardinal's servants went in before him, lighting the room with torches, and it was only then, when all was still, that Rollo crossed the threshold. Even so, as if he sensed some presence, he swung abruptly round and stared into the hallway. Brother Corvo almost laughed out loud, yet cleaved to the shadowy recess, his long white gaze unblinking. And then he saw, standing at the cardinal's left shoulder, in the instant that he shut the door, a thin black devil with eyes as bright as rubies and bifurcated tongue.

Jacopo and the friar encounter Wolf Schwanhals

TIME IS LOST AMID THE RUSH OF BLOOD AND BREATH, the pulse-thumping panic, the cries, the crash of branches, the thud of boots and crackle of pine needles. Jacopo ducks and darts and dodges, while Fra Lippo plunges past trunks with surprising speed, a legged keg careering over pine cones, his habit aswirl. They crouch behind branches, saplings, humps or tussocks as their hunters fade to phantoms in the skeins of their own shouting.

'I'll have to go back,' pants Jacopo, when the cries have vanished in the depths of the forest.

'Why?' hisses Lippo from behind his tree.

'I can't leave Scimmi.' He peers back among the colonnades of trunks, uncertain now of the way they've come. 'She's probably still hiding near the village. They might take it out on her.'

'We can't go back. I'm not even sure which way it is.' The friar's puffing, red and sweaty, his habit littered with needles like a crude attempt at camouflage. 'She's a clever cat, she'll find us.'

'She's clever all right. But she's stubborn too when her dignity's hurt.' He gives Fra Lippo a crafty look. 'What about your relics? What'll you do without them?'

'Oh, well,' sighs Lippo, then seems to cheer up. 'It won't be hard to get some more. Any boneyard will do.'

'And what was all that stuff about the Virgin's girdle and seducing young girls? It was—'

'Rubbish, absolute rubbish, my boy.' Fra Lippo looks the soul of indignation. 'The sort of filth these drunken yokels use as an excuse to kill God's friars.'

Jacopo turns to seek the way they've come.

'But he sounded so, well, so—'

'Full of Satan's lies?' The friar's hanging back as if unwilling to go with him. 'Indeed, they are a vicious gang of cut-throats.'

Jacopo commences walking, uncertain what to think, when there's a crash amongst the bushes to his right. In an instant—dagger in hand—he's at the side of Lippo, who's wrestling a long misericord from under his robes. There's a rustle of mulch behind them, then the leaves of a blighted balsam start thrashing at knee-height, as if they were besieged by midgets, and something bursts into the clearing. It's sleek, sinewy, silver and ... Scimmi, trotting toward them like a small, clawed pony, her muzzle bloody, a rat's paw gripped in her teeth. She drops it on the ground, bats at it half-heartedly, then nuzzles clotted whiskers against Jacopo's leg.

'You villain!' he says, patting the top of her head with his fingers, drawing them back stained red with rat's blood. 'That wasn't a time to go mucking about.' He picks her up and rubs at her ears despite the gore. 'We might have lost you.'

'Yes,' says the friar darkly, massaging the scratch on his hand and watching Jacopo pull a small horn from her head. He notes that the crimson wattle no longer hangs from her chin, then jerks his thumb through the trees, suggesting, 'This is the way to go.'

And go they do, trudging on through the woods and the night, their blankets, cloaks, even their tinderbox left behind them with the donkey. Luckily it doesn't snow, but the night is nonetheless cold as they huddle together in hollows of stone, Scimmi purring away between them. Nor does it get warmer the next morning, and they walk as briskly as they can amongst the wooded hills, slapping at themselves like flagellants. Tempted though they are to go down to the villages below them, they remain upon their high, secluded trails for another day and night, afraid that their pursuers, zealous as they seem, might inveigle others to pursue them. At last they descend from pines to elms to thickets of birch and alder, hot with their exertions and the sun's return.

It's after some time in this terrain, when they come upon stumps bearing signs of the axe, that they hear a cry whose pain and terror cut straight into their hearts. Jacopo stares at Fra Lippo, who gapes in turn, each almost as frightened by the look upon the other's face as by the sound itself. Somewhere ahead of them a woman screams, and almost before they realise what they're doing, they've crept to a place where the light seems less obstructed by the trees, and are peering up into an open stretch of sky as a second scream now splinters round their ears. They tiptoe forward, and peep out through the foliage toward a broad, bright clearing.

Before them lie a rundown farmhouse and a field. In this field are three cows and a man, the cows collapsed upon the ground, the man beside them with his guts splayed out. At the doorway of the farmhouse an infant lies face down, as if he'd tripped upon the step, and blood spreads out beneath him like a deepening shadow. The screams are not from these still figures, but from the woman sprawled upon her back beside the pigpen. She is no longer screaming, but merely whimpers, perhaps because a soldier in a leather helm and armour is kneeling at her head, one hand wound tight within her hair, the other with a knife against her throat. His febrile stare is bent upon his fellow, also in a leather breastplate, who grunts above the woman as he thrusts inside her, his buttocks pale and smeared with dark mud. Jacopo glances at Fra Lippo, who doesn't notice his attention, caught up as he is, eyes avid and exhausted, fist tight about his blade.

'Soldiers,' Jacopo hisses in his ear. 'Who do you think they are?'

The friar, leaning forward on a branch, intent, neglects to answer, mesmerised perhaps by the soldier's joyless grunting, the only sound beneath that bright blue sky until the woman's voice breaks once, like glass, upon the air. The kneeling figure twists her hair, about to use his knife, when a third man ambles through the farmhouse doorway. He has a crossbow strapped upon his back and, like the others, is clad in leather armour, but takes no notice of his fellows, concentrating on the flask of wine and great round cheese he carries. He stumbles on the child, looks down, then marches on.

'You'd better hurry up,' he calls. 'We're too close to the camp. We can't risk staying here long.'

His companions appear not to hear him, but everything changes when the branch that Lippo has been leaning on gives way beneath his weight, cracking like a whip and plunging him toward the clearing. The kneeling man glares round. The grunting soldier lifts his head and squints up at the sound. The third man rips the crossbow from his back and wheels about, fits a bolt into its chamber, while Lippo, winded, clambers to his feet. Jacopo too stands staring, exposed by the broken branch.

'Don't move!' shrieks the archer, his wine flask emptying its contents at his feet. Fra Lippo gropes a little at the space before him, hissing at Jacopo. 'Don't say a fucking word!' the archer bellows. 'Come forward slowly.' Then adds with infinite menace, 'As slowly as you can.'

The friar tiptoes forward, trembling plumply, hands plucking at the air. He moves with such deliberate, timid steps that he might be mocking the man's order. 'Where ...' he moans, 'where are you?' He's groping at the breeze before him as if at some frail face. 'Please, I can't see. Don't hurt a poor blind friar.'

'Gur wah dar!' Jacopo barks, nodding with his head and pointing at Fra Lippo.

'Aaahhhh ...' says the mud-spattered soldier, collapsing on the woman, whose body starts to heave and wrench with hacking, bitter sobs.

The friar stumbles off toward the trees behind the farmhouse, hands flailing in the air.

'You!' the archer screams out at Jacopo and, like some lethal fiddler, tucks the crossbow at his chin. 'Lead him over here if he can't see.'

'Gah wur dah?' he says, confused.

The sated soldier bounces with the woman's every sob.

'He can't hear you, sir. He's deaf,' moans Lippo, flapping with his arms at the dead child. 'We are the poor of God, sir, a blind friar and his mute.'

Suddenly the soldier with the knife heaves upright, laughing. 'A blindman and a mute!' he cries. 'Oh, Christ, our only witnesses.'

Then the bowman too begins to laugh, letting his arm drop, as the soldier on the ground snarls, 'Kill them,' rolling from the woman's chest. 'The mute saw it and the monk heard it.'

'I—I heard a pig grunting,' says Fra Lippo.

'Wuh,' Jacopo nods.

'Kill them!' cries the soldier, and the archer lifts his crossbow as the pair begin to run, the friar moving with amazing speed despite his blindness, Jacopo edging past him. They've almost made it to the trees, Jacopo sensing with every moment of their flight the arrow closing with a hiss toward his back, waiting to be pierced, skewered, split, as he stumbles to the foliage. He turns back for the briefest time to see the archer, neither standing nor even taking aim, but running after them, hurtling through the bushes at their heels, already on them, yet not stopping, barely glancing, just flashing past as if he didn't chase, but fled.

As he peers through the screen of leaves, it's not the bowman who commands the thief's attention. For there upon the clearing, as if they'd ridden up out of the earth, are three tall knights in armour, their horses masked in metal. One gleams white, and with such a neck and long, beaked visor that he's like some mounted swan that brandishes its broadsword in the sun. The soldier with the naked, splattered arse now stands beneath this horseman, trembling, as the sword glints skyward, swooping in a gleaming arc, unhindered by his neck, and lobs the leathered head a distance through the air. The body falls, still trembling, beside the sobbing woman, while the others ride the second soldier down, one—his helm a boar's tusked head—spitting him upon his lance, the other carving through his neck.

'Take their horses and their heads,' commands the leader, hinging back his visor's pointed beak. 'This commune's paid for order and they'll get it.' He swings his horse toward the north, then turns back for a moment, shouting, as if to tell the woman, 'I won't be disobeyed.'

All three ride into the north, leading the riderless horses after them, the dead men's saddlebags now swollen with their swords and leaking heads.

'Oh, Jesus,' Jacopo says at last, letting out a sigh. 'Maybe we should go and help the woman.'

'No, wait.' The friar's hand is shaking on his shoulder. 'Give them more time. I don't want to meet them coming back.'

They pause for some minutes, listening, until Jacopo says, 'Come on, we ought to go and help her. The man or the child might still be alive.'

'Oh, yes. Those soldiers might be too.'

'Well, there's no point sitting here.' He looks at Lippo slantwise. 'Besides, who knows what booty those men might still have on them?'

The following day the clouds draw in and the wind grows bitterly cold. Light rain has begun to fall, turning to sleet, then a soft, steady snow. They trudge up a stony incline, glad to be using a road once again, yet eager for some place to shelter.

'We should at least have taken some coats from the house,' growls Lippo, shivering in his habit.

'Well how was I to know it was going to turn out like this? It was sunny yesterday morning.'

'I said, didn't I—'

'Yes, yes, you did. You're a soothsayer ... good enough to be burnt.' Jacopo walks more quickly up the steepening hill, making the friar scurry. After climbing for several minutes they come to an inn perched on the brink of a steep descent. Smoke twirls from its roof and streams through piecemeal air.

'Let's get a drink!' calls the friar, afraid his companion might not even stop, but continue on down the road.

Jacopo says nothing, just turns from the path and heads for the door. Once inside, they move through the smoke to the kegs and hogsheads that stand by the counter—no more than a flimsy table with counting-board, beads and pitchers for the wine—where the innkeeper eyes their approach.

'Good afternoon,' says Jacopo.

'If you like trudging about in the snow,' the man replies, then chuckles as if he's performed some masterstroke of wit. 'If you like your balls turning blue and dropping off.'

Jacopo glances sideways at Lippo, saying, 'Yes, you're right, it's lousy weather,' and goes on to order drinks for them both, as well as some cheese for Scimmi, discussing the foulness of the day still further with the innkeeper, who seems a big, bluff, voluble man, eager for any excuse to laugh. They give an abridged account of their travels, discussing the virtues of cats versus dogs, till Lippo leans forward and says, confidentially, 'We had a funny thing happen,' and tells the man what they'd seen at the farmhouse. When he comes to the part with the horsemen, describing the leader's curious armour, the taverner too leans to say, in a tone of some surprise, 'That's Schwanhals.'

'I beg your pardon,' says the friar.

'Schwanhals,' he repeats, 'Baron Schwanhals, the *condottiere*. They say he's in the pay of Cardinal da Parma of Boccaperta. You were lucky you were hidden.'

'A *condottiere*? But we're a long way south of Boccaperta.'

'Don't ask me what's going on.' The innkeeper flings up his hands. 'Some say he's gathering numbers to do the cardinal's bidding further north. Some say he's simply wintering here, since the famine hasn't hit us quite so hard. Others reckon him to be taking payment from half-a-dozen communes, each vying with the others to keep him off their territory.'

'But he killed his own soldiers,' says Jacopo, 'and took their heads back to his camp as an example.'

'Yes, well, that's because he's involved in a struggle with Count Montefeltro, one of the most powerful landholders in these parts. He doesn't want more enemies than he needs, so he's trying to keep his men in check.' He gives them a crafty look, and jerks his thumb at the northern wall. 'You'll see what I mean right now if you open that window. We need a bit of fresh air in here anyway.' He nods his head and jerks with his thumb once more. 'Go on, take a gander.'

They exchange puzzled glances, but Lippo walks over, followed by Jacopo, and unlatches the shutter. He raises it just a small way, but a blast of cold air and snowflakes still enters. They stand at the window and peer out, seeing little at first but grey depths of snow. 'What are we supposed to see?' the friar calls over his shoulder, but receives no answer from the innkeeper. Instead, Jacopo jostles his arm and says, 'Look.' And he does, till his eyes grow used to the feathery blur of the gulf past the window, and he sees the shadows of far, dark armies wheeling below in that pallid void, tiny, circling and slow. There are horses and horsemen and, slower still in the fractured air, foot-soldiers, crawling homunculi. He sees cavalry merge and riders vanish in whiteness, as if constructed of snow, while troops move in to outflank each other, swirling like winds over silent white ice, like companies of cloud.

They stare at this dumbstruck slaughter till

Lippo starts to shiver, turning toward the fire; and Jacopo wonders if this is the way that a god watches pain. But he too shivers, then rubs at his arms and says, 'Let's shut the window, eh?' He pulls down the shutter and fastens the latch. 'It's getting too cold in here.'

The fall of Frederico dalla Montagna

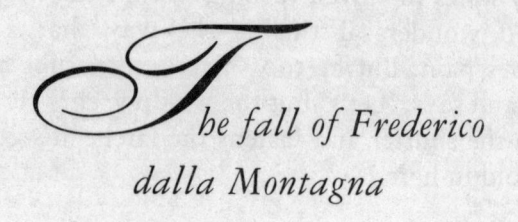

BALDASSARE STOOD AMONGST THE BLAZE OF TORCHES before the Montagna tower. The militiamen of the Porta San Stefano milled below its walls, some swinging the great battering ram on its rusty chains which creaked and grated in the cold, damp air. He watched Donato Spini, their *castellano*, dart from one group to the next, occasionally checking the weapons—even the uniforms—of his men, as if they were about to go on parade instead of storming the tower of Frederico dalla Montagna. He did not entirely trust this *castellano*. Nor, for that matter, did he entirely trust the others whom the Signoria had ordered to capture the main strongholds in their quarters of the town. Agnolo del Leone himself had been unable to vouch for the loyalty of all the militia, yet as he had said, if the Signoria moved quickly enough, the waverers would be taken by surprise and forced to follow orders by the momentum of events. When they'd entered the palazzo itself they'd all seemed keen enough, smashing benches, tables, chairs against the locked doors, until Baldassare had advised Donato Spini that they'd meet less hardship at the tower's outer door, heavy though it was, than struggling through a chain of barricaded rooms.

So here they were in the piazza, wielding the communal battering ram, the same one used on these very towers before the exile of Baldassare's father. They should have dismantled them then, as so many communes had, but instead had procrastinated. He glanced toward their banner propped against the wall, only the mouth and forepaw of the great Guelph lion now visible, and for a moment had the curious sense that he was fighting the wrong side, that some perversity of fate had positioned him behind this creature when, by every logic of his birth and nature, he should be vaulting headlong at its claws.

It was not unlike the way he'd felt when they'd first entered the palazzo, smashing through the bolted doorway only to find that they were standing in an empty building, the lofty entrance echoing about them. It was then that he had seen on the wall the massive shield emblazoned with the outlawed eagle of the Ghibellines, and felt the strange conviction that, at any other time, with any other chain of circumstance, he would have stood beside Montagna and the others against merchants such as Tuccio. Now he was to wed a wealthy merchant's daughter. He had placed the gold betrothal ring upon her finger. Nor had the nobles liked it, taking out their spite upon the woman. Stoldo dalla Montagna, Frederico's elder son, had been the worst, publicly impugning Gaia's honour, declaring her a whore and spreading other vicious lies about her. It was this that fuelled his eagerness to break into their tower.

'Get back!' cried the lookout, and Baldassare instinctively recoiled, quickly glancing up to where the lip of a great cauldron appeared at a window, suddenly disgorging a steaming sheet of water. The soldiers scattered, letting go the ram. Cheers cascaded from the tower, and two or three cried out as they were caught upon the legs and back; but, for the most part, the deluge was expended on the square's cold stones, where it settled into puddles, briefly steaming in the glow of the reflected torchlight. Then the militia raced once more to work, wielding the ram with redoubled vigour, until the hinges of the iron door began to groan beneath the onslaught, then suddenly gave way in a surge of wood and men.

Donato Spini rushed ahead among the foremost of his soldiers, and Baldassare, eager not to lag behind, lunged after him as best he could. But the battering ram, and those who'd used it, blocked the doorway, and he had to shoulder through them, past the corpses of the household's servants, until he reached the stairs. These he found absurdly narrow and clogged with further bodies, which he jerked aside. Some groaned as they rolled back behind him, but he didn't even think of stopping, gripped as he was by the need to catch up with the *castellano*. He passed through a room where some fighting still went on. A child shrieked; he thought he saw, at the edge of his sight, a militiaman cutting a woman's throat. The real struggle was somewhere overhead, and he leapt toward the stairs, so littered with the dying and the dead they seemed constructed not of stone, but flesh. He came upon a second room, where the fighting was more fierce. Here too he would have hurried on since there were only two men of the household and three of the militia. Yet, as he passed, he glimpsed the larger of Montagna's men dispatch the first of his opponents, then start in on the other, who seemed no match for him. He didn't pause because he wished to save his ally—the man was crumpling to the ground already, blood jetting from his neck.

'Stoldo!' he cried, holding out his sword. 'The last time we met, you were cringing like a dog beneath your father's orders.'

Stoldo dalla Montagna swung upon his heel; a look of shock suffused his face. He drew a shaky sigh, then grinned, recovering. 'Ah, but that's where you're wrong, Baldassare. *This* is the last time we will meet.' Without another word he flung himself at his opponent, as if hoping to profit from the speed of his attack. Indeed, Baldassare was pushed back on his heels, fighting to maintain his balance, making a shield out of his sword, till Stoldo's blade rang like a tocsin in the narrow room. Baldassare glanced sideways, seeing Stoldo's companion getting the better of the third militiaman, and decided that it might be safest to let himself fall back toward the wall. His sword inverted in the air before him, he crashed against the stones while Stoldo battered him with blacksmith's blows, blade sparking like a giant flint beside his ear. It suddenly seemed that he might die, here, against this wall, in a room he'd never seen, at the hand of a man who insulted women in the streets. His forearms ached from holding back the blows, his head was ringing from the clatter of the blade, and his breath was dry and raucous in his throat. Then, overconfident, or possibly just tired, Stoldo paused at the height of a thrust, as if to gain some added leverage, some final extra strength to break through his opponent's guard, allowing Baldassare to flick his blade up fast, slicing Stoldo's arm. It seemed a minor wound, yet made him pause just long enough for Baldassare to lunge, then thrust, then push him through the room. There was a single, sudden cry as he collided with his fellow, yet Baldassare paid no heed, chasing his opponent to the wall, where the man stood, wild-eyed, and tried to lift his sword. His arm seemed useless, though he made a futile effort to hold the weapon steady with the other.

'What's the matter, Stoldo?' sneered Baldassare, and knocked the sword away. 'You spoke so jealously of Gaia, I thought you wished to marry me yourself.' And he sank the blade in Stoldo's body so he staggered down the wall, grunting and coughing and dragging Baldassare with him. They appeared to embrace, till Baldassare struggled up, wrenching the blade free.

He glanced round hastily. The militiaman sat panting on the floor, grinning up at him vaguely, his opponent prone and seeping. The noise of battle still echoed down the stairway. Barely pausing to return the grin, he hurried for the stairs, leaping up them fast, then clambering over bodies. He found a pair of women and a child butchered in a wash of blood. For a moment he could not continue. This seemed too bloody, too scrupulously cruel, as if every member of the family must be slaughtered. Tuccio's words kept sounding in his memory— 'Keep a watch on the militia. There may be traitors.' No room he'd passed contained a living member of the household. They'd all been murdered outright. Was this the militia's zeal, or the work of some amongst it that wanted no-one left who might give evidence of treason? He rushed upward to the fighting.

Cries echoed from the tower's topmost room. Here the shouts and clash of blades, now muted and spasmodic, had the sound of single combat rather than massed attack. The voices were not those of men in battle, but the mocking cheers of an audience at some low comedy. He reached the door and found it crammed with milling bodies, no longer fighting, but merely jostling upon tiptoe as if a show were happening within. He too stood on his toes and craned his neck to see, peering over shoulders and helmed heads, across a charnel-house of corpses, toward a corner of the dingy room where Frederico dalla Montagna—his retainers dead—now held his broadsword at the ready. A cut beneath his hair oozed blood, and his face was smeared with gore, yet there was nothing beaten in his posture as he faced his foes.

'Well, come on,' he muttered, voice shaky and defiant, but neither Donato Spini, the *castellano*, nor the militiaman who prowled with him before Montagna seemed eager to accept the invitation. He snorted with contempt. 'You cowards!' The crowd began to jeer. Spini feinted with his sword.

Montagna turned to parry, and the militiaman thrust forward with his spear, slipping through his guard, his robe, his skin, pinning him to the wall as Spini, slicing through the air in one long sweep, lopped off his head. It bounced upon the stones. A cheer went up, and Baldassare shouldered past the crowd to reach Donato, till nothing stood between them but that floor of bloodied limbs. The *castellano* smirked, then cocked an eyebrow to include him in the carnage, or perhaps to say that there was now no difference—at least, that anyone could see—between their motives.

It was only later, as he stood alone beneath the eagle on its shield in the palazzo's entrance hall, that he realised such bloodshed had probably occurred all over town. He gazed at the old symbol, surprised to find himself beset with doubts about his dealings with the merchants.

In which Fra Lippo makes an unpalatable suggestion

IT IS COLD, SO COLD THAT MOVING IS PAINFUL, AS IF splinters of frost had lodged in the joints. Jacopo and Fra Lippo trudge down the hillside, a hearty breakfast doing its best to warm their bellies, though its heat is quickly lost. There's been a heavy snowfall overnight, leaving great white empty nests among the branches of the trees, and covering the ground with such a universal whiteness that the landscape looks like an abandoned room draped with dust sheets. Jacopo gazes at the valley that stretches to the north before them. It was here that the silent battle of the previous day had taken place. Now, from what he can make out across that distance, there are only scattered groups with an occasional cart, and fires burning in the cold.

As they make their way across the fields, he sees that shadows in the snow—shapes he'd thought were rocks or hummocks—are actually dead soldiers submerged beneath the whiteness. The groups that move amongst the dead are scavenging for weapons or collecting corpses for burial. He sees carts full of spears, pikes, swords, saddles and entire suits of armour; others are piled with bodies, the remains, he presumes, of Count Montefeltro's forces. These, it would appear, were defeated with severe losses. As Jacopo glances at a cart heaped high with corpses, he notes how awkward and angular they seem, not laid out neatly but scraping together like great lumps of stone, victims of a premature rigor mortis. The driver and his mate have stopped beside a large, half-buried mound of bodies, and have just leant three of them against their cart. All had fallen with their arms thrust out and now, propped upright as they are, appear caught amid the throes of some wild emotion, arms flung heavenward in ecstasy or anguish. Already stowed in the bed of the cart are a group of foot soldiers, each frozen like an armoured foetus round an arrow. The driver tries to heave two figures from the snow, a pair of archers curled together, flesh pierced by their daggers. His mate comes sidling up to help him hurl the twinned blue corpses, clattering, into the cart.

Everywhere there are these human logs, stones, statues, horizontal snowmen. Toward the centre of the field they come across a frozen horse skewered by a pike, half kneeling in the snow as if in supplication to some equine god. Still further lie the cavalry, frozen where they've fallen, each knight bound to his mount by an icy umbilicus, while peasants stoke great conflagrations to set their masters free. Slowly they begin to thaw, flesh wet and blue and drowned, stretched out upon the meadow like the amputated organs of a herd of centaurs. Yet all remain as rigid as they were; nor can the horses be coaxed from their death by the men who stoke the fires, which hiss and steam, then curl with oily smoke into the air, as thief and friar hurry past, intent, their faces turned already to the north.

As the weeks go by, the weather remains cold, slicing through the woods with bitter northern winds, drowning the sown seeds in icy showers, smothering each village under snowfalls. Beasts die upon the fields of derelict farms or huddle under roofs of huts and byres. The friar buys himself another donkey, a stubborn, surly creature raddled with cankers and bowed by Lippo's weight. He accumulates new relics—a piece of Saint Stephen at a boneyard, Nicasius at a tannery, Veronica at an abattoir—and houses each within its own ad hoc phylactery. Though he rings his bell until his knuckles whiten, such crowds as they once attracted no longer gather. Baron Hunger rules this countryside, and trophies of his power—emaciated men whose skins seem black with bruises, skeletal mothers with babies like starved monkeys, children like miniatures of Death itself—now trudge across the land.

Such a country hides its victims, who huddle in the darkness of their huts, and it's only rarely that the travellers see the famine's true extremes, as when Jacopo, driven by his own sharp hunger, batters at a hovel in the fields. There's no reply, but he thinks he hears a moan within and thrusts his weight against the door, revealing three small children locked inside, abandoned by their parents. Two are dead, and a third lies dying, mouth filled with sodden straw, while a pot of grasses boils above a smouldering fire. They hear accounts of people eating dung or pigeon droppings, each other or themselves; and the pair once find a figure lying prone upon the road, skin thin, almost transparent, like a shroud to hold his bones. At first they think he's dead, but some slight stir provokes their curiosity till they kneel and see the hollow that he's made with teeth and nose. On peering closer, they see his jaws still moving, grinding weakly with his final strength upon some blades of grass.

Through the quickness of the friar's wits and Jacopo's subtle fingers they survive the winter famine, thinner perhaps, and sick with hacking coughs, yet sturdy for all that. When spring arrives, it finds them marching still toward the north, their arthritic donkey between them. Jacopo whistles and the friar grows expansive, since the snows and icy winds are gone and the sun comes shining through. Everywhere they look, each field and hedgerow, wood and road, is lush with sap-filled growth. The oaks and elms and beeches soften with green leaves, and great white briar roses flood the woods with scent like slow explosions.

Along these roadways flecked with poppies comes a sullen army. From the huts and silage pits emerge the hungry. They scour the ripening woods and traipse in tattered bands amongst the meadows, stuffing their faces with hawthorn and hornbeam, plucking cress and nasturtium, crocus and lily in great dripping handfuls. Across the web of pathways spread the spiderfolk—limbs long and tremulous, joints swollen with scrofula—devouring what is edible, and much that isn't. Once, Scimmi has a robin torn out of her claws by a boy with parchment skin; later, skirting a green meadow, they see a group of women trudge amongst the grasses, finding roses, thistles, poppies and rape leaves, stirring all together in a rusty pot, and eating.

These people grind flour out of anything. They eat breads made from dog grass and sour wild arum. Once, and once only, Jacopo tries a loaf ground from cyclamen roots and, though he spits it out, can taste the bitterness for nearly the whole day. They find a village stupefied with bread made out of darnel, and one that's ill from flour made with bay leaves. Everywhere there's talk of summer and the great golden reaping. Few would choose to remember—let alone mention—what seed they devoured before the sowing. Their hope is a habit, the harvest's millennium that no-one dares doubt.

Neither Jacopo nor the friar proposes to do so. Yet, though the weather is fine and their colds disappear, spring is a bit disappointing. If anything, the scrounging of food has left the peasants with even less time for the friar's preaching. The only one who's truly content is Scimmi, forever darting off through the fields to gobble up mice and small birds, squirrels and moles, shrews and warm lizards. Her coat looks more lustrous, her lithe body sleeker, than they have for some time. Perhaps it is this which provokes Fra Lippo to say: 'You know, my boy, it's said that no-one in this country is buried whole any more. The best bits are saved for the pot.'

Jacopo stares at him blankly, Scimmi thundering under his hand.

'Yes, and I think it's true,' the friar continues, answering her purr with his snarling stomach. 'There's only one of us here gets adequate nourishment.' He leers at Scimmi then sidles closer, quietly hissing, 'What say we eat the cat?'

Jacopo pulls her into his lap, where she pauses from purring and stares about sleepily.

'I don't mean to sound blunt,' Lippo hastens to add, 'and I know she means something to you. But she's no longer any use in the act and she's grown so ... plump.' He looks at Jacopo sadly, then suddenly blurts out, 'And *we've* had stewed brambles for the last two days.'

Jacopo gives him a long, slow gaze, his eyes as cold as the blade at his belt. 'If you just *think* about eating her,' he says, so slowly that he might be talking to a child, 'I'll cut *you* up and eat you whole.'

The friar looks at him, then turns away, embarrassed; normally he might have proffered some scholarly argument, but says no more, and the night grows quiet except for purring.

No further mention is made of this dispute. Once or twice Jacopo notes Fra Lippo's glances in Scimmi's direction, but he puts the incident out of his mind and thinks it a brief aberration brought on by hunger. So it comes as a shock—after a fruitless search for a brook that Lippo assured him was there—to find neither Scimmi nor the friar at their camp. He hunts through the trees, increasingly plagued by the thought that he'll find her dead, or that Lippo has eaten all trace of the murder. Then he hears a loud cry and runs through the woods, emerging into a clearing where Lippo's under a tree, one hand still gripping his dagger, the other thrust in his mouth, now pink with drooled blood. Unaware of Jacopo's presence, he shouts, 'Come down, you vicious thing,' glaring into the leaves, where Scimmi stands hissing, back arched in spikes.

'Lippo, you bastard!' Jacopo snarls, springing forward, knocking the knife from Lippo's hand and kicking him in the stomach, so he grunts and sits down, unable to catch his breath. Meanwhile, Jacopo scales the tree, where Scimmi, after some coaxing, consents to clamber into his arms. Then he rounds on the friar, who's sucking in air like a massive baby. 'You ... you can't be trusted. I don't want any more to do with you.'

'H-h-how dare you hit a man of God?' says Lippo feebly.

'A man of God? And what God's that? The God of greed?' He clutches Scimmi closer to him. 'You think of nothing but yourself.'

'And who do you think of, Sir Thief?'

Jacopo makes to lunge forward, but thinks better of it, turning instead and striding into the woods.

Thus they part, and Jacopo is glad of it. He continues toward the north, making more speed than he did with the friar and his donkey. As summer quickens, the wheat and rye and millet promise a modest crop and a remedy for hunger. Yet, so famished are the farmers, that they reap their fields still green, the harvest bearing little grain and fewer seeds for sowing. But the people eat better than they have in months, and Jacopo's eating with them.

Further north, he comes upon the ruins of a village, men lying in dried pools of blood, and women with their clothes torn off, their stomachs opened. He's told that the Swabian, Schwanhals, has a contract from the Church against the commune of Topomagro, and that this is the path of his army on its way toward the town. Still Jacopo continues on until, one morning, he climbs a hill and finds a shepherd there, peering past the fleeces of his scattered flock toward a vista of flat hills and a valley with a river. At the end of this long valley are some shallow gorges where a town slopes to the sea.

'What town is that?' he asks, sure that the other must have heard his approach.

But the man swings round, surprised, then mutters, 'Topomagro.'

It's only then he notes, on the far side of the valley, the tents and pennants of the encamped army.

Tuccio parleys with Wolf Schwanhals

TUCCIO RODE THROUGH THE PORTA DEL COLOMBO, still bemused by his position. Perhaps it was the great Guelph flag flapping on the Torre del Colombo, or the pennants whipping back and forth above the gates, or the uniformed militia that lined both sides of the Via della Lana—whatever the cause, he felt less at ease with his position on the war council than he had at any time since his appointment. No sooner had his term expired as a Prior than he'd found himself elected by the new Signoria as one of 'God's Eight Good Men', the council chosen to organise the town's resistance to Wolf Schwanhals. He rode across the causeway above the rocky gullies abutting the eastern walls. He heard the clink of arms and harness from the company behind, and glanced at his companions—among them, Francesco Morelli and Agnolo del Leone—then squinted through the sunlight at the army on the plain.

It looked to be around three thousand strong, with many horsemen and the huge dark skeletons of siege machines for smashing down their walls. He saw the riders coming slowly through the haze, and wondered once again at his capacity for dealing with such men. They would know him for what he plainly was—a merchant and a trader, a man of money, not of war. So was it prudent of the Signoria to have chosen him to meet with this *condottiere*, this Swabian, whose advance from the south had provided vivid proof of his barbaric nature? What they really needed was the service of some kindred monster. But none of proven mettle could respond in time. So Topomagro's champions were men like Tuccio and old Agnolo del Leone—God's Eight Good Men—to fight the swords and axes of the German with abacus and ledger. For Schwanhals they'd be eight fat moneybags to slit wide open.

Yet they'd worked their hearts out in the last few weeks, these moneybags. The calling in of debts owed to the commune, the tax levies, the forced loans, the arm-twisting and bitterness, and in such straitened times ... no, it had not been easy, perhaps as brutal in its way as any military campaign. How the Signoria had fought itself, and then the notaries, not to mention that great stumbling block, the Council of the People, two hundred strong and every one opposed on principle to new taxes and forced loans. God knew how many friends he'd lost amongst the merchants hardest hit. Not that he himself had stinted. No, for once he'd run the risk of future impositions and made quite public the levies that he'd paid. As had Agnolo and the others. So that was what they were indeed—fat moneybags, full to the tune of thirty thousand florins, offering themselves to Schwanhals.

He reined nearer to Agnolo, who stared ahead at

the approaching riders. 'I'm still not confident,' he muttered through the clatter of the hooves, 'despite all our efforts.'

'Oh, Tuccio, you never are,' smiled the Gonfaloniere, eyes screwed up against the sun. 'And I've never seen you less confident than just before you make a killing.'

'Perhaps,' Tuccio frowned, 'but I don't like that word *killing*. After all, we're dealing with soldiers, not merchants.'

'I'm not so sure.' Agnolo raised his voice above the horses' noise. 'Remember, these aren't warriors in the old sense. They're mercenaries out to make a profit. Something like ourselves. Give them money and they're happy.'

'Well, if this *condottiere*'s a merchant in disguise, he's not going to want to damage the reputation of his business.'

'What, by breaking his contract with the cardinal and taking our offer?' Agnolo paused for an instant, then smiled. 'He might just see this as a means to test his market value.'

'Yes, and I wonder what he thinks that value is. If Pope Clement's behind the cardinal …' His words trailed away; the riders were drawing nearer by the second. Above the dust of their progress, Tuccio could see their standard, a swan breathing fire like a dragon. If this were merely a parley, he would have been loath to meet them in battle. Huge armoured horses battered the road, riding the dust like a white, roiling cloud, each man a mythical beast brought to life—metal bear, steel boar, gleaming swan—as if they came, not from the tents on the plain, but out of some crack in the air, from a world as crude as it was resplendent. Nor did they slacken their pace, but seemed to move faster the nearer they came. Tuccio feared they might ride straight on, leaving arms, hands, heads in the wake of their axes, never pausing, never slowing, but hurtling upon the town. As he slowed to a standstill, he tensed for the blow, felt the leap of his heart, only to find himself still on his horse, cloaked in white dust, hard metal faces before him. The men at his back were coughing softly, while the mercenaries' horses ducked their spiked heads. One of these riders, a fraction in front of the others, drew off his helm. Tuccio noted his long, thick neck and knew straight away who he was. The others, too, either took off their helms or flicked up their visors, showing faces as hard as their blunt metal masks.

'Baron Schwanhals?' said Agnolo straight off, addressing the man he'd guessed was their leader.

'That is correct,' the soldier replied, his Tuscan clotted with consonants.

'I am Agnolo del Leone, Gonfaloniere of Topomagro. And this is Tuccio di Piero Landucci, elected spokesman of the council—'

'Yes, yes, very pleased to make your acquaintance.' The *condottiere*'s smile was brisk and impatient. His horse gave a snort of contempt. 'But my men are eager for this campaign, and I'm no diplomat. So let's get to the point, shall we?'

Even phlegmatic, resilient Agnolo seemed taken aback. He stared at the man, seeking the means by which to continue.

'Well, gentlemen, if you don't know what the point is—' And he made to turn away.

'Surely the point is money,' said Tuccio quickly, and sensed the unease of the men behind him. 'There's no enmity between us, Baron. Why else would you march against us?'

'Now that's much better. Directness is easier.' He shifted his gaze from one to the other. 'So then, what is your offer?'

Agnolo glanced toward Tuccio and back to Wolf Schwanhals. 'We'd thought that perhaps fifteen thousand florins, with the saving you'd make in men and arms—'

A sudden uproar stopped him as the baron threw back his head and laughed, eliciting yet further guffaws from his knights.

'And we thought to give you free passage through the commune, with provisions to last for a week,' he persisted, provoking more outbursts of mirth.

At last, when the laughter had finally died, Schwanhals levelled a solemn gaze on the Gonfaloniere. 'I'd thought you might have been serious. But I see that you're wasting our time. So, really, there's nothing more to say ...'

Again, Agnolo glanced at the others, then smiled as if at some secret signal between them. 'We were prepared to go as high as—and this includes safe access to the town and up to a month's provisioning—as high as twenty thousand—' But this time the guffaws exploded before he had finished, leaving him red-faced and puffing with shame.

'Really, old man,' said the *condottiere*, wiping

his eyes, 'it would have been better not to have bothered. My men are eager to get paid and move on.' Then he looked at Francesco and Tuccio behind him, and said, voice edged with anger. 'Why should I break a contract, signed with my own good name, for so little more than the cardinal's already offered?'

'Wait then!' urged Tuccio, holding up his hand and taking counsel with God's Eight Good Men, cajoling and remonstrating till further offers were made—twenty-five thousand, twenty-seven with one month's provisions—each provoking a little less mirth and more discussion than the last.

'Name your price then,' cried Tuccio in frustration, attempting to force some commitment. 'Perhaps we can meet it.'

'I put no price on the breaking of contracts,' the baron said with a smile.

Tuccio glared, saying 'Thirty thousand. We can offer no more. Either accept it or attack us. It's all that we have.'

This sum brought no laughter at all, not even a smile, but only a hushed and lengthy debate. Finally Schwanhals turned to the burghers. 'Thirty thousand,' he demanded, 'with unlimited provisions and access to the town.'

God's Eight Good Men now muttered and squabbled, until Agnolo poked up his head and firmly announced, 'Thirty thousand with six weeks' provisions, and access to the town for no more than twenty men at a time.'

Wolf Schwanhals gazed slowly round at his captains, raising his eyebrows.

The cardinal hears bad news and Corvo confronts the cook

ON THE EVENING AFTER GOD'S EIGHT GOOD MEN had parleyed with Wolf Schwanhals, the plains to the north of the cardinal's palace seemed bathed in green light. The trees, which all winter had risen from the fields like huge frozen bloodstreams, now rustled in the warm dusk breeze. Beneath their leaves, a pair of oxen in ornamental yokes came straining down two pathways, their bright gilt harness tinkling in the air, their crimson caparisons and red felt hats giving them the look of Spanish cardinals. Nostrils steaming, shoulders working, each heaved at its towline as Rollo's barge came down the canal like a big toy palazzo. Banners that bore the Madonna, Saint Margaret and Saint Lucy roiled at its sides, and a carven Christopher, larger than a man, seemed to rise from the waves with the bow on his back. Lanterns glowed on the afterdeck and the smoky smells of cooking meats mingled with soft music, for Rollo never travelled light.

The last rays of the sun lit the cabin's slatted window where a group of deacons perched on narrow chairs. The cardinal lolled upon a throne of cushions, face tiger-striped with shadows. 'Dim those lights,' he muttered, and a deacon scurried out, for Rollo was nervous tonight, swaying from elation to despair until the news arrived from Topomagro. He placed his wine upon the table and peered through the shutters, finding nothing but the stillness of the failing light. From the cardinal's private chamber Tozzo was emerging in a shiny crimson gown, stepping from the dark like Rollo's own stretched bones. The cope, which trailed upon the floor when Rollo wore it, barely reached the jester's knees, and he slid about the room with slow, disjointed strides, like some parody of holy ritual. Such actions were worthy of a good whipping. From a hidden inner pocket, the clown produced some baubles, each hurled into the air before he drew another forth. There was a golden sun with an open mouth, a glittering orb, a carven sheaf of wheat, a bishop's mitre, a garnet-crusted sword, the Ghibelline eagle and the lion of the Guelphs, all wrought in miniature, all shining in the light. As Rollo saw them spun, not by a jester's fingers, but by a cardinal towering almost to the ceiling, he saw that Tozzo paid due tribute to his triumph. He felt a sudden lump form in his throat, and unexpected tears in his eyes. For a moment, as he watched this mute performance, he bathed in pure pleasure. Then the barge came to a standstill.

There were footsteps on the gangway, the sound of voices on the afterdeck, and a man he knew from his palace guard was ushered in. The cardinal leaned forward, felt his heart beat faster. This was it—the news of Topomagro's downfall. Yet the man appeared solemn, as if unwilling to approach.

Meanwhile, Tozzo caught each golden object in his pocket, listening on one leg like some ungainly crane while the deacons angled forward in their chairs, eyes bulging with the effort, as if they might read the messenger's lips. There was the man's muttered voice, the deliquescent patterns on the ceiling, and the changeless phrases, 'the *condottiere*', 'bought off', 'by the commune', and the cardinal's face aghast.

'Bought off?' he cried, skin sweating with a sheen of watery lights.

The messenger, uneasy, faced the silent room. 'Not a single blow was struck.'

The jester disappeared, though no-one noticed him at first, until one turned, and another, as the whole room slowly sensed his presence at their backs. There, by some actor's trick, he'd hitched himself in Rollo's doorway, a cardinal in crimson samite hanging by the neck.

Rollo breathed a bubbling snarl. 'Too far, Tozzo. This time too far.' He beckoned to the guards who stood before the entrance. 'Since he likes to get out of his depth, we'll throw the cretin overboard.' And they came bustling through, tearing the jester down from his perch and dragging him out to the deck. The cardinal swayed to his feet, upsetting his wine, lunging to see how Tozzo squirmed as they flung him over the side.

He almost reclined on the surface, his robe a bright red lily, till suddenly this mute, who'd climbed up curtains, walls, the very air, went scrabbling in panic at the fragile foam and vanished with a gurgle.

•

When the cardinal was away, the servants became masters of his palace. While some revelled in this freedom, others saw it as their mission to ferret out those miscreants who took advantage of his absence. One such crusader was Strappo the cook. Not that this cramped Brother Corvo's style, or that of several others on the kitchen staff. For here they were—Corvo, Fiducia and Speranza—reeling after dinner by the blazing oven. Strappo had gone with one of the swineherds to examine a boar he'd been fattening for a banquet, and was not expected back for some time yet. Meanwhile, Corvo had conscripted some bottles from the cellar, until, tired of wine, they'd opened a jeroboam of aqua vitae. Now they sprawled as near to the oven as they could—having devoured a whole hare between them—and stared into the dying fire as if cajoling visions from the embers. Fiducia started chuckling and tumbled off her stool.

'Ooh, I feel so light, like I could swirl up to the ceiling.' She waved a hand before her eyes and watched her twirling fingers.

'It's not the aqua vitae,' said Speranza. 'It's this grease of Naso's. It makes you feel light-headed.'

'The drink, the oil,' he murmured. 'They don't *make* you feel any way at all. They just allow it.'

Fiducia made no effort to get up off the floor, but simply flopped against the stones. 'If I was the cardinal,' she smiled, 'I'd drink my cellars dry within the week.' Frowning, she gazed down at the flagstones. 'I'd make a mess of my religion.'

'Well, if wine's the blood of Christ, it's a holy thing to do.' Brother Corvo raised the jeroboam like a monstrance in the air. 'And aqua vitae is the Holy Spirit.'

'Oh, Naso, you say the wickedest things,' Speranza giggled. The ointment on her skin was glistening in the blaze. 'Such wine must have the blessing of a priest.'

'I am your priest, Speranza, and the wine is blessed by me.' He made a ragged Cross upon the air. 'The Church says mortify the flesh and glorify the soul, yet it does nothing but *deny* the flesh. Wine, herbs and voluptuousness—these lay bare the spirit through subversion of the body.'

'Well then, Naso, I want to bare my soul.' Speranza stretched toward him, while Fiducia, cackling, drained her cup.

'The body is a fortress with five portals,' he continued, paying her no mind, 'each leading down a separate pathway. Only when we have besieged that fortress, torn down the walls and made the pathways one will we find the single spirit that resides within.'

Speranza raised his spattered smock and gripped his narrow pizzle. 'Is this the way, Naso?' she said softly, as he took a mouthful of the fiery liquor, chuckling all the while, at the very moment that the cook came through the door.

Strappo didn't waste a second, stumping past the benches, bellowing, 'I've got you now, you lechers!' He pulled a cleaver off the wall, not pausing in his stride, and rushed at Brother Corvo. 'Trouble,' Strappo cried, 'nothing but trouble. I knew it the minute I set eyes on you.' Corvo slipped out of Speranza's grip, drawing a blade from under his tunic as he darted round the fire to the far side of the oven. 'Well, Naso, I'll give it to you now.'

Fiducia scrambled to her feet, and Speranza tried to grab the cook's thick arm, but he flung her off and bustled forward. He snatched a brand up from the fire, rushing at the scullion with the cleaver raised, the flame held out before him. Corvo stood his ground, spitting like a cat, showering the cook with aqua vitae. The brand flared blue, and Strappo roared as flames snaked up his sleeve. He jerked his arm away, but Corvo was already brandishing the jeroboam, basting the cook with brandy till his clothes ignited. He twirled before the oven like a fat blue flame, then rolled along the floor.

'Like roasted pig,' snapped Corvo, grabbing both the women. The cook writhed, squealing, and they reeled into the night beyond the rear door.

In which Jacopo comes to Topomagro

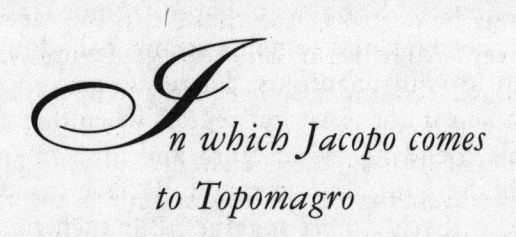

IT'S AFTER TWO NIGHTS OF SLEEPING OUT ON THE HILLS that Jacopo comes down to Topomagro. He wends his way up the dusty south road, approaching the squalid camps that have filled the ravines beneath the walls since the vagrants' expulsion from town. The warm sun, the green hills at his back, the towers, domes and campanili all induce him to ignore the pauper encampments and march on regardless. The tents of the army remain in the east, and he's heard of the peace between the commune and Schwanhals. The *condottiere* is now a guest of the Priors, who have given him a lavish reception to honour the truce.

Jacopo smiles at the thought of this feast, and Scimmi stirs in her pouch, one paw emerging, her small claws extended. He nuzzles her neck with his fingers, which she grips then releases, beginning to purr. If he didn't have Scimmi ... He glances behind at the gentle hills, sheep dotting their summits like clover, and considers his time as a shepherd, then shakes his head clear of the memory. He seems to be suffering a plague of such memories—scraping salt in Hyères, the circus in Sicily, even those wormy discussions in Kaffa with Lapo Tromba—as if so much travelling and so many strangers had peopled his world with phantoms. There are also thoughts which he cannot resist but regrets when they come, like his friendship with Laura and the games with her children, and how it might all have turned out if they'd reached port together. But such thoughts are now pointless, so he puts them quickly aside. He thinks often of Lippo, too, chuckling over the friar's cheap tricks and his talent for turning junk into wonders and then into cash. The man was a rogue and, indeed, if he'd eaten the cat Jacopo wouldn't have scrupled to open his gizzard. Yet, as time has gone by, he's come to regard him with humour, not anger, and even to view his techniques and speeches as possible sidelines of his own. Perhaps Topomagro, compared with the poorer lands to the south, might be the place to test his new skills.

He nears the Porta Santa Maria, where there's a clamour of peasants and merchants, paupers and soldiers, all crowded together in a great melee. Jacopo has heard that, with their restocked granaries and brighter hopes of peace and order, the Priors have eased the entry restrictions, creating false hopes in the hearts of those paupers expelled during winter. He walks past the lean-tos lining the road, squeezing his way through the tight crush of bodies, caressing a purse or two as he goes.

A man on a tall, covered cart and a youth with a barrow of turnips, go through. The throng surges forward, carrying with it a small group of beggars who gape at the gatekeepers. Their spokesman, a large-framed man with a tumour on his neck, speaks to the first of the half-dozen soldiers. 'Surely you've heard the answer already,' the gateman replies, raising his voice as if to inform whole tribes of the deaf. 'Unless you can find a land-holding patron to vouch for you, you can't get in without showing proof of business.'

One of the beggars holds out his bowl like a letter of introduction. 'Go on, get off!' shouts the soldier, at which the beggars start to protest and are shoved aside by the rest of the crowd that brays its derision. There's a general pushing and jostling from which, almost to his surprise, Jacopo emerges in front of the guards. 'Well?' the soldier demands with a querulous grunt. Jacopo has not thought this through. 'Well—' he begins as the guard looks him haughtily up and down, saying, 'You don't look like you've got any business in town, or anywhere else for that matter.' He makes to thrust him aside, but halts at a cry from above.

'Ser Jacopo!' says the voice. 'Ser Jacopo!'

All peer up at the wall's castellations, where the parapet holds not only soldiers but well-attired merchants and a smattering of clerics, each hoping to usher some friend through the fray.

'Ser Jacopo, you're here at last.'

This time Jacopo can see the speaker, along with everyone else, since he's leaning over the parapet, shouting at the gatekeepers, 'No, no, signori, do not turn that man away. He's a most important visitor to the city,' at which the big soldier, looking nonplussed, glances sideways at Jacopo. 'Wait,' cries the voice, 'I'll come right down,' and it's no time at all till Lippo's there, throwing wide his arms, declaring, 'Ser Jacopo,' as he totters across to embrace him.

The friar looks well, as if he's been eating heartily, and Jacopo has to restrain his amazement as Lippo grips his shoulders and says, 'You're looking thin, Ser Jacopo. All that fasting, I suppose.'

'Ah, yes, indeed,' he answers, feeling his way. 'It's been quite ... well ... rigorous.'

'Excuse me, Friar,' the guard interrupts, 'but what is this man's business?' He turns back to Jacopo. 'Just what is your business in Topomagro?'

'Well—'

'He's on a pilgrimage,' Lippo replies, as if stunned by the soldier's ignorance. 'Surely you can see that.' When the man just stares at him blankly, he adds: 'He's Ser Jacopo Passero, one-time notary to the Signoria of Arezzo, now one of the most powerful merchants in Civitavecchia. He owns any number of ships used by men like, well ... Tuccio di Piero Landucci, to name just one.'

The soldier stares at the ragged man, amazed.

'I was given this penance of fasting and pilgrimage by the bishop,' says Jacopo, head bowed as if in shame. 'If you require further explanation than this, then you'll simply have to turn me away. For I would never sully a lady's name.'

'Turn you away? Ser Jacopo Passero turned away? Just think of the Priors' reaction.' Fra Lippo gives an incredulous giggle. 'Of course they won't turn you away.' He peers sharply at the gatekeepers, who shuffle uncertainly.

'Come, good sir,' he continues, throwing an arm round Jacopo's shoulder and drawing him on to the gateway. 'The bishop's penance might be a hard one, yet it would surely not preclude your staying with our brethren at the Abbey San Francesco. We have old times to discuss ... and new ones as well.'

With one quick glance at Scimmi's pouch, he gives Jacopo a grin, leading him on past the guards and into the town.

A Sport of Kings

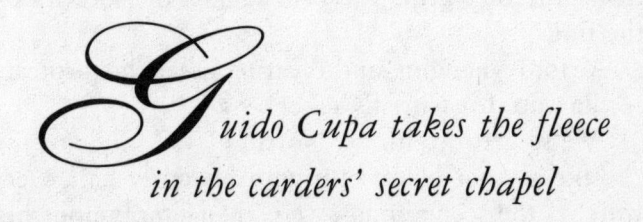

Guido Cupa takes the fleece in the carders' secret chapel

'CEPPO CASTRACANI,' ANNOUNCES GERI PINZA, running his finger down the register of misdemeanours, 'for brawling with your fellow carders, five *grossi*.'

'I wouldn't brawl if they didn't provoke me,' Ceppo protests, an accusatory hand flung out at the others around the big table.

There are bleatings, catcalls and neighings. Fists, cups, the hilts of knives pound the table.

'Come on, Ceppo, pay up!'

'No welching, Ceppo!'

'Five *grossi*, there's a good lad!'

'Increase the fine, Geri!'

Ceppo shakes his head and digs the silver coins out of his purse, then reaches across the table to drop them in the box before the shop's three ancients. Alfredo Crostadura, playing the court tipstaff, leads him solemnly back to his seat through a madhouse of shouts and whistles.

Geri looks up sternly. 'Nofri Pasquini,' he says slowly. 'For insulting the *cappella*'s good name, seven *grossi*.'

'Seven *grossi*?' cries Nofri, wrenching his arm

from Alfredo's grip. 'I appeal against the severity of the fine.'

A riot of banging and bleating greets his protest.

'Pay up, for Christ's sake!'

'We're getting thirsty, Nofri!'

Like a stout black ram with his curly hair, Geri watches the scene impassively, then simply nods his head. Nofri turns to Ciuto di Dino and the other two ancients, all seated on Geri's right.

'I have never insulted the *cappella*'s good name,' he cries, arms flung theatrically wide.

'It's said you told a pair of dyers from the shop of Bernardo Zoppo that you could outdrink any dyer in Topomagro.' There's a chorus of agreement round the table, but Geri folds his arms, unmoved. 'You were also heard to add that this was more than you could say for most of your fellow carders.'

All hell breaks loose, cries of outrage, howlings, death threats. Geri looks on, poker-faced, considering their tiny *cappella*. What else can they do but keep it as small and secret as possible, forbidden as they are to join a guild, to hold office, even to form a poor man's confraternity? So here's their little chapel of Saint Blaise, which no man may insult with impunity, whether in jest or in his cups.

'I was talking about the carders of Siena, where I worked for a few years. You should know that, Geri.' Yet he doesn't look at Geri Pinza, keeping his eyes firmly fixed on the ancients, who are huddled in conference.

At last, Ciuto di Dino pokes up his head. 'It is the considered opinion of this appeals tribunal, Nofri, that you pay the fine with a surcharge of one *grosso* for taking up the court's time.' He bangs his hand down on the table amidst cheering and guffaws. 'Eight *grossi*.'

Muttering, Nofri tosses the coins in the box, returning to his seat through volleys of back-slapping as Geri considers how much their treasury now contains. Yes, almost fifty *grossi*, about enough for a decent banquet after Guido's contribution. He knows how important all this is, these rough feasts, the laughter and, above all, the ceremony—perhaps it is their only means of strength. But, first and foremost, there is Guido's taking of the fleece. He stands and nods to Alfredo Crostadura, who ambles round the table till he's at young Guido's side. For the first time that afternoon, silence falls upon the carders, and Geri can briefly hear the hubbub from the tavern down below. Then Ciuto di Dino is placing the fleece in his arms, and Alfredo is leading the boy toward him.

Now the silence is shattered again by hooting and bleating.

'Make it a black one, Geri!'

'He likes black ewes!'

'Especially when they belong to Signor Tuccio!'

Geri raises his arms with their burden of wool, and the room goes quiet once more. They're speaking of Lucia, one of Tuccio di Piero Landucci's black slaves. He watches Guido Cupa as he saunters toward him. The boy is certainly well made—pale, handsome, robust—with looks like a noble's, even in carder's clogs. He's popular too for one so junior, and his grin keeps flashing, though he tries to suppress it, as he passes each muttered jibe.

Perhaps, as they say, the slave *is* besotted, though it's more likely carders' gossip.

With the fleece draped over his forearms, Geri extends his hands. The boy moves forward, urged by the tipstaff, till he stands at the fleece and allows his hands to be taken. Geri looks steadily into his eyes. 'Guido Cupa,' he booms, 'it has been decided by those most senior in this *cappella* that you are ready to take the fleece.' He makes no attempt to release the boy. 'But, firstly, you must strengthen that allegiance you swore when first you entered our membership. Will you do so?'

'I will,' says Guido slowly, while Geri holds his hands and his eyes, almost daring him to smile at these echoes of marriage. Indeed, it is the *cappella* he will wed.

'Do you swear never to reveal the nature of this brotherhood to anyone outside it, nor to betray its members in word or deed, nor to accept less for your work than others at your level in the shed? Do you swear by Saint Blaise, who was torn apart by the metal teeth of combs and cards which are the tools of our labour?'

'I swear by Saint Blaise.'

'Do you swear to support all actions agreed to by your brothers to improve the lot of the *cappella*, to do all you can to subvert those injunctions of merchants and foremen which will harm your brothers, and to do your best to support any brother unfairly dismissed from the shed? Do you swear by Saint Blaise, who was torn apart by the metal teeth of combs and cards which are the tools of our labour?'

'I swear by Saint Blaise.'

The litany proceeds, the carders looking on dreamily, some remembering when *they* took the fleece, some considering the beautiful Lucia, all growing thirsty and thinking of the feast. At last they hear Geri saying, 'Do you swear to join your brothers in whatever brawls they meet, to outdrink the members of any other craft in Topomagro, and to fuck whatever women, fair or foul, that you are able? Do you so swear?'

Amid a sudden shouting uproar, Guido smiles and cries, 'I swear!' while Geri drapes the fleece across his shoulders, and old Ciuto places cards with metal teeth in both his hands. From the cupboard at his back, Alfredo produces a jug of wine with which he charges—in fact, barely moistens—the vessels of all those present. They cheer and toast the boy, draining their cups at a sip. Geri cocks an eyebrow till Guido remembers, digging three days' pay out of his purse to drop into the box, and the others lumber forward to make some minor contribution.

'Alfredo, Luca, Guccio,' cries Geri. 'Food and drink for the feast.' He hands the box to Alfredo, who sweeps down the stairs to the tavern, followed by Luca and Guccio and half-a-dozen others.

Later, when the tavern has grown quiet, the carders are still roistering. To be sure, some lie sprawled in corners, and Nofri Pasquini, king of the drinkers, has flung back his head on his chair as if to crack the ceiling with his snoring. Remnants of roast mutton are scattered round the room like a puzzle to be reconstructed; a pair of cats have leapt up onto the table where chicken bones, picked clean, lie piecemeal. Guido, who'd sat for a time in honour with the ancients, reclines among his peers, the fleece now packed away.

'You know,' says Luca Peroni, 'when *we* went down to get the food—'

'Thank you, Luca,' puts in Guido, and everybody laughs, since Luca's mentioned this point several times.

'No, really,' he insists, 'you should have seen the withered-up old ewe they tried to sell as mutton. And the chickens? Talk about boilers. I'd rather try to eat old Ciuto.'

'So what did you do?'

'Oh, well,' says Luca, raising up a little in his chair, 'Alfredo just told them they could save such rubbish for the dyers. He said we weren't washers or scourers, that carders ate the finest cuts, and that we'd go somewhere else if they couldn't do any better. So the butcher says, as meek and mild as anything, "Oh, I didn't realise you were carders. We get a lot of teazlers here." Then Alfredo says, "Yeah, I hear they like it raw," and the butcher scurries off to find the best cuts in the shop.'

'Raw,' laughs Ceppo Castracani, 'that's a good one.' He casts a crafty eye on Guido. 'Not like Guido. He likes his mutton well done.'

'That's right,' smirks another, 'very well done. Sort of charred.'

'Black, you might say.'

Guido once again attempts to make light of the reference to Lucia, but this time his smile seems cool with boredom or fatigue, and silence falls upon them.

Meanwhile, at the far end of the table, Alfredo Crostadura pokes his thin, bent beak at Geri Pinza's ear: 'How much longer do you think we can afford these feasts, Geri? Some of their objections to the fines seemed only half playful.'

'And yet they found the money.' Geri watches the figure that his finger's tracing in a pool of wine. 'They sense as well as we do that the feasts are necessary.'

'Perhaps. But necessary or not, you can't get water when the well runs dry.' His mouth turns downward in a frown. 'Our money buys a little less each month. Sure, they say the cardinal's gone mad, riding up and down his bit of a canal as harmless as a fool. But he was the *merchants*' problem. *Ours* are just starting. These taxes for the loans the Priors borrowed for their bribe ... To support the feast, some men have to starve.'

'I know that too, Alfredo.'

'Even the fishermen complain,' the man is muttering, 'as if the famine extended to the sea itself.'

'Yes, yes ... we've talked about it many times.' Geri places a hand on his companion's arm. 'Things will have to change. But the only way for us to play our part is for the *cappella* to keep going as it is.'

'Well, that's true enough. But it won't keep going unless something happens fast.'

Geri sighs and rolls his eyes up at the ceiling. 'Something will happen,' he says slowly. 'Believe me, something will.'

•

The bells of compline are ringing in the squat campanile of Santa Maria delle Ruote. The small, slim figure in the cloak of *romagnolo* slips like a wraith across the bridge toward the dyers' quarter, the face a shadow beneath the rough wool, so that only the eyes gleam whitely in the darkness. The five great gates have long been shut, enclosing the town in its nightly prison; the curfew, so much more strictly enforced since the trouble with the nobles, has forbidden trespass on the streets since vespers. Lucia pulls the fabric tight about her and darts into the gloom beneath the dyers' shops. If she were caught by the watch she would be birched, and Tuccio, embarrassed by her actions, would punish her as well. So why is she taking such a risk, sneaking from her master's house, abandoning her duties, roaming through forbidden streets? Why, for Guido Cupa of course. The very mention of his name, the merest thought of him, makes something in her stomach twist and turn, her heart leap up, as if it were some creature not her own that would escape into the air. He is so lovely with his loose black curls and pearly skin, so hard and lithe, that she wants, even now, in the middle of these fearsome streets, to wind about his body like a cat.

Yet she is unhappy. Where, before, he made a show of the dangers he would face to meet her—sometimes at the merchant's house itself—now it's always she who takes the risks, who makes the effort to find the times that will suit him. She peers round her at the houses rising from the street like crooked teeth, the gaps between them breathing out the stench of foul latrines and rotting food. The Borgo Santa Caterina is not a quarter that she's used to; whereas, once, Guido tried to keep his poverty concealed as much as possible, now he doesn't seem to care. It's not that he is cruel or brutal, just indifferent, which, in its way, is worse. She hurries on toward the carding shed, convinced that nothing seems to work for her at present. She has made an image of his heart from wax, thinking of him as she melted it. She has killed a dove from Gaia's columbarium, and touched its blood to Guido's chest as she embraced him. Today she's paid a sum that she can scant afford to buy a consecrated host—stolen from a church and scribbled with her name—which she must somehow have him eat. But her faith in all these methods has been shaken, since he continues to grow distant.

At last she reaches the long, low carding shed beside the river. She skirts the wet stairs where the wool is washed and scoured, passes the spare stretching frames against the wooden walls, and enters the far courtyard where his hut abuts the shed's south-eastern end. It's little more than a lean-to in the mud-rutted yard, a place where the poorest, least senior of the carders can be on hand at dawn to let the others in. She raps the dry planks, fumbles at the small cloth pouch that holds the wafer, knocks again. For a moment she panics as the thought occurs to her that Guido might be there with someone else. Then the door jerks open and he's staring out, eyes wide. 'Lucia!' he says, and adds, as if remembering, 'Yes, you said you'd come.'

'Well, give me a warmer greeting than that,' she laughs, falling over the threshold and surprising his arms into catching her. 'I've braved the watch for you.'

'Oh, what a heart!' he says while she wets his face with kisses. 'I've never known a braver—' but she stops him with her mouth, her fingers wriggling up beneath his shirt until he leaps back, laughing. 'Stop it, Lucia, your hands are cold.'

'But not my heart.' She gives a look that's like an accusation, till he moves to take her to him, though he takes her cloak instead.

'No, not that,' he says softly, touching his lips to her neck, so she shivers a little and holds him once again. Slowly he draws away, watching as she stands in clogs and cotton shift. He sees her sombre throat and arms, smiling to himself.

'What?' she asks.

'Oh, nothing,' he just smiles.

'*What?*' she demands, arms akimbo, play-acting now—the role she knows he likes.

'Well, I'm not really sure how brave it is for you to dodge the watch.'

'*You* do it, then.'

'But in the night, Lucia, when there isn't any moon. Blink and close your mouth, and hup! you're gone. Open up again and there we have the moon and two big stars.' She smiles a long, soft smile. 'There, just like now, you see.'

'Well, you should talk,' she says, running a finger up his arm. 'You could vanish too, in the right situation.' She traces the light blue vein at his biceps. 'Say, in marble.'

'Flatterer,' he grins, then skips away to light a second candle from that already lit upon the table.

'You're always slipping away from me!' she cries, and gives a sudden grin, yet thrusts her hands behind her back to hide their trembling.

'Slipping away from you?'

'Yes,' she ventures. 'It's got so hard to see you. And when I do, you always ... slip away. Just like then.'

'Ooooh ...' And he comes toward her, holding out his arms.

'No, I mean it, Guido.' She tries to push him from her.

'Now who's slipping away?'

'No, I'm not. I just want you to tell me if you're sick of me.'

'Sick of you?' He makes to hold her once again, then stops, letting his arms fall. Watching for a moment, as if weighing something up, he slowly shakes his head. 'No, I'm not sick of you. It's just that everything's so hard now.' He leans against the table. 'I'm up so early every morning to let the carders in. Then I work all day till late ... but I just don't earn enough any more. Maybe if I didn't have to rent the combs. Everybody's trying to get a bit of extra money.' Guido sighs and shrugs his shoulders, glances at her sidelong. 'That master of yours really wants his pound of flesh.'

She reaches out to him, squeezing tight. 'I'm sorry,' she says, voice muffled in his shoulder. 'Tuccio's such an old miser.'

Grinning, he pulls away. 'Well ... he treats you well enough.'

'Just see what'd happen if he found I wasn't sleeping in the kitchen with Ambra and the others.'

'Oh,' and he traces the outline of her fingers with his own, 'you make me feel like a coward. I'll come to you next time, like we've done before, in the cellar of the storehouse.'

'It's too risky, too easy to get caught.' He couldn't have chosen a less inviting option. 'It's better in the cloisters of Santa Maria dei Poveri.'

'Yes, I suppose you're right.' It's like he's suddenly grown bored with the whole thing. 'We wouldn't want to be caught by Signor Tuccio.' He looks up quickly. 'Or that daughter of his, the one who told you off when I was there to get those bales the other day ... Gaia, isn't it? She seems like a real bitch.'

'Guido!' she chuckles, surprised by his vehemence. 'She hasn't done anything to you.'

'No, but I hate the ones like her. You'd think they were the Mother of God the way they look down on everybody else, sitting up in their loggias on their fat arses.' He stares Lucia in the eyes, his perfect features twisted in a perfect sneer. 'I mean it, I can't stand them.'

'I know,' she laughs, then sees a chance to gain his favour. 'I think Tuccio feels that way himself at times.'

'What do you mean?' he says, half smiling.

'Well, with this wedding coming up, she's been so fussy about everything. The clothes aren't right, and then the plans for the banquet, and who's been invited, or the gifts they'll be given. There's arguments all the time. And Tuccio's so moody.

Sometimes he's nicer than I've ever seen him, and sometimes it's like he wants to forget the whole thing.'

'Really?' he grins, then brushes her cheek and shakes his head slowly. 'Don't worry, there'll be a wedding all right. Probably the richest the town's ever seen. He'll starve his carders and washers. He'll cut us back to the bone. But he'll spend a fortune on her. He'll spend what he steals from us on that bitch, and on her fop as well. You can be sure of that.'

His anger is suddenly so harsh it makes her uneasy. She tries to soften his mood. 'But it *will* be beautiful. You should see the cloth for her dress.'

'A sow in samite,' he laughs. 'Well, maybe someone should teach them a lesson. Maybe they should—'

'Don't be stupid, Guido. If I'd thought you were going to be like this I wouldn't have told you.

Seeing the fear in her eyes, he holds her more closely. 'I won't say anything,' he whispers, 'I won't do anything, not if you don't want me to,' and runs his hands beneath her shift, along her smooth, slim thighs, while she blows both candles out and casts the shift aside.

'Not fair,' he's laughing, 'open your eyes, I can't see you.' Then she bites him on the chest—'Ow! Not your mouth, your eyes—' as she tears away his shirt and lays him on the table, pressing her mouth to his. 'Mmmpf ... what's that, Lucia?'

'A piece of bread that I was chewing,' she hisses in his ear. 'Now eat it up like a good little boy.'

In which Brother Corvo finds disciples

DUSK SEEPED FAINTLY THROUGH THE LEAVES. BROTHER Corvo sailed through the tunnelled dark with Speranza and Fiducia in his wake, and a light breeze brushed the upper branches like the passing of a spirit. Speranza smiled and Fiducia whimpered faintly; Corvo, with his greasy smock and hair, seemed like a pauper wizard marching through the night. He had gathered purslane, the roots and berries of black nightshade, foxglove leaves and other weeds he had not named, as both the women—apprentices attentive to his every move—watched him crush and sift and macerate his gleanings by a brook. Some he kept entire, and others cast aside but for a few small fragments, then mixed them with a paste he kept within a pouch beneath his robes. At his urging, the women had licked the bitter mixture from his fingers, while he himself had sucked away the final smearings. Now the forest came and went in long, slow breaths, swirling by like centuries of silent rain, then fixing in a moment as a leaf, a stone, a twisted root of startling clarity. At times the air above them seemed to roar like some great force, yet when they looked, there were the steady branches and the frozen sky.

Brother Corvo said nothing as they went, but hummed a tuneless monotone till the first pale stars that shone amongst the leaves were shimmering with his voice. They came into a clearing and at its centre was a tree. The women reeled beneath it, staring at its branches where strange white flowers bloomed. As they watched, they saw that these weren't blossoms but countless pallid hands, punctured through their centre like the hands of Christ, each holding in its palm a drop of blood. Then—though it was difficult to say just when—he thrust his knife into the tree trunk's side, and after seconds long enough for darkness to have fallen, they saw the hands close tight as if they withered. Then Corvo urged them on.

At last they left the forest for the dark of moonless fields. Here everything seemed devastation, for the *condottiere*'s hired soldiers were no longer in his service and scavenged through the countryside in roaming bands. Crops trodden underfoot, dead animals, a smouldering barn, rose in silhouette beside the road. Speranza and Fiducia hesitated, huddled at the centre of the open fields; but Corvo marched right on and they made haste to follow. At one point they came upon a copse of trees as bulky as a castle in the dark. He stopped there as if listening, then darted off into the night, only to return some minutes later with a Minorite's long cowl.

'Was—' began Speranza, 'was it a dead friar there, Naso?'

He turned slowly, brushing soil from the rough garment. 'Not Naso, Speranza. Corvo,' he said softly, though somehow she felt frightened. 'Brother Corvo.'

'*Brother* Corvo?' Fiducia spluttered—the beginning of a giggle—but now he was approaching and with each step he seemed to loom until his shadowed face leaned over them. Fiducia gave a queasy smile and said no more. Speranza took her arm, while Corvo turned and hurried on as if he had some destination, his habit billowing behind him.

Some time later, as a huge full moon began to lift its broken face above the meadows, Speranza panted at his back: 'Hey, Nas ... uh, Brother Corvo ... have you ... taken vows then?' He wheeled round briefly and she thought she saw a sickle grin within the hood. He swung back to the road in silence, and she added, 'Or is this some kind of trick? A false identity?'

'A false identity?' replied the back, rippling with the moving air. 'I was Naso, now I'm Corvo. Neither one is false.'

She scurried to catch up, her head now swimming soporifically behind her. 'But have you really taken holy orders?'

'Holy?' Brother Corvo chuckled. 'Oh no, there's nothing holy about them.'

'What do you mean?' puffed Fiducia, striving to keep pace.

'I mean,' said Corvo, 'that Holy Mother Church is just like any other mother. Part saint, part whore, part fool, and her goodness springs mostly from her self-forgetfulness.'

'Now that's the old Naso,' laughed Speranza, then glanced up sharply. 'That is, I mean—'

'Yes, yes, I know what you mean.' As if in punishment, he made his stride still longer. When he spoke again, it was in a voice that sounded muffled up in thoughts. 'The Church teaches of an endless war for power between good and evil, light and dark, God and Lucifer. The Cathars, reviled and now destroyed, spoke more coherently of a struggle between spirit and gross matter, God and Antigod. Unfortunately, neither Church nor Catharists are right, for both have chosen the wrong side.'

Speranza stared as if the scales had fallen from her eyes. 'You mean,' she said, half in horror and half in fascination, 'to choose the Devil?'

'In a sense,' he chuckled, slowing his pace and gazing sideways down at her. 'For weren't the Cathars right to deem the spirit good and matter evil, since all our ills, including death itself, arise from that gross stuff? It is the God of the Jews and the Church, this maker and taker of the flesh, who creates the world's evil. In fact His adversary—the Cathar's Antigod—is the Lord of goodness and the spirit. Mother Church, who thinks she worships the face of God upon His Cross, has got it wrong. Indeed, she worships His arse, and your Devil is quite other than you think.'

'I don't understand you,' sighed Fiducia, stifling a yawn.

'No,' Speranza added. 'When we were working for the cardinal, you said that we should take the ways of the flesh.'

'Urge them to exhaustion,' leered Fiducia.

'I did,' he grinned, moving along more spryly now. 'And I still do. The only means to overcome the carnal is to know it, and revile the God who took its form. For we are tied inexorably to the flesh, and only through its bewilderment will we find the spirit's path.'

He stopped abruptly, neither talking nor moving, but staring at the moon above the fields. Speranza felt awhirl with all these words and herbs. She gazed at Brother Corvo, whose head seemed circled by a lunar halo. She had never known another like him.

'Come on,' he said, and marched off once again as if he led some grand crusade as yet inchoate, to a place still unrevealed. His muddled conscripts stumbled after him through field and woodland, coppice and embankment, until they came upon a broken, harsh terrain where men had quarried deep for metal. The moon reflected green in pools among the rocks, covering the ditches and the stony outcrops with a patina of verdigris. The ground was littered with a scree of stones through which they picked their way, the women's minds still swimming with his words, when suddenly a double roaring erupted from a ditch below the road. Two great black dogs, eyes whiter than the moon, maws red and torn with snarls, came leaping up the rocks toward them.

'Bulfas! Moloch!' cried a high, thin voice. 'Get here, you mongrels!'

The creatures skittered sideways at its sound. Their growling turned to whines of protest. Yet 'here' was almost where they stood, for a figure was emerging from that pit of shadow, illumined by the moonlight. And if Speranza could have thrust it back she would have done so, since it seemed to her that she was witnessing some imp come up from

Hell. She saw the visage of a grotesque crone, as pallid as the moon, with a cobweb of deep furrows where two black spiders sat. She watched those eyes go scuttling toward Corvo while the dogs came cringing round. He, however, said nothing for some moments, gazing downward at the ditch with a small abstracted smile. The woman knotted the opening of a sack, which she thrust beneath her clothes. Speranza followed Corvo's gaze into the pit, her heart now knocking at her ribs. Deep within that dark the shadows coalesced, and there she seemed to see the outline of a woman, her outspread legs unravelling a cord that twisted round the neck of her dead child. Neither moved until, with another subtle shift, the shadows became formless once again. Then the voice of Corvo said, 'Your name ... what is it?'

'Maria,' the woman answered, bending a little beneath his gaze, then said no more.

'Maria,' he repeated, savouring the name, 'would you join us? We are looking for the spirit's kingdom.' When she cocked an ear, yet still said nothing, he added, 'We can always find a place for someone of your skills.'

She smiled coquettishly, then said, 'Why not? I've naught else planned,' so that Speranza shivered and Fiducia coughed till Corvo waved them on. The dogs—tall Bulfas and black Moloch—raced into the night as if at his command.

It was at dusk a few days later that they came upon the group of wanderers. There were perhaps twenty of them seated in a clearing, some muttering together, most staring at the ground or air before them as if into some private desolation. All were thin, a number barely more than skull and limbs and ribcage with a tissue of grey skin; it seemed to Speranza that some graveyard might have been dug up there and its whispering citizens made to mimic life by the play of leaves and light. There was, however, a sluggish stirring in their ranks when Corvo strode amongst them, followed by Maria and the two great dogs. He waited at the centre of the clearing where Bulfas sniffed and Moloch snarled until the bones flinched back, afraid. He lowered his hood and his long, lank hair went streaming down his shoulders.

'Look at you all, lying there like corpses!' he bellowed, so that both the beasts, excited by his tone, began to bite the air. 'What has brought you to this hopelessness?' he asked, softening his words to see them cringe back from the dogs. At first there was no answer, and he leant a little closer down amongst them, saying, 'I mean it. Why such misery when the Kingdom is at hand?'

Again there were the rows of lowered eyes, until someone at the far edge of the crowd said, 'Kingdom?' looking round at his companions for support. 'What bloody kingdom? Unless you call getting chased from every town in Tuscany a kingdom. You'd be hopeless too if you were poor like us.'

'Poor?' roared Brother Corvo, and again the dogs went mad. 'It's the poverty of our thoughts that makes us poor.' Suddenly a brilliant stone appeared in his hand, some kind of ruby or carnelian of enormous size, palmed at Rollo's palace. 'There is a kingdom in the west where I plucked this from a stream.'

The setting sun blazed in its heart, and the vagrants gaped to see it. 'What?' said one. 'What kingdom?'

'The Kingdom of the Spirit,' he replied, watching how the stone was sparkling in the light. 'A place with riches equal to the wealth we hold within us. And I want you to come with me to find it.'

'Of the spirit?' said the one who'd spoken first, his voice, though cowed, betraying the first signs of mockery.

'Yes, the spirit,' Corvo cried, hurling the jewel away into the air—or at least they saw the glitter of its path toward the sun—while Bulfas chased beneath it. 'A place of fleshly plenitude where the loaves are white as clouds and the sea so full of food that no-one swims there but simply lies upon the water and rides the backs of fish.' There were chuckles from the crowd and hints of interest kindled in their eyes. 'This is no story. There is a kingdom to the west—I have been there numerous times—where the pigs are so glutted with fine truffles that they turn up their snouts at an apple. And as for the people, their hearts are so generous that they make their gnocchi out of butter and tie their vines with sausage.' His audience had dreamy looks upon their faces, attempting to remember or imagine how these foods might taste. 'It is a place worth seeking. I would lead you there to help you find such riches.'

As he spoke this final word he held his hand

aloft, displaying the very jewel he'd cast away. The crowd gasped its amazement.

'I—I've been to the west,' said the sceptic at the rear. 'There are farmers there, like elsewhere, to chase you off their lands.'

'No-one will dare to chase you now!' cried Corvo in a voice that brooked no doubt. 'Who would deny the riches of the earth to the people of the earth? Come, take up sticks and staffs along the way and follow me.'

For a moment he stood before them, watching as they muttered—'He might be right,' and 'Well, it can't do any harm,' and 'What have we got to lose?'—then swung upon his heel, almost with contempt, marching westward with Maria, Moloch, the returning Bulfas, Speranza and Fiducia, until the crowd lurched stiffly to their feet in threes and fours to trail along behind.

As luck would have it, after they had travelled for some time beneath the trees, following the road into the hills, they came upon an isolated farmhouse in the midst of sloping fields. The light had all but vanished from the sky, and a purple-coloured dusk remained to show them a small orchard filled with apples like pale globes beneath the leaves. Higher in the hills there were the bushy silhouettes of olive trees, a slope of leafy vines and, down below the road, beside the lamplit windows of the farmhouse, a field of rustling hemp.

'Well, come on, don't be timid,' Corvo laughed, pointing at the apples with his stave. 'The earth was made to feed its people.' As if they'd lacked for nothing else but a command, the crowd surged forward over the stone fence and down into the orchard, where they fell like locusts on the trees. At first they were a little circumspect, each taking an apple, maybe two, muttering and munching as if to keep a secret. But soon they grew more bold, clambering in the treetops, shaking the branches, laughing and shouting one to another in the dark, as Corvo cried, 'Go on, eat up, there's lots for all.'

Then lights—a trinity of lanterns—came drifting from the farmhouse. First one and then another of the crowd began to notice, till each stopped eating, some half turning to the road as if to run. Corvo burst out laughing. 'Go on, keep eating. No man of God prohibits eating to the hungry.' Yet they paused, the apples' broken globes still in their hands, the unchewed fragments in their mouths, as the farmer and his sons came bustling up. He was a wealthy peasant by the look of him, who'd somehow saved enough to buy his own proud plot of land.

'What the fuck are you doing?' he bellowed, almost weeping in his rage, his two stout sons beside him. 'Get on your way or I'll run you through.' He was brandishing a pitchfork, while one son held a flail and the other a long scythe. 'Quick, piss off!' he spat, jabbing his fork toward them.

Most flinched back, but Corvo and Maria stood their ground. 'Do you really think you own this earth?' said Corvo. 'Or the air, or stars above it?' He then addressed the others while the peasant's mouth hung open. 'The true God owns the earth and *you* are God's deserving poor.'

The farmer, recovered from his shock, lunged forward with the pitchfork, bellowing, 'You'll see who owns this land all right,' the long robe torn by muddy tines as Corvo dodged aside. He grasped the weapon with his unencumbered hand, bringing down his stave across the old man's shoulder. One son attacked him with the scythe, but Moloch fell upon him, and Bulfas hurtled headlong at the farmer. This was like a signal to the cowering crowd, one of whom—the sceptic of some time before—came charging at the son who held the flail, a great stone in his hands. This boy, quite paralysed till then, turned upon his heels and ran, making for the house; the father too now scrambled to his feet and hobbled back the way he'd come, Bulfas on his tail. Only the youth with the scythe, torn about by Moloch and battered with a club, failed to get up. The mob, inured to defeat, began to giggle with amazement, and then to laugh, and finally to cheer, delighted with the taste of conquest. Brother Corvo waved them on, gathering the fallen torch and heading for the hemp field.

Here, without delay, he flung the burning thing among the hemp; the fire smouldered while he told them of those mysteries he considered they might grasp. He spoke to them of good and evil, light and dark, of the spirit and the flesh. As the fire built behind him, eating at the hemp and crackling as it ate, he spoke of God and Antigod, Lucifer and YHWH. Shadowed by the blaze, unmindful of its heat, he battered at their brains with puzzling words.

'There is a dark star coming,' he declared. They breathed the searing smoke, confused with burning plants. 'A thing devoid of matter, invisible to our gross eyes. Like that star that heralded the birth of God as flesh, it rises from the east.' Some began to spin, some danced, all drunk on hemp and hunger. It seemed that others danced among them in the shadows—dark, groping molemen whose eyes streamed tears, the vipers of the field that writhed upon their tails, or weevil-demons fleeing from the leaves, sucking at the air with elongated snouts and wringing all their hands.

'Yet this dark star brings not the reign of YHWH, creator of gross matter, but the blighting of our fleshly selves in vast confusion, where all of uncorrupted faith may find perfection of their spirit.' He raised his arms toward the heavens, while redolent hemp-devils blazed in ranks behind him. 'And then the God of Light will be at hand, and a sun of pure spirit will rise out of the night.'

They did not listen to his words, much less comprehend them, yet seemed to breathe them in; some went ambling to the farmhouse—where cries were heard—and others wandered off among the flames, then wandered back again. Embers fell like incandescent rain, smoking in the hair of Speranza and Fiducia, and Maria tumbled on the grass with Bulfas and black Moloch. Then the group came up out of the farmhouse, bringing with them a heavy tun of wine to mount upon the stones, till some sprawled, gulping, all but drowned beneath its spigot, and Corvo stood there, smiling.

Jacopo Passero meets Lucia

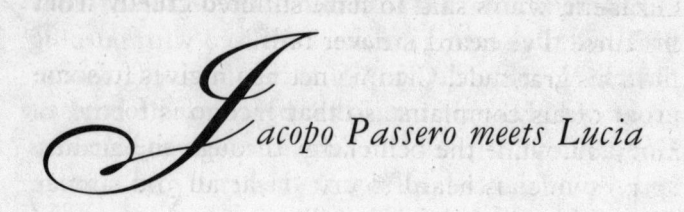

'HE SAYS THAT I'VE LET WATER LEAK INTO THE verjuice. Every day it's a new complaint. I say that it's the rotten barrel, but he won't hear of it.'

'Husbands, Genoveva, they get mean and finicky when their blood's full of bile.'

'Maybe I should let a little water into his liver,' giggles Genoveva, craning over the heads of the crowd to watch Fra Lippo's preparations.

Jacopo notes what he needs, then sinks among the shadows of his cloak and broad, raked hat. Through the hubbub of voices, the market resounds to the ringing of a bell.

'The discomfort, Gugli. I can hardly sleep.' The small, squeaky voice belies the bulk of the speaker, who completely blocks the friar from Jacopo's view. 'Tell people and they're apt to laugh, but there's nothing worse than wind.' Indeed, the air behind him is witness to his suffering.

'I know, Gianni, I know.'

'Sometimes I feel as if my guts might burst.'

'I think I know the prayer to help you, Gianni. I'll write it out on a square of vellum which you must wear about you. It's a prayer to Saint

Elizabeth, who's said to have suffered cruelly from the curse. I've heard it never fails.'

In his gratitude, Gianni once again gives fulsome proof of his complaint, so that Jacopo is forced to hurry on, while the bell clangs through the air and Lippo's voice is heard to cry, 'Hear all you sinners the word of the Lord. Hear all you sinners the word of the Lord.' He stops behind a pair of servants, one a stocky Tartar girl in a spotless cotton smock, the other a lean African. This latter, in her shapeless dress, makes him falter with her loveliness.

'Those charms that you and Nicoletta recommended,' the black girl says, 'they've worked no better than my own. At least, as far as I can see.'

'Give it time, Lucia. You're too impatient. These things don't happen overnight.'

'But, Ambra, if anything, he's grown more distant.' Her voice is soft and slightly husky. 'There's something going on which he won't talk about. With him and the other carders, I mean.'

'Well,' says her companion, 'at least it's not another girl.'

'No, but ... Here, wait, he's starting.'

Apparently satisfied with the size of the crowd, Fra Lippo has begun to preach, waving with his arms and bobbing on his toes. Jacopo hears nothing—he's heard it all before—and is, instead, considering the black girl's words. Clearly there is someone she seeks to win with love charms, someone fool enough to keep himself immune. Well, who can tell? Such charms might miss their mark and find another. But before he scurries off, there's something that he wants, some little token.

Without a moment's pause, he slips a hand amongst the bags of fruit that lie behind her feet. He finds nothing there of interest but a tiny slip of paper, which he filches in a trice. Then he draws his knife and cuts, from her string bracelet, a dangling, cheap straw trinket.

Darting to the rear of the crowd he slips into a laneway where he shrugs off cloak and hat, beneath which he is wearing a doublet and black hose. He hurries round a circuit of dark lanes, waiting in the shadows at the edge of the piazza.

'Is this not the time,' the friar cries, 'for all to seek repentance? Now that stories reach us of a plague that's in the south ...' But Jacopo isn't listening to his words, thinking instead of what he himself will say. He goes back over what he's heard amongst the crowd, of old Alfreda with her warts and loneliness, of Gianni with his wind, of Lucia ... yes, Lucia, and the fool who wouldn't want her.

Lippo is repeating that the best form of repentance is donation; a moment and, here it is, his cue: 'And now, good citizens of Topomagro, as a sign of God's benevolence amidst the thunder of His wrath, I present to you my assistant, Jacopo Passero, blessed by the Lord with special vision.' Without further ado, Jacopo bustles on in tights and piebald doublet, plucking from its sconce a torch that Lippo's lit despite the sun. He thrusts it in his mouth, as he learnt as a jongleur, then hauls it out and holds it up, expelling puffs of smoke. 'I used to eat fire,' he cries, 'till I felt it singe my soul.'

He puts the torch back in its bracket, drawing a greased sword out of his belt. 'Many times I swallowed swords like this.' He stabs the blade straight down his throat, then slides it carefully out. 'But I soon saw the way I pierced Christ within me.' Even as he sheathes it, he comes careering forward, with cartwheels, twists and somersaults, down into the crowd, where he bounces on his toes, proclaiming, 'And how I used to tumble, till I knew that I was tumbling straight to Hell.'

Having obtained their attention, he proceeds to tell them a lurid version of his travels with Orlando, full of textbook sins and culminating in a dark night of the soul before a hostile audience in Syracuse. He recounts his topple from the tightrope, his long unconsciousness, the following black melancholy, and the dream wherein the angel Michael held a fiery sword against his brow. 'From that moment there were things that I could see, things past understanding, yet true beyond all doubt.' Here he feels a moment's hesitation, for it is now that Lippo's written speech runs dry, forcing him to improvise. He stares amongst his audience, as if seeking further words, until he finds an ancient woman, skin puckered up with warts. 'I see Alfreda, with her painful rheumatism, bedevilled by some quack who treats her warts with human excrement.' He looks with infinite compassion on her verrucose amazement. 'But, Alfreda, let me tell you now, the remedy is prayer.'

'Oh, Alfreda,' cries her crony, 'how could he have known?'

Jacopo's gaze has shifted from the blushing gargoyle, seeking those whose conversations he remembers. There are numerous others whom he's chosen, some cringing as his eyes drew near them, some beaming to attract his interest. To one among the last he says, 'And you, Gianni, poor sufferer from colic,' having no trouble in discovering the massive man, round whom a vacant moat has formed. 'Distress yourself no longer, for Saint Elizabeth, earnestly besought, will happily dispel your anguish.'

He scans the gaping mouths, seeking out the morning's final choice. At last he fixes on the one he has avoided until now, the Negro slave, Lucia. She seems innocent of his attention, muttering to her companion, till he says, 'And you, Lucia, who make charms to fire the heart of a lover. Surely the charm of your beauty is enough to fire any heart.' Then he turns his eyes aside and says no more, wishing no-one else to see the object of his words. Nor does Lucia, or the Tartar slave beside her, give anything away, except perhaps for the bemused and dazzling smile that lights her face. Jacopo hasn't seen it, dragging his eyes toward the middle distance as he drones the final litany about the blessings of the Lord. Yet, while Lippo makes impassioned pleas for large donations, and even as some are given, Jacopo's gaze keeps slipping to that place where she has been, hoping not to lose her.

There are those who stare at him in silent awe, and one or two who come across to ask him how he's done it. 'I am the ignorant vessel of the Lord,' he says. 'You must ask Him.' He turns distractedly away, as if the one he seeks has gone, then finds her face before him.

'How did you know?' she asks him softly, a smile

both quizzical and radiant playing at her lips.

'I just did,' he says, drawing her aside. 'I don't know how. It simply … happens.'

'But about the charms, they—' She stops, and his heart leaps up at her black eyes, the quivering confusion of her smile, her dark, lithe body.

'Come on, hurry,' says the other girl, 'we've stopped too long already. Monna Beatrice will be angry.' In the absence of any further answer to her questions, she lets herself be drawn away.

'But I meant that,' he calls behind her, grinning, '… what I said about your beauty,' though she's already vanishing through the crowd.

He unfolds the slip of paper that he's stolen from her bag. It's merely a receipt to one Tuccio di Piero Landucci, presumably her master. If he's as wealthy as so fine a slave suggests, then his house should not be hard to find. Jacopo feels the small straw charm between his fingers, and the conviction grows within him—perhaps he really has the gift of vision—that he'll meet her once again.

Jacopo waits amongst the shadows of the late afternoon in the portico opposite Tuccio's house. He watches its facade as if his famous second sight might penetrate its stones. But not once does he catch a glimpse of the one he's looking for. Business associates and clients of her master, workmen, servants, women he assumes are members of the family, all come and go through the archways of the shop or the deeply recessed street-door. But he sees no sign of the slave Lucia. Indeed, he's somewhat puzzled by his own reactions. When he isn't actually thinking about her, she seems to hover at the edge of thought; and when he tries to ignore her, even shoo her away, she keeps drifting back, part angel, part mosquito. He's held out for no more than a day, and now, much to his own amazement and the amusement of Fra Lippo, is keeping vigil at the portal of this African slave as if she were a princess.

He's waiting while the shadows lengthen, and feels increasingly a fool. Even Scimmi deserts him, skulking off into a nearby alley. As annoyance is turning slowly to dejection, Lucia emerges through the street-door, carrying a pair of bags, one made of cloth and one of straw. She's wearing a cotton shift, identical to the one he saw her wearing at the markets, though perhaps a little longer. He feels a curious relief, as if he hasn't been quite sure till now that she is real. He wants to run across and touch her. Instead, he waits until she's crossed the street, heading to the Via della Lana, then leaves the portico and follows her.

'Scimmi,' he hisses, making kissing noises with his lips. But the cat gives him a level look and will not budge out of the alley. Shrugging, he ducks along the street behind Lucia, casting one brief glance across his shoulder and seeing the creature dart behind him through the shadows.

Lucia walks quickly down the Via della Lana, almost as far as the *podesta*'s palazzo, then crosses to the Via di Calimala, heading south toward the bread shops and the butcheries. Once or twice she swings abruptly on her heel, but Jacopo's nothing if not agile, and easily ducks aside. At last, just when he catches sight of the carcase of an ox hung out above the street, and guesses that she's making for the butcher's, she slips into a laneway full of bread shops, cakes and bakeries. He hurries after her as quickly as he can, peering first into the depths of one dim shop and then another. The air inside the lane is redolent of baking bread, like the innards of an oven, and for a moment he simply mooches, snuffling up the warmth. Then he sees her in a shop across the street. Her bags already full of loaves, she's on the verge of leaving; he scuttles smartly over, strolling past the door as she comes out. Then: a near collision, bags jostled, loaves upon the stones except for his quick thinking. 'I'm sorry,' he's saying. 'No, no,' she shrugs, a little briskly, hugging the load to her.

'Really, let me …' A dawning smile. 'But isn't it? … Yes, Lucia.'

'I—'

'You remember … with the friar, preaching in the markets.' He extends a tentative hand. 'Here, let me …'

'No, that's all right.' She looks at him and smiles with slow astonishment. 'Yes, of course I remember. You told me … Well, you look different in those clothes.'

He stands back a little, raising an eyebrow and making a slight bow. She looks at him more closely, observing his wry smile and agile movements. Not handsome, as her Guido is, but somehow interesting to look at, since his features—the corners of his eyes and lips, his narrow nose, his eyebrows—seem twisted slightly up as if mischief played behind them. His face is like that of a statue in her master's study, one of the old gods with little wings that sprout out of his feet.

'Here, I found this,' he says abruptly, holding up the small straw charm he'd taken from her bracelet. 'It was on the ground where we'd been speaking. I thought it might be yours.'

'Oh, yes,' she laughs, looking at the string of dangling gewgaws on her wrist. 'I noticed it was gone.'

'Then wasn't it lucky that I met you ... It is Lucia, isn't it ... your name?' She's smiling as she nods. 'I had a feeling I might meet you again.'

'Well, you would, wouldn't you?'

'I—' For a moment he isn't quite sure what she means, then, 'Oh yes, of course, I suppose I would.'

Taking the charm from his fingers, she laughs once more, her tongue bright pink behind her lips, and he stands for an instant, silent.

'Well, it was funny meeting you like this.' She turns toward the laneway's entrance. 'I suppose I'd better go. The cook throws tantrums if I get back late.'

'Yes,' he says, half turning with her as a streak of silver bounds up from the stones onto his shoulder. 'Oh, Scimmi,' he grumbles, while she sits there licking at her paws.

'Is that yours?' Lucia cries, staring at the cat.

'Yes.' He looks embarrassed. 'I'm beginning to wish I'd never taught her that trick. Now she does it all the time.'

'What did you say her name was?' When he repeats it, she stretches out her hand to fondle

Scimmi's head. 'She's pretty.' Scimmi takes the tribute with aplomb, not pausing in her licking. 'But I'd better go,' and she turns toward the Via di Calimala.

Jacopo starts to follow, attempting to put Scimmi in her pouch, but she slips back out, trotting at his feet like the ghost of a small dog.

'It was strange the other day,' he begins, 'when I saw you in the crowd. Quite different from the others.'

'What do you mean?' She turns, inhaling the cool air still heavy with the scent of fresh-baked bread, as if they've brought the bakery with them.

'Well, usually I get a sense of who a person is. But with you it was confusing.'

'Why?'

'Because I saw both you and … a kind of image of you. But the two were completely different.'

'Different?' she says doubtfully, shaking her dark head. 'How could they be different?'

'I—I don't want to sound ill-mannered.' He looks at her uncertainly, and she nods that he continue. 'I saw you as you are, a slave in slave's clothing. Yet the image that came into my mind was altogether different. You remained a beautiful woman, but no longer a slave. You wore taffeta and samite, gold jewellery at your throat—the finest gowns and gems, like some great lady.'

At this, Lucia laughs out loud. 'I'm not that, as you can see,' she says at last, 'so perhaps your skill deceives you.' Then she falls silent, as if distracted by her thoughts. 'Unless … but it's too stupid.'

'What?'

'Well, it's just that when I was little—from as far back as I remember, till about when I was five—I lived with a rich family in Boccaperta. I hardly remember anything about it, except that the mistress of the house was very nice. I can't recall any other children, and I think she treated me like a daughter ... Can you imagine, me, the colour that I am, the daughter of some wealthy merchant?' Jacopo seems upon the point of protest, so she hurries on, regardless. 'At least, I remember her as very kind, and having my hair plaited by the maids, and wearing gowns just like you said, of taffeta and silk. But they were the dresses of a child ...' She pauses, breathing quickly, as if she ran instead of walking.

'Yes,' he nods, then gives her time to tell him more, and when she doesn't, says, 'What happened? I mean, to change the situation.'

'Oh, she died, I think. At least, I didn't see her any more. And he started getting rid of everything. The husband, I mean. The clothes, the furniture, the house all went, and I went with them too. He sold me to a woman who lived just off the Via Gentili, near San Stefano.'

'And what happened then?'

'With Monna Carla Petriboni?' She's staring straight ahead into the shadow-blackened streets. 'Well, she didn't spoil her slaves. And she had no need for further daughters, so she worked me hard, had her housekeeper give me lessons in how servants should behave, yet still found fault with me. So it wasn't long before she sold me cheap to Signor Tuccio. But it's the sort of story you'll have heard before, and it's hardly worth talking about, and ... besides, we're there.'

It's true, they're almost at the corner opposite her house. 'I think what I saw was real,' he blurts, puffing, at a standstill.

'What? You mean me as a little girl?'

'No,' he says slowly, glancing down into her eyes. 'I think I saw you as you really are, in yourself, a beautiful, proud woman who—'

'Oh, that's stupid,' she says harshly, and then softening her tone, 'I've got to go.' But he's staring wild-eyed at the air before him, holding out his hand as if to fend off demons.

'I see something!' he hisses, beckoning her to him. 'Quick! Shelter in this doorway!' And he bustles her—bags, loaves, memories and all—into the portal of a narrow house.

'What? What is it that you see?' she breathes, at the very moment that she feels his arms encircle her, his lips upon her face.

'Why, that I will kiss you.' And he begins to do so once again, but she wriggles free, catching his chest with a pointed elbow.

'Don't you dare,' she says, and steps into the street. 'You *are* a bold one, aren't you?'

'Only where the prize is worth it. I—' But his eloquence—for this really has the makings of a noble speech—is interrupted by Scimmi's leaping on his shoulder. 'Oh, for God's sake, cat!' he cries, which makes Lucia stay to smile at his frustration. 'Yes, Lucia, wait, just for a moment.' He's struggling to unhook the creature from his doublet. 'When—' But the girl is heading for the house.

'When can I see you, Lucia?' She keeps walking, saying nothing.

'Lucia, *when*?'

She swings round quickly, a finger to her lips. 'I'm supposed to be going to the cobbler's. Tomorrow morning, on the Via Meraviglia.'

The carders discover an unexpected ally

NOW TOPOMAGRO BROILS UNDER HOT SUMMER DAYS, the longest of the year. It is the Feast of John the Baptist, and the members of the Arte della Lana march beneath the saint's broad banner with its image of the lamb, his emblem and the guild's. It is a time when day has triumphed over night, when labourer and merchant may put aside their differences to celebrate their common goals in commerce and religion. The carders from Tuccio di Piero Landucci's workshops, however, have chosen to remain aloof. Far from the guild's celebrations, they are seated outside their favourite tavern in the little piazza near Santa Caterina delle Ruote. Most of them are here—Geri Pinza, Alfredo Crostadura, Ciuto di Dino, Ceppo Castracani, Nofri Pasquini and Guido himself, as well as numerous others—all staring glumly, determinedly, out into the square. Not much is being said at present, and through the silence at the table they can hear the sound of drumming from the northern end of town. For why should they make merry with a guild which they can't join, yet which imposes its authority on everything they do?

Geri shakes his head and sips his wine. He watches the bonfires that blaze on the piazza. Some are small, no more than cooking fires for the families gathered round them. Others are quite large, such as that round which a double circle is already dancing widdershins. Nearest to the river, on the far side of the square, is one where people cast off objects of ill-omen—a knife, a counterfeit coin, a broken spindle, papers of some kind. As he watches, a woman lifts a sack which seems to struggle in her hands, heaving it up into the fire where it howls amongst the flames. He frowns, trying to hear their chanted rhymes, but the dancers' squeals conceal them. He's about to suggest that they might build a fire of their own, using the guildhall of the Arte della Lana for kindling, when his words are interrupted by some new arrivals.

Those who can, find places at the only vacant table, the rest plonk down upon a bench against the wall or simply stand about. The carders mumble to each other, and Geri's nodding grimly at Alfredo, surveying this new group. Its members seem perhaps a little older than themselves. Their clothes look better too, yet remain the clothes of working men, and some have hands that bear bright stains like multicoloured birthmarks.

'Dyers,' mutters Ceppo Castracani to his neighbour. 'What are they doing here?'

Meanwhile, Bernardo Zoppo, the owner of the dye shop they all work for, and a relatively wealthy man, is ordering jugs of wine. Geri and Alfredo give circumspect nods, and Bernardo makes them a small, constrained bow, while the rest of the men stare glumly at the fires.

'I thought you'd all be at the guild's procession,' suggests Geri, and Alfredo lifts his eyebrows at Bernardo.

'Yeah,' says Ceppo, already in his cups, and speaking louder perhaps than he intended. 'What's wrong with the taverns in the Borgo Santa Maria?'

The dyers glance in irritation at the question and, before Bernardo can give his answer, one says, 'There's nothing wrong with them. You ought to try them sometime, if you can take strong drink, that is.'

'Strong drink?' sneers Nofri Pasquini. 'Any carder's worth three damned dyers as far as drink's concerned.'

'That's right,' adds Ceppo, while the dyers snarl their protests. 'Why don't you go back to the Borgo Santa Maria and drink that piss you call good wine?'

'Ceppo ...' Geri cautions, but he's too late even now, since some of the dyers have already started forward.

'Ha, you carders!' one laughs nastily. 'You couldn't pay for more than water coloured with a bit of *canaiolo*.'

'Just so,' says another, a heavy man whose fingers bear the scarlet stains of *grana*. 'These carders can't drink water and walk straight.'

'Piss off to the Borgo Santa Maria!' shouts Ceppo, rising from the table, while Luca and Nofri follow suit.

'Yeah,' sniggers Guido, 'look at his hands, just like a slaughterman's. Go back and stick some pigs.'

At this the dyers hurtle forward, clashing with

the carders at the doorway of the tavern.

'We'll show you what carders are made of.'

'Think you can insult us dyers, eh?'

'Bastards!'

'Cretins!'

They growl as they push and shove amongst the benches. Hands grapple, fists fly, heads butt. Those not yet involved are jumping to their feet, shouting their support. The scuffle gains momentum and the families stop to watch, until a dyer tumbles back upon the dancers' fire. Suddenly the tangled men are separate once again, the dyers now on one side of the fire, seeing to their fellow, the carders on the other. The man seems fine, apart from a few singes, and they're up to start again. But Geri and Bernardo jump into the fray, knives drawn, each facing their companions.

'So help me, I'll cut the first of you that moves,' says Geri to the carders.

'Stand right there!' shouts Bernardo to the dyers, his elegant long dagger flashing with the flames. 'We're here to celebrate the feast day, not kill each other.'

'Exactly,' Geri's nodding.

But Bernardo Zoppo hasn't finished yet. 'We've stayed clear of the guild's parade to show our solidarity against the *lanaiuoli*, not to fight with carders.' He puffs out his chest and brandishes his blade. 'And wouldn't they just love it, to see us fallen into drunken brawling?'

'He's right,' says Geri, glaring at his carders. 'You're undermining the whole notion of our being here.'

'Go on,' Bernardo urges, softening his tone, 'embrace your brothers. *They* are not your enemies. They suffer from the same oppression as yourselves.'

At first there's grumbling and conspicuous attention to wounds, but gradually they sidle over, muttering together, finding places at each other's tables. It isn't long before the wine begins to flow and the mumbling turns to laughter, as they recall, then re-enact, the slapstick of the brawl.

Still, Geri and Bernardo, seated at the table furthest from the door, seem far less sanguine. 'I thought you'd be marching with the merchants,' Geri says at last.

Bernardo runs his finger round his cup. 'No, I'm sick of getting screwed. At least I can stop pretending that I like it.'

Geri ponders his wine, but doesn't drink. 'You do well out of your business. You could buy and sell the lot of us.'

'Oh, I don't know ... I do well enough, I suppose. Though not as well as you probably imagine. Expenses keep getting higher all the time.' He glances at the square, where the dancing has resumed, and then turns back to Geri. 'I could be doing better for all the work I do.'

'But you're not powerless like us. You've got some influence.'

'Well, I wish you'd tell the *lanaiuoli*.' He shakes his head and laughs. 'Don't kid yourself, Geri. I'm in the same boat you are. The dyers are kept out of the guild, yet they've got to obey every dot and comma of its statutes.'

'I know your house, Bernardo, and your workshops. You're a wealthy man by any standards.'

'By any standards? Oh, come on, Geri. You work for Tuccio di Piero Landucci, don't you?'

'Well, I didn't mean like *him*.' Geri frowns, peering at Bernardo as if he were a sum that wouldn't quite add up. A silence forms between them, tense with unvoiced thoughts.

'Look,' the dyer sighs at last, 'I'm better off than you are. Sure. But what a man like Tuccio does to his carders, he does to me as well. And not just him. All the rest of them—the members of the wool guild, the Guelph Party, the Confraternity of Saint Mark. All those who keep the seats in the Palazzo dei Dieci warm for each other. Agnolo del Leone, Marco Martello, Bartolomeo Chiaudano. They charge us, tax us, collect our rents, create the laws and keep us powerless. They've got it all sewn up.'

Geri gives him a long, appraising stare. 'I didn't know *you* felt that way as well.'

'Well, you do now, Geri. I'm nearly going mad with it. Just look at that master of yours. For years we've been fighting to break his monopoly on the import of dyes. And every time we start to get somewhere, what happens? He gets himself appointed consul of the Arte della Lana. His recent prices are going to bankrupt me.'

'Yes,' says Geri softly, nodding. Then he looks up slowly, narrowing his eyes. 'Something's got to happen, hasn't it? Prices, taxes, rents ... everything goes up and wages stay the same—'

'Well, wages aren't the issue,' Bernardo puts in

quickly. 'It's taxes—and duties, of course—that are the problem.'

'Perhaps.' Geri's gaze is doubtful. 'Perhaps. I've been talking to the peasants in the Chiasso delle Bestie. They complain of the tolls on the produce from their plots outside the town. And the fishermen in the Borgo San Pietro, too ... They fret about the duties at the Porta del Mare and the rents they have to pay to Agnolo del Leone.'

'To be sure, Geri, to be sure.'

'These *lanaiuoli*.' He reaches forward, taking hold of the dyer's arm. 'We could give them a shock, Bernardo. Carders, peasants, fishermen ... and now dyers. Instead of brawling like today, taking out our anger on each other, we could show them how we feel, make them see our strength. We aren't like Montagna and the others.'

'Yes,' says Bernardo, looking edgily around the square.

'What happened to them ... that wouldn't have to happen to us, you know.' Geri leans forward, raising his eyebrows at his companion. 'They *need* us. They couldn't massacre the town.' He shakes him by the sleeve. 'Just a single show of strength might be enough to make them listen.'

'Yes,' Bernardo mutters once again. 'But really, it's these loans that are the problem. Many say the Priors borrow big because they borrow from themselves, then have the commune pay them back at heavy interest.'

'But what do you say, Bernardo? Would you act with us? There are many who agree.'

Any answer to his question is interrupted by a

sudden howling as a large, emaciated dog, its back and tail ablaze, is chased across the square by shouting youths. The carder and the dyer watch them as they vanish down a laneway.

Geri shakes his head and chuckles. 'Every year it's the same. We must change things now, Bernardo.' He observes the dyer's frown as the howling dwindles under distant drums. 'They must let us set up guilds and grant us places in the Signoria. We'll force them if we have to. What do you say, Bernardo?'

'Force them?'

'Yes, of course. It's the only way they'd do it.' Seeing his companion's puzzlement, he makes himself relax a little, dampening the fire of his zeal. 'I've spoken with carders in a number of the workshops, and with some of the peasants too. There's general agreement that we have our procession for the Feast of Saint Blaise, our patron saint. It's there we'll make our grievances known. If they fail to acknowledge us, or worse, then we'll put the torch to some carding sheds, and even one or two palazzi.' He falls abruptly silent, then jabs a finger at the dyer's chest. 'I'm trusting you, Bernardo. If any word of this leaks out—'

'Of course not, Geri. Don't insult me. I—'

'Then will you join with us or not?'

Bernardo turns to peer round the tables, where carders and dyers, so recently eager to beat each other up, are drinking and laughing like natural allies. 'Yes,' he says slowly, nodding with conviction. 'Yes, I think we will.'

In which brother Corvo builds a kingdom and Jacopo steals a gift

WHILE THE RED COMPANY PILLAGES FARMS TO THE north, and the dispersing troops of Wolf Schwanhals prey on southern villages, Brother Corvo and his followers roam the countryside that summer like some weird scouting party for yet another company of freebooters. With the tall, gaunt form of Corvo striding at their head, they prowl the flowering highways, taking food when they need it, collecting tributes of meat and wine for Corvo's Antigod, and gathering whole pharmacopoeias of herbs for medicinal and religious purposes. This rabble, at first fragmented and directionless, slowly draw together to become a congregation—almost, though not quite yet, the spirit kingdom of his preaching—attracting to its fold other aimless souls who roam the roads in search of shelter. Under the tutelage of Brother Corvo, spurred on by his rhetoric, emboldened by his violence, these vagabonds begin to gain a sense of their own strength, to find within themselves a taste for power. Across the hillsides rumours spread of peasants murdered, blazing hemp fields, the butchered bodies of rich landlords. Tales of desecrated churches and lonely villages beset by drunken mobs begin to trail behind them, at times preceding their arrival in some isolated place, though mostly they have moved too fast for that.

Brother Corvo speaks to them of birthrights, disinheritance, the patrimony of the poor. He speaks of law as theft and of theft as restitution. He has them see how the inheritance willed to them by God is swindled from their grasp by landlords, prelates, bakers, peasants—anyone, indeed, possessing more than they. And isn't this everyone they meet? He reminds them of how the bishops of Jehovah, Lord of the flesh, now live in sinful luxury while the righteous live as paupers. 'Who then are the children of the God of Light, whose Kingdom is at hand?' He stands upon whatever ledge or stone or log he's found to speak from, casting his gaze across them and brandishing his staff. 'Why, you—the vagabonds, the outcasts, those lost to this corrupted world—you are the chosen of the Lord, none other.' Such are his words, and such the effect of the herbs he gives them, that many see the coming kingdom as he speaks. 'The world of flesh and matter, of Jesus and Jehovah, will tear *itself* apart. The Antigod has little *need* of us, for such is His subtlety that His enemies destroy themselves. Yet we may play our part.' And throughout these balmy weeks, at lonely farm and hamlet, they do not shirk their duty.

For the most part, such depredations are blamed on soldiers and not upon the minions of the Antigod. Of course, rumours slowly spread, but with such wild and curious mutations that they find small credence with the local lords. So Brother Corvo and his flock continue westward, until at last, in early August, he leads them over rolling hills and across a stubble plain toward a town above the sea, his staff held like a sorcerer's before him. There is no further west to go. Without a moment's hesitation, he marches to the town's great eastern gate. Here the guards refuse them entry, yet Corvo does not argue. He takes them past the paupers who shelter near the wall, and tries his fortune at the next gate to the north. The guards survey the tattered ranks of drabs and ruffians, the two great hounds and other mongrels trailing at their heels. They gawp at old Maria with her primrose coronet, and back once more at Corvo, saturnine and sallow with his tonsured, greasy hair and great hooked nose, then slowly shake their heads. They read aloud the Signoria's edicts, barring all but those with firm connections or contractual obligations to the commune. Brother Corvo simply laughs, a laughter that infects all those behind him and sets the hounds to belling, until the guards place nervous hands upon their swords and wave the crowd away.

Once more he does not argue, simply beckoning his minions, who growl their indignation as they wander to the river. Beggars watch them from their bare ravines as, on the Ombronetto's stony bank, they chase away what vagrant gangs they find there and take their humble shelters. Thus it is, beside the hissing, swirling waters, that they fashion their first kingdom.

That night, while the full moon strangles in a

knot of clouds, they hold their sabbath. Brother Corvo and Maria draw forth powders. Ointments, oils and unguents are rubbed into the skins of all beside that river. One among them has a wheezy set of bagpipes, another a broken drum, and they start to play exhausted cadences that tangle with the waters' purling till the tired rhythms warm into a heat and then a fever and a madness, so that many of their number swirl in circles, or join arms back to back, spinning till they fall. Powders, tinctures, infusions, inspissations—whatever forms are most to Corvo's purpose—have been cannily prepared. Henbane, heart-leaf, foxglove, the roots of mandrake and the fruit of dwale, all mingle in the blood. Some eat darnel mixed with thorn-apple, or the thickened juice of poppies, while others drink infusions of dark ergot. The dancers reel, the drummers beat, the pipers weave bleak tunes, till the guards upon the wall are peering through the dark and the vagrants shamble near.

Speranza feels a savage joy leap through her, as if it cut her heart. It seems the night is breaking down, the sky itself fragmenting. The walls and turrets of the town lurch up like hellgates, and Fiducia lies beside her, dead; until she sees it's not Fiducia but a stone that, somehow, has taken on her likeness. She sees Maria, her wrinkled, blotched old breasts and belly garlanded with flowers, riding on a drunken youth who heaves as in his death throes. Her head is spinning, and then—how long she cannot say—she flies, wind streaming through her hair, the stars aswirl about her. Here, beside her for an eyeblink, is a hag so vast that flesh rolls down her sides like cream spilled from a bucket, though there's no-one fat amongst them. Speranza feels the need to cling, since the sky falls all around her. She is sick, holding tight onto the stones beside the river, which roil and curl with serpents, some twisting up the bank. She turns and sees black Moloch writhing from a hole, dragging his dark coils behind him, while Brother Corvo seems to hover like a devil on the foam, his pale skin sweating quicksilver; and the moon, a spirit thing within the night, is glaring at her sidelong.

All is darkness at the Casa Morelli, and the night is silent but for the thin skirling of some bagpipes. A silver-plated moon is peeking round a corner of the house, illumining the window that should not be open. At first this window is an empty shadow in the pallid masonry. Then a tiny face appears, with thin, stiff whiskers and pointed ears. It turns this way and that, as if to check that nothing's there, and then the cat's whole silhouette jumps up onto the sill. Next, like some peculiar birth, the head and shoulders of a man emerge out of the shadow, his hand sweeps up the cat, and he is leaping down the blank face of the moon without a sound, landing on the roof tiles of a lower storey. They pick their way across the coping, then down another wall to reach another roofline. And so on, down they go, until they crouch above a rear courtyard where, as luck would have it, a dog begins to bark. The man, legs dangling from a gutter, leaps onto his feet as the dog snarls just below him. He turns, surveys the windows overhead, which still remain in darkness;

picking up the cat once more, he urges it along the iron of the courtyard's fence, where it strolls at ease across each spear tip, not faltering for a moment, while the dog goes mad beneath it. At this the man jumps down, bounding past the well, the sundial and the foaming dog, leaps up onto the water trough and, just as lights come on, vaults over the back fence.

'Got them,' he says, as the cat drops onto his shoulder. He takes the necklace and the heavy golden earrings from his pouch, admiring them upon his palm, then pours them back, pushes Scimmi down on top of them, and scuttles off into the silent curfew. 'Come on, we're running late.'

For tonight, as on other such infrequent nights, he's to meet the slave, Lucia. He dashes through the shadows, listening, one hand against the pouch where Scimmi wriggles on her rattling nest. All summer it has been the same, and even now, in August, things seem little changed. He'll urge, nag, lie in wait, until at last, hidden by the night, she'll slip out of the house to meet him. There are numerous places hidden from the curfew—the cloisters of the poor men's hospice, the cemetery, even the boulders at the far end of the beach. For someone—some carder friend of hers, he thinks—knows a hidden breach beneath the walls, made there by those peasants who live within the town. This carder is his rival, he feels certain of it now. At times the situation can seem almost funny. He, Jacopo Passero, free spirit, the rival of a carder for a slave. At other times it pains him badly. She gives her body, her laughter, but he can never lose the sense that she is holding something back; though once she said a name—this carder's name—with just that softness he can never get from her. Guido. She hasn't said it since.

But why go on like this? It isn't like him. He snuffles at the balmy air, the dark, warm breeze, quickening his pace. He's to meet her in the small, walled orchard off the cemetery of Santa Maria dei Poveri. The moon floods the spaces of the town with light; the smell of night blooms fills the air. She would have him, she would smile. What more was there to want? Her soul, perhaps? As though he was God Himself? He laughs softly in the silence, which is broken only by the sound of pipes and the baying of some distant dogs.

He climbs the orchard wall and drops behind it, wondering if she's waiting. Scimmi leaps as he hits the ground. He peers through the rustling dark that smells of oranges. Panic knots in his guts. Lucia isn't there, just the indolent sifting of shadows, the acid Spanish smell. Then, like a spirit from the vaults beyond the gate, her cotton shift comes drifting through the trees, worn only by the night. And now a smile, a chuckle, the soft touch of her hand.

'Did I give you a fright?'

'I thought you were a ghost,' he murmurs, her arms flowing round him and her body pressing with a most unghostly warmth. Her lips brush soft and dry against his mouth, then open, moist, into his own, the scent and taste of what? Of ... bread, as she thrusts the mouth-warm wafer with her tongue between his teeth.

'Corpus Christi,' she whispers, drawing back, while he chews mechanically and swallows.

'What—' he says. 'What is it?'

'Just a piece of bread,' she smiles, knowing that her charms have worked, yet all the more unsure of why they will not work with Guido. 'A piece of bread that I was eating.'

'You're mad, Lucia,' he cries, reaching out to hold her once again.

'Ssh, you'll wake the sexton.' She's pushing him away.

'I don't care whether—' But seeing the fear on her face he stops, fumbling at the pouch instead. 'Look, look what I've got for you,' he says softly, drawing forth the necklace, then the heavy golden earrings. 'From a palace which the king keeps only for his jewels.'

'Oh, Jacopo,' she whispers, half in fear, half in joy, while he wreathes the shiny coils about her throat. She stares at the hooked pendants in her hands. 'They're beautiful.'

'Gold suits you,' he breathes, admiring his creation. 'You should be clothed in gold.'

She smiles a wide, white smile. 'I think you're the one who's mad, Jacopo.'

'Not in the least,' he protests, rolling his eyes. 'Your natural element is gold. Your dresses should be sewn from ducats. I could see it straightaway. All I've got to do is look at you to know that you're some Barbary princess stolen from the cradle.'

'Like I said, you're mad.' Almost regretfully, she strokes the warming metal at her throat. 'But you know I can't keep them.'

'What do you mean?'

'Well, they'd find them and know I'd stolen them.' She's reaching for the clasp already, until he leans against her, drawing down her arms.

'Then *I'll* keep them,' he breathes into her ear, 'and you can wear them, and be a Barbary princess whenever you're with me.' His lips are nibbling her soft throat, hands plucking at her shift.

'Mad,' she mumbles, sighing, while the shadows whisper round them no blacker than her skin, and he enters her as if some gateway opened in the night itself to let him in.

The King of Cats and plans for a charivari

LATE AUTUMN HAS BLOWN ACROSS THE TOWN LIKE plague-breath, exhaling its contagion on the leaves until they sallow, as with excess bile, and then flush choleric red and fall, black with melancholic humours. Despite the year's decline, Topomagro is full of laughter and activity, for today is the feast of Saint Martin, and a tournament is being held on the Piazza del Colombo. Geri Pinza watches the opposing forces of the Porta del Colombo and the Porta Santa Maria take up their positions, sees three ladies strewing roses from the Castle of Love—constructed expressly for the tourney—then hears the trumpets stutter, the drums begin to thunder, and already feels the feast day turning bitter in his heart. The jousting fills him with gloom and, as he hears the splintering lances, the pleasure of the crowd, the metal horsemen tumbling with the sound of broken bells, he is overwhelmed by how easily people's hearts are won by such displays, even though it's they, through their taxes and their hunger, who pay for the prestige of the gates' rich captains. He stays to see the armies battle for the Castle, their blunted broadswords slicing up the sunlight into blinding slivers, but walks away amid the uproar as the knights of Santa Maria storm the ramparts, his back turned to their captain as he waves the Virgin's banner, and has vanished altogether by the time the old *podesta* rises with the trophy, a helmet heavy with gold wings.

Geri skirts a host of games along the route toward the Borgo Santa Caterina—a pig-run in the Borgo dei Operai, where men with wooden clubs go charging through the streets in pursuit of a squealing shoat; footraces in the Borgo dei Medici; an archery tournament in San Francesco's orchard; and at the Ospedale degli Abbandonati, the bishop funds a banquet for the poor. But Geri stops for none, intent upon the square in front of Santa Caterina delle Ruote where a number of the carders are engaging in a tournament traditional in that quarter.

He's relieved to greet Alfredo and the others since, amongst them at least, he no longer feels that he's abetting some agenda of the merchants. Yet even here he begins to feel strangely out of sorts, cursing himself as a fool and a killjoy. He stands amid the rowdy crush of bodies, seeing the competitors line up, their heads newly shaven, burly Ceppo Castracani and squat little Nofri amongst them. Their scalps are white and bald, though with a few errant bristles. He notes their hands already tied behind them, the first contestant's feet strapped tightly to the planking. He hears the wails of the tomcat nailed to the pole by the skin of its back, even as the man strains forward, thrusting at its belly with his head. The cat erupts in spitting howls, sinking its teeth in his shaven pate, claws tearing at his skin, till he loses his nerve and tries to draw away, wiggling on the planks with his arse stuck out. But Geri can no longer enjoy it, despite the roars of laughter from the crowd; and when the man jerks back with a sound like ripping silk, blood streaming from his crown, the carder feels first sickened, then shamed by his disgust.

Nofri fares no better, head torn and bleeding as he stumbles to his friends; nor does the one who follows him, nor the next; while the cat itself, though looking battered, still seems full of fight. Geri, on the other hand, has had enough, depressed by the crowd's delight, turning away as Ceppo swaggers to the pole. So, while he hears the crowd's approving roar, he doesn't witness Ceppo's triumph, the way he grinds his great bull head into the tomcat's belly, though it spits and rips and screams. Nor does he see it flagging, tongue stuck out, claws flexing, not in flesh, but in the air, its hisses fading to a shaking sigh, its body drooping as Ceppo turns and grins. All he sees is the broken creature, red mouth seeping, claws dangling shreds of skin, and there beside it the smiling man, awaiting coronation as the King of Cats, his court already cheering, 'Drink, now drink up to the King.'

The Signoria has suspended the curfew for the evening, and later there's a lavish feast provided for the worthies by the Confraternity of Saint Mark. There, between the lion of the saint and the lion of the Guelph Party, the members of the confraternity, as well as all their guests, gather at great tables in the Piazza della Signoria, while the usual crowds of oglers watch them from a distance. It's with this spectacle in mind that Guido and some others ramble through the town, their feet unsteady, their voices loud with wine and the relinquished curfew. Guido leads the troop, a wine jug in his hand; Luca, Bartolomeo, bloody Nofri and Vieri di Grazino come weaving in his wake. But their most celebrated member is Ceppo Castracani, the King of Cats, who, throughout their wanderings in the southern suburbs, received cheers and much back-slapping, though his fame has dimmed the further north they've travelled. Nevertheless, he continues to attract attention, insisting upon wearing his gilded wooden crown, which perches on his head at a most peculiar angle in order to avoid the cuts inflicted by the cat. With his thick neck, broken nose and the streamers of dried blood that trail beneath the crown, he makes a sight worth noting, and the glances they attract grow more and more suspicious the more northward that they go. He has never been the most benevolent of drunks and, while Guido, Luca and Vieri go reeling back and forth with boisterous laughter, he simply grows more silent, cleaving a straight path among the revellers they meet, his face the carven prow of a galley trimmed for war, lip curled, eyes sullen, brow caked with cracking blood.

At last, after numerous detours, they reach the Piazza della Signoria. People promenade or watch the feast, kept back among the shadows by the town militia. The event is taking place before the tall Palazzo dei Dieci, a low segment of its walls lit ruddy gold, its upper reaches wreathed in blackness, save for its topmost tower which is bright with torches in the dark night sky like a crenellated moon. Guido watches as Signor Tuccio hoes into a fatted partridge with total concentration, then nudges Luca with a smirk. He sees the pie brought out by seven servants of the commune, so heavy that it constitutes three courses in one and lets the worthies contravene their sumptuary laws; for it is layered with fried almonds, dates, spiced sausage, greased chicken and ravioli stuffed with pork, all cooked in red-hot embers.

Guido licks his lips, turning to watch Gaia, the merchant's haughty daughter, and her fiance, Baldassare d'Aquila. In the shifting golden light her beauty is intense, and she glances out toward the ogling throng, then smiles above the food at Baldassare, a measured, sidelong smile which he returns. It seems to Guido as though they relish the attention of the crowd, as if they laugh—as does old Tuccio—to take the food out of the people's mouths. He feels suddenly disgusted by the feast, the splendid clothes, the handsome couple.

'Hmph,' he snorts, convinced that something must be done to prick such pride.

'What?' says Luca, already bored.

'This wedding that's going to happen, between Tuccio's daughter and her ... clown ...'

'What about it?' The others, tired of the food they cannot eat, are also turning round to hear.

'It's a farce,' he mutters, 'the marriage of a sow to a hog. Something should be done.'

'What?' grunts Ceppo, grinning. 'What do you mean something should be done?'

'Yes,' nods Guido slowly, 'of course,' more to himself than his companions, 'a charivari ...'

Meanwhile, the friars of San Francesco have organised a meal for the deserving poor, those registered as paupers in the parish records. They come on crutches and small trolleys; cripples who walk upon their hands, legs twisted back in baskets; girls drained of flesh by newborn infants; the stumbling, white-eyed blind; all swarm toward the convent as if it were a lodestone drawing hunger. Here, at trestle tables in the cloisters and the quadrangle, they struggle for a place upon the benches as the friars dole out loaves and fill the bowls with fish stock. Emaciated children trail the bustling friars; and Fra Filippo Peppo, helping out his hosts, is brushing at their fingers as he ladles out the soup. Jacopo Passero is there as well, having given up the chance of snipping purses in the town, and is juggling in the courtyard for his gobbling audience; Scimmi, long since vanished from the convent's cloisters, has climbed into a tree and gone to sleep.

Later that night, across the river, on the square in front of Santa Caterina delle Ruote—where the tomcat's nailed up still—the drunken crowd has drifted off, leaving only those too drunk to move and some wine in sour puddles. The stray cats of the quarter come nosing round like shadows. A sickle moon's pale light shines weakly down above them as they start and flinch at every sound, then turn to sniff out food. Some pass beneath the pole, pausing to look, to hear, to catch the scent of the dead cat, then bristle and move on, slinking belly to the ground to escape their crucified brother, this Christ of cats, with neither mother nor disciples nor any tomb to rise from.

Guido leads a charivari

AFTER THE WEDDING AND LONG NUPTIAL FEAST, Baldassare goes home to check that Enzo, his servant, has prepared the house for Gaia's arrival. He stands in his chamber, surveying the bed, then restlessly paces before his tall window, peering out at the dusk and the streets below. In his mind it is morning still, and he sees Gaia, her long train afloat as she rides her white mare to the Duomo. Such a wedding! Perhaps the most splendid yet in the town. He sees her over the crowd in her gown of red samite, a shimmering flame in the autumn sun, while the town's great people come trailing after. He sees the notary robed in black on the steps of the white cathedral, waiting to read the contract aloud to all the assembly, and there, behind her veil of lace butterflies, Gaia's dark eyes.

He stands at the bed, then paces again to the window, his memory feasting once more on the banquet. He'd never seen Tuccio look more pleased, raising cup after cup of sweet *trebbiano* from his vineyards in the far Marches. With what warmth the merchant had smiled at him over the soup, hot with the scent of mullet, squid, *rascasse* and sole, their flavours swimming in that salty broth as they had swum in the sea. How he had toasted him—now they were father and son—before his lofty guests. Baldassare can smell the courses still: the huge blue tuna on its silver salver, the piglets basted a tawny gold with sprigs of rosemary in their mouths. There was the great white goose surrounded by clutches of agate eggs, and slow-boiled brill like rhomboid plates, and the gilded peacock with its fanned-out tail, throat stuffed with camphor in aqua vitae, its beak breathing fire into the air. He pictures the gifts for the guests: the chokers, the greyhounds, the monkey that climbed the embroidered plants of the drapes; and thinks of the tiff between young Marina and Beatrice, her mother—his mother—over the small white lapdog she claimed from an absent guest. How delighted he'd been by it all, to be part of them now, this family, after so many years alone.

Yet how keen he became to get away, to have Gaia here with no other soul about them. Soon she will come upon her white mare through the dusky streets. Already he hears the noise of the gathering throng, the clop of the horses and shouting of children. He peeps through the curtains and sees her below. There are cries from the crowd as she starts to dismount. 'Watch out, he's hiding in the bedroom!' shouts one, leering at his companions, so that Baldassare edges away from the window. 'There's a thief who wants to snatch your purse,' laughs another. 'And he's got a long sword,' suggests yet another. 'Prick-eater!' rumbles a drunken voice, and Baldassare darts back to the drapes.

Peeping once more, he sees the scowls that turn on a thug with a shaven head and thick, broken nose. His companions—a little less rough then he—jostle and shush him, while the crowd regains its good humour. But Baldassare pays them no heed, since Gaia arrives at the door with Marina and all of her women companions.

His servant hides in the kitchen; and shoeless, Baldassare slips to the door of his room to listen.

'Is anybody here?' calls Marina, dissolving in giggles.

The women hiss her to silence, then end up giggling too.

'He's gone,' suggests Alberta. 'I heard someone say that he rode away.'

Monna Francesca, the oldest amongst them, smiles reassuringly: 'Then you're safe, my dear. He's here no longer.'

Baldassare himself feels the pressure to laugh, hearing their voices draw nearer below him.

From the base of the stairs Marina announces, '*I'll* find him,' and he pictures her rush as Alberta cries, 'No!' then adds in a dignified tone, 'We must all proceed together.'

And so they do, looking in each of the lower rooms, finding no-one there. At last they start up the stairs, and he enters the great wooden chest by the window, shutting himself inside, then hears their feet on the boards of his chamber.

'Well,' says the voice of Gaia, 'it seems that it was true. He isn't here,' to which there's muttered agreement.

'Then we can safely leave you,' says Francesca,

'secure in the thought that you won't come to harm.'

'Well, I think he's—'

'Come, Marina,' Francesca insists. 'It's time that we left.' He pictures their comfortable nodding, hears Marina protest as Francesca adds, 'That is, if you feel quite at ease.'

'Yes, thank you ... all of you. I feel perfectly at home.'

They take their leave, bustling away down the stairs with many a whisper and giggle; before the street door even closes, Baldassare comes rising out of the chest to meet Gaia's smile above the great bed.

That night Baldassare dreams he is lying beside her after love-making. Moonlight streams through his unshuttered window, and she sprawls against him as if she's been flung there out of the moon. In the midst of his dream, he hears a loud booming. He glances up and sees that the walls are opening, cracking apart like the shell of an egg. Boom! The timbers splinter. Boom! The roof splits wide to the stars as he twists and struggles and ... opens his eyes in the dark beside Gaia.

He tries to wake up, peering about him. The room is intact. A far fainter moonlight seeps through the window. His wife lies silent beside him, undisturbed by his dream. How else could it be? Yet the booming goes on like the sound of struck metal. He thinks of pans and old pots being beaten with spoons. Now there is shouting, a chorus of cries like the wailing of cats.

'Wh—?' mumbles Gaia, stirring beside him.

He starts to sit up, lifting a hand to rub at his eyes. 'What is it?'

'Shh, Gaia. Listen.' He's gripped by a sudden fear and, still half asleep, starts to rise from the bed.

The door of his room opens slowly. Both he and Gaia watch it in silence, as if entranced. It opens on darkness, and then from that darkness ... a pallid figure, like a spirit suspended before them. They watch it glide forward, shimmering, gauzy, flowing in silk through the shadowy chamber. Deep in that gloom they can see the red lips on its waxen face and the long black hair from which there blossoms a crown of white lilies. It's a bride, or the spirit of one long dead, now come to their marriage bed. Gaia stifles a sob.

'Baldassare,' it croaks in a hoarse, deep voice. 'Baldassare, my love.'

It steps still nearer and they see all the rips and rubbish-tip stains on its gown, its mane of black hair like strands of dyed jute. Nor does the face seem to shine any more with a soft, glowing pallor, but is coarse skinned and dark, plastered with powder and smeared with grease. And the thing is no longer alone, for a figure in black, like a vagabond priest, arrives through the door behind it, bearing a club and wearing a mask.

'Just what the hell—?' Baldassare commences, but the bride slips a dagger out of its gown, blade glinting with moonlight that sifts through the window, then lunges toward him. The knife's at his throat, the priest's arms about him, as he stares eye to eye with the broken-nosed bride.

'Sweetheart,' it moans, rubbing against him, then

turns back to Gaia. 'He's not yours, you bitch. He married me first.' It nicks at his throat with the blade and, filling his nostrils with wine and stale garlic, lisps in his face, 'Why did you leave me to marry that sow?'

Baldassare sees that another has entered the room, a youth in a makeshift domino, who sits on the bed beside Gaia, prodding her with his dagger. 'You'd better put on some clothes,' he counsels. 'It's cold in the evening air.'

'Bugger clothes,' growls the bride, grabbing the arm of Baldassare. 'His servant slipped past us, running like a hare. He'll be back with the watch if we don't hurry.'

'Yes, you're right,' nods Guido, for this is who it is holding Gaia by the wrist, just as the priest is Nofri Pasquini and the bride big Ceppo, King of the Cats, his scabs almost healed beneath his black wig. 'We'd better move fast.'

Gaia, attempting to wrench herself free, cries, 'Who are you? What do you want?' Baldassare jerks to the window, almost tipping Nofri out. For a moment, he sees the men who are standing below with their saucepans and pots, all in crude dominoes, and the poor bony beast that will carry them both on its back, less like a mule than a structure of cankers and wens. Ceppo jabs at his ribs with the knife, crowing, 'Oh, so you don't want to come to Lucrezia's.' He turns to Gaia, and simpers behind his torn veil, 'You'd think he'd never been to a brothel before.'

'I saw old Tuccio down at Lucrezia's last night,' leers Nofri.

'Come on, hurry up,' says Guido, dragging his charge off the bed, from which she retains a single sheet in a futile effort to cover herself.

'We're going to help you spice up your marriage,' roars Ceppo.

'Yeah,' Nofri grins. 'Keep your eyes open, lady, you might learn something at Lucrezia's.'

Baldassare kicks out and cries, 'You filthy—'

But Ceppo stops him with his fist.

'You might learn a little less pride,' sneers Guido, 'and so might the great Signor Tuccio.'

'Don't I know you?' Gaia begins, voice trembling. 'Haven't I—?'

'Come on,' he snaps, and drags her to the door, followed by Nofri and Ceppo, who plants a big kiss on Baldassare's lips, while he reels, still groggy from the blow.

They wrestle down the stairs, where the junk-heap bride keeps snarling and threatening. They're moving fast through the lower hall when the door flies wide and the watch bursts in, pursued by the fleet-footed servant. The captain's sword is at Guido's throat; the rest race to Baldassare, who wheels on his heel and knocks Nofri down. Ceppo heads for the stairs, his lacy train behind him, just as a watchman tangles his fist in the mildewed taffeta. Ceppo heaves back, the knife in his hand, and the man falls hard with the blade in his armpit. All come for Ceppo, who struggles and shouts, his bride's gown bloody. His victim twitches and soon lies silent.

Some minutes later, before a stretcher's been brought for the corpse of the watchman, and all but

Gaia stand in the street, Baldassare peers about him, seeing no sign of the others, only the scrofulous donkey that waits with its air of incurable melancholy.

'There were others here, too,' he says. 'They were making a racket under the window.'

'I know,' the captain nods. 'Your neighbours said so. But never mind,' he adds, giving his men the signal to move the prisoners off, 'one way or another, we'll discover who they were.'

A trial and counter-trial

SOON AFTER THE ABORTIVE CHARIVARI, THERE WERE A number of misfortunes in attempting to bring its perpetrators to justice. For instance, two days after the killing of the watchman, it was reported to the *podesta* by the captain of the people that Ceppo Castracani had died as a result of running headfirst at the wall of his cell 'in an excess of shame and choler'. No more than a week after this, the *podesta* received a second report, which stated that 'one Nofri Pasquini, carder, being of a frail constitution, and having fallen into a fit of melancholy as a result of his involvement in the abovementioned murder, perished in his cell on the eve of the Feast of the Apostle Andrew from an affection of the lungs'. As if this list of misadventures weren't enough, the authorities made no headway in discovering the identities of the other members of the gang. Both Ceppo and Nofri had insisted, despite the strenuous efforts of their interrogators, that they and Guido had only met their co-conspirators at a tavern on the evening of the charivari, which had been so drunkenly spontaneous that they hadn't even discovered the fellows' names.

Guido had maintained this story too and, as if to demonstrate the grotesque coincidence of his companions' deaths, remained doggedly alive, though he wasn't looking well. Of course, once it was discovered that all three of them were carders employed by Gaia's father, there were rigorous investigations in their workshop. Not only did the captain of the people send his agents, but Tuccio conducted a personal inquisition, involving individual interviews—in the presence of a notary—with every carder. Baldassare was brought, unannounced, to the carding sheds one day in an effort to secure an identification. But he recognised no-one, for the moon had not been bright that evening; besides, the culprits had been wearing masks. In the end, those in charge of the case lost interest in discovering the identity of these accomplices who, after all, had been guilty of no more than a mock serenade in doubtful taste; an irritating enough example of delinquency, but one so common in the town that, were they to lock up every drunken apprentice who'd banged a pan outside a cuckold's window, they'd need a gaol as big as the Borgo Santa Caterina. And, when all was said and done, they had the killers.

Tuccio himself was not nearly so complacent. Yet he too eventually relinquished the search for the others, and when the time arrived for Guido's trial, his mind was focused solely on its verdict. Indeed, it had disturbed him greatly that his daughter and her husband should be attacked inside their home and, what was more, by three of his own workmen. He found it hard to resist perceiving it as an attack upon himself. Of course, he'd realised for some time that many of the carders were in cruel financial straits. They were always the first to feel a downturn. And, yes, this downturn had perhaps been longer and more extreme than most. But this was just the way things were, the way the Almighty intended. How could they be otherwise? No, such disorder must be crushed at birth by the most severe punishments. It was no excuse to say that Guido Cupa had not stabbed the man. His invasion of Gaia's home made him as guilty as if he'd held the knife in his own hand. This was why Tuccio had put such pressure on the Signoria to send a memorandum to the *podesta*, urging hanging as the sentence. Not that Sandro needed much convincing.

At the trial, Tuccio sat and listened, his face a death mask. Guido did not look well at all. He was thin, whey-faced, the skin beneath his eyes bruise-blue, his nose misshapen; and he took an inordinate amount of time to shamble through the chamber. This aside, the *podesta* moved the trial along with admirable speed. Gaia's presence was not required, and Baldassare, his servant, his neighbours, the members of the watch, all came and went with great efficiency, the evidence piling up like clods upon a corpse. Indeed, the corpse kept casting furtive, beaten looks at Tuccio, as if he knew full well who was the force that drove this trial.

When all the mummery was over and the time for sentencing arrived, Sandro fiddled with his crimson robes, making the most of the moment, and then proceeded in his soft, Venetian tones. Tuccio could not have been more gratified had he himself composed the final form of words: 'Clearly these crimes of trespass, assault and the murder of a member of the city's watch are iniquitous at any time, but that they should form part of a conspiracy against the son-in-law and daughter of such an eminent merchant, one of the town's most illustrious men, is almost tantamount to insurrection. The court, in such a case, has neither wish nor option but to impose the severest penalty. Thus it is the decision of this court that, on the last day of this present winter, the carder Guido Cupa shall be hanged in the Piazza San Stefano.'

Not long after the handing down of Guido's sentence, the carders have retired to the upper room of their favourite tavern. Here they have already grown quite riotous with wine, and a number of them wear outlandish costumes found amongst the rubbish in a wealthy part of town. Geri Pinza, for instance, enthroned as he is at the head of the table, has draped a gown of soiled brocade across his shoulders; and Alfredo Crostadura, pacing up and down before him, wears a robe of tattered samite lined with cat. There are shouts and rumbles of laughter, and some surprisingly long speeches, punctuated by bellows of assent or disagreement.

'Do we have any further charges?' shouts Geri from his chair, lifting his cup as if it were some kingly attribute, and slopping wine onto the floor.

'Yes, my lord,' Alfredo nods, till it seems he might dislodge his head. 'I also accuse Tuccio di Piero Landucci of the murder of Guido Cupa.'

'And what, uh ... things ... would the honourable prosecutor present to the court by way of argument?'

'There is no need of argument, my lord. The man is guilty by his very nature. Is he not our miserable employer?' Flinging wide his arms, he turns to the assembled throng and is virtually blown down by gales of loud assent.

'But evidence, Alfredo, evidence. After all, this is a court of law.' This time it is Geri's turn to breast the carders' laughter.

'Well, if you insist, my lord.' He looks offended, and drains the cup before him on the table. 'It's the ... er ... contention of the prosecution that Tuccio di Piero Landucci did wilfully bring pressure to bear upon a court of the commune in order to ... uh, procure the death by hanging of the said Guido Cupa, guilty of no other crime than a youthful ...' But here he seems to run out of words, shrugging his shoulders at the puzzled crowd. 'Oh, stuff it, Geri. He nobbled the court to get Guido hanged.'

'Yes,' shouts Luca. 'He murdered Guido, and he'd do the same to any one of us that was in the charivari.'

'Guilty,' mutters Geri, banging his cup down on the table.

'He knows Guido didn't kill anybody,' adds Bartolomeo.

'He pays us nothing,' cries another, 'and has us work like dogs.'

'He makes laws to make him rich and us poor.'

'He used his position as consul to get a monopoly of dyes.'

'Guilty,' announces Geri, before any more can speak, 'guilty, guilty, *guilty*!'

With the last impact of his cup upon the table, the room falls silent. Alfredo stands, mouth open, as if unsure of what comes next. The crowd sits stifling belches.

'Um,' says Geri finally, 'does anyone have any other charges to bring ... against anybody else?'

'Yes,' Alfredo pounces, 'I'll say I do.' He peers round the room to let the tension build. 'I accuse Alessandro della Casa, the present *podesta*, of complicity in the murder of Guido Cupa.'

'But ... but he isn't dead yet,' suggests Ciuto di Dino.

'Well, he soon will be,' Alfredo snaps at the old man. 'There's no doubt about that. They want him dead, and he will be. Look at how willing the *podesta* was to bow to the Signoria.'

'Guilty,' intones Geri, but then, as if the thought had slipped his mind, he adds, 'Are there any words in his defence?'

'Well,' says Vieri slowly, 'he *is* said to have owed money to Signor Tuccio.'

'Oh, well, that's different,' Geri nods. 'We'll burn him before he's hanged.'

The room erupts in laughter.

For a moment there's another silence, then a voice cries from the corner, 'I charge the captain of the people with the deaths of Ceppo and Nofri.'

'Yes, yes,' shout numerous others.

'Guilty,' agrees Geri. 'Any further accusations?'

'Agnolo del Leone,' shouts Luigi Luchese, 'for charging high rents and fucking young boys.'

'Oh, yes, yes, guilty on both counts.'
'Marco Martello,' cries another.
'Guilty.'
And so the trial proceeds, its charges growing ever more extravagant, its judgements more perfunctory, until the hootings and guffaws and poundings on the table rise to a crescendo and it seems as if there's no-one further to accuse. Then gaunt Alfredo lifts his finger in the air, shouting in a hoarse, high voice, 'I accuse the *lanaiuoli*,' so that everything goes quiet.

Having waited for the silence to become attention, he continues. 'I accuse the *lanaiuoli*, and all the great ones of the town, of using their wealth to make us poor and their power to make us weak. I accuse them of refusing us admission to their guilds or the right to form our own, thus denying us the hope of holding office in the commune and any chance to better our condition. I accuse them all of preaching charity and having none, of giving alms to the registered poor while they let their workers starve. I charge them with making laws to suit themselves and enforcing them against us.' Finally he turns from the main body of the carders, to whom he's been addressing his harangue, and confronts a rather addled-looking Geri. 'I charge them with claiming to uphold the word of God, while doing the work of the Devil.'

Geri rises to his feet, and his heavy, ragged gown goes tumbling from his shoulders. 'Guilty,' he says at last, slurring the word drunkenly. And, as if he hasn't said enough, he mutters, 'Guilty,' and another 'guilty,' then totters, gazing sullenly about him. 'A fine speech, Alfredo,' he chuckles, almost to himself, 'though I'm afraid I'm not quite in a state to match it.' He peers slowly up at them. 'Except to say, in my position here as judge, that I do indeed find all these people guilty.' He bends to pick his robe up off the floor and drapes it over his shoulders. 'I think they should be punished ... quite severely. In fact, it's something that will happen.' He bangs his fist so hard upon the table that some of them look edgy. 'This February, during Carnival. On Saint Blaise's feast day, and at Mardi Gras. I can now assure you all that plans are underway, and that the guilty *will* be punished. Palazzi will be burned, and bodies also. Yes,' and he gestures with such passion that he nearly tumbles backwards, 'the guilty should be burned in the Piazza della Signoria, the prisons opened and the gaolers locked inside ... masters beaten by their servants, riders ridden by their horses, hawks eaten up by sparrows. On such a day the shadow of the sundial should turn backwards, the sands fall upward in the glass, and time flow back to start another way. Yes, the bodies of the great will burn till they ignite their souls in Hell.'

He stops, as if for breath, and vomits. But his curious speech has started further accusations, so that Luca and Vieri are sent below for wine as Alfredo speaks once more.

*L*ucia meets Brother Corvo
and Tuccio meets the Priors

LUCIA PARTS THE BRANCHES OF THE BROOM. IN summer, they're a mass of yellow flowers beneath this section of the wall, but now—a winter's night—they're mere rustling thickets of black shadow. Here, in the town's shabby quarter round the Ospedale degli Abbandonati, there's a breach below the walls, created by the peasants who daily till the fields out on the plain. Guido showed it to her early in the summer, as if dispensing some great privilege, and hinted at a pact between these peasants and the carders. Yet she tries to shake this memory—like every thought of Guido—from her mind, and concentrates upon the task at hand, forcing the branches far enough apart that she might thrust her head out through the breach. Carefully, and as quietly as she can, she wriggles from beneath the wall, listening for a movement on the parapet above. There is none, so she eases to her feet and slips away in a watchful, loping crouch.

The night is overcast and cold, devoid of natural light, and moving through the dark ravines Lucia is invisible. She heads toward the river, guided by its voice. She is apprehensive, trembling more with fear than with cold. If it weren't for what they'd done to Guido ... but she doesn't want to let those thoughts take hold, since every time she's started to remember, to feel his touch, to see the whiteness of his skin, she sees the fists and boots, his lovely face all broken, till she wants to tear the memories from her head. She's pretended not to care, even to Ambra, who surely has some notion of her feelings. But it's Tuccio she cannot bear, the spite with which he boasts of Guido's torment, his lust to have him hanged; she has wished him dead a thousand times—prayed, cast spells, made charms—yet still he lives, while Guido hastens to the gallows.

She gives a bitter smile amid the blackness. It's no use trying not to think of Guido, since the purpose of her coming here is him. She stops and peers round her for a moment. Apart from the torches above the Porta del Colombo, the only lights are fires further to the east, most likely on the nearer of the river's banks. She picks her way toward them carefully, the ground beneath her feet increasingly deceptive the closer she approaches to their restless shadows. There's a scuffling to her right, and a high-pitched, muffled giggle, as a group of children vanish at the edges of her vision. Then, quite suddenly it seems, the world grows brighter and she's almost there.

The largest bonfire is nearest to the water, but others burn about it; the only sounds are the crackling of the flames and the snap of breaking sticks. Even the river's voice seems drowned beneath the blaze. Scattered round them are quite a tribe of people, all with the loose, hard-bitten look of vagabonds. Some lie naked near the fires, and numerous bare-arsed children go scurrying about. There's the smell of burning flesh, which comes from spitted creatures roasting in the flames. She peers closer, seeing neither sheep nor boar nor hare, nor any beast that she might recognise upon a spit. It's only once she's nearer, noting their lean bodies and sharp snouts, that she knows that they are three large hounds slow-roasting to be eaten. She turns away, approaching the tall bonfire.

All waking eyes are on her, but not a word is said. A group of women and some savage-looking dogs are clustered near the flames. One of the beasts begins to snarl, curling back its lip and baring its white teeth. Another rises, rumbling. 'Bulfas,' says an ancient voice, 'Moloch.' And then she sees the speaker, rippling in the heat, an old and wizened woman with old and wizened eyes. There is some authority about her, and Lucia approaches, trembling. When she's no more than a pace or two away, a figure, hidden by the blaze till now, comes rising up as if out of the flames. He's tall and gaunt, with tonsured hair that hangs about his shoulders, and straightaway she knows that he's the one she's seeking.

'I've been told that Brother Corvo's here.' She clears her throat to keep her voice from shaking.

'He is,' says the man, somehow confirming that she's found him.

'He's said to have a gift for drugs and poisons.'

'Poisons?' He cocks an eyebrow and smiles around the group of women. 'There are no poisons, merely quantities that poison. The keys to Paradise, cut carelessly, unlock the gates of Hell.'

She frowns in some confusion, then plucks up all her courage. 'I want you to sell me something, in the right quantity, as you say, that might poison both the soul and body.'

He stares without a word, and the crackling of the flames might be the thoughts of those about her. His smile is open, friendly, with large and yellow teeth. 'Sell?' he chuckles. 'I'm no apothecary. Nor would I presume to tell you what you want. But here you are free to find by trial upon yourself that purchase which you seek.'

She stands, uncertain for a moment, then walks across to sit beside the now quiescent dogs. 'Yes,' is all she says.

'There's something happening here that bodes disaster for us all.'

Tuccio was in full flight. Once more his name had been drawn out amongst the ten, and he was determined to exploit the opportunity.

'In fact,' he continued, 'just to give you a clearer sense of the situation, I can provide you with at least one name with no great danger to its owner, though I'd still request, of course, that it remain within this room. This man is not, at present, an informant, but he could be influential. He's Bernardo Zoppo, the owner of a dye shop in the Borgo Santa Maria del Carmine. He's been hoping to get some price concessions from me and, in the course of our negotiations, has let slip a hint or two about the plans of certain carders, all very vague, of course, and easily denied. But I think he wants to give me the impression that, with the right inducements, he might be helpful.'

'I'm sorry,' ventured Marco Martello, shaking his head, 'and I understand how upset you must be, Tuccio, about the recent attack upon your daughter, but there's nothing concrete here. It's like you said with this dyer—all too vague and easily denied.'

'No-one's trying to deny anything,' snapped Tuccio, 'and yes, it *is* vague, precisely because we've got so much to find out. But what is clear is that something dangerous is beginning, and we must make provision for our own security. What Bernardo seemed to be implying is that the carders want their own guild, as well as positions reserved for them amongst the Priors, with the ultimate aim of redistributing taxes in their favour.'

There were cries of disbelief and outrage, and for the only time that afternoon Tuccio felt he had them with him, even Marco and his ilk.

'But it goes further than that,' he added, raising his voice above the noise. 'This is a threat to the very nature of our commune. To allow the led to lead, the ruled to rule, to make the servants masters, would be to open up our gates to lunacy and evil, to turn the world upon its head and go tumbling into chaos.'

There was no dissenting voice among them. He felt relieved, smiling primly at Agnolo del Leone, who nodded his agreement, adding, 'Of course, such demands are ridiculous. Yet the dangers are quite real. The rumours that the peasant farmers are involved seem of particular concern. They have connections with some villages which blame us for their lack of bread. If they opened the gates to these outsiders when things got out of hand—'

'But what do you propose?' urged Stoldo Peroni. 'We can't just have the militia attack them all. They're the means of our own wealth.'

'And let's not forget,' Marco added with a saintly smile, 'they haven't done anything yet.'

'Exactly,' said Tuccio.

'Then what *are* we to do? Sit on our hands and wait for them to murder us?'

'What I suggest,' purred Tuccio, 'is that we keep our eyes and ears open, vote Agnolo extra funds for more informants, check every saddlebag and cart that comes into the town, expand the militia and provide them with the best Milanese swords we can afford.'

'Yes,' Marco nodded impatiently, 'but if what Agnolo says is correct, then any militia we recruit may well end up outnumbered.'

Thank you, Marco, smiled Tuccio to himself, though what he said was, 'True. You've seen the problem clearly.' He glanced uncertainly around the table, since this bit would be tricky. 'The only possibility is this. If things get bad enough, we might just have a chance of outside help. Of course, it means another loan, though I'm sure we're all agreed it's worth it. You see, the fighting in the north, around Pistoia, has just ended. There are forces there now looking for employment. It's possible that some of these would camp up in the hills outside the town, in case of an emergency.'

'What forces do you mean?' asked Marco, narrowing his eyes.

'I ... was thinking of Wolf Schwanhals.' He gazed at his companions who, for men so often eager to make speeches, now seemed strangely speechless.

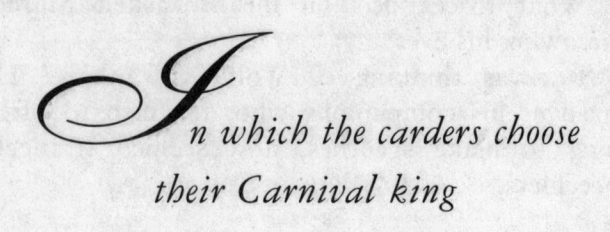

In which the carders choose their Carnival king

HIS CHIN SUPPORTED BY HIS HAND, SAINT BLAISE reclines among the long white ram's fleece of clouds high overhead. He gazes calmly down above the carders' sport and turmoil, a smile of soft beneficence upon his face, despite the iron combs and cards, the flails and bloody rakes—devices of his martyrdom—that tore his flesh to pulp and now litter the lambent surface of the clouds. Slowly he extends his other hand to cross the sky with two pale fingers, the symbol hovering above them for some moments, before dispersing in the air like sunlight. The vision too disperses, and Geri Pinza turns to watch the carders' race, the jeers and whistles erupting in the air about him as his eyes begin to clear of the sun-dazzle.

'Come on, Bartolomeo, don't just waddle. Run!' shouts Vieri di Grazino beside him.

'Go, Luca, quick! You're doing well!'

Geri spies Alfredo, a reluctant entrant, the big club bouncing at his thigh like a massive wooden phallus. 'Get a move on, Alfredo,' he bellows, 'you're running like a spavined ass!'

Alfredo half turns, grimacing, almost tripping on

the heels of the runner before him, so that Geri starts to laugh, slapping the shoulder of Vieri, who blushes at the unaccustomed intimacy.

They watch the group of runners, perhaps fifty in all, go pounding through the square before the tavern in hot pursuit of the ram that's fleeing up the lane by Santa Caterina delle Ruote. Indeed, it isn't actually a ram, but an aging wether, which should tire fast enough to spare its chasers any real embarrassment.

Over twenty workshops have turned out, despite the chill of the February day, and all have provided runners. Geri smiles to himself; this bodes well for their march on the feast of Saint Blaise, at which the winner of this race will be the king. He hopes it's someone from their shop, to add to their prestige—perhaps Luca, who's good at any game, or Bartolomeo, of such simple, splendid health that he just might come in first. Whoever it is, Geri knows that he and Alfredo will be the strength behind that Carnival throne. Alfredo has the words and ideas, while Geri has what Alfredo could never truly have, precisely because of those words and ideas—the trust of his fellow carders.

He glances round the crowd that's gathered in the square, taking note of the group from Bernardo Zoppo's dye shop, who are sharing jugs of wine beside the tavern wall. Bernardo himself, face shadowed by whiskers like smeared charcoal, seems surly and unsociable, refusing Geri's bids to catch his eye. Benno Sapori, on the other hand, with his useful contacts on the farms of the *contado*, gives him a wave and starts to stroll over, just as the wether comes clattering in.

The thing is wild-eyed and panting, slipping about on the stones. The beaters close off the square and the crowd gets in on the act, bleating, guffawing, waving their hands while the creature dithers and shies. Geri lets out a cheer as the first of the runners arrives. It's Bartolomeo, with Luca behind him; then all the others come pouring in. Bartolomeo heads straight for the sheep, which slithers away as he swings his great club and skittles a mob of wine-tippling fullers. But Luca, nudging aside a rival carder, swipes at the wether once, then twice, and finally thrice, crushing its skull with the blow.

It splays to the ground, dead in the instant. With a single voice, Geri and all of his workshop give out a cheer, joined by Bartolomeo, and then by Alfredo who's just reached the square. They shoulder their victor, hoisting him up the church's broad steps, where the priest, a fellow most willing to join the frolics of his flock, awaits with the robe of kingship, face wreathed in fatherly smiles. Luca stands bowed, like a boy at his confirmation, as the man swirls the sheepskin over his shoulders, adjusting the hood with its great curled horns.

'I procl-cl-claim you the K-King of the Ca-Ca-carders,' announces the stuttering pastor, warning his flock to enjoy the coming excesses with the rigours of Lent in mind, though his admonitions are lost in the din of their bleatings.

Luca shuffles before them, aware that the ᴐment calls for a speech. 'I declare ...' he declares ⸺oice still hoarse from his recent exertions. 'I ⸺ the coming of the carders' kingdom.' Then ⸺, as if such were sufficient for any new king.

But Alfredo and Geri are with him already, whispering in his ears, firming his face with new-found resolve. 'I declare,' he commences once more, 'that the world be turned upside down, that the great shall be humbled, the poor raised to power.' Here the priest begins shaking his head, plucking the sleeves of Alfredo and Geri; the King, wound up as he'd seemed, now runs down abruptly. 'Let the little men rise and the big men fall ... and, er ... let those who've sat on us be sat on ...' His speech trails off in a round of loud cheering, begun by Alfredo. Whatever objections the priest might have had are lost in the noise and the start of the feast.

The women and some of the carders start bringing the food—great platters of bread and slabs of strong cheese—while tapsters arrive bearing jugs of cheap wine. The slaughtermen get to work on the wether, wielding their knives in the chill winter sun; the butchers bring forward what broken-down goats and old ewes they can spare, slamming them down on the stones of the square where the carders are building their fire. 'The feasts of Cockaigne going free,' cry the women with platters of cheese and thick bread, while some—more sardonic—bear planks with dead rats, rotten herring, oats, wormy wine and old straw, shouting, 'The food of the poor, five florins a dish, the food of the poor, five florins a dish.'

'We'll leave those for the *lanaiuoli*!' roars Luca, forgetting his grandeur as King of the Carders. 'Only they can afford them.' His subjects raise up a cheer, tearing the dark, heavy loaves with their teeth.

Wine pours down throats and the first rich whiffs of the roast fill their nostrils, and a stronger, less wilful good cheer takes hold. New servitors come with the women and tapsters—carders dressed as clown princes, bishops, abbots and priors. As if the jugs contained words, not wine, talk floods from the labourers' mouths as the first burlesque dance begins—a father pursued and thrashed by his child to the whistles of the feasters. In the second a carder, uttering terrible cries and dressed like a wool merchant, gets flogged round the square by one of the fleece-beaters.

The last performance—for the time being, at least—has a very small carder arrayed as a Prior. But Geri sees little of this, since he's drawn aside by Benno Sapori, intent upon conversation.

'You know you can count on the peasants,' he says, just a bit too sincerely, as if he's put away more than his share. 'We're with you every step of the way.'

'Yes, yes, of course. We might not have had those without you,' nods Geri, observing the bright, unlawful swords in the hands of the dancers circling the Prior.

Benno raises his wine as if for a toast, and loudly announces: 'The villages of Roccianera, Maria del Poggio and Palude are willing and eager, and the breaches in the walls are complete.'

'Shh, Benno.' Geri peers round, smiling. 'I know these are friends, but we can't be too careful, can we?'

'Oh, Geri, you know you can trust the peasants. And the fishermen say they'll break with custom to march with the carders.' Abruptly his tone seems to darken. 'It's others I'm worried about.'

'What do you mean?' Geri narrows his eyes, while the mock-Prior whimpers in glittering sword-blades.

'I mean him,' Benno hisses, jerking his thumb at Bernardo Zoppo. 'I don't trust those dyers, particularly Zoppo. They're likely trying to have it both ways.'

'Do you *know* something, Benno?'

'There's nothing I know for certain, except that I'd only trust *him* to be loyal to his own interests. He's been seen at the Palazzo dei Dieci.'

'Well, that—' Geri hesitates. 'That could mean nothing at all.'

Yet he doesn't sound confident; Benno watches him, eyes out of focus, and he in turn is watching the Prior rise from his robes, dressed as a carder, to join his own killers.

Later that evening, downstairs in the carders' tavern, Geri sits with Bernardo Zoppo at a small corner table. The dyer seems uneasy, casting brief glances this way and that, as if to be sure of his cohorts' deployment about the room, yet gives a quick smile and says, 'A wonderful day, Geri, lots of wine and plenty of laughs.'

'Yes, and a good solid feeling amongst the men.' He watches Bernardo, follows his gaze on its circuit about the room. 'Still, that's only a foretaste of the march on Wednesday. Now *that* should be something. You know the Borgo San Pietro's committed itself as well?'

'No, Geri, no, I didn't.' He raises his eyebrows, half hopeful, half anxious. 'Well, that should pad out the numbers nicely. No worries there.'

Geri fills the dyer's cup again, though it's nearly two-thirds full. 'So, with them and the dyers as well, not to mention the people from the Ospedale quarter, we'll have quite a procession. Enough to make the *lanaiuoli* shit in their pants.'

Bernardo gives a humourless chuckle like a fit of dry coughing. 'Yes, indeed, Geri.' He raises his eyes, takes a sip of his drink and says slowly, 'Though I'm not really sure it's the right way to go about it, not any more.'

Geri watches him closely, seeking the gist of his words in his face. 'Not the right way?'

'No, it seems too ... provocative.'

'Too provocative?' Geri echoes once more. 'But you said that you'd—'

'March on Saint Blaise's day, I know.' Bernardo nods then looks at the fire. 'It's just, well ... things are different now.'

'Different? How are they different?' Despite himself, Geri raises his voice. 'The carders aren't paid any more than they were ... their taxes haven't gone down, have they? Or have I missed something, Bernardo?' He stares at the dyer intently, then utters a harsh bark of laughter.

'No,' Bernardo mutters, bristling at the sarcasm.

'But some change *must* have happened. After all, you're not marching.'

'Have I said I'm not marching?'

'I think so. Yes, I think you have.' Geri watches, and nods with increasing conviction. 'But just in case I'm doing you wrong—are you marching, Bernardo?'

'No. No, I'm not.'

'And why aren't you marching, Bernardo?'

The dyer turns his gaze from the fire, his features suffused with infinite reasonableness. 'I'm not marching, Geri, and my dyers aren't marching, because we think things are going too far. I mean all that flaunting of swords you're forbidden to carry, and the way they were used on the Prior in that dance. You saw the priest's reaction. He'll be off to tell the bishop, who'll take it to the Signoria.' He shrugs his shoulders and slowly shakes his head. 'To tell you the truth, I think you're teetering on the brink already.'

'Of course we are!' cries Geri, unable to restrain his anger. 'It was always going to be like that, surely you realised it. How else can we get any tax concessions, let alone our own guilds or places in the Signoria? Do we simply go up and ask? "Oh, excuse me, Signor Tuccio, but would it be all right if I took your seat as Prior?" I mean, I don't believe you're naive.'

'And I'm trying hard not to think that of you, Geri.' Bernardo gives a short, grim laugh and tosses back his wine. 'What do you honestly expect to achieve by incensing such powerful people? If you keep up the sort of antics you performed today, they'll crush you like the ants you are … like I am too. You won't stand a chance.'

'I see,' says Geri bitterly. 'Well, something's certainly brought about a change of heart.'

'Look, Geri,' the dyer urges, putting out a

conciliatory hand, 'I wish you'd see that I'm speaking with *your* good in mind as well as my own. What's going to happen after the march on Wednesday if they show no sign of bending? By Mardi Gras, or sooner, you'll be forced to use your swords. And what do you think the *lanaiuoli* are going to be doing then? Counting their money? Going to church? Shivering under their beds?' His hand is now a fist that thumps the table. 'No, they'll be sharpening their blades and getting the militia ready. And when they've had enough there'll be blood, which all the dancing in the world won't staunch, and a good many of your carders will be killed, and you'll end up choking on a rope in the Piazza San Stefano.'

There was silence between them for a moment, broken only by Geri's loud yawn. 'Well, I wish I'd known all this before.' He smiles unpleasantly, giving a snort of contempt. 'So there's risk involved and we might end up failing? All I can say is, I'm humbled by your insight. I'll bear it in mind when we've got our own guild and you're still kissing Tuccio's arse.' He gives the dyer a long, appraising look. 'Or maybe you're better off already. Maybe you found this sudden moderation of yours in one of your visits to the Palazzo dei Dieci.'

For the first time, Bernardo looks upset. 'What are you implying, Geri?' The veneer of reason has cracked, and now crumbles. 'Is there something wrong with my going to the Palazzo? Have I suddenly forfeited my rights as a citizen of Topomagro? No matter how obsessed you may be with your plotting, I still have business to conduct.'

'And what deals does that business involve, Bernardo?'

The dyer jerks abruptly to his feet. 'You know, I don't think I want to listen to this any more. I've spoken for your own good, not mine. But I suppose a man can always count on treachery to see treason everywhere.'

'Treachery?' snarls Geri, also rising. But Bernardo's heading for the door, followed by the eyes of those amongst his men still sober enough to note the speed of his departure.

The feast of Saint Blaise brings forth the parade and the rain. It does not bring forth the dyers. On the route from the river to the Piazza della Signoria they are nowhere to be seen. But everybody else is there—carders, peasants, fishermen—and Geri buries the dyers in the details of the day. Beneath the grey drizzle are drums and raucous horns as the long parade uncoils from the Piazza Santa Caterina, across the pale river and up through the throngs of the Via Gentili. The King, of course, is in the lead, wrapped in his sheepskin robe, his brow sprouting ram's horns; Bartolomeo and Vieri follow at his heels, carrying the Prior, red-robed and great-girthed, stuffed with soiled wool and as big as two men. Troops of carders march behind in time to the drums, their faces deathly with chalk, the charcoal of their eyes, moistened by the rain, already weeping blackened tears. In their hands they wave the weapons of their trade, the sharp-toothed cards and combs of martyrdom. Behind them come the peasants with their flails and levelling rakes, chanting rhymes to the beat of the drums—'Pile up the fires, pile up the pyres, pile on the liars and pile on the Priors,' or 'Thresh the great and rich, flail them till they twitch, beat and beat and beat, to make the harvest sweet'—until these rhymes that roar like drums, and drums like measured rhymes, fill every courtyard with the thunder of their passing.

Next comes the world that marches on its head, the topsy-turvy throng of husbands thrashed by wives, of lords who wait on servants, of mice that eat the great Guelph lion, its wool torn by their teeth, its face's clay already melting in the drizzle. Impossibility is piled upon absurdity, as if all order were inverted and the parade were time itself proceeding backwards, until the final conundrum—a fisherman caught by a mackerel—leads to the marchers of the Borgo San Pietro. These come striding behind their banner, a fish that holds Saint Peter's keys. And here comes their fisher-king, a moth-eaten Neptune riding in an ox-drawn boat with wheels, his moon-queen there beside him. His minions march behind them with their nets and hooks and traps, while hers—the hunters of shellfish—are marching with their lanterns. Among them, flaking and misshapen, is the leviathan itself, built from cast-off tanners' hides, its own huge bones picked clean and piled together. A Prior Jonah—bearing an uncanny likeness to the landlord of so many, Agnolo del Leone—is wriggling in its jaws, pausing in his pain to wave at friends among the crowd. This beast's patched tail is more or less the tail of the procession, a thing so long and slow it's almost sunset by the time that everyone arrives at the Piazza della Signoria. Here they beat their drums and chant their rhymes, then plant their emblems on the stones before dispersing to their homes or local taverns.

Later, when night has properly fallen and the watch arrives at last, they find before them on the steps, hacked and torn apart by hooks, combs, cards and flails, the figure of the bloated woollen Prior.

The worthies put on a show

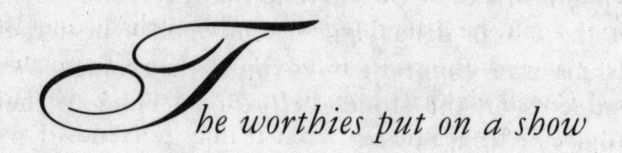

ALL THE BIG PEOPLE OF TOPOMAGRO—THOSE WHO, be they short or skinny, could stuff their shoes or vests with florins—sat in the largest chamber of Tuccio's palazzo. There were the full contingent of Priors and Gonfalonieri, as well as numerous advisers and special commissioners; there were the main officials from the Confraternity of Saint Mark, and the consuls from the town's leading guilds. Tuccio, tired from all the talking, stood at the head of the table in order to wind things up. 'The important point,' he said, hoping his tone sounded final enough, 'is that the sheer strength and confidence of our display should discomfit the seditionists. If this doesn't work, and insurrection ensues, then our response must be quick and ruthless. They have signalled the violence of their intent, and we must signal the resolve and power of our own.'

'I still can't believe their audacity, Tuccio,' said Bartolomeo Chiaudano. 'That business with the effigy, on the very steps of the Palazzo, and those traitorous rhymes. I—'

'Yes, yes, Bartolomeo,' put in Tuccio, eager to

avoid the revival of earlier points of contention. Once again he attempted to establish that conclusive, concluding tone. 'Some of what has happened might well deserve chastisement in itself, yet its only real danger lies in what it may portend. If we act too rashly, we might precipitate those very events we are hoping to avoid, yet might avoid them if we find the wisest middle path. And once tempers cool, when Lent has had its chastening influence, then there may be time to patiently seek out and punish all those guilty of the crimes that you so admirably condemn, Bartolomeo.'

'Please, not *may*, Tuccio, but *must*,' the man insisted. 'They *must* be punished.'

'Indeed ... Yes, indeed. But before you all go,' and Tuccio said this rather loudly, so that even those who dozed might hear, 'we owe a debt of thanks to one whose information we have found invaluable.' He gestured that this individual rise. 'On behalf of everybody here, I would like to thank you for your courage and sense of civic responsibility, Bernardo Zoppo.'

One week after the carders' march, the *lanaiuoli* and their friends had completed preparations for the selection of their king. It was to be by means of a tournament in the Piazza della Signoria, where the crowds had been gathering since early morning, jostling into the areas cordoned to contain them, while the sun flashed and vanished behind a host of rippling banners. From his seat with his wife in the worthies' raised stand, Tuccio observed the people's faces. He observed their amazement at the comic joust performed on a chain stretched high in the air between the Palazzo dei Dieci and one of the guildhall's bartizans. He smiled as they laughed at the fight of stilted giants in their thick, painted hauberks. Nor did he refrain from joining in their cheers at the customary battle before the Castle of Love, as the self-proclaimed Knights of Saint Mark—the most youthful members of that confraternity—galloped in triumph around the square, waving their swords and their flags of gold lions. But his applause was loudest when those stepped forth who would vie to be King, nodding as Beatrice pointed in turn to their son-in-law, Baldassare d'Aquila, and his friends, Bernardo Cuorevero and Aldo del Palagio, as well as numerous others among the town's worthies.

The armour and colours of these combatants were far more splendid than those of the 'armies', and the fighting showed greater skill and aggression, though Bernardo's blade slipped once beneath his opponent's pauldron, causing a nasty gash.

'I don't like that,' growled Tuccio, shaking his head. 'We don't want them hurting each other.'

However, most of the combats went smoothly, with Baldassare displaying panache in each of his matches, defeating Bernardo at last in consummate style.

'Oh, good,' purred Monna Beatrice, while Tuccio beamed with fatherly pride. 'He'll be King then.'

'We-ell, not quite,' he said, pointing out one final contender, who'd seemed to be blessed by freakish luck in all of his bouts thus far.

'Oh, no,' she cried, 'not him, whoever he is.' For his face was hidden under his visor. 'Apart from anything else, he's too fat.'

Indeed, he cut an ungainly figure upon his horse, and when the combat commenced, aimed nothing but farcical thwacks at Baldassare's helm.

'He's hopeless,' she laughed. Yet, just like the other opponents, Baldassare failed to make use of the openings left by the clumsy knight.

'Baldassare's been wounded,' cried Beatrice. 'In one of the earlier combats. Otherwise he'd move faster than that.'

He was finally knocked from his horse by a blow like the swipe of a cudgel. Nor did he get up before the other was judged the victor.

'I told you,' she hissed. 'He's hurt. You shouldn't have let it go on.'

'He's not hurt,' chuckled Tuccio, watching the stout man tug at his visor, which revealed the moist face of Bernardo Zoppo, as red as a helmeted lobster. 'Baldassare and all of the others agreed to it. It means that the dyers, the most pivotal group, are now with us. And not just Bernardo's own. Making a dyer our Carnival King means that *all* the dyers are with us. And the carders, along with their allies, will see it, publicly, like this.'

She shrugged, unimpressed. 'Well, I don't like it. Baldassare could have won. It's like making a clown our King.'

'Even if nothing else works,' he smiled, appearing not to have heard her, '*this* will demoralise them.'

His words were borne out by those large groups

of dyers who yelled their approval. They might well have been cheering his tactics. Nor did their roaring abate, but increased threefold when Agnolo del Leone, the gold coronet and ermine-trimmed robe in his arms, descended the stairs to crown the dyer as King under hosts of billowing lions.

Later that day, Geri stood with those on the Via Gentili to watch the worthies' parade. He waited with hosts of carders beneath the high walls of the merchants' palazzi. Those around him were poor and—though chastened at first by the size of the turnout—their squalor, their rags, the stink of their poverty now reassured him. The *lanaiuoli* were granted the luck, not just of their birth, but of one of the finest days all that winter. Still, the warmer the sun and the brighter their armour, the more the crowds would resent them. He peered around him, finding paupers infested with vermin, vagrants with broken, carious teeth, workers drunk with bad wine and hunger, all the troops of that hidden army awaiting the first real crack in the high walls about them. The sound of beaten drums and blown brass announced that the worthies were coming, and he, like all those about him, peered intently along the street.

The first of them all was Bernardo, the King, with his glittering crown and long robes. Close at his heels came the knights he'd so doubtfully vanquished, their smiles and steel blades aglitter. Next were the Priors and all of the great ones, dressed in the trappings of office or wealth. In turn came the priests and the doddery bishop, the merchants, physicians and lawyers, perhaps more elaborately robed than the rest, with their wives on their arms in opulent gowns. Banners waved and flags flew above them, while conservative craftsmen and careful small businessmen trailed along after, piously proud to be there at all. The procession surged past on the wings of its wealth, or so it appeared to Geri as he watched them vanish along the street, trailing the troops of the city gates and, lastly, the town militia. Here was no Carnival march, no freedom, no rich hint of chaos. Here was the simple display of might and God's good order as seen by the Priors—the florin, the cross and the sword, spelt out to caution the people. But the people were past the point of such warnings, of this he felt certain. He turned to confirm his conviction, and felt his guts twist as he saw, not only the ignorant paupers, but carders as well—even Luca, their Carnival King—staring in open-mouthed awe at the vanished procession.

Mardi Gras riots

MARDI GRAS—FORTY DAYS BEFORE CHRIST'S PASSION—Carnival's last convulsive shudder before the pale sobriety of Lent. Here, before the fast, the feast; before abstinence, abundance; before chastity, lubricity—all day the lords of misrule have reigned in every tavern, and the courts of fools have been in session. Parades, burlesques and banquets, till now less frequent than in richer times, have suddenly burst forth upon the town. Great bands of paupers and vagabonds have gathered to be fed at church and hospice; gangs of youths, apprentices, poor journeymen, have run in drunken sorties through the streets. Strange sights have widened every eye: a tournament of jesters armed with wooden spoons, which left four senseless on the stones of the Piazza San Stefano; a bloated man astride a wine tun, with two dead pheasants in his hands; a cripple playing Lazarus in a street burlesque; and in the Piazza del Colombo, a gigantic pair of roosters pecking at each other's painted fabric feathers. In the brothels, full as churches, the townsmen have partaken of the body, and in the streets there has been blood.

In the early evening, at Lent's threshold, the

Confraternity of Saint Mark holds a feast at its eponymous abbey. Here are meats and wines to rival Gaia's wedding banquet, though the entertainments are more extravagant. Six Venetian acrobats traverse the vaulted ceiling, and jugglers from Parma vie with Roman clowns for the worthies' attentions. Sicilian fire-eaters, like domesticated dragons, make to roast the ladies' meats, while contortionists rival southern pasta with their twinings. Tuccio, as de facto host with Agnolo del Leone, observes the goings-on with proprietary pride.

He watches Marina and Baldassare rise to dance, as a performing Lombard bear, still tethered by a chain to its master's belt, steps up onto a keg and rolls it back and forth, its feet flip-flopping on the staves. He leans against the cushions with a sigh, closing his eyes slowly. Such a pleasant evening, so long as nothing happens to disturb it. Should things go wrong, and the clog-wearers make their move, his men are all too ready. The militia is on the alert, there are weapons here and at the Palazzo dei Dieci, and the addresses of known leaders—such as those of his own workers, Geri Pinza and Alfredo Crostadura—have been distributed. But he's convinced that nothing *will* disturb them. The eruption's been indefinitely postponed. Yes, of this he feels quite certain, and tries to put all thought of it behind him, determined now to let himself relax and have his feast in peace.

Later, after the completion of their supper, they all don masks and gather on the Via del Colombo to proceed to the Palazzo. They walk with lanterns, their silks and satins rustling like the wings of fireflies as they parade past Tuccio's house, his servants gaping from the windows. The ladies wear the faces of enamelled, sequined cats, and in the lamplight's shifting glow the men walk, chatting, like elegant bears or lions. Since the curfew has been cancelled in their honour, a host of oglers gathers on the way, while the blades of the militia clank warningly behind. But the winter night is cold, and soon, beneath the sculpted brows and cheekbones, those lips not painted red have turned quite blue, so that all are pleased to finish their parade and reach the tall Palazzo dei Dieci. Here, followed by the ropewalkers, contortionists, the jugglers and the bear, they hurry inside to their Mardi Gras ball, and the militia take positions round the inner courtyard.

At about this time, in the Borgo Santa Caterina, the carders storm across the old stone bridge, their torches burning in the new moon's dark. They seem to move in a shower of flames, the whey-faced ones with hollow eyes, the painted death-masks, the cone-nosed men that jiggle like mosquito-sired demons. Stout Geri strides along, Alfredo at his side, eyes blackened with damp charcoal. Behind them come the gangs of workers from the sheds and peasants from the town, and even some who've crawled beneath the wall already, marching in their masks to the bray of wooden horns. At their head, lumbering between the torchlit houses, comes their King in effigy, a Prior stuffed with straw, his face aflicker in the orange light, the scowling image of old Tuccio. Geri peers round him at his army, listening to their laughter with deepening satisfaction.

The dozy watchmen sent to spy upon their homes had crumpled with no sound. It was a portent of the night ahead, and he stares along the darkened tunnel of the street toward the great Palazzo's tower, unseen but fast approaching.

Some way before them and a little to their left, in the Borgo dei Panettieri, yet another Mardi Gras procession is in progress. A host of children, wearing woollen cloaks and carrying long tapers, moves slowly through the streets. Two ancient friars from San Francesco lead them, conducting their chant with trembling hands as their high-pitched voices cry:

> *'In the wheat field kill the mice,*
> *In the hen coop kill the lice,*
> *In the fruit trees kill the weevils,*
> *Fire, kill the Devil's evils.'*

These children wander through the streets of baker's shops and granaries with fire in their hands, eyes solemn with their purifying task, as if spring itself depended on their presence. The friars guide their footsteps through the dark, their tapers pale reflections of the carders' torches, their voices gentle echoes of the carders' roaring cries a dozen streets away.

In the Palazzo dei Dieci the worthies' ball proceeds apace. A wide circle of masked dancers orbits the great fire; jugglers dressed like jesters lob apples past the bear, his back quite black with shadow, belly red with fiery light. Tuccio, puffing with exertion, flops amongst the cushions by Agnolo del Leone. 'Well,' he says, 'it looks as if the gamble has paid off,' and Agnolo nods his head, both unaware that, just beyond the walls of the Palazzo, the carders are erecting their swollen, grim-faced Tuccio on the Piazza della Signoria. For here, while Tuccio converses comfortably within, the faggots are heaped about his effigy's straw legs, his crimes upon its head. As the captain of the people rushes in to tell them, the straw erupts in flames, and the windows glow vermilion. The captain stands there gaping, his message never heard.

Men and women hurry to the windows. Baldassare and Bernardo Cuorevero have gone already for the weapons in the cellar.

'Riot!' cries one amongst the crush.

'The rebellion's started!' shouts another, rushing for the door, while others try to calm the mounting panic.

'They're trying to get in!'

'They'll kill us all!'

Agnolo del Leone, flushed with drink or anger, bangs a chair down on the floor so hard that, for a moment, there is silence. 'No-one's coming in!' he bellows. 'And no-one will be killed except through fear.'

While Agnolo tries to get them quiet, Tuccio confers with one of his young servants, saying, 'You know which way, once you turn off the road to Perugia?' The youth, still nodding, rushes from the room.

A host of men now swarm up from the cellar, holding spears, swords and halberds. Better even than the wrath of old Agnolo is the sight of all these warriors bristling with bright arms, so that fearful cries now turn to heartening shouts as the troops surge out the door. In the square there's nothing but the figure made of straw, already withering; far across the town they see the glow of further burning. They break up into groups, fanning through the streets, some clad half in steel and half in silk; others dressed like dandies; others yet—forgetful or uncaring—still wear their masks and leap into the dark like bulls or bears or lions, swords swinging in their fists.

Geri Pinza stands in the street beneath the burning palazzo of Marco Martello. The lower windows, like the mouths of kilns, spew out orange flame, and incandescent streamers flicker through the smoke that seeps between the roof-tiles. He feels as if his chest and face, both crimson with the heat, have caught on fire, yet he doesn't move, standing on the stones in silent contemplation of the carders' work, the torch still smouldering in his hand. In their first rush through the house, the rioters have hurled its contents out of windows, down into the street, where others put them to the torch; tapestries and carpets, leaning heaps of clothing, bolts of silk, bright rugs, the heavy canopies of beds, ignite in bright red flame. Carders, combers, washers, scourers, leap from blaze to blaze with torches in their fists. Further down the street, the children and the household's servants cringe in doorways as neighbours—some with buckets sloshing in their hands—attempt to comfort them, yet stay back from the house, discouraged by the carders' swords. Vagrants too are here already, some drawn forth by riot, some by hope of heat, but most by the thought of pilfering some object of great value from the blaze, darting at the piles as yet untouched by torches, or crouching round a fire's crackling birth, plunging in their hands for a piece of clothing or a pile of gilded buttons, only to be flung aside and threatened with a blade.

Against the black sky, where the road slopes down toward the sea, a tower is now burning. Sulphurous clouds already roil about it, and Geri briefly wonders where the blaze will stop, just what will happen if they go on with their torches. He sees some carders loading jewellery, silver buckles and sconces from the walls into a folded damask swatch, and all these questions leave him.

He rushes over, shouting, 'Leave those things alone,' and waving his extinguished torch. 'We can't let them call us thieves.'

The carders, who are men from the workshops of Marco Martello, stare at him, amazed. 'What?' demands one. 'How else are we to get our due?'

'Not by thieving,' Geri insists. 'The due of thieves is to be birched throughout the town stark naked.'

'Then it's Marco should be birched,' protests another, 'since it's him who stole from us.'

'That's right,' says the first, gathering the cloth about his spoils. 'We're taking our due payment.'

Geri knocks the damask from his fingers with the torch, then draws his sword. 'We agreed on this. We mustn't risk our cause with looting.' But now another group arrives, including Luca and Alfredo, who also draw their swords.

'It's true!' snaps Luca. 'We said that was the way,' and those behind him mutter their agreement.

'Set this junk alight!' says Geri, while the pilferers protest. Alfredo thrusts his torch against the cloth, which smokes, then starts to blaze. 'We can only lose by stealing.'

'Well, what do we do now then,' snarls one of the would-be looters, 'since we can't do much more here?'

'Burn down Tuccio's carding sheds,' says Luca, raising his torch in the air.

Alfredo looks at him and shakes his head. 'Don't be an idiot. The sheds are the carders' livelihood.'

'Then we'll burn his house. Just like Martello's. What do you say?'

'All right, let's do it.'

'Burn down Tuccio's house!'

And they're rushing up the street already, no longer bothered with the conflagration, united once again, while the servants shamble forward and the vagrants leap among the half-burnt piles of valuables.

At about this time, a group of peasants from a nearby village, having crawled beneath the walls, are forcing entry to a butcher's shop within the Ospedale quarter. When the gates give way they tumble in, then stare about them, axes at the ready. There's nothing in the courtyard but carcases that hang from hooks, though they don't let this discourage them, knocking down the door into the house, where they find the butcher and his wife already wriggling through the windows that lead into the rear lane.

'Got you!' laughs their leader, and drags the butcher down, turning as he sees the wife rush for the door. 'Go on, get her!' he yells, then hauls his man into the yard, where the woman now stands pinioned.

'We've waited a long time for this,' he says, face cracking in a broken grin.

'What ... what is it?' The man's knees buckle, and only his assailants stop him falling.

'What *is* it?' The peasant puts his knife against the fellow's chin. 'Well you might ask.' Then yanks him closer to the carcases, so his feet scrape on the ground. 'But you couldn't really give a fuck, now could you?'

'I—I haven't done anything, I—' The knife-blade, scraping at his jawbone, interrupts his protests.

'Shut up!' The man is holding the knife firm, glancing at the others as the woman starts to yell, and they pull her hair till she subsides in whimpers. 'As if the toll on the beasts wasn't bad enough, consider what you pay us. And look at the profits you've been making.' He indicates the ample house and shop for, indeed, the butcher is by far the richest of his trade within the town, virtually controlling the purchase price of any creature bought for slaughter. 'Have you seen how men are living in the villages?'

'Have you seen how men are *dying*?' cries another.

'I've got n-nothing to do with—' But now he shrivels back, chin cascading blood as the knife flicks up again.

'That's right,' says the leader, 'n-nothing, n-not any more,' and they drag him closer to the marbled slabs of meat that sway upon their hooks. 'How do you think it feels to be one of these creatures that you slaughter?' When the man just gapes back, silent, he prods him in the ribs. 'Well, *how*?'

'I ... I don't ...' The words have dribbled dry.

'Oh, well,' he laughs, eyeing the butcher, then a vacant hook, 'there's only one way to learn, isn't there?' In a single swinging lift they heave him up, then jerk him down, so the hook tears through his neck, leaving him dangling, making strangled sounds, toes fretting at the stones while his wife cries, 'Please, please, let him down.' But they truss her up with bits of twine and gag her with her blouse. They trade swift glances; then, at a nod of the leader's head, go running out the gates, leaving the woman—hands behind her—pushing with her back against her husband's feet to ease his pain.

Meanwhile, in the Via dei Panettieri, the tower of Agnolo del Leone burns forty times over in the eyes of the chanting children. The friars order them away, but some continue staring. Further up the street a crowd of paupers has besieged a wealthy bakery. Their angry voices rise beneath the fire's roar and, as the children watch, the door falls down and some rush in, others peering through the windows till they fling the baker out, exclaiming, 'Robber! Give us bread!'

'There's barely a loaf to give you,' his voice pipes thinly through the tower's roaring. 'Liar!' they cry, and yet he argues still, 'I give to charity.' But 'Liar!' they cry once more, and with a wrenching thrust they lift him up, back toward the door, and like a single starving thing come lunging after him. The friars herd their charges, leading them away, and once again their high-pitched, holy voices chant:

> '*In the wheat field kill the mice,*
> *In the hen coop kill the lice,*
> *In the fruit trees kill the weevils,*
> *Fire, kill the Devil's evils.*'

A little later, long fingers of red fire clutching at his back, Geri Pinza comes scuttling out beneath the ground-floor arch of Tuccio's palazzo. The shop's already well ablaze, and a group of carders batters at the door that leads up to the house. Servants are flinging wide the upper shutters and staring out in terror. Some shout down into the street, but Geri doesn't listen. He's seen the men approaching from the Via del Colombo, figures wielding heavy swords, half armoured in long gambesons or helms, some in cloaks of minever and some with lacquered masks still fastened to their faces. They're coming fast now, at a run, twenty, twenty-five at most, and he stares about him quickly, glancing at his workers gathered in the street—fifty carders there at least, and perhaps as many washers, all with knives and some with swords. Then the worthies are upon them, Doffo del Bene at their head, young men with training and good weapons. He sees a group of carders fall back, running, some cut down in the initial onslaught; it seems the very speed of the attack might cause a rout. He waves his torch about, abusing those retreating. But now Alfredo's there, emerging from the flames below the house with still more men, all hurling their red torches. The worthies try to ward them off, as Alfredo, Luca, Vieri and the rest come slicing in with swords. He hears loud shouting from the dark beyond the fire, and sees a mass of peasants hurtling down the street.

A rush of triumph fills him. He feels the power of the poor converging to avenge those wrongs till now unrighted. The young men rally, back to back, set upon by sickles and the best blades of Milan. Some retreat to less exposed positions, Doffo del Bene swinging his great broadsword; others simply scatter, harried by the peasants. For the first time since the burning started, Geri feels some hope. His cause swells up inside him and he rushes with his sword to join the fray. Around him now the ever-present vagrants have swarmed in, having seen which way the fight is going, kicking at the youths who've fallen to the ground and snatching their fine weapons.

In the light from the burning shop-front, Geri notes their snarling faces, grotesque as carvings on cathedral walls. A flash flicks by his eyes and he sees the sword already at its zenith. He lunges with his blade, piercing the boy's soft belly, watching how he grits his teeth, breath rattling as he falls. He wrenches back before the sword's dragged from him, eyes upon the boy's racked face; all the while he senses something different, a kind of rumbling thunder that echoes through the stones. He stops, and others round him stop as well, even those caught in the midst of murdering each other; all listen, letting their swords drop, turning slowly like somnambulists to peer up the street where, coming through the fast-converging host, they see the horsemen, swords upraised and axes hacking down, hewing hands, arms, heads, like Death's own woodsmen helmed with boar and swan. Saint Mark has brought Wolf Schwanhals.

In which Brother Corvo reaps a harvest

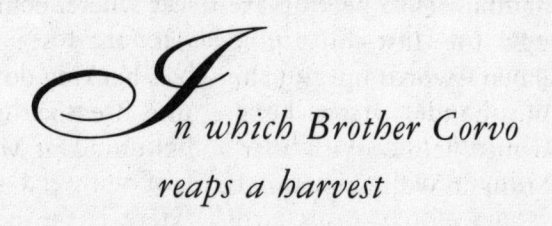

IN THE PIAZZA SAN STEFANO THERE ARE TWENTY weird trees. Each has a trunk with just one branch supported by a single brace. Each branch bears one dead fruit, and that fruit is a man, and he hangs from a rope. In this orchard of dead men that grows from the stones before the church of San Stefano, a single watchman dozes by his fire. With the moon overhead, the watchman sleeping and the Porta San Stefano locked for the night, Brother Corvo, old Maria, Speranza, Fiducia and half-a-dozen others come slipping from a laneway to the shadows of the square.

Brother Corvo, who prudently held his minions aloof from the Mardi Gras disturbances, puts a finger to his lips and bids them linger where they are. They have spent some hours dodging the town watch, creeping from the breach in the south-east walls—shown them by Lucia in payment for their poisons—and he wants no errors now. So they remain and he slips across the square, gliding from one thicket of dark shadows to the next, only the knife that glints its silver mimicry of moonlight hinting at his presence. But the watchman remains snoozing, even when the blade has slithered through his ribs, disturbing his repose for just a moment of sharp anguish. Then Corvo strides about the square more carelessly, his habit gathered round him, hands clasped behind his back, surveying those geometric trees of withered fruit like some monastic orchardist. Here is the heavy form of Geri Pinza dangling from his rope, eyes bulging in his face and his tongue stuck out. And there Alfredo, head cocked strangely down, as if his body, yearning for the earth, had sought to wrench his twisted neck out of the noose. Luca, Vieri, Benno Sapori, the leader of the peasants, and numerous others are hanging there as well. Corvo peers up into their choked blue features as if to read some oracle of Topomagro's future.

Finally he crooks an arm and his followers come forward, glancing swiftly round them. One or two now warm themselves beside the watchman's fire, but most have taken Corvo's lead, wandering among that gallery of grimaces and dangling limbs. Only Maria, Speranza and Fiducia seem intent upon some purpose, for which the ancient woman draws a knife out of her robes while the others grasp her hips to lift her up. She reaches with her spindly arms, holding out the blade toward the face of Luca Peroni, the erstwhile King of the Carders, where his tight-clenched teeth have almost bitten through his tongue. She slices once and finds the job quite easy since he's all but done it for her. Then, catching the leathery thing between her fingers, she puts it in her woollen pouch. Her work is not so quick with Geri, whose tongue, though rigid and quite purple, is perfectly intact. With him she takes her time, cutting away carefully, puffing out small gasps of steamy breath from the exertion. Slowly she completes her circuit round the bodies, omitting only those whose tongues are captive under teeth and locked behind the muscles of clenched jaws.

This harvest done, she closes up her pouch, kneading the stiff contents and smiling to herself. For they will soften well enough when boiled and leached out for their virtues. Now Brother Corvo crooks his arm once more, returning whence they've come. Nor does he glance back toward the carders, since their destiny will not be his. He has far more than desperation—or even so tenuous a thing as justice—on his side. The God of Light, like the sun behind a hawk, is with him, and the shadow too that comes out of the south to do His will. To the east of the town he hears the pipes still skirling, guiding his party back to their provisional exile, and for the moment he goes to them.

THE LORD OF LIGHT

Brother Corvo prepares for battle

DAWN, THE BEGINNINGS OF SPRING, THE EAST A WHITE light, a hole in the dark from which a cold wind comes like the breath of day's waking. To the east of the town, on a bare, stony hill, figures move: a flapping of rags, a spare-jointed stamping, shadows cast against light. As if day mourned its birth, the song of the wind is the whining of pipes and the cry of cracked voices. A fire rocks and shivers, coughs sparks into the paling sky as the figures circle round it like a dance of moulting birds. One, the crone Maria, feeds its flames with odd gobbets—a buzzard's cut heart, vervain picked barefoot under Taurus, a donkey's pizzle, blessed wine mixed with spittle—and the blaze leans out toward her in the wind, opening its red maw. The dancers reel and stumble as if drunk, baring their teeth to laugh. Brother Corvo, with a reddened stick or bone, covers rags in lists of words. Fiducia, having found the power of talismans and amulets under old Maria's guidance, moves among them draped with hangings like a human shrine—sprigs of rosemary to ward off hostile spirits, heliotrope to silence slander, a hare's foot for the soothing of wild dogs, mistletoe against arraignment, and five nettle leaves to warrant safety from all fantasy. She, like her companions, turns her eyes to Corvo as he rises from his writing.

Bending for a moment by the fire, he speaks the words of consecration to a heap of bone and feathers. He lifts the buzzard with its heart cut out, holding it above his head, wings spread—a burlesque cruciform for adoration—before he hurls it at the flames. His people stand watching in the ashen air; Maria comes to help him with the pile of scribbled rags, lifting them up and flinging them amidst the heat, where they fall, then briefly seem to float until they fall once more, these namings, as their owners fell from Heaven into fire. The crowd washes back, mindful that the burning of such words might free the spirits which they name. They wait to windward; the fire, whipped and kindled by the blast, yearns down toward the town with smoky sighing.

Corvo stands before them, opening out his arms to guide the streams of embers, crying, 'Fall upon them in Your light as You fell from Your twin God, YHWH, Tetragrammaton, God of darkness and gross matter. Fall upon them in the brightness of Your being, whom some call Lucifer, and others Satan, and yet others foul Beelzebub. Fall upon them and ignite their darkness with Your light, tear their gross flesh with teeth of purest flame, Apollyon and Abaddon. Bring forth Your great powers, Asmodeus, Berich and Azazel, and deploy those princes despised by Your dark twin, abandoned by His world, and variously cursed as

Dagon, Thammuz, Moloch, Belial, Baal and Mammon. Call up those mysteries out of exile from the shadowed world, Heradiana, Demogorgon and Abraxas ...'

Here some sap-filled branch or badly balanced log, or spirit reluctant to be summoned, disturbs the fire with a splintering crack and fountain of red sparks, so that Corvo's flock begins to moan and cower in the brightening dawn. He towers over them, throwing up his hands and shouting, 'Here me, Prime One, for Your time has come and we are here to serve You. O, Lord of Light, send forth that shadow of Yourself, that pestilence which rages from the south and east to nullify all flesh. Destroy this town, infect its people's blood with fevers, their flesh with sores, and in the agony of death fill every heart with black despair against the God of matter, that He may die within them. Grant us the privilege to lead them in the path of Your wise spirits, Tabuel, Adin, Tubuas, Raguel, Sabaok, Uriel, Simiel, Floron ...'

And so he continues into morning. The members of his flock, watching that descent of fiery spirits on the town, feel their hearts catch fire, each one a black and burning coal within its grate of bone.

Lucia takes Jacopo to Corvo's kingdom

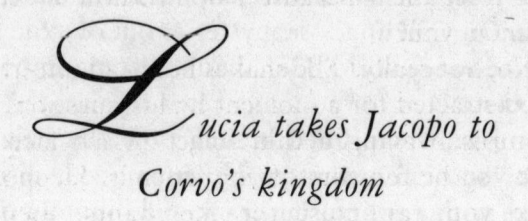

TWIN FIGURES ON THE MOLE AT TOPOMAGRO, silhouettes, their backs a little silvered with pale light. Behind them, the rising plateaux of the town with the starry Bull astride its towers, and the moon a skewered onion on the Duomo's campanile. The black sea lies before them like a breathing beast, its dark reflected in their faces as they sit and watch it, tethered by each other's arms, the slow waves lapping at their feet.

'Come tonight,' insists Lucia. 'Tonight's a special night for them, a kind of sabbath.'

Jacopo watches her white eyes, like moons of mercury within her shadowed face. 'I've said no, Lucia. These friends of yours, they're witches, or worse. I don't want to go and see them.'

'You're scared?' Her laughter starts as a soft carillon, but ends with a brazen echo. 'I wouldn't have thought it of you. My little thief a coward.'

For a moment he looks offended, then slowly smiles and says, 'But that's the point. I *am* a thief, just like the merchants are thieves, and my friend, Fra Lippo. I'll trust a thief because I know what he wants. But these friends of yours, these witches ... I don't trust them because I don't know *what* they want. Do you?'

'No, not really.' She shakes her head uncertainly, as if distracted for a moment by his question. Then she turns, waving a thin finger in his face. 'But don't you be too sure of *your* friends, Jacopo. You think you can trust the merchants, men like Tuccio?' She spits into the hissing waves, and snaps, 'They're pigs. I know what he's like, I work for him. The trouble with you is, you want to be like them so you steal their possessions. Thieves like you look up to them as better thieves ...'

Shaking his head, he holds out his hand toward her lips. 'That's not true. I don't admire Tuccio. I hardly know anything about him. I—'

'You hardly know him? Isn't he obvious enough to anyone who's not a fool ... one of those men whose silky smiles hide the heart of a vulture. Look at what he did—what he *had* done—to Guido and the others.' She turns away, and when she speaks her words sound choked. 'I saw him strangled on that rope, his eyes bulged out ... his beautiful soft eyes ... and his lips all twisted as his body turned ...' She stops to get her breath, panting thick, dry sobs. 'If I could have that done to Tuccio ...'

'Lucia ... sshhh, come on,' he whispers, wrapping his arms about her, nuzzling his face into her tight-curled hair and rocking back and forth, back and forth, upon the stony pier. 'There's nothing can be done, not now. Don't make yourself feel worse.'

For a time she weeps; her tears add their paltry matter to the sea, and Scimmi watches as they plummet, nosing at the air. Jacopo croons his words like whispered lullabies. Suddenly she gives a sniff and sits up straight. 'Jacopo,' she says at last, nodding her head slowly, 'you're right. This isn't any use.' She holds him tight and strokes his hair. 'Come ... it's time you went with me ... to the sabbath. They know so much of healing and of herbs ... and of so many secret things.' She kisses his cheeks, his lips, his eyes, wetting him with fragmentary tears, till he feels himself begin to nod in slow agreement, already rising as she goes.

'What tricks have they been teaching you?' he laughs, tucking his unwilling cat beneath one arm and reaching out his other for her hand, skipping to keep up as she marches off to skirt the moonlit walls.

The fire is so large that it seems more like a hill of molten gold. Caves of saffron and dark crimson burn within, and its twin lies shimmering by the river's shifting waters. Only the figures that move around it reduce its size as they draw nearer, vague shadow-spirits drifting through its vapours. Some, naked or arrayed in rags, go reeling by like drunks, their bodies larded with dark oil. Lucia smiles at one or two and waves toward some ancient hag who fails to notice, preoccupied with pushing off the dogs that sniff her skirts. A group beside the river passes around a bowl, each taking a small sip then handing it along. Others, stretched beside the fire, let children rub their flesh with unguents, chatting all the while. One, barely visible behind the amulets that clothe her, comes across and stands before Lucia.

'Here, this is for you,' says Fiducia, holding out

what might be cuttlebone strung upon some twine. Jacopo sees faint letters written on it. 'It will help you to win favour with everyone you meet.'

Lucia takes the talisman and the woman grins up eagerly, eyes bright with what might almost be infatuation. 'Go on, read it!' she says, watching Lucia scan the letters, then peering askance at Jacopo who cranes to see them too.

```
S A T O R
A R E P O
T E N E T
O P E R A
R O T A S
```

Lucia squints at the powdery forms, then frowns. 'But what does it mean?' she demands, frowning harder still, as if the meaning had been hidden in the soft, calcareous shell.

'Oh,' says Jacopo, seeing something there, and Fiducia glares at him, speaking up fast before he can tell Lucia.

'Read it down,' she instructs. Lucia parts her lips once more, as if to make a protest, but Fiducia swiftly adds, 'Now read it left to right, then read it backwards from the bottom, then—'

'But I can't read!' Lucia snaps, as if that sealed the matter.

'Well, nor can I,' proclaims Fiducia, unsurprised, 'but that's of little consequence. Its strength remains unchanged. Brother Corvo told me how it works.'

'It reads the same all ways.' Jacopo peers at the shell.

'Well, of course it does.' Fiducia barely looks at him, already turning the talisman about. 'You see these letters on the back?' But her words are interrupted by the growling of first one dog, then another. A pair of massive hounds begin to bark at Scimmi's pouch, then suddenly the hag comes up with flaming brands, driving them before her. Jacopo notes the other creatures near them, some cringing from the barking dogs, some taut, some passive—cockerels in cages, ravens, jackdaws, birds of many sorts, and other cats and yapping dogs, a goat, a tiny hedgehog, rabbits, moles and hares—all captive at the blaze, eyes flaring with its swelling.

'Now hurry,' says Fiducia, 'you should be oiled before he comes.' With no further effort to explain who 'he' might be or why they must be oiled, she leads them to the children by the fire.

Most among the camp have already been anointed, and the children lounge as near as they dare beside the fire. Some seem dazed, but most are laughing as if drunk, staggering about and giggling over things invisible. A boy and girl—seven years old, perhaps, or eight at most—agree to oil him. They help him from his smock and shirt and then start dragging at his trousers. He waves them off, clutching at his belt and wondering what madness has induced him into this. He sees Lucia naked, stretching by the fire as a pair of infants lard her with their pudgy hands. Beckoning back the others, he has them oil his torso only, while he strokes poor Scimmi, her eyes red circles of reflected flame, her back still ridged and hackled.

They crouch beside him, fingers sliding with a slow, mesmeric rhythm, as if the long anointing soothed their spirits. He too begins to feel a little dazed, perhaps by their massaging hands, the heavy air, the heat and passing night. Soon he has the sense that he is drifting, floating, wafting like a cinder in the fire's currents, till his eyelids open into golden light and spices fill his nostrils. Suddenly there's movement all about him, figures rushing from the fire, Scimmi scrabbling at his chest. 'Come on!' Lucia hisses, while pipes begin to screech and wail. 'He'll be here any moment.' Once again he can't help wondering who this 'he' may be, beginning to resent 'him' as he's pulled into the dancing, slow as yet, but growing faster by the minute.

The ring of witches narrows and then widens, twirling him about in counter-clockwise circles till he feels that he is spinning, not on rocks and earth, but through the fiery spheres. Nor has he any sense of passing time, since they turn against the sun; then 'he' of whom they spoke rides in upon his horse, which rises like a wave before the flames, a spume of grooms gripped tight upon its harness to bind it to the earth. A tremor passes round the ring, the dancers' eyes all fixed on 'him', heads twisting as they spin, while Jacopo—despite his jongleur's skills—feels bile rise in his throat.

Brother Corvo sits in stillness, witnessing the frenzy. Then he stands up in the stirrups, eyes watching every face, and brings a slaughterman's long blade out of his habit. The circle falters, slowing, some stumbling as they turn to see him hold the knife aloft. He grips the stallion's mane, leaning forward as it shies, and draws the blade in one slow, silky pass across its throat. At first there's nothing, no reaction, just the breathing of the dancers; then the creature seems to sprout a ruby collet, a thing so fine that it might well be some reflection of the flames. But soon the collet is a pendulous, rich necklace, then a bubbling panoply that floods the stallion's breast, and the beast is walleyed, snorting bloody foam and jerking from its handlers. It tries to leap, to buck, but plunges in their grip; it rises trembling, head arched back, its teeth a tombstone grin before it flounders, and Corvo goes down with it. Yet, when the handlers part, and the horse lies dark in its own blood, he stands there, silent, shadowed by the blaze, as if its heat consumed the creature's flesh and left his fleshless form.

What a splurge of sacrifice ensues. The necks of fluttering jackdaws, ravens, doves, are wrung before their cages; goats and dogs are clubbed down where they stand, cats strangled. Hares shriek beneath the knife and moles grope into death. Jacopo winces from the killing, reeling in the din of yelps and cries, hands tight on Scimmi's pouch, pushing down her head as she attempts to peep. He sees a hoopoe, wings spread wide, its heart cut out, and at the outskirts of the fire's light, a hedgehog writhing on a needle. Figures slick with sweat and oil hurl roosters, pullets, pigeons, at the flames where, cooked upon the wing, they fall or fly like massive embers. Some dance with grotesque steps, their faces painted with the creatures' blood; others hold the bodies in the air as if in mourning.

Corvo, with the flames ascending at his back, raises a great chalice, lifting it above the crowd before he drains it dry. Other groups pass round crude goblets of their own. The crone, the woman with the talisman, and several more besides, arrive with pitchers full of liquid. A number of half-naked men and women, proffering a cup, already gather round Lucia and Jacopo. She takes a draught—he sees her swallow—and passes it to him. He stares into the brackish, oily depths. 'Come on, Jacopo,' smiles Lucia. 'Hurry, drink it up.' He feels their watchful eyes and tips the goblet back, takes one small sip then makes to pass it on. The group sits watching him, impassive, and the man across the circle lifts his eyebrows, tipping back his hand to indicate that he should drink more deeply which, since death is in the air, he does without demur. The bitter, bilious liquid slithers down his throat and he hands the cup along. He feels himself begin to heave, but holds it firmly down, his shoulders slightly hunched, lips glistening and pursed.

Some among them, after their communion, begin to dance once more; others simply lie upon their backs, eyes wide and features working. He turns to face Lucia, who flings her arms about him, plants a kiss upon his mouth and then, just as he tries to hold her, leaps among the reeling ring of dancers, stumbling for the fire. He makes to follow her, but sinks as if he's loaded down with weights. When he looks again, she's gone. He tries to rise once more, then feels the turning earth, the rush of space inside his head and, legs still moving like a toppled bug's, falls flat upon his back.

He lies there, drifting in a slow anxiety, washed and worried by the voice of the black river. Somehow, out of that wash of waves he feels a movement, a warmth that, breathing, crawls across his belly and his chest. He slowly lifts his eyes, which seem to flutter like the wings of insects with the effort. He feels the silky touch of fur against his cheek, and at the very moment that he looks into her lemon eyes, Scimmi rubs against him, swaddling him deep within the thunder of her purring, kneading his chest with her needles, though he cannot feel them. He turns toward the fire and sees Lucia speaking with the hooded man; then further, to the river, which sings now with the hissing voice of flames. It winks with sliding lights—the pieces of the broken moon—which drift apart then merge, then float up smoothly from the blackness into air. Pale-bellied fish break surface, descend in plunging arcs, others swim and slip out of the depths toward the stars. He shuts his eyes, feels rushing waves of heat and seems to see, as if his lids were made of glass, Lucia, her black fur pale with silvery light, tail swishing like a cat's, as she rides a flippered fish and waves a flag of shadows past the moon, white as a skull in the speckled sky.

Lights flash across his sight and he writhes to flee the sound—the rumbling breath, the heated roaring in his ears. His eyes flick wide then flutter shut, revealing Scimmi or Lucia, her long, lithe, limber body stretched upon him, a moving sheath of silk that closes like a razored mouth. Her pointed teeth, her topaz eyes, are mirrors to the flames that crackle as they mate, her fingers scoring slits, red trenches, shreds of skin. Writhing as he is, his eyes roll round like taws, reflecting shadows, fire, the men and women strangled by the claws of cats, the hedgehogs and the smiling hares that skewer them with needles, their gizzards spilled by long-beaked birds. Pale pigs are snuffling up their hearts like glistening truffles, and a great black goat, crouched before the flames, turns torsos on a spit. He draws his breath to scream, hears nothing but the roar of heat and a crackling voice that seems to say beside his ear, 'Lucia, take heart. Kill him soon, or don't come back again.'

Tuccio eats orange sherbert

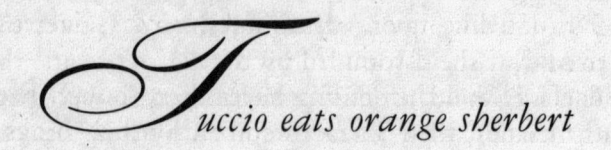

Marina sat in the rear loggia of her father's house, pushing back the wisps of hair the evening breeze displaced beneath her wimple. In her lap she stroked a tiny fluffy dog, Dame Fortune's gift from Gaia's wedding. She smiled at the small thing, ruffling up the fur between its ears so that it wriggled and flicked its pink tongue at her fingers. She heard the clink of the cups and the low, earnest words of her father, Bartolomeo Chiaudano and the physician, Francesco Morelli. She paid little heed, turning to the stand that supported her book, a translation from Florence of Chretien de Troyes' romance, *Yvain*. But her thoughts wouldn't focus, distracted by her anger at her father's change of attitude. Since Gaia's wedding she had found herself curtailed on every front by both her parents, her erstwhile freedom in her movements, dress and speech abruptly checked, subjected to her father's acid tongue and her mother's gorgon gaze. 'Don't use phrases like that, they're not becoming to a girl your age.' 'Try not to shout, Marina, and stop rushing round like a child.' 'No, Marina, I insist, you really should dress more demurely now. What's charming at fourteen may be a disgrace at sixteen.' And so they went on, determined now Gaia was married that she'd soon follow suit.

The idea held little appeal for her, though she wasn't certain why. She wanted to do other things, though again, she wasn't certain what. Her father's stories of sailing the sea to Sicily, Spain and Africa, or Baldassare's tales of Venice and Roumania, these fired her thoughts and made her burn to travel. The stories she read of knights and enchantments, like the one before her now, made her want to dress in gleaming steel and ride out on adventures. To be a knight in strange realms ... the very thought made her curl up her toes with delight. Somehow the women, sitting in their castles, doing their embroidery, waiting for news, didn't appeal to her at all. Perhaps if you could find someone who'd take you with them on adventures ... but this happened neither in the stories nor in the lives of Baldassare and her father. No, the more she thought of it, the less appealing marriage was, especially since it seemed to call for speaking softly, and never running, and wearing gowns so thick and long it felt as if she waded everywhere in water. But it was hard to know just what to do, besides staying in her father's house forever or entering a convent. She stared unseeing at her book, then nuzzled briefly at the dog's soft fur. It whined and wriggled with excitement, till she shook its front paw, saying, 'Why is it, Palla, that the more attention I give you the more you start to cry?' She glanced toward her father and his friends, who might have smiled to see her talking to the dog. But they were taking no notice, too engrossed in their discussion. In fact, her father was ordering Domenica to bring some ices.

'Our slave girl, Lucia, has become quite an expert at Arabian sherbets,' he was saying. 'She makes them from our own eggs and oranges, and the ice from my cooling tower.'

'Yes, Tuccio,' laughed Bartolomeo ruefully. 'Before you say another word, I'll admit it, I was wrong about the cooling tower.'

'Did you hear that, Francesco? Bartolomeo admitting he was wrong? You're a witness to this, you realise.'

'All right,' Bartolomeo smiled, reddening a little, 'it was a good idea. Though let's wait and see this evening's results.'

'Have no fear, it's a specialty of the house.' Tuccio sat back beaming in the temperate air. With Domenica gone and a brief silence falling round the table, he returned them to their topic. 'You were saying, Francesco, about the letters you'd received on the sickness to the south?'

'Well, that's just what I was going to tell you,' Francesco nodded, growing suddenly solemn. 'It's no longer confined to the south. My friend in Genoa informs me that it's raging there, and there are rumours of some isolated cases in Pisa.'

'Pisa?' said Tuccio. 'From what we hear, isolated cases don't stay isolated long. If it's in Pisa, it could soon be here as well.'

'Yes.' Francesco stared distractedly toward the north, as if the sickness might be seen approaching like a storm across the hills.

'I don't know,' said Bartolomeo, shaking his

head doubtfully. 'I haven't heard that much of it really. Sometimes it seems to me that you physicians are so hemmed in with illnesses yourselves that you get things out of proportion.'

'That's not altogether wrong, Bartolomeo. But this, I think, is different.' He sighed and took a little sip of wine, then gazed at both of them. 'For those who've had their ears to the ground, these rumours have been building for some time. More than two years ago there were stories coming from the east of a pestilence in Cathay. Millions were said to have perished. And each month these stories said the plague was coming closer, sweeping on through Persia and then Tartary, Syria and Byzantium, sparing neither heathen nor Christian.'

'But there's always illness breaking out somewhere,' protested Bartolomeo. 'To put each separate case together, as if they were all one pestilence descending on the world, is to court disaster and encourage panic.'

Francesco stared at him and seemed about to raise his voice, but took a deep, impatient breath instead and spoke with slow deliberation. 'To ignore the facts, Bartolomeo, is another form of panic.' He raised his hand as Bartolomeo made to speak once more, adding, 'The magnitude of this cannot be doubted—the stories are simply coming from far too many sources. From Sicily, for instance, where the towns on the western coast are said to be all but deserted, and where war almost broke out between Messina and Catania over the protective relics of Saint Agatha. Or from Naples, where it's said that sixty thousand people have already died. In Genoa, after the docking of some suspect galleys, the sickness took a hold and now hundreds are perishing each day ...'

His voice had grown so urgent that Marina listened closely, her thoughts distracted from her personal fate to that of the whole world. Francesco's words had made her fingers tense and nervous, twisting tight in Palla's fur until he yelped.

'Yes,' said Tuccio, 'my Barcelonan agents have written that it's there. My Venetian office writes that Venice too has been infected.'

Francesco shrugged his shoulders. 'Oh, yes,' he said, 'and from the reports of my colleagues in that city, the Doge, Andrea Dandolo, and the Great Council have ordered strict control of immigration, setting up a quarantine of forty days at the Nazarethum. They've banished the dead to graves on the remotest islands and forbidden beggars to exhibit corpses.' He leaned a little forward, saying almost in a whisper, 'And they've even—would you believe that things could come to this?—allowed surgeons to practise medicine. Can you imagine it? Those barbers dealing with physic's subtleties, the complexities of humours, drugs and planets. Chaos is surely descending on the world, and with the speed of an avenging angel.'

'But these are great cities you're speaking of,' Bartolomeo argued, 'trading ports with ships from every land, full of riches and corruption. Surely we're too small, too humble, to provoke God's wrath on such a scale.'

'Then we may provoke His wrath on a scale more like our own,' suggested Tuccio, 'and still have no-one left alive within our walls. From what I hear of this pestilence, it makes no comprehensible distinctions, killing all it can in one place and slowly moving on.'

'But why?' Marina blurted from her corner, frightened by an image of the sickness as an army, Death mounted like a general at its head.

They turned toward her, surprised to hear her voice, as if they'd all forgotten she was there. For a moment no-one knew quite what to say, till Tuccio replied a little testily, 'How can anyone know that, Marina? Such questions are beyond us. Only God can know their answers.'

There were splutters of indignation from Bartolomeo Chiaudano, who finally burst forth, 'Well, I'm not so sure about that, Tuccio. Such suffering must surely be a punishment, and what else can a punishment be for but sin? A plague of the proportions suggested by Francesco can be nothing less than God's chastisement for our wickedness.'

'Oh,' uttered Tuccio, throwing up his hands, 'well, yes, of course that's true ... I wasn't questioning that ...' He glared at Marina, who started playing with the supine dog. 'What I meant,' he explained, turning to the others, 'was that we can't really fathom what's behind it, what's causing these things to happen ... you know, through what mechanism God works. Can we, Francesco?'

The physician adopted a lofty expression, then puckered his brows and lips in a frenzy of concentration. 'It's very hard to say as yet,' he announced at last. 'As far as I can glean from my correspondence, there are numerous opinions, to put it mildly. Some say that the corruption of the soul infects the body. Though most agree that this cannot explain the thing entirely, since virtuous priests and dutiful physicians are said to perish, while men of ill-repute steal off scot-free. Most hold that it is something far more general—a corruption in the air itself, which travels with the winds from realm to realm, destroying where it rests.'

'But what corrupts the air if not the sickness of the souls that dwell within it?' Bartolomeo pursued, his tone so comical with puzzlement that Marina thrust her face in Palla's fur.

'Well, once more, opinions are divided. Some, following Galen's work on epidemics, say the corruption has resulted from putrescence caused by deaths from earthquakes in the east. Others agree about the earthquakes but say the air has been made toxic by fumes out of the earth. Still others blame agents of the Devil—witches, Jews and lepers—for releasing potions in the air, while the most learned lay the agency upon the planets.'

'Mmn,' Tuccio nodded solemnly, 'that's the way that I incline as well.'

'Yes, indeed. For I have it on good authority that members of the Medical Faculty of the University of Paris believe that the corruption is a result of the conjunction of Saturn, Jupiter and Mars in the house of Aquarius, a very dangerous situation, I'm sure we'd all agree.'

'But what can be *done* about such a disaster?' Bartolomeo cried. 'We can't reverse the planets.'

'Certainly not,' agreed Francesco, almost as if he enjoyed the intractability of the problem. 'There are those who say it *is* insoluble, such as Ibn Khatimah, a physician from Granada who maintains that at the core of every outbreak of the plague the corruption of the air is absolute and irreversible, incapable of ever sustaining light or life again. Though others are not so gloomy.'

'Yes, Francesco,' nodded Tuccio, clapping his hands together, his voice grown suddenly brusque. 'Yes, all this is very interesting. But I'm a banal and practical man who grows frustrated in the absence of practical solutions. The question is, what do we do here, now, short of changing planetary motions, to safeguard Topomagro?'

Francesco glanced up blankly, just as the sherbet arrived. 'Ah, sweet sanity at last,' smiled Tuccio with some relief, 'after all these sombre notions.' He watched Lucia place the bowls upon the table, each with its ball of sherbet as small and dark as a tangerine. 'Marina, I'm sorry, I was thoughtless. Would you like one too?'

'Yes,' she said, barely conscious of his question, Francesco's words still rattling in her head. 'Thank you.'

'Well then, come and join us,' he commanded, waving Lucia away and Marina to him, so that she came and sat down at the table, the dog still cradled in her arms. He nodded at the others, saying, 'We'd better start before they melt, good manners or not,' though his encouragement was hardly needed by Bartolomeo, who'd already picked up his spoon.

'Delicious,' he sighed through a mouthful.

'Yes,' agreed Francesco, 'so cool and sweet on a balmy night. With a friend like you, Tuccio, who needs to purchase passage to the east?'

Grinning, Tuccio sheared off some sherbet with his spoon. 'But to get back to what we were saying before ... about what we might do to safeguard the town. I'm concerned about the inexperience of the Signoria. If the pestilence reaches us, do you think they'll cope?' He raised his eyebrows for their answer, slipping the sherbet between his teeth.

'There are some good men there,' said Francesco, 'including two of the commune's best young physicians. I've heard they're considering restrictive measures.'

Tuccio pursed his lips, as if in disagreement, saying, 'Lucia's used bitter oranges. I'll have to speak to her about it.'

'No, not at all,' and 'Oh no, they're excellent,' the others protested, Francesco adding, 'It's just that your palate's been too pampered by good food.' So their host shrugged, and was seen to try a second portion.

'What did you mean, "restrictive measures", Francesco?'

'Oh, well, from what I've heard, a number of things ... though none is more than a suggestion as yet. For instance, they've foreshadowed an ordinance restricting visits to infected states, like those of Genoa and Pisa ... so that access to the town would be denied to those returning from such places. Or again, there's the notion of forbidding imports from infected areas, things like bales of wool, linen goods, corpses for burial, of course, and ... What is it, Tuccio?'

Both men gazed with some dismay upon their host, whose face at first seemed stricken with disapproval, his eyes wide, mouth gaping, cheeks red with excess choler. 'Tuccio?' But now his face had turned dead white, while he gripped then clawed his throat, emitting tiny choking sounds as if he couldn't breathe. Marina threw the dog away and lurched up from her seat, but Francesco beat her to it, leaping round the table with surprising swiftness, shouting, 'He's breathed the stuff into his lungs.'

Tuccio was staring, his small eyes bulging. Francesco, straddling both his legs, thrust a spoon straight down his throat. Tuccio gagged and heaved until, with a sudden spluttering groan, he spewed the sherbet up. Francesco stood back, sweating, wiping at his doublet with a napkin, supporting his friend with his one free hand.

'He should be all right in a minute,' he murmured to Marina, who was close to tears. 'He's had no more than a nasty fright.'

Certainly, groaning as he was and glaring round in horror, he seemed to have received a *very* nasty fright. And though the vomiting relieved his physical distress, he showed no signs of real recovery. In fact, he started thrashing on his chair and neither of his friends seemed able to restrain him until Gino and Domenica, alerted by the cries, came running to the room. 'Quickly,' cried Francesco, as Gino took his place, 'we should bring him to his chamber. It may be that the strain has caused more serious harm.'

He urged them forward, shooing the remaining servants from the doorway. But at a cry from Marina he turned to find her staring, not at her father's raving departure, but at the floor, where the small white dog, its tongue still stuck in a gobbet of sherbet, lay dead with goitrous eyes. 'Marina?' he said, peering first at her, then after the merchant, then fixing his gaze upon the slave girls, Ambra and Lucia, still loitering at the door.

*In which Corvo considers
the Pestilential King and Jacopo
attends an execution*

BROTHER CORVO STANDS ON THE HILLTOP, HIS HANDS at his sides, his long hair turned into whips by the wind. On the plain below, his disciples mill by the river, and beyond them crouches the town. He stares at the sky, his bent nose whistling in the unsettled air, while high overhead the clouds rend and tear or flash like steel in the glare of the sun. Grass, trees, river, the flags of the town, the festering sea—to the rim of the circled earth, all is in flux but he, here at its heart, on the hub of its raised navel.

His gaze remains fixed, as if it would pierce the moving blue spaces above him. He peers beyond to a blindness of brilliance and shadow where the twin Gods are once again fused, as they were at the start; though not now in the slow, clenched circling of birth—one light and one dark—but gripped in a murderous combat. And he is the singular witness here below, where the elements echo that battle, and no-one may know of the victory of light till they've passed through the darkness.

To the south, beyond the horizon, he sees the plague rising up from the plains like a swarm of black locusts. Turning, he sees it fly from the spires of the great northern cities, a tide of sick souls that floods through their streets. From the north and the south the dark waves come, and he waits on his hill for their breaking.

He stands at the storm's bright centre, a rod of iron for its lightning, chosen as he is by the Twin of Light to bring destruction like a beacon. For now he is death's own lodestone—the Pestilential King.

Jacopo barely stops to draw breath. He has followed the cart all the way up the Via Gentili, jostling through crowds, past the Duomo, past the house of Francesco Morelli, where he pauses a moment, staring up at the windows in sudden grief, since this is where he'd once stolen a necklace to give her. The crowds line the street, hooting and jeering as the cart passes by, enjoying the morning sun, the air's excitement, the bright savage smiles that flicker between them. Some buy sausages, pancakes, cups of sweet rosewater, cracking jokes with the vendors till the thief feels lost amongst enemies. He thinks of Gino, the steward, and his slanderous tongue; of the housekeeper, Domenica, who'd implied that the boy, Guido Cupa, was Lucia's sole lover, as if he himself had counted for nothing. There were others, to be sure, but no-one was *more* her lover than he. But mostly he thinks of Ambra, the young Tartar slave. How pale she had looked at the trial, like watery cheese, and how limp, barely able to stand before the *podesta*.

A cry goes up from those around him—some draw their breath and avert their eyes, and some stand higher on tiptoe to see—as a scream erupts from the rickety tumbrel. He keeps his face hidden, sick with the crowd's febrile chatter, thinking not of the killing to come but of Ambra, head bent before the *podesta*, telling the court of Lucia's love charms, her potions and rituals and stolen church wafers, weeping to tell how the slave would slip from the house at night, only to come back at dawn, strange in her speech and smelling of ointments. She too embellished Lucia's love for the carder, speaking of how she had hated their master since Guido's hanging, as if the whole speech were Tuccio's trap to confirm the girl's guilt. She'd lusted for Guido, there was no denying it, and she'd hated her master as well; but this doesn't mean she'd attempted to kill him. Nor is he dead—both he and his malice are thriving.

Her scream fills the air between the high walls. He thrusts through the mob amid curses, pushing past women, children, stout men, as if something pursued him, some fury that cries with her voice, that knocks loaves from men's hands and upsets cups of wine. For what else makes him witness her pain but the hope of some miracle, some reprieve of the angels, some means of escape? San Stefano's dome is almost in sight, and it's here that she's sentenced to burn twice over as poisoner and witch. Yet who else would save her, even if they could? Not the crowd, all hooting and jeering at the edge of the street, nor the guards, much less her tormentors. Nor would the priests intervene on behalf of a witch, nor the Signoria, whom Tuccio holds in his purse. There is only he, Jacopo Passero, master thief, to steal her from them. And yet he dare not ... no, not even to go to the cart and support her, since he might be suspected of witchcraft himself and be burned in her ashes before San Stefano. He remembers a time when accusers proved wrong in their charges had suffered in place of those they accused. But not any more. Now the charge itself was sufficient, and although they might furnish no case at all, the accusers could walk off scot-free.

All this seems so much prevarication. He's a burglar, is he not? A master thief, the top of his trade? So why can he not steal Lucia? He glances about at the gobbling crowd, at their fat-smeared faces, at the militiamen down on the street with their halberds, and knows the question requires no answer. He tunnels under their arms, past the jut of their hips, trailing the squeaking cart like a lone, hungry fish in the wake of a ship.

He hears her cry out, hears the howl of the crowd, and this time can't stop himself looking. He sees the old cart, the driver prodding the ox with his whip, and standing, arms lashed to the rough timber sides, Lucia, still gripped in the pincers held by the man behind her. His partner is drawing his own metal tongs from the bucket of coals at his feet, holding them out before him so that even those people high in their houses can see the points glow red in the air. Then he plunges them into her flesh, giving quick, vicious twists, while she whimpers and writhes, crashing down on her knees to the floor of the cart, skin crisping, fat curling up with a smell of cooked meat. The man lunges forward, her blood steaming up from the red-hot tongs, then wrenches them back, uprooting a thick wad of flesh as she screams and the crowd pours forward with grim fascination.

Jacopo shudders, jerks back like a tortoise, head low on his shoulders. It's as if he's surrounded by monsters—no better himself—unwilling to help, to save her, to put a stop to her torment. If he had a thousand hands with a thousand knives he'd plunge them all in their hearts. But he hasn't and can't, and must watch her yet in his mind, her dark skin ragged and gaping, her body ablaze at the core of his rage. For who above all makes her pain and his helplessness? Who but her master, Tuccio di Piero Landucci? He thrusts up his head and peers about, yet sees neither him nor any other great man of the town; then catches a glimpse of her bleeding body and turns his eyes away, thinking he smells her burnt flesh. A sickness of pity fills him, of running his fingers over her wounds, hearing her scream; for a moment, he thinks of her beauty, of how he'd caressed her and heard her low sighs, her cries in his ear, and sees her astride him in the pale evening, a thing of such sweetness and strength that, seeing her broken, trembling and bleeding ... He turns away to be sick, vomiting over the shoes of some vendor to cries of disgust and loud laughter.

'Can't take it!' cries one.

'Spoil it for others,' says another.

'Don't come near me!' shouts a third, pushing him off, so he crouches amongst the mob at the verge of the square, wiping his mouth and his chin, peering about him to find that he's there, at the steps of San Stefano. He shoves his way to the shallow portico, surveys the piazza. A ring of militiamen keeps the crowd back from the stake, and with them their captain and Otto the Nark, a one-time informer to the captain of the people, and now the town's executioner. There's no priest, no dignitary, no sign of Tuccio, just the cart bouncing over the stones with the crowd churning after. The militiamen let the cart clatter through, but push back the rest with their halberds. Jacopo watches the men in the back take hold of Lucia's arms. Even from so far away he can see how she winces, her wounds like red and white birthmarks spotting her skin. They fix her hands behind her, pulling— almost lifting—her down from the cart. When her feet touch the ground she nearly collapses, eliciting protests from Otto, who limps across on his mismatched legs, his infamous temper flaring before him, as he roars at the pair to take her full weight. They do it roughly, dragging her quickly over the faggots and up to the stake, while Otto the Nark comes lurching behind, binding her tight with a chain, trussing her up like a beast to be slaughtered.

He does it so fast that the crowd seems unready, chattering still as he lights the first flames, then suddenly falling silent, hushing each other, leaning eagerly in, like some revelation might be at hand; or as if, in fixing their gaze on her final moments, they might glimpse the flight of her unshriven soul. Now there is only silence, then the first wisps of smoke and a fireside's crackle as Otto jerks back, waving his luminous brand. The fires roar up and a screaming begins; the crowd starts chatting once more, peering into the conflagration, where she flickers and shifts, a dancing black shape at the hot orange core, as though heat had melted her chains and, immune to the blaze, she moved at its heart like a shimmering salamander. Jacopo's strength has run out. There will be no rescue, no sudden eruption of courage, no descent from the heavens, and he turns tail and runs. He slips past the throng with his hands to his ears, feeling only the dumb, chilling numbness of stone, as if the air, the wind, the sky, his heart, were made of stone. Slowly, far from San Stefano, the anger begins, and the bleak resolution. Lucia's life had been stolen from her. And who was the thief? Her master the merchant, Signor Tuccio di Piero Landucci. Jacopo knows that he will not kill him. Yet *he* is a thief as well, and craves a thief's vengeance. The merchant had stolen a thing beyond wealth. So he in turn must search the man's treasures and steal such a thing. For all men, even a merchant like him, hold something as priceless.

The pestilence comes to Topomagro

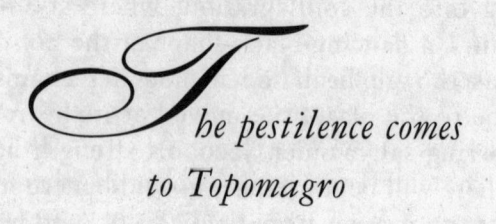

'HEAR ALL YOU SINNERS THE WORD OF THE LORD, hear all you sinners the word of the Lord ...' and on and on the loud voice cries, while the bell tolls out above it. The families of fishermen slowly arrive in the Piazza San Pietro, drawn by the bait of that clammering bell in the hand of the portly friar. Fra Lippo Peppo has cast his net wide, surprised by the size of the crowd, and remembering Christ's words about 'fishers of men'. Despite the length of his stay in the town, he's not preached near San Pietro, and is here a fisher of fishermen, raising his voice to bring in the catch and grieving Jacopo's departure. He's a worry, that lad, going back to his thieving; though what can Fra Lippo do but preach him a sermon, something which might sway a village but, sad to say, not his old partner. So the friar must addle his brain after new routines, solo sermons which might keep him free from his brothers' suspicions.

'Hear all you sinners the word of the Lord.'

It was tempting to fall back on relics. After all, they were something he felt at home with, unlike his recent routines with Jacopo, which felt dangerously close to feigned magic. But relics worked best for itinerant preachers; townsmen, in contrast to ignorant villagers, were fickle in their faith. Indeed, many presumed that this was why the plague was so vicious among the cities. Be this as it may, the fact remained that his brothers at San Francesco seemed less than totally trustful. True, once Jacopo had moved to other lodgings, their suspicions had waned. Nevertheless, some scurrilous claims concerning his work had filtered back to them, and he'd never quite managed to undo the damage. So relics, if considered at all, should be used only sparingly.

'Hear all you sinners the word of the Lord.'

And they gather in silence, facing the preacher upon the church steps, the bell in his hand with its tongue hanging out. For a moment he waits there, struck dumb, then suddenly flings one arm in the air and draws it across the breadth of the sky. 'The hammer of God is loosed on the land!' he cries, his voice so loud that it hurts his throat, such that only a consummate effort of will can keep him from coughing. 'And high in the air over Naples, Messina, Venice and Rome an angel weeps with a fiery sword, laying low with the pestilence all of no faith. Have no doubt, this sickness is almost upon us, even as I speak. Who can be sure that the soft, warm breeze that blows in your face is not the breath of God's angel, breathing contagion amongst you?' He pauses to let the notion sink in, while several fishermen stare with mistrust at the air about them.

'Thus I urge you to pray to the Lord and to Saint

Sebastian, the patron of those afflicted with plague. Yes, pray with me now to this goodly saint, this merciful healer who, at the hands of the Emperor Diocletian, was shot through with arrows like plague-sores, who was healed by the pity of Saint Irene, yet martyred at last by that unrepentant emperor. Kneel, I say,' he commands, waving the crowd to its knees while he draws a deep breath and commences, not the traditional prayer, but a torrent of horrors, visions of death and decay from the tales that he's heard of the plague.

A stumbling, yet heartfelt 'Amen' redounds from the crowd, whose blanched, frightened faces stare up to discover what counsel Fra Lippo might give. In raising them back to their feet, he beams such a radiant smile that they feel reassured. 'My friends,' he says almost gently, 'it's been vouchsafed to me by my order to bring here among you— that you might know God's mercy—a rare and sanctified thing.' He takes from his robes a small wooden casket from which he extracts ... it's unclear just what, though it looks like an old bit of stick. All eyes turn toward it, some wide with anticipation, some pinched with myopia. 'For here, passed down through the years, is the end of an arrow—still with a bit of its fletching—drawn by Irene from the saint's holy instep. I've been sanctioned to let you come near it, this splinter of hope, for a gift of no less than one *grosso*, that you, the people of the Borgo San Pietro, might receive its grace and be safe from the plague. I have also a small selection of crosses, some made from juniper, some from sandalwood,

some from laurel, and if you step forward, I—'
A shout from the throng stops his eloquence. For a moment Fra Lippo prepares to flee, afraid lest some gang of unsatisfied customers out of his past has abruptly resurfaced. But most pay no heed till a man, hurrying through the crowd, bounds up the stairs so smartly that Lippo can't resist flinching.

'Friar, come quickly, please,' he implores, 'it's my daughter.'

Still ill at ease, he allows himself to be led down the stairs, through the crowd, to the hub of their interest, where a girl of twelve or thirteen is lying flat on the stones, her face flushed red and covered with sweat, eyes strangely unfocused. She moans then cries out, pressing a hand to her arm, while the people mutter and stare at Lippo.

'What is it?' he says uncertainly, and the father now brushes her hand aside, tears back her sleeve and reveals, there in her armpit, a taut, fierce bubo. He draws back her elbow still more, so she wriggles and kicks, almost catching the friar a blow on the knee as he gazes in horror.

'It's the sickness,' says one behind him, already bustling away.

'The plague,' another confirms, starting back.

'Quickly, Friar,' the father pleads, 'get the arrow of Saint Sebastian.'

So he scuttles off with no time to think, suddenly afraid, as if the thing he's invoked for so long has come to settle its claims. In the midst of his fear, as he casts about for his broken old arrow, he can't help wondering how well it would work to have someone collapse, just like that, then revive at the relic's touch. If only Jacopo might be persuaded ...

'No,' says Jacopo, shaking his head. 'I'm sorry, Lippo, but I want to stick with my natural talents.'

'And what are they worth unless used in the work of the Lord?'

'That's just what I'm doing.' Jacopo shrugs and wrinkles his brow. 'Certainly more than if I was working with you.'

'Oh, now, don't be offensive,' the friar says sadly, taking a sip at his wine. 'But while you mention it, if you're going back to thieving, for God's sake steal a better vintage.' Then he glances up sharply. 'And what do mean, you'll be doing God's work?'

Jacopo leans back in his chair, opening his arms to embrace the whole room with its cracked, broken walls, its unshuttered window, the sound of the woman singing next-door. 'I've got all I need here. I couldn't find a thing to steal for myself. No, any stealing I do from now on will be for the Lord.'

'That's perilously close to blasphemy,' says Lippo severely and, ignoring his laughter, continues: 'How can you possibly steal for the Lord? It's against His commandments.'

'Not if my theft is the way that He punishes one of His sinners.'

'Who?' Lippo asks, eyes narrowing over his cup.

'Tuccio di Piero Landucci, the one who had them murder Lucia.'

'Oh, that Barbary slave you lusted after.'

'Don't say that, Lippo,' he snaps, leaning over

the table, more than a little drunk. 'If you'd seen how she died ...'

'No, no, I'm sorry. I shouldn't have said that.' He shakes his head slowly. 'I'm an idiot.' After a small silence, he looks up and says, 'But it's not for you to punish him. The sickness is here already. If he needs punishment, God will see to it.'

'Then why did they punish *her* with such cruelty? If they believe in the justice of God, why not leave her to hellfire?'

'Because they see themselves as God's agents,' says Lippo, raising his eyebrows as if it were obvious.

'Well, my friend,' smiles Jacopo, 'that's just how I see myself.'

Fra Lippo regards him over his cup, and shrugs. 'I'm not so sure that any of us should be punished. Things happen almost before we know it. We are what we are, and they happen. Or perhaps we should all be punished. Either none or all of us are sinners.'

'Well, that's what they say, isn't it? That we're all sinners ... all guilty of our parents' first sin and must die of it.'

'That's what they say,' nods Lippo, pouring more wine from the pitcher. 'Just like they say that the plague's sent to punish our sins.' He pauses, listening to the song that floats through the air from the room next-door. 'But I'm not so sure. That young girl I saw this morning ... she'll probably die. Sometimes I think our first sin lay not in disobeying God, but in seeing Him as jealous and wrathful ... a punishing king.'

'But that's what He is, at least sometimes, when we do wrong.'

'Yes, indeed, that's what they say. But when we try to act like this God, to make laws and seek justice, then we end up like a race of vengeful fathers, hurting ourselves, as if our first sin weren't disobedience but misconception.'

'I—I'm not sure what you mean,' says Jacopo, scratching his head, a comical frown on his face. 'You speak as if we'd made God and not the other way round.'

'No, no, not that,' protests Lippo. 'I mean that we don't see Him clearly, and that our poor sight makes us fear and stumble, like blindmen in a world of light.'

'But surely, then, God should lead us, should—' But his words are cut short by Scimmi, who leaps from the floor to his lap, to the table, overcome with impatience at the piece of cold sausage that sits at its centre. 'You little thief!' he cries as she jumps to the floor with the meat, shaking it like a rat in her teeth.

'Strong words, Mr Thief,' laughs Fra Lippo, stooping to stroke her sleek back, till she snarls and sidles away, dragging the sausage with her. 'You don't really want to go back to burglary, do you? Why not join me in preaching God's word? We'll start travelling again, ahead of the plague, though not too far ahead. This latest idea ... it's a good one.'

'I've told you already, I'm going to stay and take care of Tuccio.'

'Leave it to God, Jacopo, leave it to God.' And

so the argument goes, around and around in diminishing circles, while they gradually finish the wine and Scimmi devours her sausage.

The first in sight are the dogs, Bulfas, Moloch and a dozen other wolfish, manged or mad-eyed creatures sidling down the street; some snouting the air, some with raked hackles, others cringing low and bent and vicious, as if they could slip unseen beneath their spines. Then comes Brother Corvo, tall and hooded, the sword of some dead captain slung about his waist, and no more fraction of him showing than the tip of his hooked nose, seeming, like the dogs, to sniff the tainted air. Behind him walk Speranza and Fiducia, one garlanded with daisies and wild roses, the other hung with herbal amulets and talismans with scribbled nostrums. At their heels, the hag Maria ambles, breathing songs to the unravelled skirlings of the pipers in the rear, a naked baby in her arms, its gummy grin an echo of her own, a toothless moonsmile on its great, round, pallid face. And now what others come behind her down the shuttered street—tall, gawky goons in rags, muscled thugs, shit-smeared infants pocked with sores, dames scabious and naked as their first wandering mother, cracked blitherers, gibberers, sad loons with swimming eyes, dancers back to back, and slatterns decked with feathers and butterflies' plucked colours. For here, through the Borgo San Pietro, on a feast day written in no calendar, comes Corvo's new-found order.

The houses stare with dead men's eyes, each window blank and shuttered, and to the west the heavy stonework of the wall looms up, devoid of movement. Doors clench on silence, and the gaping mouths of alleys breathe a dampening putrefaction. On the street there is no movement but the sift of lightbeams through the smoke of smouldering rags, the burning clothes and linen of the unseen occupants. Brother Corvo is alert to all, to the bodies of the rats that lie among the refuse, to the dead cat sprawled upon the stones, a heap of rat guts spewed before it. He hears, beneath the burden of the pipes, the dearth of birdsong and, once or twice, a cry that spatters through the broken jalousies. For here he smells death, the descent of flesh, the coming of his kingdom. Air flutters round his ears, the faint winds not winds at all, since bodies die behind these walls, and give up their souls which, even now, come whizzing through the air like moths of lambent fire, comets made of glass, so delicate and light that any hand might seem to catch them. Slippery and quick, soft as shrimp pried from their shells, they flicker for whatever vacant womb they may, and seek a further birth into the flesh. But with the pestilence upon them what womb is there that won't soon die? And what hand is now more powerful to mould them in their nakedness than that of Lucifer, the God of Light?

Corvo pauses while the dogs go bounding forward, each vanishing around a turning of the road. He can hear their barking above the whine of pipes as he approaches. And then he sees it, the great black body sprawled across the opening of a laneway. Bulfas and Moloch hesitate uneasily, sniffing at the air; a number of the smaller dogs, taut, half starved and nervous, dance around the giant's corpse, yapping and snarling, leaping toward it in sudden darting forays till their muzzles graze its skin. But the ox remains inert, unmoving, reeking where it lies. A stench, not of putrescence, but of the pestilence itself hangs heavy in the air, driving all away but the hungriest of hounds. Huge carbuncles, big as melons, rise from its coarse hair and weep dark, noisome fluids on the stones. The procession moves past quickly, disturbing only briefly the storm of flies already gathering above the body, then rounds a further turning and enters a small square.

Here, on the flagstones, is a basin carved with two crude griffins, a paltry thread of water dribbling from its spout. Once again the mongrels start their snarling, teeth popping at the figure lying there. But Corvo will not pause, despite the murmurs at his back and the dogs' redoubled paroxysms. He strides straight on, eyes shadowed by his hood, merely noting the dead beggar stretched beneath the fountain, as pallid as the ox was dark, sores streaming with the same black, brackish stink. Crowded on the square's far side, creating a great din, is a horde of revellers dancing jigs and drinking wine. It's for their riot that he's making, the frayed parade regrouping in the rear, the pipers hugging harder to their windbags, the willing hounds relinquishing their prey and bounding forward, ears flung back and red tongues lolling.

Neither the irruption of the dogs among them, nor Corvo and his motleys, cause the revellers much consternation—their senses are too benumbed with wine—and the newcomers merge amid their number like the mingling of twin rivers. Brother Corvo notes as well the way each back turns from the fountain, the way each voice is raised and how the fiddles scream, as if to drown out any sound that is not theirs. This crowd, for all its noise, turns resolutely inward, and no pronouncement short of the last trump would wake it from its riot. He sees the way the dancers do not dance, but stagger; the way the speakers do not listen, but rant in mutual monologue, as if all language but their own were fraught with peril. Some, a little further up the narrow street, wear bits of costume, and one—a tall, fat figure with a rumbling laugh—is got up in a death's-head mask from Carnival or All Saints' Eve. He performs ridiculous dances with surprising ease, whisking through the crowd on slippered feet, wobbling his big belly and slapping at his arse, a grin fixed thin and lipless on his face. All the while he carries a great cask of wine, filling up each drinker's cup in turn and laughing fit to burst at their slow capers.

'Lord Death,' breathes Brother Corvo as he passes, 'why do you make them drunk?'

'Well,' says Death, suspended for a moment in his pouring, 'dead on your feet, dead to the world, dead drunk—it's all a matter of degree. Besides,' he adds, still playing up his part, yet turning to his task once more, 'we fatten swine before we slaughter them.'

Corvo smiles and marches forth, secure in his faith. For now, as summer builds to its full heat, the

Pestilential King comes unannounced, surveying his sad streets. And still he is an exile in his own dominions. The plague has far to go before it captures the town's heart. The dead remain too spare about him, and he must wait until their souls fill up the air like shoals of silken fish. It is the final dark before the new God's dawn. Beneath his mantle Corvo smiles once more, head lifted as he hurries on, listening for souls.

Fra Lippo lies supine on his pallet in his small white cell, no companion with him save the Psalter by his side and the crucifix upon the wall. Even these he does not see, floating as he is in fire. Pain waxes and his bones are candles brightly lit, then wanes into a raw, parched whimper. Once, amid this waning, an old priest peers from the oily air, pushing at his lips and thrusting in the wafer, which crumbles on his tongue like dust. Crusted with chrism, the dry cicada fingers touch his skin, the dove-voice mutters rituals. Lippo strives to speak some fragment of confession, but the words drown in his throat. And then the priest is gone, and flames erupt once more. He sees a black inquisitor come leaning from his lectern, listing charges of false promises, fake relics and deceitful healings. Eyes yellow in his fevered face, he sees reliquaries, phylacteries, arks, shrines and monstrances gape wide in crypts and on the altars of a thousand churches. He sees the relics of apostles rise in admonition. The phalanges of Saint John the Baptist's finger wag in anger, Saint Blaise's jawbone drops with disappointment, and Saint Margaret shrugs her sacred scapula.

All rise against him in his pain—the saints he's mocked, the villagers he's swindled, the brethren he has lied to—all decrying him among the streets, laughing at his anguish as they lead him bound and burning. At the height of the procession, as Lippo begs for mercy, the relics join together in a climax of collision—a rib of Saint Sebastian, the wristbone of Saint Paul, Saint Stephen's battered cranium, the ulna of Saint Chrysostom, Saint Barbara's pelvis, and many, many others from the friar's repertoire— all towering above him in a rage of accusation. His hands are bound by Otto the Nark, while the aggregated saint, monstrous with its extra teeth and missing ribs, pours scorn upon his head, the flames already rising as he cries, burning in his flesh, his guts, swelling till he feels that he will burst. And then he does, spewing stench across the air, the town, his sheets, deflating like a broken bladder, feeling weakness and relief, watching the red heat and Christ who hangs upon His cross within it. He watches while the flames abate, then drops back on his bed, no longer seeing the nailed crucifix but feeling it against his back as if he hung there, dead.

When he steps down to the ground the flames have almost faded, like the countless sombre leaves of a grove that glows at dusk. He moves in fear through this wood of burnished trees, coming to a clearing with a small, dark stream where a figure stands in silence. He steps a little forward and then pauses as this figure, shrouded in a deep blue robe, begins to turn. He feels afraid, then sees it is a simple girl, one of those he'd meet in any village. He starts to smile, but something causes him to falter, something in her face, her eyes, some sorrow that he can't define, which seems not young, but ancient. She looks at him with disappointment so complete and depthless that his eyes turn slowly inward, and he feels not fear but a desperate grief, a mourning for a life now lost, missed chances irredeemable. He stands there, failed, waiting to be finished like any flame snuffed out as she slowly smiles with such a fullness of acceptance, her arms held wide toward him, that he stumbles forward, clumsy in his gratitude; but she is no longer there, as if her loving eyes were his, and his the arms extended to the foolish, hungry-hearted world which bursts in light about him.

Jacopo discovers the means of his vengeance

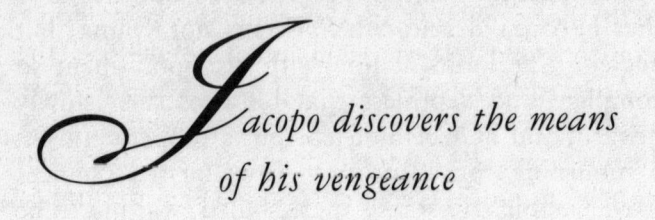

TWO NIGHTS AFTER THE BONFIRES, THE STREET dances, the high jinks and low comedy of the feast of Saint John the Baptist, Jacopo Passero climbs the tall roofs at the rear of the house of Tuccio di Piero Landucci. Scimmi leaps intermittently into the darkness, slipping from shoulder to sill to rushy flagstones, reconnoitring shadows and sleepers, sniffing the air for snoozing dogs, then perching back on his shoulder like a sleek and silvery moon-beast. He is angry as he scales the stepped rooftops, thinking of Lucia and the flames that killed her, and the patient vengeance of her master. Yet he has to rekindle these images daily, as if, deprived of his will, they might fade of their own accord. For now she seems vague in his mind, like something he thought he had known, but hadn't.

Perhaps the death of Lippo, no more than a few days back, has obscured her memory for the moment, the figure of the fat friar as insurmountable in death as it was in life. He thinks of the time that Lippo and he were chased through the woods by those villagers. Then he shakes his head slowly, recalling how he'd found him, already dead by the time he arrived, the priest brushing past as they met at the door, his pyx tucked under his arm. For a moment, he'd felt the room lurch about him, the floorboards tilt at his feet, as if he stood once more below decks on that death ship, watching Laura die. Of course he'd known the plague was here, but to have it suddenly before him, to see it stamped like a brand on the face of his friend ... it was more than he could bear, and he'd fled on the heels of the frightened old priest.

He clambers up to the second-floor rooftop, tiptoes over the tiles, skirts the stale, smoky mouth of a vent, and starts the next ascent. He thinks of Tuccio somewhere within, peacefully dreaming of some new scheme, feeling no guilt at all at crushing Lucia and having her burned at the stake unshriven. Tuccio, who hadn't even deigned to be there, content to do business while others killed her. Well, if Jacopo succeeds, his contentment won't last past tonight. However, even as he climbs the third-storey tiles, he feels the numbness within, the fatigue that erodes his resolve, that tells him to go, to cut his losses and leave the sick town before his luck runs out. For the very wildness of the feast-day crowds had seemed to echo their fear, as if God had condemned them already to die for their sins. But if anyone's sins might warrant such death, it was men like Tuccio, whose greed created the wealth that would help them flee to secluded villas. Yes, he's seen it all before. And tonight, one way or another, he'll make sure the merchant pays.

He stands before the windows of the lightless, topmost storey, listening for sounds from sleepers within. All is quiet, just the faint soughing of the night wind disturbing the silence. He reaches forward and tries the shutter of the nearest window. It's firm on its catch. Hugging closer to the house, he shifts a little sideways on the tiles and tries the next along the wall. It eases upward as he lifts it. He peers through the shadows but dares not let the moonlight in. He drops Scimmi onto the sill, urging her forward. She hesitates, sniffing the room within, then leaps down noiselessly, vanishing into the gloom. She's gone for a while and Jacopo's growing impatient, lest the lure of food scraps found in a kitchen might prove irresistible, when suddenly, out of the dark, she leaps on his shoulder. 'Oh, Scimmi,' he breathes, 'I wish you wouldn't do that.' But she's down again smartly with quick and quizzical tail-flicks, along with the pert, impatient mews that tell him the path is clear. He lifts the shutter higher and steps in behind her, finding an empty bedchamber, most likely a guest room. He checks the only cupboard—there's nothing but linen and one extra counterpane. The same is true for the rooms on each side, and he follows Scimmi along a dark passage until he comes to a larger doorway, through which he discovers Tuccio's library.

Though the windows are wide to the starlight, he strains to make out what lies on the merchant's desk and shelves. There's nothing but letters and quills, candles and codices, not even a casket of coins or bill of exchange to encourage him. He's here, not to pilfer, nor even to find his fortune, but to make Lucia's killer suffer for his crime. What he requires is something of fabulous wealth, something valuable both for its monetary worth and its beauty, something a man might invest his pride in—a possession that Tuccio loves. He slips silently out of the room, back to the passage and down the steep stairs that he finds at its end.

He passes a narrow kitchen, some passages probably leading to quarters for servants, then loses Scimmi somewhere between an echoing hall and the cavernous depths of a dining room, neither containing one object worth stealing without a horse and cart. It's in a lower kitchen that he spies her, crouched above some sleepers by the dying fire. She's gnawing at chicken bones—he hears them crunch from across the room—and refuses to come when he beckons. So he leaves her where she is and heads off down a darkened corridor.

The fact is, men like Tuccio keep their treasures near them when they sleep. For this reason, Jacopo ignores all further rooms, looking just for the principal bedchamber. At last he finds a corridor with three tall, carven doors, each closed upon a room adjacent to the rear loggia. It's here, in one of these, that the merchant will be sleeping. He listens at each door in turn—imagining a massive ruby ring or a casket carved in chrysoprase containing a great treasure—but hears nothing from within. After much procrastination, he tries the middle door, twisting the handle and pushing his weight inward, peering quickly round the silent room. Pale light is sifting through the open window, revealing a dresser and a high, closed bed. He strains to catch a sleeper's breathing, creeping nearer as he listens. Perhaps he should simply sort through the drawers as softly as he can. Yet he can't resist just one quick look and draws aside the corner of a curtain, peering at the bolster. For the bed holds nothing but a faintly musty odour, and he turns to the dresser, deciding that the chamber is the older sister's, the one who recently got married. He slides out drawers, groping at the contents, finding only some cheap spare linen and heavy bolts of cloth, some of it expensive—rosato, velvet and scarlet, sewing silk, and taffeta—the sort of thing whose theft would merely irritate the merchant.

He slips out of the room, glancing at the doors shut tight on either side. He decides to try the one on his right, moving gingerly along the hall once more. Again he listens; again he hears nothing. He turns the latch and enters, pausing at the threshold as if the merchant were already rising from his sheets. He finds himself inside a room still smaller than the first, containing one large chest and a bed with open curtains. But this bed is not empty. Jacopo stands staring, the door half closed behind him. A girl lies curled beneath the thinnest cotton cover, a swathe of heavy hair unfurled across her pillow. Her lips are slightly parted and her palm lies cupped before them; as he stands unmoving, he seems to feel her soft, warm breath against his cheek. She looks so slight and lithe, her back a little arched, one thin leg drawn almost to her chin. The moonlight frosts her hair, her skin, and he can't help smiling in the shadows, seeing how she curls about herself, so silvery and spare, like some feline thing become a girl. Yes, he might almost reach to stroke the fan of hair upon its pillow.

Turning to the chest before the bed, he pauses. What is it that Tuccio might value most of all? What is it that he himself would hold of greatest worth? Rare jewels have sparkled in his own thief's hands, but what loss would make him weep? What necklace, piece of gold or diamond? No, he's never cared *that* much for these. Perhaps the only thing, now that he thinks about it ... yes, the only thing that he might weep to lose is Scimmi. Indeed, his cat.

He turns back to the bed where sleep has flung the girl. Oh yes, he'd love her desperately if she were his. Just as Tuccio must love her. A new awareness fills him, floods him with conviction: here is the thing the merchant would most hate to lose. Suddenly a shudder moves her, a great, slow, shaky sigh, till her knees and tiny breasts and narrow ribs arch upward through the sheet, a gesture so voluptuous in such a skinny thing that he hesitates, distracted, before he draws his knife. But how to steal her from him? To kidnap her ... would be madness. He holds the knife before him, moving from the shadows. He couldn't hurt her, yet ... A sudden gasp comes shaking from the bed. 'Wh—?' Then he has her tight between his arms, the blade already glinting in her eyes. And he feels the rushing of her breath between his fingers, the trembling of her hands, or possibly her heart, while he keeps on saying, 'Ssshh, it's all right. Don't be afraid. I wouldn't hurt you,' and countless other such assurances until, between the words and knifeblade at her ear, she slowly quietens down. There's a long and awkward pause where she just breathes and he says nothing, gripped together, waiting in the silence. She mumbles something soothing through his fingers, and he says, 'Will you be quiet if I let you go?' As she nods against his arm, his grip relaxes slowly.

'Wh-who are you?' she whispers, watching as he gets up from the bed and stands before her, the knife still ready in his hand. 'What do you want?'

'I ... uh ...' he stares about him, unsure of what to say, then thinks of Scimmi thieving in the kitchen. 'I'm, er ... looking for my cat.'

'Looking for your cat?' she says, more loudly than she'd meant to, and he puts the knifeblade softly to his lips. 'With a dagger in your hand?'

'I'm sorry,' he hisses, fumbling the weapon back into his shirt. 'I got frightened. It looked like you were going to cry out.'

She does not seem reassured, her eyes wide and glistening with tears. 'You're here to steal something, aren't you?' She holds up her hands as if to fend him off. 'Not that I think it's always wrong. Some people have to steal, I know. I'll give you something if you like.'

He smiles, abashed, gazing down at where she wraps the sheet about her. 'Yes, you're right. I was here to steal. And I am a thief.' He holds out both his hands, as if to show that they are empty. 'But I won't steal from you now.'

'Why?' she asks, and looks a bit suspicious, opening her mouth to pose a further question just as something flashes through the half-closed door—a spirit at high speed, a sudden rush of moonlight on the floor—and springs up to his shoulder.

'Oh,' he gasps, a comic gape upon his face. 'Scimmi! How many times ...?' He turns toward Marina. 'She does it constantly.'

Marina's fear and mistrust have become a wary smile. 'I see that you really were looking for your cat.' She laughs uncertainly.

'Though why I'd want to find her I couldn't tell you.' He tucks a finger under Scimmi's chin. 'You little wretch!' But she takes no notice, simply sitting on his shoulder and licking at her paws.

'But you're here as a thief, aren't you?' the girl pursues.

'I was,' he nods, stroking Scimmi softly. 'But not now. It's always harder once you ... well, once you get to know the people you were going to steal from.'

'So you do it a lot?' She looks afraid once more, as if regretting that she's asked.

'Only since my parents died.' He hangs his head in sorrow. 'When the pestilence struck Naples ... I couldn't stay there any longer. Ever since, I've been running from the plague, heading north, doing what I can. I've wandered the roads all through the south, with a troupe of travelling acrobats for a time, then helping a poor friar I met upon the way.' He gazes up with a look so sad that it might stab her to the heart. 'And sometimes I'm reduced to thieving.'

She stares at him, mouth open, fancy taken, not by his feigned sadness, but by his wanderings. She sees the wayside inns, the hedgerows by the open road, the forests in the hills, and thinks of all those strictures grown tighter by the day. Her father's admonitions, her mother's watchfulness, the long, thick prisons of her gowns, and riding side-saddle, accompanied everywhere she goes by beady-eyed attendants—all the hemming-in that she has had to bear since Gaia's wedding comes flooding in upon her.

'What's your name?' she asks, eyes softening.

'Jacopo,' he says. 'What's yours, my lady?'

She sees the acrobats, the squares and towers of far towns, and is taken by a sudden lightness of the heart. 'Marina,' she answers, half frightened by the weird joy she feels. 'Marina di Tuccio Landucci.'

He notes the softness of her smile, her eyes' bright eagerness, and knows that, yes, he might just steal her from her father yet. 'Well, Marina, perhaps—' But his words are interrupted by Scimmi, who leaps down from his shoulder to the bed, arching her back and rubbing at Marina's hand. The girl, distracted, starts to stroke her. 'She's lovely. So smooth and silky.' And she holds her in her arms.

'You're lovely too,' says Jacopo lightly, yet with feeling enough to make her look up quickly, breath catching in her throat. She sees his thin, dark face, his sharp blue eyes that seem to slant a little upward like a slightly puzzling smile. He reaches out a hand and runs it over Scimmi's coat until he finds Marina's fingers, brushing them lightly with his own, then closing slowly round them. She blushes, looking down, heart racing in her chest, and draws her hand away. He seems to chuckle and Marina looks up sharply, yet finds his hard, bright eyes all creased with laughter, and wants to put her hand out once again, as if she'd never moved it. But already he's scooping Scimmi up into his arms and stepping to the window.

'Marina,' he says softly, holding up the cat, which wriggles in his grip. 'If I should lose this wretch again ... well, I think I'll know where she might be. Can I come here first to find her?'

Marina hesitates, watching him uncertainly. 'Does she often ...?' Then lets her question fall away, closing her eyes instead and nodding slowly, 'Yes, I leave my window open.' And floods him with the candour of her gaze. 'But you must be careful.'

'Oh, yes,' he whispers in return, smiling with a wide, white, hungry smile. Turning to the window, Scimmi still beneath his arm, he peeps out once, flashes back a final grin and slips into the dark. Marina gazes after him for no short while, wishing and yet fearing that she might have followed, not into the town's walled shadows, but out into the endless silver night.

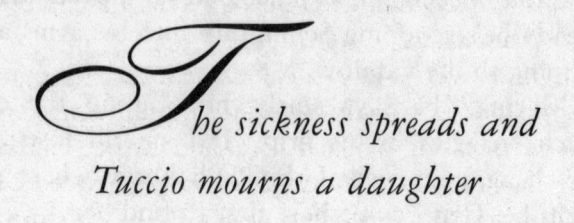

The sickness spreads and Tuccio mourns a daughter

AS THE DELPHINIUMS AND DAFFODILS, LILIES AND crocuses had blossomed in the woods beyond the town, and the poppies, harebells, buttercups and dogroses had sprouted from the grass in sprays of colour, so the flesh of those who lived close by the Porta del Mare and the Porta Santa Maria had thickened with the first rank blooms of pestilence. At first the fishermen of the Borgo San Pietro and the workers of the Borgo Santa Caterina had been the only ones to feel the blade of that dark gardener, falling back into the earth like grass stalks mown and scattered. But as the petals blackened on the boughs and fruit came forth, as apples slowly deepened to a full, rich red, and lemons, nectarines and peaches swelled upon the air, so the buboes grew upon the flesh of those inhabiting the eastern quarters of the town, in the Borgo dei Lanaiuoli and the Borgo dei Medici e Farmaciste. Now, in the heat of midsummer, the pestilence went stalking through the streets of the wealthy, taking not just fishermen and carders, slaughterers and dyers in its passing, but merchants, traders, bankers and physicians, as if its initial hesitation before the ranks of men had been no more than a catching of its breath.

There were fiery sermons from visiting friars, supplications to Saint Sebastian, public prayers for the intercession of the Virgin, and gifts to charity by the most unlikely individuals. Huge bequests were made to San Francesco, and the bishop led processions up and down the town, a great flock of merchants, craftsmen and labourers barefoot behind him, swathed in coarse wool and beating themselves with short knotted cords. Their voices swam up through the hot summer air in long prayers of penitence, and Saint Barbara's thimble—produced from the depths of the Duomo's crypt—bounced at their head in its crystalline casket. Even now this same bishop, old and feeble though he was, had left his home of so many years to go to Valence, where he hoped to enlist the prayers of His Holiness, Clement the Sixth, on behalf of the town. Nor, in this outbreak of piety, did the people omit more mundane forms of caution, since the Signoria wrote page upon page of new regulations to ward off infection. Many shut themselves up in their houses, shunning their neighbours, or sought protection from the poisonous air by burning incense each night in their chambers, or by walking the streets with packets of spices pressed to their noses. Yet neither prayer nor penance, drug nor decree, seemed proof against pestilence.

In the town's poorer quarters, the cemeteries filled with bodies, so that queues of porters formed in the churchyards, their biers piled high with unburied corpses. Deep pits were dug where the indigent dead were heaped in layers and covered with dirt. People collapsed in the street and lay there untouched; each morning discovered new rotting corpses, like leftover nightmares, laid out at their doorways by terrified neighbours. Kites, crows, buzzards and jackdaws squabbled and flapped amid the decay. However, these too contracted the sickness, wobbling away through the alleys and streets, collapsing like drunks, their feast unfinished.

The stench of the dead lay over the town like the carious breath of some long-dying god. For a time the wealthiest quarters were spared the plague's more drastic excesses. Here were neither buzzards nor jostling queues of porters nor trenches stacked with bodies. Affluent funerals retained their dignity, though recent legislation left them smaller than before. In the Borgo dei Lanaiuoli the plague did not slaughter wholesale but crept each night from house to house, choosing its victims with a connoisseur's care. With time the infection spread faster, till even the town's most opulent streets held their matinal dross of dead bodies, and increasing numbers of merchants deserted their homes and their commerce to flee for the north. Now people died more often alone, abandoned by relatives and friends, most likely discovered by neighbours, not usually with their eyes but with their noses.

When Gaia fell ill, Baldassare did not flee, though it seemed that God sought to purge him of adoration, so much did the illness afflict her body. He had worshipped her beauty and fierce pride; now, as the sickness gained ascension, it slowly turned her into its image. First, in her groin, a bubo swelled out like a smooth purple head, then formed a twin in her armpit, a third in her neck, till she groaned with each tide of blood that pulsed through her. A fever swept her on the second day, and soon her sweat, infected with plague, almost drove him out of the room. Her saliva and breath held the stench of decay; and then the illness took hold on her bowels, and she swam in such muck that only perversity—less kindness than self-destruction—drove him to clean her up. Raddled with fever she raved, mired and mottled with taut red wens that thrust from her skin like bloodied snouts, her flesh so pocked and shamed that it seemed she'd been ravished, not by a mortal man but by some demon crawled from the Pit.

Francesco Morelli lanced the bubo under her arm and did his best to drain it, drawing away a thick black blood and greenish scum, which he caught in a golden cup. Despite her screams, he tried sealing the wound with red-hot steel, but met with no success, for the boil throbbed more fiercely still. He put plasters on each of the buboes, some made of resin and arum roots, some of amethyst powdered with snakeskin, and some that smelt like excrement. But most he bled her, attempting to drain the plague from her veins. He thought it attacked her liver, fleeing to the groin—that organ's first emunctory—and bled the vein by which it fled. Then he said the heart was poisoned, and opened the vessel that leads to the armpit. Next, with the brain's emunctories swelling at ears and throat, he cut the veins between them and let the black blood out. Yet, for all his expertise, the only thing he achieved was her suffering, and he gave up in despair.

Her mind came and went, igniting like fire then shrivelling to ash. Once, when the pain sawed deep through her bones, she started to moan, 'I've failed ... failed in everything.'

'What?' cried Baldassare, rushing to the bed. 'Are you ...?' And then said nothing, waiting, uncertain.

'This bed,' she breathed, 'I'd have come to this bed in childbirth.'

'And will yet,' he assured her, grasping her hand.

'No, I've failed.' The whisper flecked her lips. 'What have I given life to in this bed?' As she lay back, choking, exhausted, he heard the slaughterer's knife in her throat, its cold blade rattling.

'Gaia,' he cried, shaking her shoulders, 'to yourself, Gaia. Give life to yourself.'

At first he thought that she hadn't heard, since her limbs went stiff and her skin blanched pale as ice. Then her mouth gaped, muttering, 'It doesn't matter ... it doesn't really matter,' as she sank into silence.

Tuccio stood at her coffin in his long black mourning robes. Beside him were Beatrice and Marina, and a little further forward, Baldassare. The Duomo was cast in evening gloom, the catafalque ashimmer with a galaxy of candles where the coffin waited like a shadow lost in light. Tuccio surveyed the scene about him—the chanting monks in coarse-spun habits, the priests in albs and broad black copes, the crowded nave—and mourned for Gaia's absence. Always, when the family was together, he'd been conscious of her presence, of her beauty, like a brightness that attracted light, drawing every eye. Now she was smothered up in darkness and not even one last glimpse of her was possible. At any other time she would have lain amongst the light in her most gorgeous gown, and those last rays of sun that broached the coloured windows, cobalt and blood-red, would have lit within her hair. Today they lit no more than dust motes, as tiny as the souls of fleas ascending in the air. The town so shunned the victims of the plague, and there was such suspicion that corpses, openly exposed, might cause contamination, that he had been prevailed upon to shut her up in wood for the procession and the service. Of course, he had ignored the rules forbidding all but family at the funeral ... and, indeed, so long was the cortege, and so elaborate the bier, and so many the monks and priests and candles, that it was like the rites of some great general from another time ... Yet, somehow, it had not felt right. Of the townsfolk, corrupted by the sickness and their fear, precious few had shown her due respect, barely turning to acknowledge the procession, and some appeared to derive more mirth than sorrow from her passing. Even the streets seemed out of sympathy; some stinking with great plumes of greasy smoke from burning heaps of rags; some strewn with corpses dumped upon their doorsteps, awaiting tardy porters; others resounding with the scrape and bump of tumbrils piled with ill-made coffins, as if they were the town's main industry. He had almost felt—with death become so familiar and obscene—that such a grand procession was a habit from another, slightly foolish time.

He opened his mouth in mechanical response, following the words in Beatrice's Book of Hours, glancing up to watch the monks and black-coped priests all gathered at their lecterns with their great antiphonals.

'*Si iniquitates observaveris*,' they chanted while he thought of Gaia lying in that darkness, face shrunken with her illness, deaf to their singing and blind to their tears. That it should happen now, when she had only just been married, when her child—his grandchild—might already have been forming in her womb ... It was too pitiful to think of.

'*Magnificat anima mea ...*'

The Canticle of the Virgin swelled into the air, filling the dome with its round, rich song, and his eyes dropped to Marina at his side. She must not die like Gaia. He would protect her at all costs. For the moment, he must stay to safeguard shipments from the East. But as soon as he could they would leave Topomagro, and all would then be simpler and less hedged in with fear.

'*Qui Lazarum resuscitasti*,' he intoned, letting himself be lost among the words of the Office, drifting with the ebb and flow of voices, till Beatrice turned the page to move on to the versicle. '*Et ne nos*,' he began, but faltered as he saw the picture facing him. For here was Death in person, grinning upward from the vellum depths, surrounded by a border packed with fruits and living flowers, yet himself skeletal, with an arrow raised above his head and holding out a gift. Tuccio peered closer and saw it was a mirror. Yes, the painted figure held a mirror to him; and he seemed to see his face reflected there, as if Death held him in his hand. '*A porta inferi ...*' He felt a sudden chill, a shiver in the bones. Perhaps he wasn't well; he'd felt fatigued of late, with headaches and sore legs. This might have been a sign, an omen, something sent to warn him of his avarice. Was he willing to die for those shipments? Would such stubborn protection of his profits gain him a secure place in Paradise? He knew the answer well, and resolved to pledge a wealthy benefice to Santa Maria dei Poveri.

Soon the Office of the Dead was over, and all gazed up from Gaia's coffin in its pyre of gold candles, facing the altar instead, where the priest commenced the Requiem, hands clasped before the chalice with its square, stiff pall of linen. Almost from the start, seeing those pale stones before the altar, Tuccio felt his thoughts slip from the service, sensing instead his daughter's sorrowful displacement, as if, right there and then, he could hear her wailing in the dank, black stone, pauperised in death amid the cold humiliation of Santa Maria dei Poveri. For here was the thing he'd been remiss in, and now it was too late. He'd never dreamt that she'd be first to die. He'd long assumed that mantle for himself. And how might one expect a man of business such as he to fix his thoughts on death? It was something better left to God. Even as his fortune grew beyond this little church, he'd not provided for the death his change of status now demanded. And thus his child must suffer. In the midst of all his grieving, his blood began to boil at the thought of that old bishop. 'Oh no,' the priest had said, the very one who stood before them now, 'we may say the Mass here, of course. But she can't be *buried* here. Not without the bishop's final word. And as you know, he's on a pilgrimage to save the town.' A pilgrimage? To save the town? To save his skin more like it. The doddery old fool had never done a thing for them, not even against that rabid cardinal, when his voice might well have held some sway. And now he'd scuttled off to Clement's castle near Valence—a town yet free from plague— as fast as he could get there, depriving Gaia of a place before the altar of the Duomo.

Well, thought Tuccio, fussing at his mourning robes, he'd better get back soon to approve her relocation from the church to the cathedral, or he'd see no more Landucci florins. So the merchant ranted in his mind, wringing his hands together more than clasping them in prayer, already making plans to gild the altar of Santa Maria dei Poveri, to beautify its walls with murals as a shrine to his dead daughter. But then the Requiem was over, almost before he'd noticed, and the Absolution had begun. Tuccio watched the pair of acolytes hold back the priest's dark cope as he blessed the bier and shook the aspergillum over it, moistening the pall with holy water. He watched the censer trail its scented smoke above the coffin before the bearers came to lift it from the catafalque. He heard Beatrice's cry of grief, saw Marina's shoulders tremble, while Baldassare, grey as ash, went slowly forward. Then he too shuffled after, through the nave, toward the night, feeling once again a shaft of grief, then fear, as he watched that shut black box. It seemed so small, too small for Gaia's life, and he felt the urge to open it and look inside, just to see if she was there. Yet he trudged on stolidly enough, catching a glint of candles from the transept and thinking how dark the nights would be in that poor church, alone in the cold stone.

In which Jacopo pursues Marina and Brother Corvo pursues a vocation

THE WIND, STRANGELY COLD FOR THE SEASON, BLOWS in from the east like a thick, black tide. It buffets the house in sudden gusts, while cloudscraps, briefly luminous, twist across the moon's pale face and the night grows shifty with shadows. For Marina, all this movement is truly a godsend, as if God might actually side with daughters against strict fathers. In her bedchamber, in the heart of the darkened house, the rush and bustle of air hides the murmur of words, the sibilant hiss of twin breaths, as she and Jacopo speak softly together. He reclines on his elbow, between the bed and the window, as if concealed from a sudden intruder; Marina leans toward him, whispering among the covers, her long dark hair spilling over her cheek and tumbling halfway to the floor.

'It's like being in prison,' she's saying. 'The padlocks and chains are invisible, but they're here all the same.'

'He's afraid of the plague,' he answers, watching her quizzical eyes. 'And so am I. It makes good sense to stay inside.'

'But *you* go out and you aren't sick.' She gives

her head a sulky shake. 'And he goes on with his business but remains in perfect health. Then there are others who stay in their houses and die in bed. I don't think it makes any difference. If God wants you to die, you will.'

'Well, there's no denying that,' he says slowly, then gives a wry smile. 'Though why God preserves a thief like me, while so many priests are dying ... I don't know how you'd explain that.'

She watches his thin, dark face, and says with a laugh near to mockery, 'You might have virtues that only God sees ... and those priests might have sinned without your knowing it.'

'Perhaps. But I know my own sins well enough.' He watches her closely, sensing the moment is right, that the jewel lies couched in its casket, awaiting the thief's quick hand. 'I've stolen from more wealthy men than I can count, men who might have given what I stole to charity.'

'Or fed their faces with it,' she laughs, and the soft, silver sound rings in his heart like a bell. 'I've heard the friars preach of rich men's sins. Some say that God has provided enough for all, that the rich steal the bread of the poor. I know little of these things ... but perhaps you're stealing back what they owe you.'

He looks at her, so sweet and young in her soft, clean sheets, then thinks how her father tormented Lucia, thrusting her into the flames. 'Perhaps ... Yes, perhaps these Fraticelli may speak some truth. But the life of a thief is a shiftless one.'

'You say that, but to me it's something more.' She leans closer to him, and he sees the rich gold of her back and thin shoulder, feeling the urge to touch her. But he knows the dangers of greed to a thief and freezes his heart with the thought of Lucia. 'It must take courage to travel from town to town, a stranger everywhere, with no-one to trust and only your thefts to feed you.'

'Courage,' he says softly, 'or desperation.'

Her eyebrows cock in a question and, with a confidential air, she twists a little closer on the bed. 'But tell me what it's like to climb into someone else's house at night, when there may be watchers there or servants or armed men?'

'Better than climbing into a house in broad daylight.'

'No, really, tell me. How does it feel, slipping through a window, not knowing what's inside, or whether you'll be killed or captured?'

'Like entering anything,' he shrugs, 'anything that's new, that you don't know. Then you take whatever you can.'

'Yes,' she smiles, 'that's what I like, instead of simply *being* there, just waiting.' She nods and plumps her fist down on the mattress. 'I think I'd make a good thief, Jacopo. I can climb, I can be as … as quiet as a mouse. I wouldn't be afraid … not any more than anybody else. And I …' She peers about, seeking inspiration, then lights on Scimmi, sleeping beside her in the rumples of the counterpane. 'I'm as nimble as a cat. I can see in the dark. Just ask anyone.'

He chuckles, shaking his head doubtfully. 'So,' he laughs, as if humouring a child, 'you'd come and be a thief with me, Marina?'

'Yes,' she says without a second's hesitation. 'Yes, I would.'

He feels the pearl, the priceless treasure, icy in his fingers. A silence grows, a dangerous silence where scruples might be born. He lets it linger for an instant longer, then says more solemnly, 'You really would, Marina?'

But now a greater silence gathers, a hush where even the wind on the shutters is drowned by their heartbeats. She stares at the room's dark walls, the corners deep in shadow, and feels the closure of a lidded coffin, as if, for just that moment, she were Gaia shut inside its blackness. Never before had she felt close to death until she'd seen her sister buried, until she'd heard the silence of the room next-door and gone to Gaia's house and found it empty. And now to wait, to stay here week after week, knowing nothing beyond her books and her needlework, waiting till the plague-breath finds her ...

'Yes,' she says once more, 'I will. I'll be a thief's apprentice.' For some moments he says nothing, watching, calculating, waiting till she takes it back, makes a joke of it, bursts out laughing; she stares at his face and thinks of the roads and towns and wide-open windows, the fear and excitement, sensing the hard, dark heat of him beside her, and the joy she wants, here, in the very shadow of the plague, lying at Death's threshold.

'That wind is cold,' she says, and he feels quite giddy with triumph, as if the jewel he'd sought were his even while he strove to steal it.

'Yes,' he murmurs, 'very cold,' and rises slowly from the floor, gently peeling back the counterpane to slip between the sheets, entering as carefully as any thief might broach a casement, still clad in smock and hose, and catching one quick glimpse of her smooth body. 'So cold for summer.'

'Oh,' she gasps, 'your hands,' yet doesn't move as he draws nearer, but shivers into giggles, while Scimmi stirs and squeaks with irritation.

The criers, the bailiffs, the watch and the militia are soon so small in number that the streets are left to those who have the strength to take them. The chaos at the gates grows wilder by the day, so that vagabonds and wandering paupers slip easily into town. Ruffians, inured to the harshest of lives, find sudden wealth as nurses to the rich, those wealthy merchants or their wives abandoned in their final sickness. But most in number is the horde of porters, the self-proclaimed sextons of the plague, who heave the biers, boards and barrows piled with corpses through the streets. These men, for whatever price they might demand, haunt the infected chambers of the dead and dying, the foetid pits, the mounds of heaped contagion, dressed in graveyard mire like a host of carrion crows. And first among them are the followers of Brother Corvo.

He and his disciples have prospered by the plague, using its protection to penetrate the town. Somewhere he has found a great dark horse with heavy hooves, which he rides among the laneways, his pack of snarling mongrels at his heels, as if he were some lord upon the chase. And his sextons, dragging at their carts and makeshift biers, come swarming up behind, sniffing out the dead. There are fortunes to be made by those who have the gift of menace and no fear of the plague. He knows the pestilence for what it is—the judgement of the Lord of Light, devourer of the flesh—and rides its dank, black power as an angel rides the storm. Its breath will not destroy him, but puffs him up with purpose like a wind fills out a sail, driving him toward its glory. He revels in these signs of the kingdom close at hand, this interregnum before the Pestilential King's accession to the throne. Before that moment, however, there is work to do.

See him riding, surrounded by his sextons, down a laneway in the Borgo dei Medici e Farmaciste. See the tall, fine house of ashlar rising up before them, its heights obscured by the blackness past their torches. See the servant who has beckoned them on, drawing back from the snouts of the grumbling dogs, their long spines quilled with fanning hackles. While Corvo grins beneath his hood, this figure mounts the stairway of the portico, where a door has opened to reveal a maid. Her smile, begun, now freezes on her face at the sight of the grim sextons already filing past her. She makes to shut the door but finds it will not close, opening it once more to seek out the obstruction, seeing there before her the tall, gaunt, monkish form and falling back before him. He sidles through, moves down the long, broad hallway, barely registering the whines of the impatient dogs behind him, and then the sudden thunder of their fighting. He follows the reflection of the torches on the ceiling, past unlit sconces, candelabra, darkened chambers, toward the stink of sickness. He can sense it in this house, the death they've come for. And then he enters the lit sickroom.

A boy lies on a massive bed surrounded by tall candles, his body in a knot, his dead face livid in the drifts of waxy smoke. The lump upon his neck secretes a thin black blood, and his sheets as well are blackened. There is the father, too, a prosperous man, beside the bed, his soft mouth anxious in the nest of its neat beard, his wife as white as marble by his side and, between them, their small daughter. All seem frightened in that funereal hush, watching the still body as if it might arise at any moment. The sextons, dressed in their dark rags, crowd forward round the bed like uncouth mourners. Fabio, their foreman, shuffles up, his chin thrust out beneath his cap.

'Twenty florins to cart him off and another ten to dig the grave,' he barks, as is his way, peering hard into the man's pale eyes, which blink, yet barely seem to register the offer. Instead, his wife, brow crinkling with a frown, steps forward just a little.

'Thirty florins?' she says, the question thick and husky, formed from swallowed sobs. 'But that's absurd. Do you seek to make your fortune from our sorrow?'

'Sixty, or we take the girl as well.' All his men press in, while Fabio grins and rolls his eyes at the young girl, who thrusts her face into her mother's belly.

'You—you wouldn't—' begins the woman, half in horror, half in anger, but the father lifts a calming hand and shakes his head.

'Of course he would,' he murmurs softly. 'I can see that he's a man who knows his mind.' He turns toward the sexton. 'Sixty florins? Well, I know you do a dangerous job ...'

Fabio grins and nods approvingly, withdrawing the hand already reaching for the girl, while the man steps back to rummage in a casket on the dresser, and his wife glares after him. The child, saved for the moment from the plague pit, peeps behind her mother's skirts, observing, not the sextons, but the shadows by the door where Corvo stands in silence. He, in turn, looks back into her fixed blue gaze, feeling the fever in his veins, the power in his blood, and seeing—as the child now parts her lips to speak—her black, split tongue, the demons at her side, one green, one red; then sends the plague upon her.

Marina braves the plague

JACOPO CROUCHES BY HIS FIRE IN THE SMALL COTTAGE he has commandeered near the Ospedale degli Abbandonati. Although it's the height of summer, the flames rage hungrily beneath the smoke hole, devouring picture-frames, old wooden drawers, expensive chairs and other pieces of scrap, since he has somewhere heard that the air should be kept hot and dry to guard against the sickness. He sits sweating in the silent room lit only by the blaze, his face suffused in the sweet smile of ownership as he surveys his little house, one of the hundreds which death or fear has caused the owners to abandon, so that houses and whole districts—as well as orphans—may now be called '*abbandonati*'. Yet Jacopo is smiling still, surveying the Flemish rug spread on his floor, the glitter of the little French enamels, the walnut chessboard with its gilded figures. Yes, the sickness has been kind to him.

It's a burglar's paradise, Topomagro, with so many houses now deserted. But even here in his sanctuary, surrounded by such wealth as he has never known before, he can't help wondering about the nature of it all, about so many dead while he still lives. He has seen the good defeated, shrivelling like sinners in the fires of the plague, while thieves, no different from himself, now thrive like kings upon their pillage. And though he would not pray that thieves might perish, such justice niggles at his notion of how things ought to be, as if somehow he had hoped, through all his theft and cunning, to reach some place of certainty within the world—only to find, among these dying priests and nobles, physicians and rich merchants, that no such place exists.

Feeling suddenly enclosed, he steps to the window and props up the shutter. He peers out into the restless night, its curfew long since broken, hearing distant shouts, sensing the shadows that go slipping through the darkness. They are adrift inside the town's stone walls, floating with the world like prisoners on a plague-ship. But floating where? He looks upward at the stars. Fra Lippo said the world sat at the centre of a host of spheres like the skins of some vast onion. But you may peel and peel an onion's skins and never find its centre. And, indeed, the world itself may be just so. When Jacopo stares amongst the stars, he finds the friar's notions hard to credit. In this town he feels almost as he did upon that boat, drifting through the stars' exhausted light, sailing out into the deepening dark; though now the sea they sail contains no beacon and no shore, only blackness upon blackness to the end of night. And of their captain in this endlessness, where kindness dies and cowards are the sole survivors? Is he cruel or simply foolish, or has he perished long ago?

He bangs the shutter down and sits back at the

fire. Such questions are confusing, if not dangerous. The world is as it is, and thoughts like these—no matter how real they may seem—reduce it to a shadow of itself. He feels uneasy, nervous, the proprietary pleasure he had felt before completely vanished. He picks up a stick to prod the flagging fire, tapping it against the hard-packed earth where it echoes with a hollow thud. Then he hears a knock upon the door. He starts up with the stick gripped in his fist. Who would it be? There's no-one that he knows here. Some rag-end of the militia tipped off about his thefts? Another thief, perhaps, come to try his luck? Only Marina knows he's here … He darts over to the door, lifts its latch, swings it open, and finds the girl upon his doorstep, peering nervously about her. She rushes past him, throwing off the long black cape in which she's draped, then huddles by the fire, shivering from some cause that cannot be the cold.

'A fire?' she cries, half laughing, half in fear. 'Surely it's too hot. You haven't got the fever?'

'No, no,' he blurts, moving quickly to her, 'it's a cure for the air's corruption,' then takes her skinny shoulders. 'But why are you here? It's too dangerous in the streets. You know I said I'd be there later in the week.'

'We're leaving,' she says softly, lowering her gaze from his. 'He's finally listening to my mother—she said she'd leave alone with me if he didn't want to come. So he's wound up all the business that he can and we're leaving on the Sabbath.'

He looks down at her dark hair, her delicate, quick face, and finds no words to say.

'I don't want to go!' she cries, a rich man's pampered daughter; then says more gently: 'I climbed out of the window ... His agent in Milan has bought a villa in the countryside. It's said to be free of sickness, and we'll stay there till the plague has gone from Tuscany. It might be years. I might be old when we return.'

'Marina,' he chuckles, lifting his fingers from her shoulder and brushing back her hair. 'It might be safer if you went.'

'No, Jacopo.' She shakes free of him, and paces round the room. 'I don't want to go with them.' A silence falls, in which he feels unsure of what to say; she, uncertain too, starts peering at his treasures— the chalices, the gilded casket, the painted panel. 'Well,' she says at last, 'you've got some nice things here ...' Then pauses for a moment, thoughtfully. 'And that's my father's chessboard!'

'Oh, well, that style's quite common—'

'No it's not. It's his, you thief.' But she's smiling, more confident now, a slight, lithe figure little taller than his shoulder. 'I want to stay with you.' She looks into his eyes, takes his fingers in her own. 'I want to stay here, to hide until they're gone. And you can teach me how to thieve with you. I'll be your apprentice burglar.'

He stares into her stubborn gaze and shakes his head; then slowly—very slowly—starts to nod, until his gloomy thoughts all vanish and, surprised, he laughs out loud.

The wealthy are deserting Topomagro in great numbers. They load coaches and wagons, carts, tumbrils and the backs of asses with their treasures, rumbling out beneath the northern and the eastern gates like the retreat of some prodigal army, glittering in silk and damask for fear of leaving the least piece of their best cloth behind. But Tuccio has not yet joined them—he and Beatrice have been gripped by frenzy since the disappearance of Marina. They send out Gino their steward, and all the servants they can spare; then free such men as Luigi Pucci and Niccolo di Lapo from their duties in the business so that they might join the search. Tuccio curses that Baldassare, so hopeless without Gaia, has already fled the town, but calls upon the help of all his friends who've not yet left, men such as Francesco Morelli and Bartolomeo Chiaudano. The captain of the people and the *podesta* have long since scuttled off, but there remain the poorer members of the town militia, whom the merchant harries into action. He is terrified lest the girl's been taken by those predators collecting in the town— the vagabonds that grow in number by the day, the renegade sextons and the tribes of looters. Yet, though Tuccio's methods might have worked before the advent of the plague, now all is chaos, and every system he had mastered is now mastered by disorder.

Days go by, the Sabbath passes, and another, but Marina stays unfound. He sends word to what agents and *fattori* remain in neighbouring towns, but not a clue—not the slightest hint—turns up to indicate her whereabouts. At last, in spite of Beatrice's protests, he knows they've done enough. No mortal father could do more. Even his wife eventually admits she must be dead or gone; why else would such a happy girl have vanished so completely? They finally settle for the explanation, first mooted by Francesco, that she's been so frightened by the plague, so overcome with terror, that she couldn't bear her father's hesitations any longer and, of her own volition, has taken flight. The physician can supply a number of convincing anecdotes of similar behaviour, so that both the parents, at first distraught and then reluctant, finally surrender to his urgings, spurred on perhaps by a new, more virulent form of plague which attacks the lungs and kills within three days. Thus it is that Tuccio, taking out his worries in a last, obsessive fit of locking and securing, leaves his house to journey into Lombardy, accompanied by his wife, his servants and his slaves, but not his daughter.

One final misadventure—or perhaps it might be better called an irritation—awaits them at the northern gate on the day of their departure. A great crush of wagons stands crippled in the road where an overloaded bullock-cart has snapped its axletree; Tuccio's convoy is stuck, unmoving, in the Piazza San Stefano. Here, Father Rocco della Rocca is ranting from the summit of the church's steps. There is a large, impoverished-looking crowd before him and, fired by his captive audience among the carts, he is delivering a sermon which seems more full of bile than wisdom. 'Mammon,' he declares, waving an aggressive finger at the wagons. 'There are those within this town who recognise no other god. This is no exodus like that from Egypt, sanctioned by Jehovah. This is the flight of wealth and luxury, inspired, not by God, but by the demon Mammon. It is the very vanity the pestilence chastises, the very avarice and lust for florins. Do you think you can escape God's punishment, all you who sit upon a pile of gold within a cart and leave the town that nourished you to die?'

Tuccio watches as the preacher waves a hand in his direction, the mob's eyes following his wagging finger. 'These are the very men who built the city's palaces, with towers to protect their wealth.' His voice has risen almost to a scream. 'Towers of Babel all! Temples built to men's own splendour, as if they themselves were God.' He crouches low above the crowd, his voice a threatening rumble. 'But there is only one God—He who directs the pestilence against His foes to cure men of sin. And are there those who truly think they can escape His wrath with horse and wagon?' Then he laughs—a blood-curdling sound—and the crowd laughs with him. Luckily the convoy starts to lumber forward, though not quite fast enough to miss his final words. 'For those who think they can escape God's wrath will escape Him only where they must escape all hope as well: deep in Hell's dark pit.'

The crowd is clearly enjoying itself, relishing his invective against the town's elite. He continues, jumbling up the gospels in a bitter stew of camels and needles, penance and peacemakers, though his words are garbled by the creak of wheels on stone. A dogfight starts round one of the dead bodies left neglected in the square. The priest's long obloquy is lost, his audience distracted; for Tuccio, the snarl and rumble of the dogs is the plague's last fanfare at his exit from the town.

Of course, not everyone chooses to leave Topomagro, even when the plague's more lethal strain appears. The poor, ravaged by both sickness and hunger, too often lack the will, the strength and means to seek out greener pastures. Master craftsmen stubbornly refuse to trade their hardwon businesses for lives as vagabonds in towns full of strangers. Some maintain that the communes nearby are just as cruelly set upon by sickness, and that they're better off remaining in the town where they are sure, at least, of roof and bed and some degree of caring. Father Rocco della Rocca says the worthy man might live a full life's span within a lazaretto, while a sinner might ride to the ends of the earth on the fastest of stallions and still perish. Francesco Morelli finds reassurance only in his own small well and secluded garden of rare herbs. And the old Gonfaloniere, Agnolo del Leone, having stored provisions in his basement at the onset of the plague, has bricked up every door and window of his tall palazzo and lives within its fastness with his family.

Jacopo, on the other hand, feels that he inhabits a land of Cockaigne. For here, as in Paradise, the mansions open wide to every pauper, their echoing chambers full of treasures left in haste. He and Scimmi stroll through breathless hallways, where crystal, gold and silver lie scattered for the taking. Sometimes, however, this abundance has a shock or two in store, as when he scaled an ivied wall toward an upper window, snapping back the hasp and scurrying inside. From the street the house had seemed both dark and silent, but slipping through its rooms with Scimmi in the lead, he heard strange noises coming from within; at last, following a labyrinth of hallways, he peered from a window high above a courtyard where torches lit a host of figures in elaborate copulation. Another time, in a splendid, tall palazzo, quite dark and well-secured, he followed Scimmi to a bricked-up room. Convinced that it must hold some fabulous possession—a thing too great with gold to carry in a cart—he chipped away at the bricks all night until, at dawn, a mass of makeshift wall came tumbling down, and he too almost tumbled when the odour hit him. Scimmi's ears flattened and she dived into her pouch as Jacopo tiptoed forward, peering in to find—on exquisite carven beds—the rotting bones of two small boys who must have fallen ill then been entombed to seal the plague inside.

Nevertheless, he's bringing home increasing booty to Marina, who starts to venture out as well, almost doubling their nightly haul. Their tiny cottage is soon crammed to overflowing; then—true daughter of a merchant—she sensibly suggests that they should leave it as a storehouse and move to more commodious accommodation. Thus they take up residence in one of the quarter's most opulent townhouses. But, no sooner are they there, surrounded by the choicest of their treasures, than Jacopo starts to question the point of all this theft.

What can he really do but stroll amongst it, laughing at the merchants who'd left it all behind? Every day the town becomes more dangerous, with cut-throats laying claim to whatever house they can. Vandals roam the streets, setting animals ablaze, defiling the altars of any intact church. The plague's new form strikes terror in each heart, so that priests desert their flocks, men their dying wives, and parents their sick children. The town is full of cries, and it seems an endless time since the Priors nailed their laws about the streets, these edicts now in tatters and the Priors long since gone.

One evening, while slipping past the Palazzo dei Dieci, Jacopo sees a bonfire in the square. Youths and girls are dancing to a wild, discordant music; some falling down with drink or sickness, others coupling in the shadows of surrounding porticoes. Suddenly a pack of hounds comes loping from the square's far side, tearing at the dancers' flesh—as if that of corpses were in short supply—while gangs of ragged creatures, waving sticks and flails, come rushing in behind like beaters at a hunt. There are screams, spilled blood, bodies hit with staves and savaged by the dogs. Cowering in the shadows of an alley, he sees the tall, gaunt horseman riding through the slaughter, and knows the man at once. It is the monk—the one he saw when he went amongst the vagrants with Lucia—now seated on his stallion as if he ruled the town.

As soon as it is safe, Jacopo slinks away, sickened by the violence he has seen. It's as though the pestilence has worked its way into their souls, corrupting all within. Only now does he suspect that he, the thief, may be no safer than any other townsman from the plague's worst thieveries. Thus it is that later in the evening, lying by Marina, he dreams that he falls ill. He feels the searing fever and the hammer of his blood, the skin so tight with poisons that he knows he must soon die. And yet he doesn't, floating now in dreamy peacefulness, surviving and recovered. He turns to rise out of his sickbed, but he cannot move, discovering—as he slowly lifts his eyes—the eyes of others near him, dead as painted stones. There are limbs of withered marble—grey, mottled torsos that stretch into the dark above him and below. For, living yet, he has been cast into a plague pit. How he thrashes to be free, breaking out of sleep, still sweating in the fever of his fear, to find Marina there beside him, moaning, wringing wet, a bubo bright beneath her outflung arm.

*In which Jacopo is faced
with a difficult decision and
Brother Corvo takes control*

BROTHER CORVO RIDES AS TO THE HUNT. HIS DOGS and minions swarm before him, clearing a passage for his coming. He loves this smooth relentlessness, this hurtling progress through the town; it reminds him of the God's—and of his own—apotheosis, which comes so quickly on him now that he sees it as a presence, like the dark, approaching end of this long street. Here, beneath the midday sun, the flat stone walls are shadowless, the arcades thin as paper, as if the world of flesh were but a mural to be peeled from revelation. His dogs' cries scorch the air, and figures vanish in their fear—a grandam waddling for a laneway, a torso bustling off on clumping arms, a blindman racing headfirst at a wall. All give way to the apocalypse as he careers toward the Piazza San Stefano.

At the piazza, unaware of Corvo's coming, Father Rocco della Rocca shouts his daily sermon. His surplice is damp from the sweat of his exertions, and the usual crowd of paupers is listening on its knees. 'Pray!' he bellows. 'Pray that this town may one day soon gain absolution. For worst of all are they who use this just chastisement as a means to spread their heresies. Oh, you well know such heretics would shrivel in the flames of Mother Church at any other time. Yet now, amongst the scum and pus, they thrive.' It's at this point that Brother Corvo's forces burst into the square, followed by their leader. The priest, barely pausing to draw breath, extends an arm in their direction. 'Ah yes, good brethren of the poor,' he cries, arm trembling with his passion, 'the Lord has brought the apostate before us.'

But the good brethren of the poor are busy scuttling for the shadows of unguarded alleys. Brother Corvo walks his stallion to the stairs, gazing upward at San Stefano's great maw, its campanile's needle pricking at the sky. Father Rocco wears a sharp, defiant look, yet backs away toward the portal when the dogs begin to snarl.

'No, Rocco,' Brother Corvo says at last. His voice is soft and mild, a sheath that hides a blade. '*I* don't serve an evil God, just Him whose time has come.' The priest can catch the glitter of a grin beneath the cowl. 'It's now you who are the heretic.'

'Blasphemy,' says Father Rocco in a tiny voice, then clears his throat and cries more loudly, '*Blasphemy!*'

Corvo sees the creature leaning downward from the tower. 'And, unrepentant, you must pay the price of heresy,' he murmurs, even as the snaky, lashing thing coils down to bite the cleric's heart. The man jerks backward with a grunt, while smoke curls darkly from his surplice. The rope between the tower and his chest begins to smoulder; another arrow hurtles from the far side of the square; then another, twirling with its rope already smoking, as yet a fourth comes hissing from the church's portal. Even as the fatted cords begin to blaze, the cassock flares and the priest is burning at the centre of a fiery web, while the four militiamen put away their bows and Otto the Nark limps forward with his axe.

Corvo beckons to the beggars, his voice as smooth and silky as the oil upon the ropes. 'Come, do penance,' he beseeches, 'and learn the true God's word.'

By the second day of Marina's illness, Jacopo knows she'll die. Buboes have formed in her neck, her groin and armpits. He has seen it all before— the twisting and the thrashing in the yellowed sheets, the stinking sweat, black piss and rancid oozings, the fierce, shining boils, the pain—and he doesn't want to see it any more. She cries out loudly and he hurries to her side. He wipes her brow with kid-gloved fingers, smoothes her hair with her softest brush, drips water from a cloth onto her lips, resolving all the while to leave that night. For she will die, there's little doubt about it, and he may well die too if he remains to nurse her.

On the third night of her illness, Marina ascends to Heaven. She sees clouds, great heavy stormheads brimming in the sky, and wafts up through them. She sees sunlight streaming over plains of blinding luminosity, and flutters up beyond it. She sees a halo of unbearable brilliance, and enters through its circle, where she finds the face of God. This face,

His face, is like a cliff arisen from the sea, a sun arrayed in rainbows, dissolving every cloud; and it softens with her father's watchful smile. 'Marina,' it says gently, 'Marina, My dear child.' And now she sees angelic hosts in spirals of bright song, one with the face of Luca, the household steward; another like the cook, Domenica; and yet another like Luigi Pucci, her father's plump accountant; for she knows that Heaven needs such useful angels. Then she sees the Virgin sighing with her mother's smile, her eyes a little sad, as if she'd let her down. 'My child,' the Father says once more, 'you make Us drink a bitter cup. We see ingratitude within your heart and know great disappointment.' And now His golden face grows crimson, while lightning wreathes His brow. 'Your loveless soul has made Us wrathful: for this you stand condemned.'

'Condemned to what?' she cries, with a sound that seems no louder than a sparrow's cheep.

'Condemned to die and go to Hell!' her Father's voice is booming, even as she falls, tumbling past the bothered flocks of angels, down through Heaven's circle, past the plains of light, the stormclouds and the sky, until ravines of smoke enclose her and the fiery Pit lies open as she screams, a hoarse and howling high-pitched cry that echoes through the night.

When he hears this sudden scream, Jacopo's heading for the door, his shoulders burdened with a massive sack. He feels the hairs rise on his neck, and Scimmi peeps at the bed from beneath her pouch flap. Some sort of reflex drops his treasures to the floor, propelling him toward her before he knows what's happening. 'Marina?' he mutters, thinking she might die right then and there. But her eyes are open. They stare at him in fear. 'Oh, Jacopo,' she whispers, and lifts her hand toward him. What can he do but take it? He feels her fingers, soft and hot, just like a flustered child's, and gazes at her face. Despite the sweat and stink and pain, there's still a loveliness about her; or maybe it's these sufferings that cause her shaky smile to touch him so he has to turn away. Why? Why should he stay and run the risk of death? There are thousands dying in the town and she is only one. Why should he add his number to the toll? Lucia ... he conjures up Lucia burning in the flames, put there by Marina's father. But now he sees himself, silent in the throng, running through the streets in fear, never turning back. And Laura ... he sees her also, dying in the galley's hold while he remains on deck. How often did he go to her? How much did he delay?

He untwists his fingers from the girl's, rising with a curse. Such softness is too dangerous. He's a thief and, like his Scimmi, has nine lives ... but tenderness might be the finish of each one. He hears Marina gasp, and reaches for the sack of gold. 'Jacopo,' she whispers, 'Jacopo,' till he sees her once again, in moonlight, in her chamber, as he slips in through the window; or climbing up a wall behind him, supple as a cat; or twining her lithe legs about him, laughing as he enters like the gentlest of all burglars. He hesitates ... since Death might steal her from him ... trembling with the urge to turn, aware that, if he does, he might never be the same sly thief again. He feels the sack against his hand and tugs it from the floor. It clanks and tinkles with a hollow sound. Then he lets it tumble with a clatter from his fingers, turning on his heel and slipping to the bed, where Marina merely flinches as he smooths her dark, damp hair.

By the following day he's sure the plague won't settle in her lungs as it does in its more lethal form. But on the fourth night of the fever, returning with some food, he rounds the corner of their street to find her high above him, lit up by the moon, and clambering along the second-storey ledge of their tall mansion. 'Marina!' he shouts, but says no more when she gives a start and almost tumbles. Instead, he scurries up the stairs, along the passage to their chamber, then peers through the window. She's some way out along the ledge, bent above the roadway as if drunk, a sack across her shoulder, from which she takes small, gilded gewgaws, dropping them from time to time onto the stones. 'Mar-i-i-i-na,' he croons, gently beckoning her to him. At last, after one or two more objects clatter to the road, she turns to eye him vaguely.

'Marina,' he says softly, 'what are you doing out there?'

'Oh, it's you,' she sighs. 'I thought it was the owner.'

'The owner?'

'Yes.' She turns to cast some trinkets to the ground. 'The owner's coming back. I've got to hide the evidence.'

'Ah, yes, the evidence,' he nods, sidling slowly after her along the ledge. He takes her hand. 'But dearest, didn't I tell you? The owner wrote to say he'd be away for six more months.'

'Oh, no,' she murmurs, and seems to shake her head, yet lets herself be guided to the window.

'He did. I'll let you see the letter.'

So the argument proceeds, with Jacopo wheedling and Marina demurring, somehow edging backward through the window to the bed, then in between the covers where he takes her in his arms and holds her till she sleeps.

No sleep is ever long, and by the fifth day of her illness he knows that she'll soon die. The buboes have grown monstrous; she slips into a stillness much like death, only to wake an hour later, flinging out her arms and shrieking like a parrot. She raves and rants and whimpers with a mania he remembers from the galley: the last frenzy before death. During a period of no more than half an hour, amid a series of long, thick, ragged cries, the buboes burst, pouring forth in such a putrid mess that he exhausts himself with retching. Then it's over and she's panting out her final gasps.

He stands beside the bed, holding her weak hand, waiting for the breaths to fade and die. He stands perhaps an hour, maybe two, listening to the trembling of her breath that slowly grows, not fainter, but more steady, until at last he sees she isn't dead, just sleeping deeply. It's only some time later that he thinks to loose her hand. As he does, her eyelids flicker open, and she gives a smile that, shaky though it is, shines dazzlingly above her trickling sores, and whispers, 'I want to rob the

Palazzo dei Dieci,' then rises weakly on her arm. 'I'll need a challenge now I'm better.'

Brother Corvo, his kingdom come, has set up court in the Palazzo dei Dieci. Enthroned within the great reception hall, surrounded by his minions, he waits the coming of the Twin of Light. Speranza, Fiducia and the ancient hag, Maria—all his loyal ones—deck his throne with tributes from the town, as Moloch and Bulfas and the hosts of other hounds go ranging through the torchlit chambers. Otto the Nark and his unkempt militiamen run the commissariat; a conscripted clutch of apothecaries brew elixirs, draughts and unguents to Brother Corvo's orders. It is these potions that make him introspective in the evenings, lounging back in that great hall, encircled by his court, observing subtle changes in the murals round the walls. He likes the one that shows the Priors at their table, mirrored in the heavens by Christ and all his saints; it tells him how the rout of one must be reflected in the other. Best of all he likes the picture of the town within its fields; not for the town itself, nor for the Virgin and her angels who sit stiffly in the sky, but for the curious, enlarged depiction of the herbs and grasses in the foreground, as if the artist had some special fondness for these weeds—chervil, fennel, hyssop, poppy, henbane, nightshade—even to the painting of the bees that drink their wonders. Though most might see just one or two of these small creatures, the depredations of some vandals have chipped the mural's paint and the fields are speckled with the golden stone beneath, so Corvo sometimes seems surrounded by the buzzing of a swarm.

Tonight, however, he stands on the tower and scans the wide town. San Francesco, the Duomo, San Pietro, Santo Spirito—all the churches are burning, the houses of heresy crimson with flame. Campanili fire the sky like flickering candles, and the Duomo's baptistery, cracked like an egg, is hatching infernos. Pillars of smoke twirl up under low vaults of cloud, their groinings lurid with heat, as if the whole town were a shrine to the imminent God. For His coming is near, Brother Corvo can feel it. His powers fill the air. Strange shapes ignite in the glowering clouds and fly through the fiery glare. And no place on earth is exempt from this cleansing: Corvo sees Venice—the forms of the Spirit Twin stalk its canals in a spiralling mist—and sniggers at Paris, where King Philip's doctors name Saturn the cause of the plague. He giggles at Basle, where they blame the town's Jews and burn them alive in sealed buildings. And he laughs out loud at Pope Clement, in his cope and false crown, crouched in a circle of fires at Avignon. For the Pestilential King has ascended the throne, and now he chuckles above the dark town.

A great act remains unaccomplished, the greatest of all: he himself must pass through the cleansing fires, even as others have done. He turns from the town and walks through the halls, drawing his lackeys about him. 'Come, we will ride!' he commands, distracting himself from the trial he must face, and strides to the courtyard to gather his hounds. Mounting his horse, he rides through the gate, his pack and his beaters before him, hurtling down the deserted streets where feasting jackdaws squabble and hop, while he swats the air with his uplifted sword. As they enter those streets where men dare to walk, they drive all before them, clubbing some back to their houses, cutting the tardy down, till they come to a square with an inn on one side where a small group of looters is loading a cart with hogsheads of wine. The pack roars in with the beaters behind, and Corvo circles, waving his sword, while the men at the cart make a show of resistance, their hands and legs torn apart by the dogs, the beaters' cudgels cracking their skulls, the hogsheads splintered to mingle their wine with the looters' spilled blood. Some slip away, only to find Corvo waiting, driving them down to the broken fount at the heart of the square. Here, joined by his troops, he harries them into the damp, mossy bowl where they slither and slip, cudgelled to pulp, till the basin's as red as a wine vat in August. Corvo now turns in the saddle, facing the sea, then the hills, then the roads north and south, seeing only the bright, blinding future.

The pursuit of Marina and Jacopo

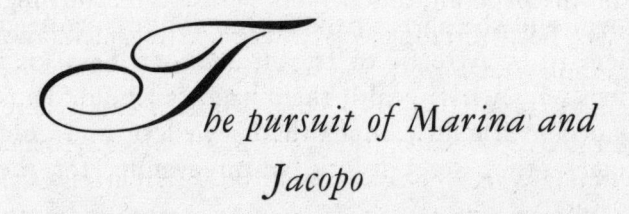

IT IS THE DONKEYS THAT FINALLY DECIDE JACOPO TO leave. He finds them in the stables of a house full of corpses, where they've been languishing beside an empty manger and a trough of mossy puddles. Of course, they're simply the last straw—his reservoirs of greed and courage are virtually depleted. For nearly every second building reeks of rotting flesh, or otherwise stands empty like a body with no soul. A charnel stench hangs over all, and some of those ravines beyond the walls have all but vanished, their rocky pits and furrows filled with corpses, while carrion-birds arrive in clouds of whirring wings. It's the violence of the looters, however, that most spurs him to leave. His rival thieves and the renegade sextons show such cruelty that he's too afraid to enter those palazzi where the pickings might be richest. Worst of all is the gang of that crazed friar whose coven he'd once been to with Lucia: it's as if their madness ruled the town.

Marina is more ambivalent. A curious elation fills her, a wish to live life to the full, as if survival of the pestilence has rendered her invulnerable. She can't help feeling that, no matter what, she will not die. At last, however, he convinces her to leave the town, and she agrees to keep the donkeys, to feed them till they're fit to travel and then help load them with what wealth their bags can hold. Thus loaded—with little more than jewellery and gold florins—they set out one warm evening for the northern gate.

They lead the donkeys silently, watchfully, through the wary lanes. As they pass just north of the Piazza della Signoria, a dog comes trotting round the corner of a street behind them. It props, woofs softly, then gives a sudden bark, causing Scimmi to peer from beneath her pouch flap. Another dog appears at its shoulder, then another, and another, pacing forward with their progress and belling like cracked steeples. Tempted though they are to move more quickly, they hold the donkeys steady, the dogs still barking, though keeping at a distance. A little further back, a man steps from the shadows. He holds a large, rough stave and watches them in silence. A second figure joins him, and a third, followed by yet others. The pack of dogs starts snarling and the men move closer, so that neither thief nor girl can bear the tension further and mount their frail donkeys, which they batter with their boot heels. The beasts lurch forward as their riders kick them harder, and the hounds bound after them at once. Jacopo, with Marina close behind, turns left into an alley, glancing back to note what dogs have followed and seeing the tall rider who watches the pursuit.

Brother Corvo sees them clatter down the alley. He sighs and smiles contentedly, his hands a little numb upon the reins, since he knows he used a touch too much rye fungus or drank too deeply of the blood-of-God. Yet, can one have too much wisdom, be profligate with grace? Shaking his head slowly, he rowels the champing horse, flying down the alley behind the vanished beaters. His ears ring with airy songs, the cries of fleeing souls. As the sheer walls rush by, lights burst as if doors opened for angels to peep out, bright faces snouting forth with smiles that warp in toad-mouthed grins. Arms beckon, wave, then yawn like maws, grunting, bleating, cheering him on, till he is doubled up with laughter on his hurtling horse, sailing down the alley in a foam of ghosts. There they are, his beaters, lolloping before him; and further on, the dogs already closing on their prey's ungainly shadows. One of the donkeys stumbles and the man who rides it pauses, swinging in his saddle as the pack comes snarling down. Teeth snap, flesh tears. The donkeys roll their eyes and bare their blunt white teeth, falling to their knees as if in prayer to some crude deity. But the man and woman have leapt down to the road, running through the dark with just the beaters following, the dogs distracted by the wheezing donkeys. Corvo spurs the stallion harder, harrying his men, vaulting their white eyes to ride his quarry down. They won't escape, for the walls are once more cheering, the laneway swirling with its coils about their feet, while the sky—the black night sky beyond the eaves—is pierced by God's eye of silver light.

The pair rush blindly through streets of shuttered windows. They flee along whatever lane seems meanest, diving through the shadows of rank alleys, as if to lose themselves meant losing their pursuers, until—the sounds of hoofbeats somewhere near—they almost run into the rear of a cart. At first Jacopo fails to realise that it's moving, then hears its axle creaking. 'Ugh!' he shudders, peering at that wagon full of corpses. 'It's too narrow to squeeze past.'

'Over here,' Marina hisses, diving for a doorway, rattling at the handle. But the bolt has been thrust home. They hear the baying in the laneways roundabout.

'Here,' says Jacopo, wheeling to his left. But that way hoofbeats echo, while cries erupt behind them.

'The cart,' she sighs at last, and with no hesitation dives toward it, pushing back pale arms and knees and feet to burrow in. He makes to follow, pauses, thinking that it might be safe for her—after all, she's just survived the sickness—while it could mean death to him. Then a hound howls close at hand. He grits his teeth ... stops breathing ... and leaps up on the cart, colliding with a wall of rock-hard limbs, peeling them apart, nudging under sore-pocked, icy skins, remembering his dream and clenching shut his eyes as tightly as a mole's. Scimmi gives a soft, protesting squeak, and he pats the pouch's fabric. He hears Marina whimper and reaches for her hand, but grips a stiff, cold claw instead, groaning as the cart goes jiggling on, the face above him peering down in glassy-eyed reproach.

Just moments later Corvo stands before them, his horse's flank toward the cart. He lifts a pallid hand. The driver halts his two old nags with much loud fuss and racket; but, when he sees that shadowed face he seems afraid, while Corvo in his turn stares down, caught suddenly within the cloud of putrefaction. The nostrils of the wagoner are plugged with wads of cotton, rendering him immune to the foul stench. Brother Corvo, on the other hand, reels upon his horse, too much affected by the evening's potions.

'Have you seen a man and girl come running by?' he asks, his words so slow that, to the wagoner, they drip with menace. He knows the sextons' methods.

'Ah, no,' the driver says. 'These laneways are deserted.'

'You've seen me, haven't you?' And Corvo gives a bilious grin, then leans down from his horse.

'Yes, I have ... I truly have.' The driver nods emphatically as Corvo draws his sword. But now a pair of hounds come snarling round the cart, darting at the corpses, their voices deafening in the narrow laneway.

'Hey!' shouts Corvo. The hounds hunch lower, fawning up at him with whining cries and thrashings of their tails. Another, just below his horse, yelps sharply at the cart, so the stallion shies a little, and with the flat of his long blade he lays the dog out cold. Then suddenly the thick, ripe smell starts churning in his gut and he wheels the horse about, shouting at his men: 'Come on, it doesn't matter. We've got other fish to fry.'

A little later in the evening, when the wagon stops at last outside the city walls, the driver leaves his bench and limps round to the rear. Grumbling of the plague and Brother Corvo, he reaches out and hauls a body from the pile, dumping it roughly on the ground. He grasps another by its stone-cold hand, dragging it down too, and then another. Settled now into a slow, familiar rhythm, he stretches up once more and clasps his fingers round a foot ... that feels ... quite warm. The toes retract, and then the body—a young girl's—sits upright with a fierce stare.

'Excu-u-use me!' it says. 'If you don't mind!'

Then a man sits up beside her, looking round and muttering, 'There's been a terrible mistake.'

'Mistake? Culpable negligence, if you—' the girl begins, but the driver is already backing from the cart, shaking his head then scuttling off toward the town.

Marina bursts out laughing. 'His face ...' she says, and Jacopo's laughing too, though he wastes no time in grabbing an old jerkin off the bench and scrubbing at his skin, rubbing as if he'd scour to the bone. She's already pulling at the harness, and he hurries round to help unhitch the ancient nags so they can ride them to the north.

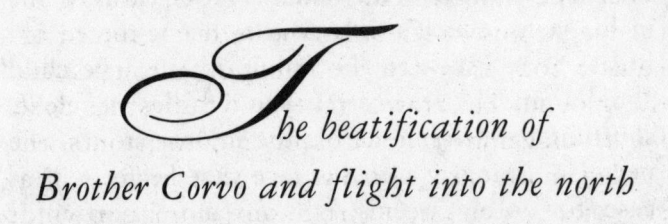

The beatification of Brother Corvo and flight into the north

TOPOMAGRO LIES SILENT, SUBMERGED IN SLEEPY peace. Dawn shimmers like water at the tops of its towers; and from a high window in the Palazzo dei Dieci, Brother Corvo looks down on the shadowy rooftops of houses below him. Vines green the walls of mansions and churches, and the woods to the east are thick with new growth. He turns to gaze north, a swallow's quick shadow skimming his face, while a skylark descends in a silvery fanfare over the square. The world seems renewed, as if cleansed by the plague's pure fires. Swifts soar and glide, and souls ascend through the liquid air like rain streaming up from the depths of the earth. The world is no longer the same; the Lord of Light now sits on the throne and His mercy reigns triumphant. Only the final act remains to be done. Here Corvo wavers and, quick as a pin, regret pricks his eyes and fear stays his breath. He swings from the window, already reviling his moment of weakness: he is no God made flesh and this is no pallid Gethsemane. The flesh of the Pestilential King must suffer the ultimate cleansing that he, above all, may spring from Death's belly pure in spirit ... He sees the shape at the doorway and his blood turns to bile in his veins. But it's only Maria, her withered old breast giving suck to the failing infant. The child squalls and writhes, yet she cradles it close, shuffling toward him across the smooth stones. She peers so strangely into his face that he feels ill at ease, for nothing seems right any more; nor will it till he does what the Lord demands. She stands with the infant clenched in her arms, casting her strange gaze upon him. And then she darts forward while his hand slides down to his sword hilt. Yet he feels, not her blade, but the scrape of her old parchment lips on his cheek, then the moistness of spittle or tears. He stands unmoving, stares solemnly down and, abashed, she turns away. Now he gives a harsh laugh, since the time has undoubtedly come for his transfiguration.

Jacopo and Marina ride north on their nags through the lush summer country. At first, with the city behind them and hills all around, they somehow thought to ride free of the plague into fields ripe for harvesting, fresh and renewed. And indeed, in certain valleys away from the highway, and on certain lonely hills, they find farms all busy at the harvest, fatted pigs in pens and, out in the meadows, flocks watched by their shepherds. Yet even here, in these havens, they find themselves chased by dogs set free from their chains, or by grim peasant faces and hands waving pitchforks, as if they came from a tainted world to bring the sickness with them. Mostly they find the plague's leavings. They ride by peasants fallen at their doors or lying in the road or heaped in a field, as still as the ruins of scarecrows. Some have been torn by dogs gone wild; most form tattered perches for the birds, with neither handmaid, priest nor doctor to attend their final breaths. All along the road abandoned cottages, with jackdaws hopping in and out their windows, lie desolate as skulls amid their unreaped fields.

Animals have fallen victim too—swine decaying in their swill, shorn sheep abuzz with flies, bloated lambs, dead cows with spring-born calves still nudging at their udders. Mostly the beasts roam loose in the wheat, their bellies full with the ungathered harvest—plump oxen, dyspeptic goats, sleek sheep, all living well amid the chaos.

The thief and his apprentice traverse this desolation, these textbook farms for fools, where the crops are left to rot and the beasts roam witless, waiting for some ending to the madness. Stubbornly it goes on; although, for Jacopo at least, it's not the desperate thing that it might seem, since his eyes are fixed, not on the world, but on Marina. He loves the way she rides astride her horse, just like a man, as if in argument against her woman's skirts. She seems so willowy, so whippet-quick despite her winded nag, and nothing that they see defeats her smile for long, which goes on flashing back at him like light flung off a blade. She sings and jokes and tries to urge her plodding hack into a run with such loud gusto that he can't help thinking, in spite of his delight, that it's a ploy to blind her to the ruin ranged about them. But this itself is joy, just like her jaunty riding, or lithe, sly climbing up a rich man's wall, or the way her narrow breasts curve up to meet his hands. He watches the infected land go by and sighs with pleasure, convinced that Hell might turn to Heaven if he were damned with her.

'We should keep going,' he says at one point in their journey, 'toward Savoy. We should go into the mountains where the air's clean.' He looks at her and grins. 'Maybe we could work as acrobats ... I've done it once before.'

She swings round on her nag's bare back, one hand upon its rump. 'And we've had a lot of practice climbing walls.'

'So,' he says, 'the mountains it is then. A good long ride.'

'Oh, well, I don't know about that.' She waits for him to catch her, reining to a standstill with the cart's clumsy harness.

'It's a long ride, all right. You'll know it by the time we get there.'

'No, no,' she laughs, pushing at his arm. 'I mean the way we're going. I was thinking we might go to Lombardy.'

'Lombardy?' He looks doubtfully toward the north. 'The plague's up there as well.'

'In parts. But not in others.'

He nudges his horse forward, squinting at her sideways. 'And hasn't your father bought a villa in the Lombard countryside?'

'He has,' she says, then smiles a broad, bright smile. 'And we could go there. I reckon we could find it.'

'Go there?' he cries, incredulous. 'To your father?' He laughs out loud. 'Oh yes, I can see it now. "Jacopo, this is my father, Tuccio di Piero Landucci, the wealthy *lanaiuolo* from Topomagro. And, *babbo*, this is Jacopo Passero, the well-known burglar, who stole your daughter from you." Of course, he'll reward me on the spot.'

'But he will, Jacopo, he will.' She grips his arm and pulls him to her, so he nearly tumbles off his horse. 'As long as we do it right.'

'What do you mean? I don't aim to survive the plague to get thrown into a dungeon.'

'No, it wouldn't be like that.' And she too stares toward the north. 'We could say I'd run away, that after Gaia's death I'd grown so frightened of the plague that ... with my father waiting there to finish with his business ... I'd fled in terror from the town.' She turns to him, her eagerness increasing with the telling of the tale. 'And then, while fleeing through the countryside, I fell ill—I came down with the plague—finding shelter in an empty cottage ...'

'Ye-e-es,' he says doubtfully. 'Where do I come in?'

'And while I was dying of the illness ... regretting my desertion of my family—'

'Praying for forgiveness,' he smiles, warming to the story.

'A young man found me, a man of honour and nobility—'

'Brave and handsome—'

'Sweet and kind—'

'Clever and cunning—'

'No, no, Jacopo,' she cries, 'clever, perhaps, but never cunning.' She holds up a finger, seeking inspiration. 'Oh, but he was strong and kindly, nursing me through my illness, bringing me food and water, risking the plague himself in order to care for me.'

'It's true, my love, all true.' He catches at her hand to kiss it.

'And through his ministrations I survived.' She brushes his long fingers with her lips, while the horses snort and dawdle.

'Yes ... yes,' he laughs, 'and more ... He owns a castle in Romagna, but it was ravaged by the plague and then by looters, and he had to flee so fast ... that he's now reduced to penury.'

'In fact, a reward might be in order—'

'For the saving of the merchant's daughter—'

'Or the offer of her hand in marriage, as in any proper tale ...'

He looks at her, his mouth a little open, then gives a beaming grin. 'Oh yes, Marina,' he declares, 'this plan has possibilities.'

And so they journey northward, refining the story as they go, adding details, pruning back the more transparent lies, reducing Jacopo from noble lord to merchant's son. Their tale provides distraction from their travels through that land, engaging them with its imagined pathways as they ride at night by lightless villages, or by day past ransacked wagons, or once, beneath a hillside where kites wheeled round and round above a blighted fortress, which—unknown to them—housed the rotting corpses of Wolf Schwanhals and his men.

•

At the centre of the great reception hall in the Palazzo dei Dieci, in the middle of the heavy bed he's had his minions bring there, Brother Corvo lies burning. Invisible flames rise around his long body, filling his ears with a ceaseless hum and buzz. He stares with fevered, glassy eyes about the hall, and yet exults, triumphant in this cleansing. He peers at the mural of the town amongst its fields, where vetch and vervain, henbane and hyssop, tangle on the wall as in some massive herbal. He watches the small bodies of the painted bees, listening through the humming in his ears; soon his vision or the room begins to swim, and there, amid a net of emerald stems, a tiny bright gold speck peels off and hovers through the air.

His followers—much depleted by this second strain of plague—watch about the bed, though standing further from him than they might, as if his burning drove them off. He has no sense of them, seeing only those bright legions that have gone before, that urge this final breaking of the chains with which the Dark God bound him to corrupted matter. And like any cutting of a cord, like any birth, its debt of pain must first be paid. Once freed, he will be glorified to dwell within the Godhead as on a brow of light. He grins amid the stink of sweat and follows with his gaze the slow, erratic path of the approaching bee.

Even as he watches, the tawny speck grows larger, then looms beneath the ceiling's beams, its beak and dusty body like a furry golden dragon's. As if from the roaring of its wings or the cloying of its breath, it brings a heat that makes his sight turn red, until the room begins to swirl and he falls into a depth of spinning darkness. Some hours, days or seconds after, his eyes snap open into crimson light. It's the noise that seems to wake him—the angry, buzzing drone of wings—since the Palazzo dei Dieci has faded from his sight, replaced by the shape of its true nature, the symmetric, towering walls that rise on every side, the seamless, fiery light, the overwhelming sweetness. For here, all about him, are the cells of some great hive, where huge-eyed heads come lolling out of casements and monstrous bees soar, hovering, in droning arcs from chamber to dark chamber. His body seems ablaze with pain, and fear shudders through him; yet this is just as every birth must be, since he can see already how the swarm attends each honeyed cell, each creature driven to its ministrations, part scorpion, part nursemaid.

Fire fills his chest, as if his spirit, impatient for its glory, might flare up out of him. The swarm moves slowly in; some turning through the air, some gliding, tiger-striped, from their deep chambers. And then they plummet, swaying in a wind of dust and bilious sweetness till they hover just above his bed, and one, a little nearer than the rest, drops down onto his chest. He feels the breath go out of him, the fires heighten; the thing, encumbent there upon him, squats above his heart as if to hatch his cloistered soul. He cries out once then starts to retch until the creature swings about, its belly quivering, its striped back arching up. For an instant the great barbed sting hangs tense above his head, then plunges, lancing down into his chest's hard centre while the bee bucks upward like a stallion, wings flailing at the air. The sting tears from it, and the swarm goes soaring to the hive's dark cope as Corvo shouts and bubbles, the slow blood belching out. 'Lord,' he gurgles, 'Lord,' already sucking like a landed fish, mouth circled in an O, yet seeing for himself the black blood swilling from him, rising in a tide above the bed, his mouth and snorkled nose.

Coming down from the hills of Emilia onto the Lombard plain, Marina and Jacopo know that at last they have reached the lands of good health. For this is just how it seems as they gaze across that great expanse, its pastures green and golden in the early morning sun. They pass lush meadows where farmers lead their cows to milking, and dewy fields already trodden by stout peasants armed with scythes, where sheaves of wheat or oats stand bound in ranks like captive armies. They skirt a broad canal, its barges almost sinking beneath their weight of goods, and pass through hamlets with their houses empty, not from pestilence but because the villagers are talking in the street or busy with the harvest. The sky shines over all, no longer like a punishing bright eye, but like a deep blue benediction.

They frequently rehearse Jacopo's role as scion of a merchant family, though necessity still tempts him to occasional theft. Once, loaded with some wine and spicy ham, they wade into a yellow field to join the harvesters, who happily accept them at their midday feast as if no breath of sickness ever entered this rich land. They proceed to tell their hosts the tale they have concocted of Jacopo's wealthy father, his misfortunes on the road and loss of all he owned. It's a romantic confection and the workers are attentive, not one amongst them showing any sign of disbelief. Indeed, they even drink to the recovery of his fortune, amid sundry other toasts.

But mostly they keep it to themselves, refining its broad outlines, adding details as they ride. Marina coaches him in what she's gathered of her father's business, and he teaches her to juggle. 'What goods could a merchant make a profit on if he bought them here in Lombardy?' she might ask, leaning backward as she rides, twirling the painted wooden balls he's given her and smiling with self-satisfaction.

'Wheat, barley, linen,' he shoots back. 'And armour, naturally.'

'All right,' she smiles. 'What would your agents be out to purchase in, say, Roumania?'

'Furs, wax, metals, sandalwood ... ouch!' he says, as Scimmi, stretching on his lap, kneads him with her claws.

'What about alum?' she suggests. 'It's vital to his dye shops.'

'I was going to say that.'

'Oh, well then ... you'd have no trouble guessing what your competitors were after if they went to both Perugia and Arezzo?'

'Fine veils,' he yawns, raising his eyebrows at the easy question.

'Or Lucca?'

'Brocades and silks, of course.' He glances slowly at her, then shrugs his shoulders. 'Come on, Marina, how about a hard one?'

She pauses for a moment, creasing her smooth brow, almost dropping the blue ball. 'Ve-e-ry well,' she says at last. 'Which guild would you have to join if you wished to make a decent profit out of silk in Florence?'

'The Silk-makers' Guild,' he grins, as though it's all too easy.

'No, Jacopo. It's not as obvious as *that*.'

'In Florence?' He hesitates, considers, then swings about to face her. 'Don't you remember where I come from? Why should I have to know which guild to join in Florence? It's a foolish question, Marina.' He lowers his voice a little. 'Besides, how do I know your answer's right? You were only a child in his household. How can you be sure you know these things?'

'Because I listened,' she laughs, never pausing in her juggling. 'Because I'd hear him talking with his friends.' She casts him a sly glance. 'You marry a man because he's wealthy or has a little influence. But you listen carefully to whatever you might hear since he may need good advice.' She gives a low, quick chuckle. 'Or he might be just plain thick.'

He watches as the balls go round and round, unsure of what to say, then suddenly starts scrabbling in his bag. 'You cheeky wretch!' he cries, bringing out a yellow ball and then a brown, slinging them amid the ones she's spinning till she shrieks and almost falls. And yet she somehow catches them, slipping both into the widening ring, her laughter joining his until the sound is all about them.

Soon, among the farms and townships, they are asking for the villa of the Tuscan merchant, Tuccio di Piero Landucci, 'who has come here to escape the plague'. There are many errors and false starts until one day they find a small, walled town whose name Marina seems to recognise, where a local priest points out a pathway to a further valley. Here, as flocks of birds fly in the sun, their wings reflecting light then dark, then light again—like the signals of a secret language—they see a villa high above them. They urge their weary horses upward till they stand upon the threshold of its open gates. Ivy and clematis strew the old stone walls, and vineyards climb the hillside to the low, pale villa, which seems to drift among a mass of leaves. They ride in through the gateway, along an avenue of shadows, wondering if it's yet another fruitless errand. Already they see a figure coming from the house, and then another, and behind them several more. They watch the first one walking faster, then the second, both now moving at a run between the vines, until her father starts to wave—who would have thought that he could move at such a pace?—and then her mother, her soft mouth beaming, and Tuccio's peaked miser's face quite bright with wind-smudged tears ...

EPILOGUE

When the plague had finally done with Italy, trailing its skirts across the Alps to Germany and northern France, Topomagro lay exhausted. Nearly half its fishermen, labourers and peasants were now dead, and the countryside was devastated because of the neglected harvest. Famine followed close upon the sickness; the price of food and labour soared to unknown heights. Thus, though Tuccio delayed returning till the spring of 1349, he found the town in tatters. Numerous of his friends had died, including Francesco Morelli who'd remained to do what good he might. Many of his competitors had also perished, while some of his surviving friends—those who, unlike him, had stayed—quite openly disapproved of his desertion of the town. One of these was Agnolo del Leone, who had sealed himself, with all his family, in his tall palazzo in the Borgo dei Panettieri. None of them had died, as if the plague were really no corruption of the air at all, and old Agnolo had stepped from his locked tower, younger it seemed than ever, to take charge of the town's recovery.

Despite his loss of friends through death or

disapproval, Tuccio at once saw how to prosper from the shortages. His months in Lombardy had not been wasted, for he'd established many good connections—and gained many an obligation—among the rich farmers of wheat and barley in the region where he'd stayed. Nor had his capital, his agencies abroad, his access to ships and credit, been disastrously affected; while his wits seemed honed to steely keenness by the plague. He imported the cheapest Lombard grain and sold it dearly in the town, arranging further shipments from the hard-hit south. Of course, like everybody else, he found the scarcity of labour led to wage demands that seemed exorbitant, yet he even found a way of turning this to his advantage. For now he used his agents in Iberia, Roumania and the Barbary coast to buy up slaves as cheaply as he could, and then sold them at hitherto unheard-of prices in labour-hungry Tuscany. So efficient was the operation that he even quarantined the slaves as a safeguard against re-importing plague. Thus, taking advantage of the rise in prices while keeping his wage costs down, he quickly added to his wealth in such a way that, whatever minor cost to his prestige his flight had meant, he gained a firmer hold upon the town than in the past.

Jacopo too appeared to profit from the plague, since Tuccio took him into both his home and business. At first, though grateful for the young man's kindness to his daughter, the merchant had found him lacking in his grasp of commerce, at least when pressed beyond a certain surface glibness. He assumed that this had resulted from his family's negligence, and his poor opinion was confirmed when Jacopo confessed that, just before the plague, his father had been listed as a bankrupt. Nevertheless, the very survival of the boy had shown a certain toughness in his make-up; he undoubtedly had charm and, above all, Marina delighted in his company. So it wasn't long before Jacopo had convinced the merchant that the pestilence had sobered him, that he now perceived how puerile his understanding was, and wished to mature into a successful businessman as quickly as he could.

With Marina's pleading on Jacopo's behalf, and the fact that most of his *fattori* had either died or fled, Tuccio had him manage his dye shops, and there Jacopo had the sense to lean upon the counsel of the foremen, learning all he could from Tuccio's accountants. What he lacked in expertise in that first period of labour shortage, he soon made up for with his thief's ability to pilfer workers from competing shops, using whatever incentives came to hand and showing none of Tuccio's reluctance to pay his men high wages. Indeed, it wasn't long before the merchant saw his virtues, and Jacopo, forgetting old resentments, even enjoyed his gruff approval, though not as much as the nostalgic pleasure of slipping from his room into Marina's curtained chamber.

Aware that the sickness might return at any time, Tuccio made donations to the Church, giving freely to its hospitals, its programs for registered paupers, its trusts for the dowries of orphaned virgins and, above all, to the funds it sought to reconstruct those churches burnt by Corvo. Nor did he ignore the Confraternity of Saint Mark, which had grown quite wealthy on bequests from its dead members, though much of its money—through Tuccio's stern influence—went to damaged churches. In the light of such good offices, the town's new bishop readily complied with Tuccio's demand for Gaia's reinterment in the Duomo. And he happily agreed to celebrate the Mass himself at the wedding of Jacopo and Marina. Tuccio's single stipulation was that all must wait upon the Duomo's renovations, a demand to which the couple painlessly acceded, snuggled nightly as they were in Marina's bolted chamber. In fact, this wedding—when it finally occurred in 1351—was perhaps more sumptuous even than Gaia's, as if it were a feast to mark death's end, with the laughing, crowned Marina the accession of new life. Though babies came less quickly than the family might have wished, it was such a period of happy domesticity—with Jacopo's dedication to the dye shops and Marina's running of the house Tuccio had bought them—that even Scimmi seemed to grow a little fat from overeating, or so her master said, until the night she bore a litter of six kittens in their bed.

This period of harmony was interrupted by the death of Beatrice, Tuccio's wife of so many loving years. He woke one morning to find her dead and cold beside him with no sign of what had killed her. With his daughter married, his closest friends all perished in the plague, and now his wife no longer with him, Tuccio began to change. His movements echoed round him in his mansion like the rattlings of a die within a cup, and he devoted lonely evenings to redoubling his great wealth. Yet even this could not provide him with his former sense of purpose and, increasingly, night after night—sometimes at the most eccentric hours—he would call upon his daughter and her husband. He lavished presents of ever greater luxury upon them, and gave Jacopo commissions of more and more importance, as if he wished to buy the love that death had taken from him. Sometimes he drank a little too much wine, then started speaking volubly of grandchildren, even insisting that the pair would live more comfortably back at his palazzo. Forbearing as they were, they soon became oppressed by his continual presence, growing restless in the comfort and confinement of the town.

They first expressed this feeling with unexplained excursions up the walls of their new home, trying tricks with ropes slung from the roof, performing acrobatics and ambitious feats of juggling. Scimmi herself, now smaller than her offspring, seemed also to have caught the wanderlust, vanishing for nights on end and snubbing her young cats. It was around this time that Baldassare and his falcon reappeared at his farm. Marina introduced him to Jacopo and, as the days went by, they spent increasing time among his meadows, where he taught them the art of falconry. Soon they stayed whole weeks amid the summer hills; while at home their behaviour seemed most curious, for many were the moonless nights that they would vanish from the house only to return some hours later burdened with fat sacks.

It wasn't long till Tuccio was grumbling, complaining that Jacopo was rarely at his shops; and, though Marina might contest this, her husband found no answer but the arching of an eyebrow and the nodding of his head. Nor did they attempt to change their habits, so that Tuccio's complaints grew more insistent until, one night when the moon was new, they packed some bags with clothes and food, with balls and tumblers' tights, put Scimmi in her laundered pouch and pinned a note upon their door, avowing love, gratitude and an overwhelming urge to see the world. Thus it was that they slipped from Topomagro, taking the eastern road upon two fine, high-mettled horses, the stars so bright about them that it seemed the heavenly city was no more than a gesture's length above the hills.